Safe Haven

Maddie James

SAFE HAVEN

MADDIE JAMES

Copyright © 2016, James, Maddie
Safe Haven
Media > Books > Fiction > Romance Novels
Digital ISBN: 978-1-62237-454-0
Print ISBN: 9781622374892
Digital release: March 2016
Editor, Deelylah Mullin

Formerly titled, *Wind Ridge*

Author Note

Some stories fly from brain to fingers to computer screen. Others take their good ol' time in coming. This book falls into the latter category.

The storyline for *Safe Haven* came to me while living in central Kentucky horse country, back in the 1990s. Nearby, was a small country farm named Wind Ridge. There was another horse farm, complete with Federal style mansion, down the road in the opposite direction. Supposedly, the new owner was a foxhunter, and stories were, that he ran his horses and hounds over neighboring fields and land, much to the irritation of the locals.

The juxtaposition of those two things—the small country tobacco farm and the stately southern horse farm—wove their way into my head and a story took wings. Over 100,000 words later, the story was finished, but sad to say, it lay fallow in my computer for many years. Other stories had their day, blessed by the publishing world, but *Safe Haven* stayed hidden from public consumption.

I always loved the story; however, it was written at a time when I was still learning how to write. I knew it needed a lot of

TLC but I also *needed* to tackle the story again, embrace it, rip it up, and let my editor have her way with it. So, I did. *We* did. Now, I am so pleased that Bekah and Collin's story is finally ready to share with you.

Please know that this could be considered a period story. It starts out in the 1980s and picks up again in the 1990s. It was a different world then, in Kentucky, and elsewhere. Tobacco farming has changed quite a bit, and of course, access to cell phones was limited. You'll probably notice other differences that date the story. Overall, I think you will find this a suspenseful, and satisfying, happily-ever-after!

Just one more thing—many thanks to my fantastic, super-editor, Deelylah Mullin. This was a challenging project for both of us, at best, but this book, this love story, is so much better because of her.

Safe Haven

Rebekah McCauley is back home after ten long years of living and working in New York City. She left the Big Apple under circumstances she'd rather not share with her family—not yet, anyway—and wants is time to heal and recover from the mess she'd made of her life. Luckily, her grandparents' Kentucky bluegrass farm, *Wind Ridge*, provides the safe haven she craves and the solitude she needs to heal.

Collin Kramer, the foxhunter next door, seems determined to infiltrate her peace and invade her quiet sanctuary—not only with his noisy hounds running amok over her land, but with his Alpha male, take-charge attitude running roughshod over her wounded heart.

But as Bekah softens to Collin's conquest, Collin realizes his own toughened heart needs mending. And just when he thinks he has that conquered, as well, all hell breaks loose. Poisoned horses, a gutted hound, and a barn fire are only the beginning. When Bekah's farmhouse burns to the ground too, they know someone is serious about destroying their lives.

But who?

Whose past has come back to haunt them?

Prologue

S *ummer, 1982*
  Woodford County, Kentucky

"I'm going, Mama."

Rebekah McCauley stood hands on hips in the center of her family's kitchen, watching her mother peel potatoes for supper.

"I've worked hard for it. I'm going."

Her arms dropped to her sides as she moved across the kitchen. She stood next to her mother and observed the rhythmic movements of the knife skimming off potato skins. At once, the tempo stopped, and her mother's hands lowered to the sink. Bekah looked to the older woman's thin face and saw her staring at the curled peelings.

"You'll never come back."

Bekah's gaze fell to the sink. The skin sagged from her mother's bony hands. They were wrinkled, rough, and callused, sprinkled with brown age spots, nails chipped and broken—dry and hard. Old.

Bekah had seen those hands peel at least a million potatoes. She'd seen them gently pull tender tobacco plants out of their beds, then swiftly separate the plants to be set with one hand, while she pushed another plant into a setter cup with the other faster than anybody around. She'd watched them make garden and chop weeds and bust open a feed sack with ease. She'd seen them gently pat her father's shoulders after a long day in the fields, and then wipe away tired tears when she thought nobody was looking.

But Bekah was always looking.

Yes, I'm leaving.

"I need you here, Rebekah."

I guess you do. You need me to cook and clean and feed the chickens and tend garden and any of a dozen other chores that a woman does on a farm. You need me to talk to you, to share things with you—to be your daughter.

She looked into her mother's eyes. A small tear balanced on one lid, daring to spill down her mother's cheek. Bekah placed an arm about her shoulders and felt them sag. Those shoulders, along with her father's, had withstood the worst of their existence since before she was born.

Again, her gaze fell to the fingers still gripping the potato and paring knife. Bekah folded her own hands around her mother's, the potato and knife rattled into the sink. The soft, supple young fingers smoothed over the older ones Bekah's were graceful, artistic—hands made to curl around a paintbrush or a pen, not pull plants or toss hay bales. Her nails were well groomed, and although they had seen their share of dirt and paint underneath them, they weren't abused as her mother's.

In twenty years, mine will look like that.

"The scholarship will pay for everything, Mama. Money won't be a problem for you or Daddy. It'll pay for tuition and books and meals and housing—anything else I need, I'll work for it. You know I'm a hard worker. And I *will* be back."

When her eyes lifted to her mother's face, Bekah saw what she suspected was fear. Her mother's gaze dropped to their hands—Bekah's smooth, youthful ones, and her mother's dried up prunes. Bekah watched a lone tear start a silver trail down her cheek. Maybe it was a memory or a daydream that occupied her mother's thoughts, Bekah wasn't certain, but it held tight for a long moment.

"You're only seventeen," she said. "And it's so far away."

"I'll come back, Mama."

A longer silence followed. Her mother was struggling. She turned and looked deep into Bekah's eyes, perhaps seeing herself, or someone she once was or wanted to be. Slowly she turned back to the sink, picked up the paring knife and the potato, and began peeling again.

"Then go."

"You're sure?"

Eyes closed, she gave a quick nod, and flew into the peeling rhythm again. Then for one last time, she stopped, rested against the sink, and turned.

"You go and get that education. You go and make something of yourself, Rebekah McCauley. Lord knows I always knew this day would come. You've said ever since you were old enough to go to the fields that you couldn't wait for the day to leave this farm. You've worked hard, got good grades, and now this scholarship—there's no way I can say no. Much as I'd like to now, hear? It's just that I can't.

"You've always had big dreams. Your daddy and me and the boys will be fine. We'll all be here digging in the dirt until the day we die, I expect."

She glanced off out the window, looking toward the fields. "No. No, you go be somebody."

Bekah watched her mother's face. The lines around her eyes crinkled with each word. Her firm lips moved matter of fact, and Bekah knew she was holding back tears.

"Just promise me this. Don't you ever forget where you came from, Rebekah McCauley. Don't forget what you're all about. You go to college. You get all that education you want, and you make something out of yourself, but don't forget your roots, Bekah, don't forget your roots."

The last potato skinned, her mother rinsed her hands under the running water, made quick work of drying them on her apron, and then turned to tend to the other dinner preparations. Bekah watched as her tired frame moved about the kitchen. She looked so much older that her forty-three years.

Don't worry, Mama. I won't forget.

* * *

The Calumet Club
Lexington, Kentucky

"Son, I can't tell you how pleased I am."

The wine glasses tinkled as rims slightly touched. The toast was for him, a celebration. Collin Kramer fidgeted in his chair as he listened to his father's praises. Too pleased. And his father never was too pleased with anything. But Collin wasn't a fool. There was no conceivable way his father was going to give in that easily.

Veterinary school had been a trade-off for a double major in business administration. He flew through the pre-vet program and was set to leave for Ohio State in August. That is, provided his father didn't renege.

The running of the family business had been a sore spot

since Collin was old enough to realize he wanted none of it—which was young. He'd rarely seen his father growing up. The man took no time for pleasure, and little for family. He was the prime definition of a workaholic; his children were not a priority. No, the bloodstock agency built by his grandfather—identifying stallion-and-mare combinations most likely produce winning thoroughbred racehorses—was never one of Collin's favorite topics of conversation.

He loved his horses, and his hounds. Animals he understood more than humans, sometimes. He'd never had a hound or a horse he couldn't communicate with or understand. He couldn't say that for some people he knew. The degree in Veterinary Science he was about to pursue was his only dream.

That is, if he could pull tonight off without a hitch.

His father turned to Herb Kilpatrick, his closest friend. Herb and his wife Carolyn had been friends of the family for years. Collin's mother and his two sisters, Katy and Jennifer, rounded out the celebration party. Collin, the guest of honor, winced as his father spoke.

"Double major, you know Herb. Business and pre-vet." His father had already downed the dinner wine and was on to something a little harder. The bourbon made him flush, enhancing his ruddy complexion. Collin's shoulders slumped as he noted how his father emphasized the word *business*. "Don't know what he'll do with all that education though. Seems a waste." He turned directly to Collin, his face stony. "But he's damned determined, that boy of mine. Damned determined."

Father and son locked gazes for several seconds. Collin could almost hear his father's teeth grinding in rhythm to the slow blues tune playing in the background of the country club restaurant. The lines in his father's face deepened. His jowl tightened as he set his jaw. *Much older looking than fifty-one.*

The liquor, the work, and the stress—all had aged him far beyond his years.

Collin wanted none of it. "Father...."

"Collin?" His mother, obviously recognizing the signs of tension between father and son, quickly changed the subject. "Did you know Erin is back in town?"

Collin's gaze stayed hooked with his father's a moment longer, signaling the subject was not closed. They would return to it eventually—likely sooner than his father realized. His attention shifted to his mother.

"Erin? Really?" Katy rolled her eyes from across the table and Collin grinned.

"No. I didn't know. When did she get back into Lexington?" *Erin.* Miles of flawless, golden skin and platinum hair swept across his mind's eye. She was two years older than him, and when she was sixteen, at least ten years older in sexual experience.

Ah, Erin. She taught him well. The Kilpatricks would have died had they known his first sexual encounter had been at fourteen in their bedroom with their only daughter. Not to mention what his own parents would have thought.

He turned to Carolyn Kilpatrick. "Back from France so soon? I'd have thought Paris would suit her nicely."

"Oh, it did. A little too much I'm afraid. She's running through her trust fund a mite more quickly than my daddy intended. Even though she's twenty-four, I have some parental control until she's thirty." Carolyn screwed up her face and looked off past his shoulder. "I had to call the shots and order her home. Poor Daddy would be turning over in his grave had he known what she was doing with his money. Sometimes I think she used art school just as a pretense to live in Europe."

Collin arched his eyebrows, and then took in his mother's warning look. Her head jerked slightly to the side, and he knew he'd better not touch that one. *Maybe Mother knows a whole lot more than I give her credit for.*

With a shuffling of salad plates, the waiter began serving the main course. The party settled down to eating, forks clanking softly on fine china, drinks refilled, a low hum of chatter around them. His sisters, Katy, the oldest at twenty-five and Jennifer, the baby of the family at eighteen, conversed softly among them-selves. Collin was content to eat. He didn't intend to cross his father tonight, at least not here. If he could bear the tension around the table long enough this evening, he would settle the score in the morning. He was going to vet school whether he used his father's money or not. He would work himself through if he had to. Plenty of people do it, he thought. *I can do it.* What he couldn't do was live the rest of his life minding the family business. There was no way he was going to look seventy when he was fifty.

Hours later, back at the family home, his mother's screams woke him with a start. Images of Erin's silky body vanished from his head as he groggily shook off the erotic dream. Collin bolted upright and threw himself toward his bedroom door in one motion. His mother stood in the hallway, sobbing.

"Mother?"

She slowly lifted one hand and pointed toward the open door of the master suite, her other hand covering her mouth. He saw Katy by the bedside, the phone to her ear. As he cautiously walked down the hall and through the door, realization hit him. He knew what he would find.

His father lay in a heap on the bathroom floor, curled onto his right side with his right arm pinned beneath him, his other hand splayed upward across his chest. His father's eyes were clamped shut, his face contorted in frozen pain. Deep lines etched across the reddened, tightened, leathered forehead.

Collin leaned over him and touched his face. Ice cold. He'd lain there quite a while. No doubt, he was gone.

Along the fringes of his mind, he heard Katy confirming information with 9-1-1. Time marched dizzyingly swift around him.

His father was dead.

A siren screamed softly in the background.

His father was dead.

Shards of his life drifted away.

Dead.

His dream.

Dead.

His father. Was dead.

Chapter One

S*pring, 1996*

"Damn coyote."

Collin cursed, wind pulling at his hair, his thighs tightly gripping the flanks of his reliable gray, the horse's hooves pounding like thunder into lush Kentucky bluegrass. His arms strained against the fabric of his lightweight jacket, held close to his body. A strong hand firmly clutched the horse's reins, keeping total control over the animal.

Keen eyes watched as the coyote slipped into the briars ahead and disappeared. His foxhounds followed, but the animal wouldn't linger. This one was crafty. There was no way that coyote would stay put. The animal intended to lead his hounds astray, even if it killed him in the process.

Years ago, a coyote was unheard of in Kentucky—but with their recent eastward migration, they were now quite common, and a cunning one would lead a pack of hounds deep into the river cliffs never to be seen again. Collin knew that. Bred to chase, the hounds would take after anything that ran—fox or coyote, it didn't matter.

Today, on what he thought was a leisurely jaunt on a brisk afternoon to exercise his horse and his hounds, he was not in the mood for it. He'd be damned if that mangy cur would lead his prized hounds into the river.

The hounds slowed, then howled and pawed at the ground around the thicket, hungry for their prey. Collin brought his prancing mount to the pack, calling them off their quarry—then suddenly, following a flash of dirty gray, they were off again.

They moved as one, Collin and the stallion, a huge mass of raw sexuality and power, each sensing the other's thoughts, movements, and intentions. The huge beast raced toward the pack, the wily coyote leading his hounds further away. Collin knew he had to call them off soon, had to get their attention before the animal took them where he and his horse couldn't go.

Perspiration beaded his forehead then dried in the wind. His muscles ached with the thrill and tension of the chase, although this chase was not welcome. A normal romp with a fox and his hounds was what he lived for, what he loved. And even though he knew both his horse and his hounds were at risk, plunging at breakneck speed across his farm, he relished in the chase.

As usual, when riding and keeping his hounds to the fox, his body grew tight with exhilaration, his mind sharp with concentration. Every sense heightened. Every nerve stood on high alert. Adrenaline coursed his body, spurring him on. He concentrated on the pack before him as blood pounded through his veins, surging through every capillary and artery. Heat rose to the surface of his skin.

The experience was one of dominance and power.

The hounds yipped and barked as they chased their prey,

hot on the scent of the animal. They raced hard against the wind roiling out of the gray afternoon sky in the west. A spring thunderstorm threatened. Collin narrowed his gaze as the coyote leapt the rock fence bordering the edge of his farm, and silently swore.

The hounds hesitated, jumping and clawing at the wall, and then scrambled over.

Damn it! Without thinking, and in one swift movement, he guided the stallion up and over the fence.

Collin saw nothing but the pack of hounds in front of him, the lead hound straight on course with the coyote. He was hell-bent for leather on seeing this thing to the end. He'd seen other hunters give up on the hounds, hoping they would come home eventually. Not him. Nothing would stop him.

Nothing.

The tireless hounds raced on, oblivious to their surroundings, the horse closing in fast. The coyote, now on open ground, ran for his life. Collin would never kill the animal, but the coyote didn't know that. He could almost sense his fear. He imagined the trembling in his stomach, the panic shaking his legs, the hounds breathing hot down his neck.

He urged the horse on. Hooves churned the soft Kentucky soil as they jumped another fence and galloped onward. Collin vaguely noticed a building to the right. He ran onto different terrain, shorter grass, smooth ground, gravel—but his eyes never left the coyote. Thunder cracked in the distance. A flash of lightning splintered the air.

An ear-splitting scream pierced the buzz around him, and everything came to a sudden and abrupt halt. A contradictory feeling of silent slow motion and mass confusion sped over him as the hounds ran circles in agitation. The horse sidestepped excitedly, then another scream and a feminine slew of curses penetrated the unnatural silence.

The coyote scurried off to safety.

"What the..." The past few minutes his mind had comprehended only one thing—the chase. Now, he diverted his attention to the ranting and raving female standing before him.

Rake in one hand, hoe in another, she shouted incomprehensibly, flailing her arms.

His inspection of her started from her dirt-clodded work boots, then slowly traveled north to her muddy blue-jean clad knees, and upward to a man's ragged chambray work shirt tied at the curve of her small waist. His perusal followed up the front closure of her shirt. Two button snaps at the top had popped open during her tirade revealing a wisp of white lace and the top of a fully rounded, lily-white breast.

Collin paused, and grinned.

His gaze resumed its trek up a delicate, slender ivory neck to rest on an angry, but extremely beautiful face. Coal black eyes spat back at him, and her long inky ponytail held high on her head with a red bandanna, whipped with the breeze coming from the storm.

My God. Gorgeous.

The coyote was forgotten.

He sucked in a breath. Was she speaking? Yelling.

"...and if you don't get your slimy, blue blood ass off my property, I'll shove this rake where the sun don't shine!"

He heard that last piece very clearly.

Collin remained solid in his seat, enjoying the dominant position—still smiling but glaring back at the delicate, yet willful woman. His horse pranced.

Spitfire of a little country thing.

She turned, dropped the hoe, and picked up a clod of dirt at her feet.

Nice ass.

Her gaze shot back as if she'd heard his thought. Her eyes

narrowed and she scrutinized him as he sat above her. Her gaze traveled from his breeches at her eye level, to his face. He stared back, a smile tugging at the corner of his lips.

She fumbled with the clod of dirt, flexing and gripping. Then she did something Collin thought unthinkable.

Threw it.

"Git!"

The dirt clod spun out of her hand like a second baseman hurling a ball toward first. The hound promptly yipped off behind his master when hit—and in the next instant, Collin leapt off his horse and exerted all the control he could muster not to grab the woman and shake the tar out of her. His fists clenched together tightly at his side. He felt the grin vanish from his face.

"Don't you ever..." he snarled.

"Then get those damn mutts out of my garden," she spat back, their noses inches apart. Collin felt the venom of her words, along with her heated breath against his face. Blood surged throughout his body, his breathing quickened.

This was an incredibly beautiful woman.

"...and get your horse off my property *now—*" she held the glare, "before I call someone to remove these beasts for me. I'm sure the pound could shelter them for the night."

Anger gained speed and raced from the ball in his chest to his pounding head, then suddenly he realized that he was a little more than angry. He was aroused. He wanted to touch her. He wanted to reach out and grasp her hips to pull her close. He wanted to crowd her breasts, feeling the rise and fall of her chest against his. To lower his head to hers, even closer, his lips barely centimeters from her full pouty mouth.

He wanted to steal a kiss. And more.

Thoroughly enjoying himself, Collin chuckled inwardly.

The cool depths of her eyes stared back, but she never flinched. *The woman doesn't give up easily.*

"Nice spunk. I like that," he whispered.

"You're trespassing," she hissed. "I should call the sheriff right now. I should have you arrested." She didn't back down. She barely even blinked. "And of course, you're going to have to pay for the damages."

Damages? Hell.

Collin stepped back. The woman stumbled slightly as he did so. He threaded all five fingers of one hand through his hair and glanced about. A trail of petunias led from the front porch of her house to the garden slightly behind it. The garden rows had been neatly marked with seed packages at each end. Had been. There would have been a variety of vegetables come summer. His hounds had torn the garden to pieces. One look told him it had been more than just a morning's work.

There was no longer any resemblance of a vegetable plot, only a mass of seeds and seedlings, ripped up tomato plants, seed potatoes sporting half-grown plants, and onion sets. The hounds continued to dig.

And she hadn't stopped talking. "If you don't get those animals out soon," her hands were placed firmly on narrow hips now, "I have a promise to keep with that hoe and a certain area of your anatomy."

Thunder rumbled through the heavy air. Fat raindrops fell around them. The wind picked up and the woman adjusted her shirt at her neck.

Collin sensed her seething anger. He almost felt sorry, but surely it was just a few seeds and some plants. At least it wasn't August and fully ripened vegetables. At least now, she could start all over.

He waved his hands. "All right, all right. No need to get

violent. How much?" Collin reached into his back pocket for his wallet.

The woman glared.

He contemplated her still-angry face. There was a certain rural flavor about her that intrigued him. Yet, there was something classy and sophisticated too. Maybe it was the contradiction in the pristine white scrap of lace peeking out from the dirty work shirt. Or her flawless porcelain complexion. Or ruby red lips.

He cocked his head to one side, wondering what made this woman tick. She still hadn't answered him.

"I said how much. I will pay for the damages." Collin focused his attention to his wallet and fumbled with a few bills.

The woman stepped backward and picked up the hoe from the ground. "Forget it, just leave." She held his gaze for a few seconds longer, and then turned toward the old frame farmhouse.

He took a step toward her, a little miffed at the sudden turn of events. "No, wait. I said I'll pay." He didn't like it when people walked away from him.

She stopped and slightly turned. "And I said forget it. I will be happy if you just keep on your own side of the fence from now on. Your dogs, too."

Collin stomped to her side, grabbed her arm a little too harshly, and spun her around to face him. Her eyes sparked something akin to surprise and fear. "I don't think you understand. Do you realize to whom you are speaking? I'm a man who takes care of his obligations. I damaged your property and I said I'll pay. Now *how much?*" His voice grew louder with each word.

She jerked her arm free. "*Look*, I know who you are, and I don't give a damn. I'm not impressed. I know what you are doing and why you are doing it, and I want to get something perfectly clear." She nosed closer. "I don't *want* your damn money. You couldn't *pay* me what all that was worth. I just want you to leave. Get it? Stay off my property. And if you know what's good for you, you won't lay another hand on me, mister."

She stepped backward.

Collin laughed, dismissing that last statement—although there were a lot of ways he'd like to lay his hands on her. "Honey, everything has a price. Now how much?"

"That's where you're wrong. Not everything."

"No, that's where *you're* wrong. I could buy and sell you. This farm too." He glanced about. "In fact, the acreage here could make a nice little addition to my place. Like I said, *everything* has a price, darlin'. Now name it."

Anger washed over her face like a waterfall. Through gritted teeth she returned, "Not this farm. Not this woman. Now, leave."

Collin backed up two steps and lifted his hands in a gesture of surrender. "Sorry, honey, didn't mean to get you all riled. It's just a garden, just a few plants and seeds. I thought I'd be neighborly and...."

The woman shook her head slowly. "Take your stinking animals, *all of them,* home with you and go play in your own yard. Now I see what everyone has been talking about. You are the most self-centered man—and frankly, I think that's pretty sad." She turned and then whipped back again. "And don't call me honey!"

Collin watched as she rushed toward the house, stomped up the wooden steps, shoved the hoe into a corner by the door, and let the screen door slam shut in final retort. Obviously, his reputation had preceded him.

But she amused him. Just like a fox. The exhilaration of the chase. A familiar fire burned deep within his abdomen. His fingers ached to touch her again. His lips desired, no yearned, to make contact. They had been so close. He'd almost captured her intoxicating lips with his. He wished he had.

This wasn't over yet. Not by a long shot.

The hunt was on.

* * *

Growing up, Bekah McCauley had lived all her life on Kentucky soil. The past ten years, the exception. Still, *never* in her life had she met up with someone so full of himself as the man who just rode roughshod over her garden. Not even in New York. Not even Matthew's insolence compared to his.

I thought I was getting away from all that.

From her bedroom window, she frowned, watching the lone figure ride across the pasture, the hounds in fast pursuit. The wind howled and she silently wished the storm would blow up quickly, dousing his hot head in an icy spring rainstorm.

She guessed Joe was right. The old farmer next door had warned her about her neighbor. She'd heard an ear full about Mr. Collin Kramer, that was for certain. At first, she found the stories hard to believe, but now felt they could all easily be true.

All Joe could talk about was Kramer's lack of respect other people's land. More than one of the neighboring farmers had encountered him running foxes over their freshly plowed fields or tobacco beds, tearing up everything in sight, and then whipping out big bills as he had done today. He'd even cut off all access to the creek from his property. Many of the older men had fished there since they were boys, but when Kramer bought the farm last fall, he put up fences, guardrails, and no trespassing signs preventing their entry.

The women just talked about his arrogance, along with the fact he was the best-looking man to arrive in these parts in years. Not that Bekah had noticed anyway. Her gaze trailed the figure as his horse leapt back over the rock fence onto his own property. Her breathing slowed, even though her thoughts returned to his muscular thighs. She'd had an eye-level view of them earlier. She imagined those muscles rippling underneath his tight breeches, gripping the horse's sides tighter as they soared over the fence.

No, she hadn't noticed a thing.

Glancing toward a dark sky ready to burst with rain, Bekah felt her own mood turn gloomy. It wasn't supposed to rain today. The almanac had said so. It was supposed to be a good day for planting, the almanac had said that too—and she had so wanted to do everything right. Her anger boiled.

How dare he.

How dare he ride in here with those beasts, and that lousy-looking piece of horseflesh, and that inflated attitude of his, and those sexy, baby blue, bedroom eyes? Her breath caught and she shook her head.

Turning from the window, she sat on the edge of her grandmother's bed. Elbows on her knees, she leaned forward, her chin resting on her fists. Pay for the damages? How could she put a price on that garden? She'd spent days planning. She'd spent all yesterday morning trying to find just the right seeds and plants, carefully picking what she wanted, agonizing over the right ones. Not to mention spending the last bit of cash she had on them.

Prior to that, she had plotted out her garden, trying to remember what her grandfather said about planting potatoes next to corn or next to beans. Then, she'd had to find an almanac, because she knew her grandparents always planted according to the signs. She had never paid much attention when they were alive, but now that they weren't, she wished she had.

Joe plowed the garden and she'd repaid him with a decent, home-cooked meal, something he hadn't had lately since his wife, Maggie, was off visiting with an ill sister. The potatoes were in the ground on Good Friday. Joe had helped then, too. Her grandfather would have been proud. She hadn't been able to pay Joe yet for his help, even though he said he didn't want anything, because money had been a little tight lately—which was why she was growing the damn garden in the first place!

Maybe she should have taken the bastard's money.

No. If I let him pay me, he'll think he can run over my land anytime he wants. *I'll not prostitute my grandparent's farm in that manner.*

A gnawing rippled across her abdomen and Bekah absent-mindedly rubbed the tender area with her left hand. Her ulcer. It hadn't flared up in weeks. But then again, she'd not been this angry in weeks. Not since the big fight with Matthew. Not since she'd quit her job at the magazine and chucked the high society life of New York City, and headed back home to Kentucky with her tail firmly tucked between her legs.

Here, her grandparents' farm waited, and welcomed her with open arms. *Wind Ridge.* Her grandfather had passed not long after she left home for college. Her grandmother retired to a nursing home a year later and died ten months ago. They had entrusted everything they owned to her, their wisdom so great to recognize that her itchy feet were only temporary, and she would someday come home needing a place of her own to heal. She would be eternally grateful they had the insight to see that and not lose faith in her, and she'd be damned if she would turn her back on them now.

Bekah was determined to make a go of the one-hundred-twenty acres she now owned. And she would do it all by herself. Not only for her grandparents, but also for herself and her future.

After all, she was a fighter. She wasn't used to giving up, and this was no different. She had fought bigger battles and won.

She was the only person in her family to attend college. She had wanted it so desperately, and she'd worked hard to make the grades—and it had paid off.

After graduation, she'd landed an entry-level position at the magazine, unusual that someone so young and inexperienced would work themselves up the ladder so quickly. But she was good, and they knew it. She fought tooth and nail to land the art editor position, and so as soon as there was an opening, the job was hers. At least that was what she thought had happened at the time. Within five years, she wound up with a good salary, a comfortable apartment, glamorous friends, plenty of nightlife, a big fat ulcer, and a scheming rat of a boyfriend who dumped her as soon as the going got tough.

Damn him anyway.

She'd managed all that, nothing was going to keep her from successfully running this farm. Nothing. Especially not her neighbor across the fence.

Or Matthew. No one.

Bekah rose and walked to the oak dresser across the room and stared into the beveled mirror. Nothing she could do until the storm blew over. Outside, at least. She hadn't asked for credit yet, but it looked as though she might be about to. She'd pulled her retirement funds from the magazine, but the check hadn't arrived. Farmers lived by credit, she knew that, and she had been putting off the inevitable. Her parents had an account at the feed store all her life. It was just the asking.

A quick ride into town might dispel her anger and clear her head. The feed store would still be open, and there were a few other things she needed. She'd treat herself to dinner out if she'd had the cash. *Looks like I'll be visiting the bank in the morning.*

"Dinner for one. An exciting thought." *Woohoo.* She frowned, staring at her reflection, brushing her hair and retying the bandanna catching the ponytail. She laid a soft hand across her tummy. "Well, you know what they say, Bekah? You are your own best company."

* * *

The storm blew over with only a sprinkling of rain. Collin watched from the barn as the angry charcoal clouds rumbled by overhead. His face stung from the wind and slanted raindrops whipping around him as he retreated onto his own land. Was it really the wind, he thought, or the bite of the woman's words that stung so badly?

What was it she said? That he didn't care about anyone or anything but himself? Ridiculous. She didn't know him. There wasn't a man around who donated to various charities like he did. Kept up a good image, the old man used to say. And hadn't he just bought uniforms for his nephew's soccer team? Kramer Bloodstock looked great emblazoned across the back. Good for advertising.

Collin ran all ten fingers backward through his damp hair and glanced from his barn across to the neighboring farm. He barely saw the green painted tin roof of her old farmhouse through the distant trees. Slim rays of sunshine filtered through the dark remnants of thunderclouds, brightening the afternoon sky.

Who am I kidding?

He turned back to the inside of the barn, pacing the width from stall to stall where he'd just fed and rubbed down his horse. What *did* he really care about? Stopping abruptly, he faced the stallion. Most riders preferred a mare or gelding to a stallion, but not Collin. He enjoyed the power the animal offered. It matched his personality.

Placing a hand next to his muzzle, he stroked the animal with warmth and caring. His animals, yes, he did care for them.

For years, all he needed was his horse and the hounds. And the agency. As much as he hated it in the beginning, he came to thrive on it. But at thirty-six, was that enough? There was a gnawing, a growing hunger he couldn't explain, eating away at him. Had been for the past few years—and he couldn't deny it any longer. He needed more. He owned the farm, his animals, and a successful business. There was a steady stream of women.

Yet, something was missing.

Slowly he strode toward the open barn door, leaned against the center post, and looked once more across the open field. A chilled breeze wafted off the storm and cooled his burning face. He followed an old pick-up truck as it made its way down the gravel lane from the neighboring farmhouse. The vehicle turned onto the paved road toward his own property. As the truck rambled past, he caught a glimpse of red bandanna and silky black hair flying out of the truck window.

Chapter Two

"**M**et your neighbor yet?"

Bekah glanced up from the flat-filled table of tomato seedlings to look into Butch Baker's teasing eyes. She'd known Butch and his family since she was a child. Their feed store was always on the list of places to stop when her parents came to town.

She rolled her eyes.

"I take it that's a yes."

Bekah straightened and selected one container of tomatoes and one of green peppers, eyeing him all the way as she stepped toward the counter to pay. "You take it right."

He followed her and then rounded the counter to the other side, shrugging. "You don't look happy about it." He glanced to the vegetable flats. "Didn't you buy tomato plants yesterday?"

Bekah let out a long breath and set the plants on the smooth wood surface. "No, I'm not happy about it, and yes, I bought tomatoes yesterday—and green peppers, and corn, bean, and squash seeds."

Butch scratched his head. "Something wrong with them?"

"No."

"You need more then."

"No."

"You helping Joe with his garden?"

Bekah signed and shook her head. "No."

For all the years she'd known Butch Baker, she'd never thought him as a pest. Even in elementary school, and then later in high school when they were a couple. When she left to go to college, she feared he would make a spectacle of himself when they broke up, but he didn't. Today though, he seemed to be going overboard. Maybe it was just her nerves. Perhaps it was the fact that she was going to have to ask him for credit.

Asking her old boyfriend for credit at his father's store was just a little much. There wasn't anything between them anymore, of course. Butch had married Peggy Harrison a year after graduation, and they now had three kids together. Bekah just knew he would feel obligated, even though half the town had credit here. She didn't know if she could bring herself to do it.

She was the superstar. *She'd* lived in New York City. She was, according to the local grapevine, supposed to have made tons of money while she was there. So much money that she could afford to quit her fancy New York job and come back and live in the lap of luxury on the farm. According to them, she had it all. Little did they know that she had barely escaped with her health, her sanity, the small amount of money she had in her checking account—and literally the clothing on her back. There was no lap of luxury at Wind Ridge.

"Then why?"

"Because the bastard and his stinking dogs tore the hell out of my garden." Her high-pitched voice rang throughout the empty feed store. She hadn't meant to sound so forceful, but she wasn't in the mood for conversation, or explanation.

Butch eyed her from the few short feet across the counter.

"Ah, I see. You've definitely met up with the infamous Collin Kramer."

She chewed on her lower lip and shifted from one foot to another.

"Yes," she snapped, then regretted her outburst. "Sorry Butch. Just not in a particularly good mood this afternoon. I need to look for few more things. Can I keep these here?" She motioned toward the plants she'd already selected.

"Of course."

The bell on the door clanged loudly. She watched Butch's eyes widen as he glanced to the front of the store. "Help yourself, Bekah," he stated as he slowly brought his gaze back to her. "Can I find anything for you?"

"No, I'll find what I need." Bekah turned on her heel, and her gaze skidded off the eyes of the man approaching. *Kramer. Shit.* She stopped, sucked in a steadying breath, and stilled the tremor that shot up through her chest. As he passed, she looked to the floor and kept walking. His arm brushed hers and Bekah ignored the sensation left by that faint touch.

Collin headed for the counter. "Mr. Baker, I need some vegetable plants."

Butch chuckled. "Funny Kramer, you don't strike me as the gardening type."

Bekah stole a glance in their direction. Kramer's back was to her, giving her the advantage of watching him from behind. His broad shoulders stretched wide over his narrow waist and hips. His long legs sported muscular thighs, evident even from underneath his khaki trousers. And his ass, tight and high, and—

Bekah jerked her gaze back to stare at the cabbage plants. *Damn it, Bekah!*

"Not for me."

Bekah risked a glance to the counter area. Collin turned and smiled. She sneered back.

25

"Look." He turned back to Butch. "I need tomatoes, peppers, onions, oh hell, I don't know—whatever is normally put out this time of year." He turned briskly again. "What do you suggest, Miss McCauley?"

Bekah narrowed her gaze and heaved out a sigh. "I don't give a damn what you buy." Her cheeks heated, her throat suddenly grew tight.

"Can't you give your neighbor a little gardening advice?"

"I'll give you advice..." Her voice trailed off, but she stood her ground. The last thing she wanted was drama.

Collin took a few steps forward. "Look," He sucked in another breath. "I'm trying to make amends here. You won't accept my money, let me replace the plants."

"Not necessary." Bekah pushed away from the rows of flats and crossed her arms over her chest. This man violated every principle of her upbringing. He stood for everything she just ran away from in New York—greed, jealousy, control—

Fucking control.

"I think it is."

She breathed deep, looked past his shoulder, and let her breath out slowly. Bekah shook her head. "I told you earlier today, I'll take care of it."

"Let me do this."

"I don't need your help, Mr. Kramer."

"I didn't say you did. I feel responsible."

"Don't you get it? I don't want your help. I just want you to stay on your own side of the damn fence."

"Stubborn woman." The two words whooshed out of his pursed mouth. Collin swiveled toward Butch. "Baker, fix her up with whatever she needs and put it on my bill." He turned to head for the exit.

Bekah stepped forward. "No. Don't do it Butch."

Collin whirled. "Do it."

"No!" She faced him.

"I've already given the order."

"Order?" She punched out a breath. "And you're so damned used to getting what you want, aren't you?"

"That's generally the way it works." He inched closer.

"Well not this time."

"Really?" Collin chuckled.

"No."

"And why is that?"

His tongue swiped across his lower lip and Bekah's pulse quickened. "Because you've never had to deal with me before."

Butch hooted from behind the counter. Collin glanced to him and then back to Bekah. In one swift motion, he grabbed both of Bekah's shoulders. As he hauled her body into his, his lips descended, searing down on hers. Hot, steaming, smoldering liquid heat enveloped her mouth.

Well, shit! Bekah tensed up. Her hands shot up between their chests and she pushed with all her might, but his arms were wound too tightly around her. His tongue dipped between her lips. Testing, taunting... She felt like biting it, but her eyes closed involuntarily, and she found herself returning the kiss as fervently as he gave it. Hot breath escaping, flesh mingling, lips tasting. Push-pull. A tug-of-war, a battle of wills, each trying to outdo or perhaps dominate the other.

Or prove a point. Butch whooped again from behind the counter.

Collin released her and took a step backward, steadying her. "And you, little lady, have never had to deal with me before."

He moved her to the side then, walked past her and out the door. Bekah swung around wildly, took two steps, and halted. Suddenly she didn't know what to do with her hands, or her body. The bell slowed its ring after the door slammed shut. She whirled back to Butch.

"Get that stupid grin off your face."

"Sorry Bekah, it was just—"

She shot him a look.

"Do you want the plants?"

She shot him another one.

"I mean the ones you picked out earlier?"

No, she couldn't. She thought she could come in here and do it, ask for credit, but she couldn't. She didn't want anything from anybody. Not now, not ever.

"No. Not today. I'll come back." She turned briskly and headed toward the door.

"Bekah? You all right?"

All right? She didn't know if anything would ever be all right again.

Too antsy to go home, Bekah ended up at her parents' an hour or so later. The drive to their farm, just on the edge of the next county, calmed her. The weather was still cool in the after-noons, but Bekah rolled down the windows and slid the back glass of her truck cab wide open anyway. She drove slowly, letting the wind pull through her hair, now released from its bandanna tie and flowing in waves around her shoulders.

She loved visiting her parents, especially since she had spent so many years away from home. But on this evening, she was not expected. Nor were her brothers, their wives, and their five collective children. Though her parents were both thrilled and surprised to see everyone, they didn't balk at pulling together an impromptu family gathering, everyone pitching in to do what they could to get the evening meal on the table.

The diversion of family was wonderful, but after mentally fighting the noise and frivolity, along with the sheer lack of a moment's peace, Bekah decided to beg out early. The thirty-minute drive home worked wonders to defray her ragged nerves.

The silence was bliss. After the day she'd had, she figured she deserved it and intended to prolong it as long as possible.

About a quarter of a mile from her farm, she rounded a sharp curve. To her right was a deep gully, leading down into the creek. She slowly drove over the bridge and drank in the evening sounds of dusk falling.

Bekah itched to be a part of it. She stopped her truck in the middle of the bridge and absorbed the calm. Crickets sang along the water's edge, the stream rippled and popped gently over the rocky creek bed. On impulse, she pulled over to the edge and got out.

"Collin Kramer be damned," she muttered and climbed over the guardrail and down to the creek, totally ignoring the 'no trespassing' sign.

Upon reaching the water, Bekah took off her worn tennis shoes and socks, cuffed her blue jeans at mid-calf, and sat on a huge boulder near the edge. She plunged her feet into the creek's iciness, sucking in a quick breath. Her toes wiggled and stretched out as far as possible as she glorified in the simple pleasure it gave her.

The rock was large enough to lie back on and she did, letting her feet dangle over the edge. Bekah laid back with her eyes closed, one arm flung across her forehead. The last rays of sun reflected a reddish glow from the evening sky, but soon, even that left. She lay perfectly still, not wanting to spoil the peacefulness of her sanctuary.

Her life had been full of so much turmoil the past few years. She needed this. Drifting into a semi-dream state, she lay listening—insects chirped, a branch rustled, an animal howled in the distance. Her body relaxed against the cool stone, almost melding with it—her feet and legs united with the stream, her soul one with nature.

The tendons in her neck expanded, loosening their tight

hold, water lapped at her ankles and the crickets drummed their near-silent serenade into her head.

The image that appeared behind her closed eyes was one of sheer masculinity. The close-set eyes ridged in low, firm brows called out to her on a wicked whisper, the depth of their blue as icy as creek water. Russet curls lay damp against his forehead. Firm, thin lip—and the tongue that swept across those lips just before he kissed her.

He threw back his head and laughed. A haunting melody. Laughing at her? A chill traveled her body. She shook herself and sat up straight, pulling her feet out of the rushing waters, rubbing her arms briskly to chase away unnerving sensations that had enveloped her body.

Probably time to get out of here.

But as she stood, the eyes remained, and for the third time that day, she came face to face with Collin Kramer.

* * *

Collin watched as his neighbor pulled her pick-up slowly to the side of the road and parked against the guardrail he'd installed a few months earlier. He'd put it there to prevent exactly what she was doing now—trespassing. Everyone wanted to park there to walk down to the creek to fish. They bothered his horses pasturing in the next field, and the late nighters were a nuisance.

But that didn't stop Ms. Rebekah McCauley.

My God. Is she taunting me, or what?

A huge sycamore near the creek's edge hid him from her view, but he watched as she stretched her blue jean-clad legs along the boulder. Dainty feet dipped into the rambling waters. Coal black hair tumbled around her shoulders, mimicking an ebony waterfall.

One delicate arm lay across her forehead. He watched, knowing she couldn't see him, although he was close enough to observe her shallow breathing. Her chest lifted and fell rhythmically, almost in sync with his own. The chambray shirt she still wore hugged each breast, tightly cupping her flesh into rounded mounds, teasing out from a gap in the snap closures.

Collin drew in a deep breath, and then exhaled, slowly. He fought off the prickling at the back of his neck. His heart kicked up a quick beat just watching her. Something gripped his gut—a warning?—and then every corpuscle in his body surged lower.

Fantasies would get him nowhere at this moment. He had set out to remove one female trespasser from his property and that was what he intended to do.

Rounding the tree, he moved straight to the boulder, stopping only when she leapt off the huge rock. They stood, gazes locked for several seconds, and then Bekah sat on the rock again and began pulling on her socks and shoes.

"What are you doing?" He broke the awkward silence.

"Leaving."

"Good."

She tugged the dry socks over her damp feet. "You think a guardrail is going to keep people away from the creek?"

"At least on my property."

She glanced up, then back to her shoes. "And you're so concerned that people stay on their own property?" She rose, took a step back toward the hill and her truck.

Collin tugged at her elbow, turning her to face him. "People should be considerate of what doesn't belong to them."

She glared. "Like how? Like ripping through freshly planted gardens?"

"I offered to pay for the damages."

"And that makes it okay?"

"It's more than other people do around here. When I first

bought this place there was nothing but beer cans and trash all over the creek bank. I cleaned it up. I don't want to have to do it again."

She shook her head. "You've missed the point entirely. I feel sorry for you." She moved back up the hill, her small round derriere swaying from side to side. He did nothing but stand and watch for a quick moment. She nearly disappeared into the dusk as she approached the guardrail. He caught up with her just as she reached her truck.

"Wait."

Bekah opened the truck door, and put it between them, one foot resting on the floorboard.

"Look," she said, her gaze meeting his. "I don't like you. I don't like what I've heard from my neighbors. I don't like what you did to my garden, and I don't like that I can't go down and enjoy the creek anymore like did as a kid.

"I don't think you understand what life here is all about. People take it easy. We help each other out and don't ask for anything in return. We let them fish in our ponds or in the creeks that run through our land. We're simple, caring, friendly folk who only want to live our lives in peace and solitude. And we don't like trespassers any more than you do. The only difference though, between you and us, is attitude. And frankly, most everyone else around here thinks yours stinks."

She sat, slammed the door shut, and let out a huge breath.

Collin laid both arms on the open window and leaned into the cab space. "Let me get this straight. You don't like me because of what you've heard about me, or because of what happened this afternoon?"

"Both." She stared ahead.

"And you don't like my attitude?"

"For starters."

"And you don't think I have any redeeming qualities at all, like neighborliness and so forth?"

She looked him straight in the eyes. "I haven't seen any evidence so far."

"All right."

Collin held the glare a little longer. Then, he reached into the cab space and touched her bottom lip ever so slightly.

"What about my kiss?"

She jerked away at his touch. "Insignificant." She looked ahead and twisted the key in the ignition.

"You enjoyed it."

"Tolerated it." She shoved the truck into gear. "You might want to move."

Collin stepped back, pulled his hands away from the truck, and watched her head down the road.

Chapter Three

Miss Rebekah McCauley....
Collin sat in the overstuffed wingback chair in his den and thought about his neighbor across the fence. Since he'd bought this farm six months ago, he'd had no indication the neighboring farm was occupied—until the stable hands started talking about the hot woman next door. Even Pete had mentioned her startling beauty. More than once, he'd overheard the conversations in the barn speculating why she'd moved there, if she were married, and what it would feel like to press themselves between her thighs.

Only they didn't express their desires in quite those terms.

He shook off that notion and rose, pacing the room, finally stopping at a floor-to-ceiling window that faced her farm. He stared into the night at the one illuminated window on the second floor of her house. That same notion had crossed his own mind over the past day—and it was increasingly disturbing. He stepped away from the window.

He didn't need the distraction. He'd bought the farm to get away from the city, away from his mother and sisters, and away from Erin. This was his solitude and his salvation. Here he could ride, hunt, exercise his hounds—whatever he felt like doing without answering to another woman. Women always wanted things. And now, there she was, across the fence, another woman. A damned beautiful—*strikingly beautiful*—woman who within the confines of one day had sent his libido whirling into oblivion.

Except she wanted nothing from him. Which was a good thing.

For him.

He didn't need another woman monitoring his comings and goings. He didn't need the possessiveness, the fawning over him, the sucking up just to get something *from* him. He didn't need *her*. He might *want* her, but he didn't need her.

Yet, he was intrigued. The three times today they'd met had not been entirely coincidental. In fact, he'd planned the second meeting, and the third he couldn't have stepped away from if he'd wanted—which he didn't. No denying, he'd likely invent some way to get close to her again, even though it was the worst thing he could do right now.

Christ. What was he thinking?

Collin stepped to the bar, poured himself a bourbon on the rocks, and then sank again into the chair. Glancing around the wood-paneled walls of the den, he perused the fox hunt prints, the formal furnishings, the oriental rugs, the brass wall sconces and chandelier—and questioned the sanity of a man like himself living alone in a home such as this. Kentucky blue-blood existence in all its finery. Of course, he'd had the money to purchase it, so why not?

For show. Status symbol. Business. Hell, why?

He entertained, yes, occasionally, but did that warrant this Federal-style monstrosity?

He was a loner. Didn't make sense. He just didn't *need* all of this—excess.

His gaze drifted to the window he'd just stepped away from. Why the hell had he allowed himself to get so caught up with business that he'd forgotten about his life? Only to end up alone?

Why *hadn't* he ever married? Why was it he'd never found himself a wife, someone like Miss Rebekah McCauley across the fence, who would keep him happy both night and day? Why didn't he have a family to share this with?

His father, of course.

Same reason he hadn't gone to college. Why his dreams of being a vet were squashed the moment his father passed away. Why he'd pushed anything remotely related to his own personal life and satisfaction away as soon as the funeral was over.

His life ended the day they put his father in the ground. He'd buried his true self deep, right along with his dad, and even though he'd vowed he would never be his old man, he'd become exactly like him.

Collin rose and tossed back the contents of the tumbler, then set it on the wooden bar. His father had gone and died on him, that's what happened. He stood and stared at the squatty glass, his breath deepening. In one quick and deliberate motion, he swiped at the tumbler, hitting it with his palm, sending glass and ice cubes flying. The thing hit the wall and ricocheted to the oak floors, shattering into a thousand pieces.

Just like his life.

He *had* turned into the spitting image of his old man—like it or not.

* * *

Bekah had left her bedroom windows open during the night. She winced as her feet hit the chilly plank floor beside her bed. As she passed the window—dawn breaking orange and pink on the horizon—she glanced at the farm across the pasture, and quickly away again.

Sleep took several hours coming the night before. She'd repeatedly played the day's events over in her mind, lingering over the remembrance of Collin's lips against hers—and felt disgusted because the kiss had aroused her. And then again, by the creek, when he'd touched her lower lip with his finger—his touch had done something to her then, too.

She didn't need this. Bekah padded across the floor, pulling her warm terry robe around her, and then padded down the stairs to the kitchen. *I came here to get away from Matthew. From men. I'll be damned if I'll get caught up with another man again for a long time.*

"Breakfast," she muttered. "That's what I need. A good country breakfast to start my day and several hours of work on the farm."

She pulled her grandmother's iron skillet off a hook above the kitchen work island and placed it on the stove. Turning to the refrigerator, she removed a carton of eggs, a pound of bacon, a can of refrigerator biscuits, butter, and jam.

"Need to clean up that garden first." She started making a mental list. "Get plants. That means addressing the credit issue. Then I need to work in the barn, maybe clean out that old tool shed." She turned the heat up high under the skillet and began layering thick slices of bacon across it. "Then after that, I need to mow the yard, weed-eat, work on cleaning up that back porch."

The list was longer than the day.

The bacon sizzled and Bekah breathed in the aroma. Closing her eyes, she pictured herself in her mama's kitchen, waiting for breakfast. Every morning had started out with bacon and eggs. She wasn't sure she'd had a breakfast like that since she'd left. She opened her eyes and glanced to the potato bin.

"Fried potatoes. Yes, definitely, fried potatoes."

For the next fifteen minutes or so, she cooked, humming to the radio on the counter, and planning her day. So, content on her task, she didn't hear the car drive up or the footsteps echo across her side porch. Just as she was ready to scoop up scrambled eggs from the skillet onto her plate, a loud rap sounded at the door.

She jumped, and then spun toward the sound. Her gaze landed on the man standing on the other side of the screen door.

Kramer. Shit!

She just stood there. Then finally, she set the plate down on the counter, wiped her hands on a dishtowel, and padded in her bare feet to the door and opened it.

For another long second, she paused, just looking. "Isn't it awful early for you to be up annoying the neighbors?"

He jerked a nod and stepped into the kitchen. Bekah glanced outside. "What, no dogs or horses?" She turned back to face him.

He grinned and shook his head. "Not a hound or horse in sight. You made that quite clear yesterday."

The screen door slammed shut as she let it go. Bekah crossed her arms. "I believe I included you in that statement."

"So, I'm not welcome?"

"You're uninvited, and it's early."

"Oh, so I need an invitation?"

She blew out a breath.

"What if I offer up an apology for yesterday?"

"Which part of yesterday."

He eyed her. "All of it."

"That still won't wrangle you an invitation."

Collin glanced around the kitchen, his gaze landing on the stove. "Not even for breakfast?"

"Sorry," Bekah returned. "I only fixed enough for one."

His gaze remained fixed on her for a moment longer, then he strode across the kitchen to the stove. "Looks like enough for the both of us."

It was true and Bekah knew it. There were enough eggs, potatoes, bacon, gravy, and biscuits to feed an army. More than enough for the two of them. But she really didn't want to sit across from Collin Kramer at her breakfast table this morning. She ignored that possibility. "What was that about an apology?"

Collin picked up a piece of bacon and turned his back to the food, leaning up against the stove. His stare met hers as he bit off a bite of the bacon then turned to pick up a morsel of fried potato. "I was thinking last night—"

Oh. You, too?

"—that I was probably a little out of line yesterday."

Resigned, she stepped across the kitchen, pulled down another plate and handed it to him. *Might as well eat. I'll just have to throw it out to the dog anyway.* "And which time are you referring to?" She picked up a mug. "Coffee?"

He nodded. Bekah poured two cups and set them on the table. He filled his plate then sat. She filled hers, retrieved forks and knives for them both, and settled across from him.

They ate for a few minutes, and then Bekah broke the silence. "I believe you were trying to make a point?"

He smiled. "Uh, yeah." He pointed to his plate with the fork. "This is really good. You cook like this all the time?"

She shook her head. "No, and you're avoiding the subject."

He took another bite of potatoes. "How did you learn to do this?"

"My mother," she said finally. "And what about that apology?"

He ignored her question. For the next few minutes, they ate in silence, and Bekah refused to let him get her goat with the silent treatment.

40

He chewed up the last bite of eggs, buttered a remnant of biscuit, and then placed his knife and fork in the center of his plate. Finally, he sat back and looked at her. "That was great. Thanks."

"You're welcome. Now. You were saying...."

He smiled. Bekah wished he wouldn't.

"I was saying that if you want to visit my creek, fish, or whatever, you can. Anytime. You don't have to ask."

"And...."

"And I guess I acted like an arrogant...."

"Asshole? Sonofabitch?"

His eyes twinkled. "You might say that."

"I just did."

"Yeah, I guess you did."

Another lingering silence crept between them. Bekah studied him, sitting there, so damn out of place in her kitchen. How did this happen?

He didn't appear to be such an arrogant sonofabitch now. In fact, he seemed relaxed and calm. Like he belonged sitting at her breakfast table in her kitchen. Or somebody's kitchen. Suddenly, Bekah didn't like the notion of that. She rose, gathering their dishes while silently reminding herself that she didn't want this.

Any of it.

She set the dishes on the counter and ran a sink full of hot, sudsy water. After slipping the dishes in, she turned. "So that's what you came over here at seven o'clock in the morning for?"

He rose and stepped closer. Facing her, he leaned each hand against the counter on either side of her. "In part."

Just a little too close, Buddy. "And what's the other part?"

"I found myself wondering what it might be like between us if you weren't mad at me." He inched closer.

His eyes were too damn blue. "And how do you know I'm not still mad at you?"

"You fixed me breakfast, didn't you?"

"I fixed *me* breakfast," she returned.

"But you let me share it."

"I was coerced."

His gaze fell to her lips. "I seem to be good at that."

"That's what I understand."

"I usually get what I want."

"I've heard that also."

"And I really do want to kiss you again."

Bekah rolled her eyes. "Really?"

He lifted his right hand to her face and cupped her cheek. "Oh, yes."

Bekah pressed her hands up between them, pushing him slightly away. "One quick question." He waited. "I need to know about this creek thing."

"What creek thing?"

Bekah cocked her head. "What do you get in return?"

He shook his head. "I don't want anything in return."

"You sure?" Bekah sure as hell wasn't. Ever since he made that statement, it had bothered her. It wasn't until just a minute ago that she figured out why.

"Of course, I'm sure."

"That doesn't sound like you."

He brushed a hair from her cheek. "And you know me so well?"

"I don't know you at all, and I really don't trust you, which is why you need to back off and keep your kisses to yourself."

"What are you saying?"

She pulled away and stepped aside. "I'm saying that I think you have ulterior motives. I think *you* think that if you allow me to go down to the creek, that I'll let you come over here with those damn hounds anytime you want."

Collin simply stared. "I guess you would think that, wouldn't you?"

"Well, if you were me, what would you think?"

"I'd think someone was being kind and neighborly, that's what I'd think."

Bekah turned and stepped toward the door. "Like hell you would. You'd be just as suspicious as I am." She opened the screen door. "It's time for you to leave."

"Appears so." Collin exited to the porch.

"And don't come back without an invitation."

"Same here," he called over his shoulder.

"No need to worry about that," she whispered. *Arrogant bastard. Drive your damned Mercedes out of here and don't come back.* "I know where I belong."

Chapter Four

The envelope was small and simple, mixed among sale bills, coupons, and the electric bill. Addressed to *Miss Rebekah McCauley,* there was no return address. No canceled stamp. No stamp at all. Someone had placed it in her mailbox.

Bekah sat still in the cab of her truck. Saturday morning shopping chores accomplished, she stared down the narrow country road. Her brother had floated her a small loan until her money arrived from New York. One obstacle removed for the moment. She looked down at the stack of mail sitting beside her on the worn leather seat. She picked up the unstamped envelope and gently tore open the small white linen flap. A large hunter-green monogrammed *K* jumped out against the stark white paper. She unfolded it and read the flowing handwritten script inside.

An invitation.

Don't come back without an invitation.

Well, well. Mr. Collin Kramer had invited her to a little get-together. A luncheon and hunter-jumper show. A charity event. Two weeks from today at his farm.

Well, how nice.

Bekah shoved the invitation into her pocket. Luncheon indeed. The last thing she wanted to do on a Saturday afternoon was play tea-time with a bunch of Junior-Leaguers in last year's Derby dresses and large-brimmed hats, their handbags neatly tucked into the crook of their elbows. Or rub noses with the jet set as they discussed their luxury cars, their nannies, or their children's private schools. Not it this lifetime. Not anymore.

Bekah clutched and braked the old Chevy, gave it some gas, then drove slowly up her gravel drive. She squinted as she drew closer to barn and focused on the older model black Ford pick-up parked beside her garden. The tailgate was down, empty flats discarded in the bed of the truck. A hoe and rake leaned against the side.

As she slowed and stopped, she looked for the owner, but didn't see anyone until she stepped out of her truck and rounded the corner of the house. An older man, probably in his sixties, jumped as he met her there, startling them both. He held the end of her hose in one hand, a small stream gurgling out of it.

"Excuse me. Who are you and what are you doing?" Bekah asked.

"Pete, ma'am. Pete Lawson."

"What are you doing here, Pete?"

He dug a grimy red bandanna out of a back pocket and swiped his forehead with it. "Mr. Kramer sent me over here, ma'am, to do this for you. Said it was a surprise." He shook his head. "Sorry I didn't get it all done before you got here. Hope I didn't ruin everything."

"Mr. Kramer, huh?"

"Yes'm." He turned to the garden plot. "Everything suit you all right?"

Bekah followed his gaze. "What in the world?" She stepped

a few feet closer to the garden. Nearly everything was back where she'd had it. Except the potatoes. She feared they were too far gone to take root again. She turned back to face him. "Actually, it looks wonderful. How long did this take you?"

Pete Lawson scratched his head. "Well, the boss and I, we got over here just after you left this morning. He raked for a while, I marked the rows, and we both planted. He had to leave about thirty minutes or so ago, I guess." He pulled on the hose and began walking toward the garden. "Just need to put a little sprinkling on top and then I'll be out of your way."

Bekah stood and watched the man's back as he methodically doused the soil with water. The spray wove back and forth forming an intricate pattern of drips and splashes on the dry earth until they all ran together. "Pete?"

"Yes'm?"

"You said your boss and you did this? Mr. Kramer, you mean?"

"Oh, yes ma'am. Said he thought it was high time we started being a little more neighborly."

Bekah narrowed her gaze and looked past Pete to the Federal-style mansion across the pasture. *Neighborly my foot.*

She watched Pete finish his task and then leave. A few minutes later Bekah pounded on the front door of the mansion. She glanced behind her at her old truck in the circular drive, parked beside a late model Mercedes sedan, and realized how out of place it looked. *Everything money could buy...* She examined the two hound statues flanking the entrance. Large ferns graced the porch, along with an outdoor wicker settee and a couple of wooden rockers.

Money. It all comes down to money, doesn't it?

She tried to peek in the sidelight but could see nothing. She banged harder this time.

"Something I can do for you?"

She swirled. Collin stood at the bottom of the porch steps. She gasped, startled at the picture he made standing there below her. His dirty faded blue jeans cupped and tugged at all the right places. He stood with his booted legs slightly apart, one hip jutted out slightly. His plaid flannel work shirt gapped open low at the neck; his sleeves rolled back high on crossed forearms. His hair looked slightly damp and curly around the edges; perspiration ran down the side of his face.

He looked rugged, tough—and tall, dark, and handsome—all at the same time. Not at all like Bekah had ever seen him.

"Uh, yes." Her tongue had obviously forgotten its function.

"Well...?"

She shoved her hands into her bib-overall pockets, connecting with the invitation. Realization hit her. "Oh!" She jerked it out of her pocket and her mind back to her original intentions. She shoved it at him. "What is this all about?"

His gaze dropped to her hand. "They call that an invitation."

"I know that."

"So what are you asking me?"

"I'm asking you why? Why did you send it?"

Collin unfolded his arms and stepped on the first of the four steps up to his front porch. "It seems that we stand on formality around here. I just thought I'd be...."

"Neighborly?"

"Actually, yes."

"And you replanted my garden today because you just wanted to be...."

"Neighborly."

"I don't understand."

He rose one more step. Face to face. If fire could spark blue embers, they would be his eyes. They electrified his entire face.

"You don't?" He paused and seized her gaze. She couldn't move if she wanted to. "I think you do."

Abruptly, Bekah stepped backward. "I just wanted you to know, being neighborly and everything, that I won't be there. I decline. RSVP and all that." She brushed past him and bounded down the steps.

He called out. "Other plans?"

She reached the truck. "Not really."

"Afraid you're going to be a bit out of your league?"

Oh, he didn't just go there. Bekah swallowed, opened the truck door, and lifted her gaze to his face. "I'm not out of anyone's league." She lifted her chin. "I've got other things to worry about. A farm to run. I don't have time for parties."

Collin brought his hand up to his chin and rubbed his slight growth of beard. "You know, if you're worried about something to wear, my sister is about your size. I could call her and...."

Bekah slammed the door shut. In two steps, she crowded up against him. "You pig-headed ass! How dare you. You know nothing about me, or my wardrobe. Are you so embarrassed now that you've invited me that you need to cover your tracks in case I show my hayseed upbringing?"

"Rebekah, that's not it, I...."

"Too bad buster, hillbilly or not, I wouldn't miss this little soiree of yours for all the gold at Fort Knox. I'll be there, with bells on." She turned sharply and jerked open the truck door. She fell into the truck cab, started the engine, and sped around the circular drive, not waiting for a response from Collin.

Oh my God. What have I done?

She'd just dug her own grave, that's what. *Dammit!*

* * *

His name was painted on the office door. The nameplate on his desk had his name engraved on it, too. Every paper on the desk bore the Kramer Bloodstock logo. Why then, didn't this office really seem like him?

For over fourteen years now, he had lived in this space. He had eaten there, slept there, and once, during a late-night session with a very willing assistant, had risky sex there. Big mistake. One he was lucky hadn't cost him a chunk of the business. He had been young then. Too smart now to let that happen again. She was long gone and forgotten. Like too many others.

Collin sat behind his desk and perused the memorabilia he'd gathered over the years. An old family photo taken at the lake. His dad's putter in a corner by the door. His riding helmet and crop sitting in the glass-doored cabinet.

Year after year, he had replaced his father's belongings in this office with his own. Piece by piece, he had taken the old man apart, dissembling a life of greed and indulgence, and recreating the man Collin remembered as a young child. Over time, he had replaced the bad parts of his father with faded memories of a youthful father figure. The man before the business had overtaken him. The only man Collin chose to remember.

Now.

He closed his eyes and laid his head back against the cool leather of the desk chair. He'd hated what his father had become. Collin hated that he had fallen into his footsteps.

Now *he* was the bitter young man, deeply embedded in this money trap.

The money. His mother threw it up in his face daily. She had made it apparent from the day after his father's funeral that she expected to maintain her lifestyle, and that it was up to him to keep the business going. It was a family business, she reminded him—one that his grandfather had started, and their standard of living was to be upheld. Katy and Jennifer were no different. Their father had not been around emotionally for them, but he certainly had been there financially. And they all, his mother and his sisters, expected it to keep rolling in. Katy had finally married, but beneath herself as her mother so frequently put it, and needed financial assistance now and again. Jennifer would be a sponge forever. At twenty-eight, she still lived at home, worked part-time in a dress shop, and spent the family money faster than he really cared to think about.

And his mother—well, she'd had plenty of suitors over the years. None of which stayed around long enough to take her off his hands. He hated thinking like that, but it was true.

But they were not unlike the other women in his circles. Money was a prime asset for any single bachelor in his social circle. Money was what attracted them and what kept them. It was what made the pretty little blond spread her legs for him in this office that night. It was the thing that brought any woman he'd ever intimately known to him. Horse people bled money. And in his business, he had to bleed money, too.

So he did.

He'd played the part. Like an actor on a stage, he had dressed the part, spoken the part, and became the part. He flashed his gold cards, escorted the rich to the races, and the parties, and the dinners. He drank the right drinks, ate the right foods, frequented the right nightspots, and became like them. He became important. He became desirable.

He became his father.

Some days he hated himself for it. Other days he didn't.

Some days he never wanted to give up this lifestyle his father had handed to him.

Collin opened his eyes. He stared across the room at a picture taken when he was six. His father stood behind him, cradling his son within his arms, hands helping to guide a baseball bat toward a hurled ball. Broad smiles stretched across both faces. Collin could only stare at the picture—taken just before his father took over the business from his father, before he lost sight of what was important in life.

He rose and crossed the room to the window and stared out. If he ever had the chance to be a father, he wanted to be a real father. He had promised himself years ago that when the right woman came along, he would sell out and go back to school. To hell and back with the family business. His mother and sisters would have to fend for themselves—or horrors, get a job. But the right woman never came along, and now he was buried too deep to claw his way out.

Automobiles whizzed by on the street below, rushing toward their destinations. Sometimes, on days like today, he wanted to join them. He wanted to get in his car and drive away fast—extremely fast. He wanted away from the leeches, the money-grabbers, the backscratchers, and backstabbers. Some days he wanted out badly.

His chest grew tight. He rubbed at the tension with his open palm, breathed heavily, and then turned abruptly, leaving it all behind. It wouldn't happen. He would never leave. He was past the point of no return.

Collin sat again and picked up a stack of papers and his pen. This was where he'd end up. Where he'd stay. He had no choice. He might as well live the life he had—play the cards dealt him. No matter what.

He placed the pen to the paper. *Did* it matter what anyone thought? It never had before. He closed his eyes again and saw Bekah's face, just after she'd leapt up off the boulder by the creek, her features softened in sleepy relaxation.

She was real. And he'd been a cocky SOB.

* * *

Bekah threw the size five dress across the bedroom. It hit the wall and slid down to the floor, adding to the existing heap of clothing there that also didn't fit. She turned and looked at her reflection in the full-length mirror and grimaced as her gaze fell from her face to her chest. The lace cups of her bra overfilled with her heavy breasts. She lifted a hand and ran one finger across the top. The past four months had changed their shape, the areola deepening in color and spreading wider around the nipple. They were full and tender, but probably a good bra would help that. The sexy underwire was going to have to go. Time to go shopping.

Her hand fell to her thickening waist and the other joined it. No one could really tell yet, she knew. Her abdomen protruded slightly with a nice little baby bump, her waist expanding just enough to prevent her size fives from fitting perfectly. Even the weight she had lost from her ulcer had come back on quickly, especially since her arrival back to the farm. She'd left her bird-like New York appetite there. Here she needed to eat to keep up her strength, to make her living. Here she ate as she did as a child. Her petite frame showed every added curve. The addition of a growing baby would become apparent very soon.

Bekah lovingly caressed her abdomen. She'd never been one of those women who hated the thought of being pregnant because of a fear of fat. She'd always thought pregnant women looked happy and fulfilled. She didn't mind gaining the weight at all.

She'd need to tell her family soon, though, and maybe then some of the pieces would start coming together for them. Telling her mother would be the hardest, but once she told the whole story, once everything was out in the open, they'd understand. Maybe.

Being pregnant at twenty-nine and unmarried, might prove more than a little embarrassing. At least here in Kentucky—in

New York no one would have batted an eye. But at her age birth control was readily available, and it wasn't that she didn't know how to use it, she did use it. She'd somehow gotten pregnant anyway.

Bekah's eyes darkened as she looked at her reflection. She sat on the edge of the bed, arms cradling her abdomen. This baby meant more to her than life itself. This baby represented her freedom, her flight from captivity, her roots and family values and stability all rolled into one. And she would do anything to protect it. This baby would grow up as she had, learning to love the things she loved, mixing old values with new ideas. This baby would learn to love the smell of fresh dirt and know the difference in planting corn and setting tobacco, as well as to distinguish a Renoir from a Picasso. The baby is the reason she came back. The baby is the reason she's still whole.

Bekah closed her eyes and the terrible scene came back. The lobby filled with people was a bit overwhelming. Mostly women, only a handful of men. Those men that were there sat stiffly beside their women, leaning over occasionally to say a few comforting words, eager to get the whole thing over.

When she'd heard her name called, her breathing quickened. The life within her jolted suddenly and silently screamed. Bekah followed the nurse down the narrow and cold, mint green hallway, and followed her into the small cubicle. The examining table had a small pillow at the top. The stirrups were in place. A large metal piece of equipment sat next to the table end. Bekah's breathing deepened. She was hot and light-headed.

The nurse repeated words to her and pointed to the table. She couldn't hear them. A loud internal scream filled her ears. Perspiration beaded from her forehead and her eyes filled with tears.

She gasped and sobbed, pushing away from the woman, and

ran from the clinic. Later, she faced the consequences of her decision when she told him.

"I didn't get the abortion."

Matthew glared through the dresser mirror as he loosened his tie. His dark eyes caught and held hers, and her stomach lurched. "And why is that, Rebekah?" His dark gaze held her to her spot.

Finally, she broke away and looked to the floor. "I've made several decisions, Matthew. I want to talk about them."

He turned and she caught his stare again. For five years, this man had been her entire life. They'd lived together for nearly that long. She knew him better than she knew her brothers, and she knew damn well he didn't want to hear what she was going to say.

"Stay here tonight and talk to me Matthew. We've got to get this ironed out."

"I think you've already made your decision, Rebekah. No need to discuss further." He stripped off his dress shirt and pants and laid them neatly across the foot of the bed. He stood before her in his boxer shorts and socks. "I'm taking a shower."

Bekah touched his arm as he turned away. "Matthew?"

His voice rose. "I've got a business dinner, Rebekah. I'm due in forty-five minutes. Business, remember? The thing you used to crave? The thing we had in common? The thing we both agreed we'd put into this relationship? Business, Rebekah—not a baby."

"I know, Matthew, but things changed—the circumstances are different now. We have to talk about this."

"No, we don't." He pulled away and walked to the bathroom, turning at the door. "You know how I feel. I've made that perfectly clear. If you want to stay with me, get the abortion. If you don't, keep the baby and leave. Don't expect me to support it or you. Don't expect me to be a father because I won't. If you have this baby, Rebekah, it's yours. If you want to keep it, don't be here when I get back."

The door shut quietly, without pomp and circumstance. Matter of fact. Just like Matthew's speech.

She heard the rattle of the pipes as he turned up the hot water in the shower. For a while, she sat in the upholstered chair by the window and looked out upon the city. Waiting. One tear streaked down her face. She had known. Deep down, she had known. There was only one thing left to do.

Get out.

While she could.

If she could.

Chapter Five

Bekah breathed on the lens of the binoculars and then wiped them clean with the corner of her bed sheet. She put them back to her eyes and focused, targeting her gaze across the pasture to Collin's farm. Trucks pulling horse vans had arrived steadily for the past hour.

Squinting, she directed her attention to the party tent at the side of the house. Workers assembled the monstrosity yesterday afternoon; the caterers had arrived early this morning. A few guests mingled about, drinks in hand. They were the reason she was spying. She focused on the women, taking in every article of clothing worn, and mentally putting together an appropriate outfit out of her less-than-stellar wardrobe. One that would fit, but beyond that, one that would knock the socks off Collin Kramer.

Why it mattered, she didn't know.

Yes, she did.

Ever since he made the crack about asking his sister for something for her to wear, she felt she needed to prove a point. She was not ashamed any more of her roots, who she was—it wasn't that, at all. It was that he assumed about her because of what, or who, he *thought* she was.

Bekah dropped the binoculars and then jerked them back to her eyes. Kramer stepped into her line of vision. She focused again and greatly magnified the image he created. Dressed in full hunt attire, his white breeches hugged his thighs, fitting closely to his legs until disappearing into shiny black riding boots. He wore a red jacket and white shirt; his riding crop tucked under his arm. Bekah watched as he stepped up to a platinum-haired woman, smiled, and placed a protective arm around her back. Kramer drew her body into his; she moved into him, spoke into his ear as he did. Bekah concentrated on the lines of his face, a slight dimple in his chin, various small wrinkles around his eyes and mouth. Firm thin lips moved as he spoke, occasionally showing glimpses of pearly white teeth.

He leaned toward the woman and placed a lingering kiss on her cheek. Bekah's insides turned to mush.

She lowered the binoculars.

A rash of emotions rattled through Bekah. Her breathing deepened. Her chest heaved. And that *alarmed* her more than it aroused her.

She took one more look. Collin's fingers traced the woman's backbone, the action sending delightful pleasures down her own spine—and she realized, abruptly, that she *was* aroused more than alarmed—

And perhaps a little bit jealous.

Stepping away from the window, she tossed the binoculars on the bed. With determination, she walked to her closet.

Approximately thirty minutes later, Bekah turned her old Chevy into the circular drive at the Kramer estate, looking ridiculously out of place. The Chevy, that is, not her. She was certain she had *cleaned up nicely*.

Sleek trucks and horse vans stood parked beside the house

in the pasture. Several expensive cars lined the drive—Mercedes, BMW, a Porsche. Bekah chose to stay right where she was, at the end of the line near the road. She didn't plan to stay long.

Stepping out of the pickup, she smoothed her dress and dusted dirt from the floorboard off her heels. With self-manicured fingers, she pressed a stray hair back into the roll at her nape, and then walked several yards up the drive. At the corner of the house, she made her way to the party tent. The crowd had grown since she'd last spied, so it was easy to lose herself among the throng. Her rusty New York instincts were sharpening as she made her way through, nodding and smiling occasionally. She knew how to work a crowd, and just for a bit of liquid support, she stepped into the tent and found the bartender. She needed something to do with her hands, and her mouth was suddenly very dry.

"Club soda with lime, please," she requested. He handed her the drink and a napkin. Bekah stepped away from the bar and perused the crowd.

A hand touched her elbow. Bekah jumped. "Nice little Saturday afternoon get-together, don't you think?" She turned to the voice. A dark-haired man held out his hand. "Justin Walker."

Bekah smiled her best smile and extended hers. "Nice to meet you Mr. Walker. I'm Rebekah McCauley."

"Justin, please."

She hesitated, studying his face. "All right."

"So, what do you think? Nice little party, or what?"

She eyed him suspiciously. "I think so. I've only just arrived, but it seems...nice."

Justin smiled. "Everything Collin Kramer does is nice." Then he cocked his head to one side. "I don't believe I've seen you around one of these events before. This is a close-knit group. Everyone knows everyone else." Then he leaned closer and whispered. "You're not a party crasher are you?"

She grinned. "Actually, I just met Mr. Kramer. I own the farm next door. I moved in about three months ago. And no, I'm not a party crasher. I have an official invitation. Shall I produce it?"

He grinned back. "No need, Ms. McCauley. I'm sure you would be well-received on your looks alone."

"You are too kind, sir." She smiled and tried to keep up her end of the casual banter, politely chatting for several minutes but her gaze skittered about the tent in search of Collin. Several times, she had to back away from Justin Walker as he invaded her space and insisted on touching and crowding her.

Bekah had planned to keep her guard up. She wanted to know *exactly* where Collin was and approach him when he least expected it. But Justin insisted on conversation and acted as though he wanted to keep her attention for quite a while, which made it difficult to keep her eyes on the growing crowd. Then when she least expected it, Collin stepped directly in front of her. She took two steps backward and tilted her chin in the air.

Collin slapped Justin on the back. "Justin, old man. What in the world's been keeping you? What's it been, three or four months? We've got to get together soon and blow off some steam."

Justin laughed. "Kramer, you old SOB, you know I don't have time for you, and when in hell do you ever have time for anything but work and those hounds?"

Collin shook his head. "Hell, if I know. It's one thing after another. If it's not my mother, it's Erin. A real pain in the ass sometimes, that woman."

Bekah took in the banter. Collin looked slightly past Justin, his gaze settling on her. A blank stare came over his face, then acknowledgment. Justin followed his stare, hooked his hand in the crook of Bekah's elbow and drew her closer into the trio.

"Just talking with your new neighbor, here. Why haven't we met before? Been keeping her to yourself?" Justin turned to Bekah, his voice lowered. "Sorry, we didn't mean to leave you out of the conversation."

"It's perfectly all right. I'm just on my way out." Bekah directed her statement to Justin but locked her gaze with Collin's.

"Miss McCauley." He drew the words out slowly. "I see you did make it after all."

Bekah's gaze narrowed. "I managed to squeeze this in between the gardening and the milking."

A broad grin spread across Collin's face. They stood for several seconds, their gazes fixed on each other. Then a shout sounded from behind.

"Kramer! Let's get this show on the road!" An older man dressed in hunt attire grabbed Collin by the arm and spun him in the opposite direction. Collin tore his gaze away from hers as the man led him away from the group.

Taking advantage of the diversion, Bekah backed away from Justin and slipped out of the tent. She'd had enough. This was not her crowd.

She headed for her truck. *Mission accomplished.* No need to linger. No desire to socialize with that *close-knit* group. She had every desire to go home and get out of her uncomfortable clothing.

Stopping alongside her truck, she closed her eyes and sighed. Her shoulders slumped and one hand fluttered to her temple. Collin Kramer was the sexiest man she'd ever known, and dammit, she was jealous of the blonde she'd seen him kissing earlier. Right now, more than anything, she wanted to stay and just watch him.

She shook her head.

No. It's my emotions. Hormones. I don't want that.

She threw off the thought about the same time she heard her name spoken behind her.

"Rebekah." She turned and faced Collin. Her gut drew into a tight knot.

"Don't call me that," she hissed.

"Okay," he said softly. "What do I call you?"

"Not that."

"Why?"

Bekah closed her eyes and shook her head. It didn't matter. She didn't want to get into it. Time to leave. "Never mind. Thank you for the lovely party, but I need to be going." She opened the truck door.

"You're beautiful."

Shit. Don't let him woo you.

She stared ahead, ignoring the tingling running up her spine. "Not the hayseed little county girl you expected?"

He shook his head slightly. "I don't know what I expected. Certainly not...."

The desire she'd chased away earlier morphed into an emotion she should push away but found difficult to define. Anger? Maybe. Pissy and sarcastic? Definitely.

"Oh, you didn't expect this little Valentino dress and diamond earrings? My shoes are Marc Jacobs and my bag is Gucci, if you're curious. And if you want to go even further, not one stitch of my clothing was bought at the local discount store. Not even the underwear and especially not the stockings." *Not that you would ever have the opportunity to find out.* "And absolutely nothing is borrowed."

"Reb... Look, I'm sorry. I didn't mean to insult you. You are stunning. I just hope you didn't spend a lot of money trying to impress me."

Bekah laughed. *"Impress you?* It's an old dress, Collin, I've had it for years. Impressing you was the furthest thing from my mind. Granted, I'm not into horses and I don't drive an expensive vehicle or live a lavish lifestyle." *Not anymore.* "But I'm a real, living, honest-to-goodness person. A person with feelings and needs, deserving of the same type of respect any other person gets. And there's a lot more to me than you know."

He stepped closer. "Then how do I get to know the rest of you?"

It wasn't an invitation. She hadn't meant it that way. She ignored the suggestive comment and stepped backward against the truck. "Not seeing people for other than face value is quite sad, but what's worse, I think there is probably a lot more to *you* than you know. I'd like to think that there's more than this shallow shell of a man I see standing before me."

He took another step. "Oh, there's a lot more to me than you know, honey. A lot more."

He thumbed her cheek and trailed his fingertips to her neck. His body pinned hers against the truck. He tilted her head up with his thumb and pulled her face toward his mouth. Fire ran through her as he attempted to kiss her.

She quickly pulled back. "Don't."

His fingers rested against her cheek. "Why not?" he whispered.

Her cheek tingled; his fingertips raked alongside her face. A raging war was going on inside her. She *wanted* him to touch her—and she *didn't.* "You are always pushing yourself on me. Don't you get it? I don't want you to do that."

"Really? Isn't this one of your needs?"

"What?"

"You said you had feelings and needs, Miss McCauley. Isn't kissing one of them?" His gaze captured hers and Bekah could do nothing to prevent what happened next. He leaned in and captured her lips, unleashing a desire so powerful it nearly shook her.

Her heart pumped as his hard, lean body pressed closer. He moved his thigh to push caressingly between her legs. She wanted to shove him away at his forwardness.

Couldn't.

What was worse, she wanted it.

The kiss deepened. Her lips parted and his tongue dipped inside, exploring. He groaned and Bekah mingled her tongue with his. Collin placed both hands on either side of her face, pulled back, and gazed into her eyes. Bekah exhaled slowly.

"I want to get to know you better," he whispered hoarsely. He leaned in and lightly skimmed her lips with his again. "Will you let me?"

Bekah pulled his hands away from her face, holding them in her palms. She curled her fingers around his hands and gazed deep into his eyes. It took everything in her not to say, yes, come home with me, make love to me—now. Get to know every part of me. She didn't. Too complicated. The baby. Matthew. Her past too raw.

"Not until you begin to know yourself," she whispered back. *Prove to me you're not another Matthew.*

* * *

Bekah slept soundly until the yipping of mutts broke the silence. At first, she thought she was dreaming. A large gray horse with a rider whose eyes bore down on her thundered through her brain. A rider whose lips captured hers in a fire so intense she thought they had fused as one.

The barking grew louder, and her own old hound-dog howled into the night along with them. Her eyelids flew open. Bekah lay still for a few seconds, orienting herself to the sounds beyond the darkness of her room. The moon shone bright through her window, casting a yellow stream of moon dust on the worn plank floor beside her bed.

Dogs! She leapt from her bed and dashed to the window. Her entire yard swarmed with dogs! Barking, yelping, howling, digging damn fox hounds.

"Kramer." Bekah gritted her teeth as she spun away from the window. She pulled on a pair of sweatpants, leaving on the T-shirt she slept in. Her feet slipped into canvas tennis shoes, she flew out the bedroom door and tripped down the narrow staircase.

The screen door slapped noisily behind her as she rushed off the porch into bedlam. The night was cool, but she didn't notice much; moonlight guided her way. All she saw were the damn dogs—twenty-five or thirty hounds crawling over her yard and garden. The soft earth of the garden ripped up by clawing paws and rooting noses.

"Git!" She ran toward the garden waving her arms and managed to scoot a few of them away. She threw a look toward the darkened house across the pasture. "I don't believe this."

She stood, hands on hips, deciding her best course of action. Some of the dogs had decided to take it easy and plopped themselves down in the yard; others roamed and howled at each other and the moon. Back to her kitchen she ran, hoisted a fifteen-pound bag of dog food on her hip, and then headed back out to the barn. Her old hound perked up his ears and howled.

"Shut up, Barney. We're just going to share a little." Three of the dogs sniffed behind her. If the other dogs would follow into the barn, she could pen them inside until Collin came to pick them up.

She sat the bag down by the tobacco barn door, and then turned to open it. Once propped open, she picked up the bag again, elbowed the light switch, and set the dog food down near the stripping room door. Looking around her for a pan or large container to put the food in, she found none. Barney, half St. Bernard and half Golden Retriever, gently loped into the barn and studied her. "There's got to be something in here," she said. "Ah heck, let's do this, Barney."

She ripped the package open and dumped the dog food out on the ground.

A cacophony of howls split the air around her. In the distance, a solitary coyote bayed long and mellow. Bekah turned to face the howl. Each dog around her stood alert, ears perked, nostrils flaring, and howled back at the animal. Several of them took off into the dark night.

"No! Come back here." Bekah dropped the food bag and ran off after them, trying to call them back. She feared if they ran off into the night, they may be gone for good.

Kramer would blame her for that too. *Dammit.*

She had to keep the rest of them from leaving. She sprinted back toward the barn where she entered mayhem. About a dozen of the hounds, and Barney, had found the food. Low growls sounded when one dog ventured too close to another's claim.

Bekah let out a long, deep breath. Perspiration beaded from her forehead, even in the cool night air. She swiped her face with the back of her hand, exhausted. "Barney! Come here."

She hoped to hell and back he'd come.

The dog lifted his head and with what seemed like reluctance, loped toward her.

Thank you.

She grasped the dog by the collar and tugged him forward as she headed out of the barn. With a backward glance, she closed and bolted the door.

"Now let's get your master over here."

Bekah walked toward the house, her gait a bit slower than

earlier, Barney herding her along. Suddenly, the wind had been taken out of her sails. Within seconds, the twin beams of headlights turned up her lane. She stood and watched as the vehicle raced toward her. She halted, the beam catching her. The vehicle slowed and stopped.

She just stood there. Waiting.

* * *

Collin slowed his truck as he came to the end of the drive, and then braked to stop. Bekah stood like a specter in front of the barn. The white light radiated her pale skin, and a soft breeze gently ruffled her loose, waist-length hair. He opened the door and stepped out, studying her face, and simultaneously taking in the exhausted aura that surrounded her. As beautiful as she was, even in sweatpants and a T-shirt, her features drooped. Of course, it was the middle of the night, and she'd obviously been roused from sleep. Goose bumps noticeably prickled her arms and a few hairs around her face curled in dampness.

"Are you all right?"

She nodded and waved behind her. "Some of them are in the barn. The others took off after a coyote. Barney and I are headed back to bed."

Collin shot a glance from her to the hound, then into the night. "They'll come home." He then looked back at her. "Why didn't you call me?"

"I was about to."

Her breathing seemed a little unsteady. He nodded and shifted his weight to the other leg. "Do you mind if I leave them in your barn until morning? I'll just check on them now and..." *Shit.*

Her eyelids fluttered and she took a faltering step sideways.

Collin lunged and grasped her arm. The hound lumbered off to the porch.

"You're not all right."

She shook her head and batted his hand away. "I'm okay. Just...tired."

"I'm not so sure about that." Collin guided her toward the house, silently damning his hounds and whoever had pulled this latest stunt. "You need to lie down." He was surprised that she leaned into him, but still protested all the way.

"I'm fine. I can make it. It's okay."

She stopped short and looked at him. Before he realized what was happening, her eyes rolled back into her head and within a second, she crumbled to the ground.

"Bekah..." he whispered. Collin gathered her into his arms, carried her across the porch and kicked the door open, and then passed through her kitchen to lay her on the sofa in her living room. He pulled an afghan off the back of the couch, tucking it snugly around her. He touched her face with the backs of his fingers, brushing away damp, sticking hairs. Her skin was hot and clammy.

He went to her kitchen and spotted a roll of paper towels underneath the cabinet. He tore off a few, folded them, and ran it under the cold water. Upon returning, he sat beside her and dabbed her brow with the cool towel.

She looked so small and fragile. He left the towel on her forehead and brushed a long strand of hair away from her face. His fingers intertwined with the long section—silky and soft. His gaze fell on her face. His breathing deepened and he watched her chest evenly rise and fall. Something deep inside him burned. Not only a lustful, sexual burn, for it was that, but a slow, steady fire that gradually built each time he saw her. A fire that banked and smoldered when she wasn't around, but quickly ignited when she was. It quickened his heart rate and blurred his senses.

With one finger, he traced a line from her cheekbone to her lips, lingering over their ripe fullness, feeling her warm breath blowing soft over his fingertips.

"Sweet Rebekah..." he whispered. "What you do to me..."

* * *

Bekah's tongue ran over her lips grazing his fingertips. If she laid there with her eyes closed, she could take pleasure in his caresses and attentiveness. With her eyes closed, she didn't have to admit that she liked him touching her. But she opened them, breaking the spell. "I told you not to call me that."

He leaned forward. "Then I'll ask again. What do you want me to call you?"

"Bekah. Just plain old Bekah."

Collin grinned. "Bekah it is. Just plain old, though, you'll never be."

She attempted a smile. "Thanks."

"How are you feeling?"

"Better."

"What happened?"

Bekah scooted up to a sitting position. "Not sure. Just suddenly felt lightheaded." She removed the paper towel from her forehead and the afghan dropped to the floor. "I'm recovering from an ulcer, but I think I just got hot, and the night was cool...."

"You shouldn't have tried to round up those hounds by yourself."

"I didn't do a very good job of it anyway."

"They've got a mind of their own." Collin threaded his fingers through his hair. She studied him and realized he looked tired too. "Look," he continued, "if you don't mind them staying in the barn until tomorrow, I'll pick them up then. I've got some repair work to do before I get them."

"Repair work?"

Collin narrowed his gaze. "Someone cut through the chain-link around the kennel. Before I bring them home, I need to fix that. It may take putting in a whole new section of fence, but I can get someone on it early."

Bekah gazed at him inquisitively. "Why would anyone do that?"

Collin laughed. "You of all people ask me such a thing?"

"I don't understand."

Collin rose and paced in front of her. "It's not the first time this has happened. At least this time they didn't lead the hounds off with a dead fox tied to the rear axle of their truck. I lost ten good hounds that time. Or crowbarred the locks off the pasture gates. I found my horses down the road one morning. I'm just hoping that since the hounds didn't venture off too far from home, they were just let loose. Maybe I'll get most of them back this time. Hopefully that coyote hasn't run them off too far either."

"I still don't understand."

Collin stopped pacing. He crouched down to eye level with her, placing his folded arms across her knees. "I'm not well-liked around here, as you know."

Yes, she did know. "But that's no excuse for what happened tonight. I spent most of my summers here with my grandparents. I know these people. I can't excuse that kind of behavior."

"Tell it to the sheriff. He might listen to you a little more than he listened to me. I don't seem to be high on the priority list."

Bekah studied his face. "I don't like what I'm hearing."

Collin stared, his eyes boring into hers. "It's a fact of life,

Bekah. Some people feel things are better off handled in their own ways. I guess someone around here thinks they're going to run me out by vandalizing my property—or running off my hounds and horses. But I'll fight them every step of the way. And I'll tell you right now, it's not going to work."

She didn't doubt it for one minute. She watched his eyes turn cool.

"Wait a minute." She sat up, nearly toppling him backward. "Are you saying that you think that I...."

He grimaced and shook his head. "Hell no. That's not what I meant. I didn't mean to imply anything."

"Well, that's good because no matter what kind of issues we have between us, I would never do something like that."

Collin grasped her hands and tugged her closer. "I know," he said softly. "Bekah, dammit, I know this is crazy but every time I see you, I want to kiss you."

"Collin, that is not something that we...."

He leaned in and brushed his lips across hers.

Bekah's eyes closed and liquid heat simmered throughout her body. *I can't do this.* Her mind battled her heart. Passion battled all reasoning. This is not something she needed to encourage.

But Collin urged her backward until she lay on the sofa. His gaze bored deep into her eyes. Hesitating for a moment, he slipped his hands under her T-shirt, and when Bekah didn't protest, he raised it over her head and tossed it aside. Then slowly, he moved his palms down her hips and swept away her sweatpants.

She let him.

His touch was rough silk against her skin. She craved it. Wanted more. Perhaps it was because it had been such a long time since someone touched her like that—*like this*—that she let him. *Wanted* him to touch her, and more. Perhaps her wacky hormones could be to blame.

A smoky haze crossed Collin's eyes as his gaze traveled over her full breasts. His hands skimmed her sides making her shudder. He traced her naval with a forefinger and then slowly moved up her torso to palm a breast. Bekah closed her eyes and arched into him.

The night was the problem. Lying here now, with him hovering over her, every hormone in her body screamed with need. She knew she shouldn't let him continue. She was powerless to stop it.

Didn't want to stop him.

In the light of day, she would probably regret it.

Threading her fingers through his thick hair, she pulled him closer. Her pelvis rocked against his thigh, cradled between her legs. He groaned leaned closer. All the while, she thought how crazy this was—and how wonderful this was. For the first time in ages, she felt so uninhibited. So alive. So free.

Free. She'd been craving freedom for years, hadn't she? She was free to make this choice right now—*today*—even if it was the wrong one. After all, it was just sex, right? No reason why she couldn't enjoy a little physical pleasure, right?

But no... Her brain shouted inside her head how careless she was being. Her body took over reasoning, however, and she tumbled deep into the abyss.

Collin whispered, "God, Bekah. Since that first day I saw you standing in that damn garden.... I want you."

Bekah's desire soared. Her fingers found the buttons of his shirt and slowly unbuttoned until they were free. His gaze burned into hers as she worked her way to the bottom and pushed his shirt off his shoulders. He tugged the tails out of his pants and threw the shirt aside. Both their fingers fumbled with his belt buckle and fly. Both pushed, pulled, and tugged until he was naked beside her.

Collin's face took on a seriousness she had never seen before. Again, his gaze traveled the length of her body. He spanned her waist with both hands. "So perfect," he murmured.

Bekah's exhaled, and cupped Collin's cheek. "Come here."

Her heart pounded. Her brain screamed for her to back off, to tread slowly. Her body craved attention and her heart affection. Knowing she shouldn't be putting herself into this situation, Bekah shook off all of reasons why she shouldn't, and let him take the lead.

Collin straddled her. She rose to meet him as he descended. A deeply passionate, lingering, emotional kiss passed through them. Fueled by the kiss, Bekah reached between them and captured his hot, throbbing cock in her palm, and tugged him closer.

Collin broke the kiss with a gasp. "Damn, Bekah..." he hissed. Sitting back, he skimmed his hands down her ribs and hips, removing the remaining lace that covered her. A shiver raced through Bekah, leaving her a quivering mess beneath him. His eyes wild with desire, his hands ran between her thighs, spreading them. He dipped a finger inside. Her eyes closed in pure ecstasy. He moved in and out and played with her clit. Her body ripe with need, she shuddered as he brought her to a rapid climax—small incoherent moans and gasps escaped her lips.

Before her quivering stopped, he entered her with a firm thrust. Bekah clutched his back and curled into him, then they both fell back against the couch. He rode her like a stallion thundering across an open field. She held on, along for the ride, their bodies meshing in passion and pleasure.

With a small grunt and one long, thorough thrust, he shimmied and pushed against her, groaning his satisfaction. Her hands smoothed and stroked his back, hugging him to her. They lay still for several minutes. Each daring not to be the first to break the spell.

Collin lifted his head and slid off to the side, cradling her body to his, and sandwiching her between him and the back of the couch. Their eyes held fast and for several minutes—they touched and caressed. Then Collin broke the silence.

"Bekah, I...."

She searched his face.

He huffed out a breath. "Hells bells. I'm sorry. I didn't use a condom. *Jesus*."

No worries. The deed is done. "Not like I have them laying around," she said. "Don't worry about it."

"Well, I will."

She put a finger to his lips. "Don't. I appreciate your concern, but no harm done. Seriously."

"You're on the pill."

She hesitated. "Something like that."

His gaze danced over her face. He trailed a forefinger over her lips, his breathing coming in shallow bursts. "You, are a mysterious woman. I want to know everything about you."

Bekah raised her own finger to his lips and said softly. "There's nothing mysterious about me."

He shook his head. "Everything about you is a mystery. Who are you? What you want for the future. What makes you tick. Tell me the Bekah McCauley story."

"It's pretty boring."

"I can't imagine that." He stroked her arms with his hands. "Tell me all about you."

Bekah rested her hands against his chest. One finger rose and traced the outline of his raised nipple. "I'll make you a deal." Her gaze moved back to meet his. "I'll tell you the Bekah McCauley story, and you tell me the Collin Kramer story."

He stared and his hands stilled. "I don't talk about my past."

"Why?"

"Because it's just that, the past."

"And sometimes that can have everything to do with the future."

He shook his head. "Not mine."

"You're wrong." *Just like Matthew.* Bekah slipped out of his grasp, threw a leg over him, and moved off the couch. She picked up her shirt and sweatpants and hurriedly pulled them on. "Relationships are a two-way street, Mr. Kramer. To build one, both people have to give and take. That's the way it works."

He rose and jerked on his jeans. "Relationship? Who in the hell said anything about a relationship?"

Bekah's mouth dropped. "Excuse me, but what just happened here? What was that sweet talk all about? Your words were heading there, Mr. Kramer, even if your heart wasn't."

Collin zipped up his jeans. "It's called sex, Bekah."

She crossed her arms. "Oh, sex. Right. How stupid of me. I guess it would be too much for you to call it making love, huh?" Well, so much for the direction of her thoughts earlier. This would be a lot easier if she just thought of this little escapade as nothing but sex. Besides, she didn't need a relationship, nor did she want one.

His eyes shot surprised daggers at her. "It just might."

The daggers pierced her heart. "Well, maybe that's the way you operate, but I don't. Usually. So, if sex is all your after with me, you can forget it from now on. I'm not an easy lay." *At least not usually.* "I just made a huge mistake here. Sorry to waste your time. And mine."

Collin grinned slyly. "You're a liar."

"About...?"

"About not being an easy lay. Generally, it takes me a couple of expensive dinners to get into a woman's panties. Thanks for saving me the cash."

Anger heated her face. "Get. Out."

"My. Pleasure."

"And Mr. Kramer, when, *and if,* we ever decide—which is highly unlikely—that there can be more to this relationship than sex, I might be willing to discuss my life with you. But I expect you to give back. I want to know all about *you.* I want to know what makes *you* tick. I want to know about *your* past. And until you can give me all of that, emotions, caring, give and take, don't you or your dogs or your condomless penis come sniffing around here ever again. Got it?"

Collin saluted and headed for the door. "Loud and clear, Miss McCauley. Loud and clear."

Chapter Six

Bekah tugged at a reluctant weed and then sank back onto her heels. Closing her eyes, she rolled her head from side to side, loosening the kinks in her neck. She had to forget it. Had to forget *him*. As far as she was concerned, the sex they'd shared was non-existent. She wouldn't think about how his hands felt on her body. She wouldn't think about how his lips felt on her lips. Or anywhere else. She refused to think about any of it, ever again.

A relationship?

How in the hell did she think, even for one fleeting moment, that she could have a relationship with Collin Kramer—or with anyone for that matter? Why had she even said the damned word! No man, least of all a man like him, was going to be sympathetic to her situation. *Crazy.* Hormones. It had to be. At least she'd place the blame there. Only once had she ever succumbed to a sexual encounter with such wild abandon—and that hadn't turned out well, either.

And it would never happen again. Her future held only one other person—her baby.

Besides, she didn't need a man.

Bekah gently pushed the loose soil around a wilted pepper plant, amazed that the simple act gave her so much pleasure. Six months ago, she would never have given a thought to doing menial tasks such as this. Six months ago, she would have been behind a desk, checking photographs, layout designs, and copy for the magazine. She would have done lunch with the other editors.

Bekah looked at her hands. Dirt clung to her knuckles and compacted beneath her nails. She rubbed her hands together, loosening the soil, inspecting her chipped nails. There was a time when it would have horrified her to go to work with a chipped nail. In New York, there would never have been an opportunity for dirt under her fingernails.

Matthew would have cringed. He loved her long slim fingers. He had insisted on lengthy nails. So much so that weekly manicures were a necessity, not a luxury. When he came into her life, she had been a starving artist, working out of a small apartment she shared with another girl in Greenwich Village. She worked in watercolors mostly then—sometimes oils. She always had paint all over her hands, deep in the crevasses of her knuckles, outlining and staining her nails. Matthew detested that.

After finding one of her paintings in a small shop in the Village, he'd searched for her, wanting to commission more. Which he did. Within a few months, he had moved her out of the Village and into his Manhattan apartment. Soon after, she'd landed the job at the magazine. It was then that Matthew started controlling every facet of her life. Her life took on a new direction.

Only when the pregnancy complicated their lives had Bekah realized the control he'd had over her. She sometimes wondered if half her successes were her own hard work—or came because of Matthew's influence. Bringing a child into that complicated, coordinated atmosphere was not something she could do. Her child needed room to breathe, grow, and develop on his or her own—not in the shadow of a control-freak like Matthew.

Bekah plunged her hands into the dark soil again, scrunching the dirt between her fingers, digging deep with her nails. The earth felt cool. Her skin showed through the dark soil in patches of white. Bekah smiled. They looked so much better. She brought them closer to her face and breathed deeply. Her lungs expanded. Her hands smelled of rich soil and earthworms. Clean and fresh. She delighted in the fragrance. Such a basic, primal smell. The land. Every farmer's heart and soul.

And this land was hers.

She rubbed her hands together and stood, loose dirt sifting downward, and headed toward the house. When she reached her kitchen, she washed her hands in the white porcelain sink, and then dried them on a nearby towel.

There was a box in one of the spare bedrooms. One of the few possessions she'd brought with her from New York. Funny how she hadn't opened it before now—but it was time.

After a few minutes, Bekah located it and lifted the box to the bed. The cardboard had been strapped tight and marked *fragile, handle with care* for the flight home. She ripped off one strip of strapping tape and tugged on the top. Finally, she pulled back all the flaps and emptied the container of wads of clumped newspapers.

On top were several canvases wrapped in brown paper. She removed the coverings one by one, studied them, and sat them on the bed. The landscapes. A couple of still life. A rare self-portrait. Studio art, mostly. Each one told a story. Each one a part of her past. She smiled as she held them in her hands, reminiscing. She touched them and caressed with featherweight fingertips.

Last she pulled out a large wooden case. She'd had it since junior high school when her parents had given it to her for Christmas. She laid it on the floor and opened it. Inside were the finest paintbrushes, oils, acrylics, watercolors, pastels. All her art supplies. Bekah smiled.

Her old friends were back.

* * *

Collin stared at his ringing desk phone. That phone and his cell were the bane of his existence. Every second of the day, his smart phone alerted him to some sort of incoming message. Text. Email. Voice. Someone wanted of piece of him. Always. Early in the morning, late at night. Didn't matter, he was always here—working. Forgetting. Or trying to, anyway.

For two weeks he'd worked his ass off at the office, pushing away everything else. Here he didn't have to think. His mind went into automatic pilot, going through the daily routines, playing the game, entertaining the clients. Here he was safe from *her*.

From Bekah, and her haunting eyes.

When he went back to the farm, he wasn't safe. Every time he glanced out his bedroom window, he could see the outline of the old frame farmhouse in the moonlight. Sometimes the light from her bedroom window called like a beacon in the night, making it even worse. He imagined her lying in bed. He could see her shape through the bed sheets. His body pulled and tugged to go to her.

He wouldn't.

Some days he felt drawn to her while he stood on his lawn,

or in the doorway of the barn. His gaze always rested on her farm. His thoughts of how her body felt beneath him, soft and supple, her hair fanned out around her face as she looked up at him. And *the way* she had looked at him. Her ebony eyes held emotions he'd never seen before. It frightened him, especially since he wasn't sure what kind of emotion he reflected into those eyes.

He let the phone ring. Who would be calling at this hour anyway? His administrative assistant left hours ago, so there was no one to screen his calls. Hell, he'd let the answering service get it.

Collin closed his eyes and laid his head back against the leather chair. He'd mentally gone over her last words a thousand times. She didn't want to see him again until he could tell her everything. Well, he just couldn't do it. Not even for another chance at loving her.

The damned phone kept ringing. Collin snatched it up on the sixth ring and held it to his ear.

"Sugar?"

Breathing deeply, he closed his eyes. "Hello Erin."

"Sugar? I miss you. Where have you been keeping your-self?" Her voice dripped with a slow, southern saccharin drawl.

"I'm busy, Erin." He opened his eyes and stared across the room. He wasn't in the mood for Erin tonight.

"Oh, pooh. Now why don't you forget all that for a while. It's after ten, honey. I'm just a little bit lonely over here. My God, it's been at least a month since we've...."

"Erin," he raked his fingers through his hair, "I can't. I'm working. I just can't shift gears like that, besides, I'm not in the mood...."

"I can always get you in the mood, sugar."

That she could. Maybe he needed a diversion.

"I'm wearing that little red number you picked up for me a while back, remember?"

That he did. He swallowed hard and checked his wallet for a condom—although he knew Erin had them at the ready. "Be there in twenty minutes."

She opened her apartment door before he knocked and was on him like a cat—clawing, panting, licking. It was always this way between them. Since the first time.

He'd had other women, but he and Erin always saw each other between relationships. Sometimes during, if the relationship wasn't exclusive. They shared an incessant sexual pull and had for years. Chemistry, Collin guessed. It wasn't love. It was convenience. Erin was convenient, and she never demanded anything but his body in return.

She pulled at his clothes, removed his jacket, and threw it to the floor. Her fingers played at the buttons of his shirt. He kicked the door closed behind him.

Collin went through all the motions. His hands played over her body. The scarlet teddy sank off her shoulders and nestled around her waist. His shirt spread wide open; she toyed with his zipper, her mouth trailing down his chest. His hands settled on her waist under the teddy.

Her face turned up. He stared down into the ice-blue eyes, the tanned face framed in silver-gold. "Kiss me," she ordered.

His face dropped closer, but he by-passed her lips, letting his mouth trail down the side of her cheek to her neck. Collin closed his eyes and saw Bekah. He felt Bekah beneath his palms. Terror ripped through his abdomen.

He dropped his hands and stepped backward.

Erin pulled away and studied his face. Her gaze played over him for several seconds. Then, her hands slid down his waist and dipped inside the waistband of his trousers, the fly unbuttoned and unzipped. Her gaze never left his. She reached inside and felt the soft mass of flesh there.

"What's this?" Her eyes narrowed.

Collin pulled away. Her hand slipped out. He turned, fastened his fly, and buttoned his shirt.

"I don't think I've ever seen you in that state before. You're usually as hard as a rock before you even get to my door."

Collin picked up his jacket. He stared at her for several seconds. Plastic, so unreal. False this and fake that. Hair, nails, teeth, breasts, anything that money could buy. Was anything there actually real? Why hadn't he seen it all before?

Before there hadn't been Bekah.

"I don't think you'll ever see me in any state ever again, Erin. It's over. All of it. Over." He turned toward the door and jerked it open.

"What's her name?" Her voice lost its southern belle politeness. Hard and cold.

Collin stared for a moment longer, and then walked out the door.

"You'll be back," she yelled after him through the open door. Collin halted and turned back slightly.

"No, Erin. I won't."

"I don't believe you, you always come back."

"Not this time." Collin turned and headed for the condo elevator.

"You will be back," Erin hissed. "You will."

* * *

The sun shone bright, the sky clear blue with puffy cotton-candy clouds. Perfect day for a picnic. Bekah breathed in a long satisfying breath. Memorial Day get-togethers were a tradition around here—with her family and in the community—and not since she'd gone off to college, had she experienced one.

It was time. And yes, she'd admit she missed them. Too long.

Bekah shoved the truck's gear into park and sat staring ahead at the small country church, built over a hundred years ago, on land given to the church by her father's grandparents. The building set in the center of a two-acre lot, at the cusp of a ridge. Behind the church, rolling hills carried themselves down to the creek bottom—the same creek that ran through Collin's property. The hills were green, the trees full of leaves and teaming with birds. April and May had delivered several inches of rain, presenting June with warm but pleasant temperatures, although bordering on humid.

But wait until July, she told herself. They'd seen nothing yet in the humidity department.

She glanced to the casserole dish sitting beside her on the seat and exited the truck. She turned to slide the dish, wrapped in a thick towel, toward her.

She steadily made her way from her truck toward the church, carrying the steaming casserole, and nodding greetings as she made her trek across the lawn. She knew the procedure. She'd visited her grandparents' graves this morning, placing fresh floral arrangements on each. There would be food, laughter, and conversation all afternoon. Volleyball for the young, and horseshoes for whoever wished to partake. Sometimes, someone would bring a croquette set.

She'd walked this same path hundreds of times when she stayed summers with her grandparents. The folks around here were always planning some sort of *homecoming*, they called it, always held at the small country church. It was the only place with a lawn big enough to hold the entire community, and a kitchen to store the food in until it was time to eat. Lots of food, plenty of people—the sunny afternoons always ending with warm starry nights, soft conversation, and sometimes a little music, depending on who happened to bring along a guitar or a fiddle.

Bekah deposited the dish on a wooden picnic table, chatted with a couple of women for a moment, and hummed to herself as she returned to her truck. She lowered the tailgate, jerking her sundress up slightly and hiking one knee upon it, and then leaned forward to grasp the edge of the cardboard box that held two pies, paper plates and cups, and a package of napkins. With one hand bracing herself against the bed of the truck, she hooked the box with a forefinger, then two, and dragged it slowly toward her. When she could fully take hold of the box, she did so and eased it to the edge of the tailgate, settling her feet back again on the ground.

She cradled the box against her abdomen and turned. From across the lawn, her gaze landed on his, drawn to him like a magnet. Their stares locked, and involuntarily, Bekah leaned against the tailgate and set the box down on it. And sighed.

Collin smiled. Broadly.

She closed her eyes briefly and blinked, the only way she could break the connection between them, then gathered her wits and picked up the box. She headed straight toward the side lawn of the church, bypassing him, and carried the box swiftly and surely toward the back door. *Lord, give me strength.* Her insides were jelly. Her entire body trembled with thoughts of how he made her feel.

Be strong, Bekah.

* * *

Collin watched as Bekah pulled up the hem of her yellow dress and eased a knee onto the tailgate of her truck—her other leg lifted off the ground slightly behind her. He grinned, if not outwardly, then to himself. Her delicate foot encased in a strappy leather; her bare calf peeked from beneath the edge of her dress. He imagined walking up behind her and trailing his hands up that shapely leg until he reached her panties.

But of course, he wouldn't. Not yet, anyway, and definitely not here.

He smiled again as his gaze ran over her rounded derriere, swaying from side to side while she inched the box toward her. Then she hopped down and the show was over—until their eyes met.

Bekah had held his gaze for a moment and then glanced off, returning to her task. Dismissing him. But she had seen him, and he'd bet the bank she'd felt the charged atmosphere between them, as much as he had.

He'd be patient. She was angry still, he was certain. And why shouldn't she be angry with him? He'd been an ass.

A fucking stupid ass.

He had come to a sudden conclusion the night before. He'd no clue the difference between having sex and making love, prior to Bekah. Before Bekah, he'd only had sex.

After *making love* with Miss Bekah McCauley, his trysts with Erin seemed shallow. Hell, that's *exactly* what they were. No substance. Just sex.

Lower than shallow.

And no matter what he'd said to Bekah that night over two weeks ago, it *was* making love, and he couldn't get it—every second, every touch, every stroke of her insides—out of his head for anything.

And he didn't want to. He didn't want to erase that night from his head. And he sure as hell hoped she was as captivated by their lovemaking, as he had been.

The tough part now would be convincing her of his sincerity. Opening himself up to her was going to be the only way she'd come around.

If I can do it.

* * *

In the church basement, Bekah set the box on the countertop with a thud, then immediately regretted her action. The glass pie plates clanked together. She let out a small breath, hoping she hadn't broken them and ruined the pies. After pulling out the paper products, she lifted one then another, examining them for breakage. None. With a sigh of relief, she placed them back in the box until later in the afternoon.

She had arrived early. Only a handful of people came to help set up. Her grandmother was always one of those people. So why was Collin here? Why *in the hell* would he be here in the first place? Bekah shook her head and turned back toward the door.

She busied herself for the next two hours, helping set up tables outside, organizing the dishes of food that came in, separating deserts from main and side dishes on the long paper-covered tables. From time to time, she caught a glimpse of him. He spoke among the men and helped set up the volleyball net. He even played a game or two of horseshoes with Joe. She watched his pale green golf shirt twist with the muscles of his back as he threw the shoes, sending a small shiver down her spine. She noticed how his blue jeans nicely hugged his ass. Once or twice, his gaze caught hers and her heart jumped.

Why he was here was beyond all comprehension. And what he was doing to her each time their eyes met set all emotion on edge.

A gentle breeze toyed with her long ponytail and billowed her cotton sundress. She had tried on every pair of blue jeans she owned, but they were just too snug. The bib-overalls were the only other piece of clothing she owned that were comfortable, but not for today. The sundress—one she had picked up in town at a discount store—was the obvious and best choice.

Bekah smoothed the dress around her with her hands, cradling her abdomen as she did so. This was how she wanted her child to grow up—the same way of life she had grown up in. If only she hadn't been blind for so many years to see how lucky she'd been then. If only she hadn't wasted so many years trying to find happiness, when like Dorothy, it was waiting in her own back yard.

"Bekah, honey, would you check the kitchen to see if there are any large serving spoons? Some of the dishes don't have any." Bekah blinked. She glanced sideways at Joe's wife, Maggie, her daydream broken.

"Oh, sure. I'll be right back."

Bekah rifled through the drawers in the kitchen, finding only three extra-large spoons. As she shoved the last drawer closed and turned back again toward the door, her breath caught in her throat.

Collin blocked her path. With feet crossed at the ankles, he leaned against the doorjamb, arms folded across his chest. His eyes grazed hers, and his lips turned up in a wicked, but very sexy, smile.

Bekah leaned a hip against the countertop for support. "What are you doing here?" she breathed.

Collin studied her for a moment, then shrugged. "Came to see if there was something I could help you with."

His eyes sparkled and Bekah's chest tightened. "No, I mean, what are you doing here at all, not just in the church." Her mouth was suddenly parched.

"This is a community gathering, isn't it?"

He stepped forward, slowly. Bekah's heart pounded. "Yes,

but I wouldn't have though it your style. Not to mention the community and you seem to have never seen eye to eye."

"And I'm trying to remedy that fact." He stood before her now, peering down into her eyes. "I guess I'm trying out the simpler things in life these days. You know, get in bed with the country folk."

Bekah felt her eyes grow large and her neck warm. Angry, she brushed past him while Collin grasped her arm. "Bekah wait, that's not what I meant. That came out wrong."

She whirled back and jerked out of his grasp. "I know damn well how you meant it. Screw the little country girl, try out the simple things? Well, this is one little country girl that is hands off, understand?" She took off toward the door.

He quickly followed. "Bekah stop. Damn it stop, please, for just a minute. That's all I ask, just a minute."

The pleading of his voice penetrated deep into the recesses of her heart. He sounded almost sincere—and for some insane reason, she believed him. She turned slowly.

Collin stepped forward. "I didn't mean that the way it sounded. I seem to be saying many things I don't really mean lately. I'm sorry, I don't want to hurt your feelings."

Bekah stared. "Then what *do* you want?"

Collin raked a hand through his hair. "Bekah, look. These last two weeks have been hell. I'm trying here... Trying to show you that there is more to me than you think. Trying to look at things a little differently and slow my life down. Because of you. Hell, none of this is coming out right."

He backed away and turned.

Bekah studied his heaving shoulders. He *was* trying. "You could start by explaining the other night."

He turned, his gaze catching hers and holding. "Yeah," he dropped his head, looking to the ground. "I guess I could."

Bekah waited. "Well?"

* * *

Collin took a deep breath. He had to be honest. "Bekah, you frighten me. When we... When we made love, and it was making love, I felt more. Different than I've ever felt with a woman. It scared the hell out of me."

Bekah eyed him skeptically, her arms crossed over her chest. "And?"

"And I didn't know how to react. I didn't know what to say or do, so I said something stupid. Please forgive me."

Her gaze didn't flinch. "Okay," she whispered softly.

He stared into her eyes for several seconds. "Really?"

Bekah nodded.

"Could we start over?" he murmured.

"We can try. Slowly. As friends. And that means no sex."

Collin cupped her chin in his palm. Involuntarily, she moved closer to him. "I want to try," he breathed. "Friends first, if that's what you want."

"Yes. Are you ready for the give and take, Collin? Can you talk about yourself—your dreams, your goals, your past?"

Collin drew back and looked deep into her eyes. "I'm ready to try. That's all I can give you right now. I need time."

She nodded. "I can give you time."

Collin smiled.

* * *

He stuck close to her all afternoon. During the blessing, he grasped her fingers, and held her hand. Bekah's heart turned a somersault, but she quickly released his grasp. They took their turns in the food line and mingled with some of the community members. Bekah ignored the remarks and the leaning, whispering heads.

This was too small a community for their budding relationship, er friendship, to go unnoticed. Was she ready for this?

A part of her wasn't. Hell, she was carrying a baby, and not his. Had she really considered the complications a relationship with Collin right now would present?

No. She hadn't. But today, she didn't want to think about it.

Today, his attention was nice, welcome. She'd deal with the aftermath tomorrow.

The afternoon stayed cool, a breeze blowing steadily over the ridge—the same ridge Bekah and Collin's farms followed, only farther down the road. They sat on a blanket underneath the shade of an old maple. Bekah brought her knees to her chest, her arms clamped around them, and leaned against the tree. The entire picnic scene lay before them.

She turned to Collin, watching the expressions on his face as he took in the volleyball game several yards away. His blue eyes sparkled all afternoon. Bekah's breathing slowed and deepened as she watched him. He made her feel so alive—and so confused. Nearly two weeks ago he had practically told her she meant nothing more to him than a willing partner. What had changed all that?

Why had she so quickly changed her mind about him? One brief apology and she was nearly putty in his hands.

He turned to face her. "What are you thinking, Bekah?"

She shook her head. "I'm not sure what's happening here."

Collin lowered his gaze. "I know I'm not sending very good signals. It's just that I..." he looked back into her eyes. "I don't know how to do this."

"Do what?"

"Date you, or whatever. I want this thing between us to me more than casual. I've just never had that. I'm not sure I know how. Bekah, I've always had women... It's just that with you, I don't know what to do first. I've never had... Dammit. This is hard."

Bekah laid a hand on his arm. "Collin, I'm not an old-fashioned china doll. I'm no different than any other woman out there. I don't know why this is so difficult."

"You're different."

She looked him hard in the eyes. "No, I'm not. Maybe what's different this time is you. We don't have to be in a rush. We need time. Friends first, remember? Both of us need to get to know each other, and perhaps, learn how to open up to one another."

He closed his eyes. "I don't think I know how to open up."

"That street probably runs two ways."

"You have deep, dark secrets you need to divulge?"

She stared at him, then glanced off. "Not necessarily deep, but I have secrets," she began. "I'm sure we both have things we need to share. Right?"

Collin cleared his throat. "Talking about myself and my problems is not necessarily something that I find easy to do."

Bekah faced him, then trailed a finger down his smooth cheek. "You will. And I can be very patient."

Collin tucked a finger under her chin and pulled her closer. He leaned in and brushed his lips lightly on her cheek. "Thank you."

She nodded, warmed by his affectionate touch. Standing, he pulled her to her feet. His arms lingered around her back for several seconds as his gaze played over her face. He sighed. "I'm feeling very lucky today."

"Why is that?"

He fiddled with a tress of her hair. "Because you're allowing me to share this day with you."

Her heart pounded. "I'm glad you're here."

Collin drew her closer. Bekah let her forehead drop against his chest, then glanced toward the church crowd.

"Wonder if there's apple pie left. My stomach's beginning to rumble."

Bekah groaned and smiled at the sudden change in the subject. "Oh, I couldn't. I'm stuffed already, but I'll walk over there with you."

Collin placed a protective arm around her waist as they turned toward the volleyball game. "Wait, I forgot the blanket." Bekah turned and took two steps back toward the tree. She picked it up and turned just in time to hear someone shout, "Heads up!"

Bekah turned toward the voice, but before she had time to react, a teenage boy came careening toward her. The volleyball hit her square in the stomach. And the boy, focused solely on the ball, flung into her chest-high and sent her flying backward into the tree.

Her breath exited her body with such force she immediately gasped, her lungs screaming in agony. She crumbled against the base of the tree, the boy rolling off to the side, apologizing. She could barely hear him over the ringing in her ears. Everything was out of focus. Collin was by her side, whispering her name, and simultaneously calling the boy every other name in the book.

When she tried to inhale, a searing pain crossed her chest. Her body shook involuntarily. She panicked, grabbing Collin's arm. "Relax Bekah," she heard him say. "You've had the breath knocked out of you. Take slow, easy breaths." She tried to do as he said. Soon her body responded. "Okay now," she heard him again. "Take one long deep breath...slowly. That's right, sweetheart. You're okay."

Bekah again did as he instructed. After several minutes, her body relaxed as oxygen spread throughout her lungs and the fuzz started to clear. She noticed the crowd of people standing around her. Her hand flew to her abdomen. She sat up and looked at Collin. "I want to go home."

The crowd started to disperse. "You need to sit right there," Collin instructed. "Give yourself another minute, and then I'll drive you home."

Her heart beat wildly. Her hand still held tight, itself against the life growing inside her. "No," she tried to keep the panic down in her voice. *Was the baby okay?* "I've got to go now, I'm all right."

"Then I'll drive you. We can pick up your truck later."

Bekah stood up, probably a little too fast because her head started to pound. This whole afternoon was ridiculous. She hadn't thought of the baby all day, and if Collin were around, she wouldn't. The baby needed to be her top priority. How could she have put herself in such a situation where the baby was in danger? How could she have forgotten such a thing?

Collin Kramer took up too much of her head, her thoughts.

"No," she said a little louder and a little more forceful this time. "Collin, look, this whole thing is a big mistake. I'm sorry, but it won't work. I can't explain to you why, it just won't." She started walking away.

"Bekah?" he shouted. "What are you talking about? I'm not going to let you drive home like this."

Bekah noticed several heads turning at the sound of his raised voice.

She turned back. "You don't have anything to say about it."

He followed her to her truck. She got in and slammed the door. He got in on the other side. "I don't understand this. Talk to me. What's happening here?"

Tears stung Bekah's eyes. "Nothing happened, Collin. And nothing is ever going to happen between us. Not because of you, but because of me. I can't get involved with you. It's complicated. It's best you understand that right now."

"Secrets."

"What?"

"You said you had secrets."

She shook her head a little, her head still fuzzy. "Yes. Maybe. But right now, I—"

"You want to go home." Collin's words interrupted soft and sweet. "Bekah, you're upset. Let's talk about this later."

A tear spilled from one eyelid. "There is no later, Collin. I want to leave now."

"I'm following you home."

"Don't."

"I'm going to make sure you're home safe, whether you like it or not."

"I guess I can't stop you from doing that."

"No, you can't. I'm not giving up. Not until I know what this about-face is all about."

She stared for a minute. Nausea bubbled up in her abdomen. "Will you please go?"

He did, holding her gaze for a long moment before backing out of the truck cab, shutting the door, and standing on the outside looking in. Not budging.

Bekah started the engine, and without looking at him, drove slowly out of the parking lot. She watched him in her rearview mirror as he crossed the parking lot and got in his own vehicle. She swore silently as he turned onto the road behind her. But he only followed her as far as her farm, slowing at her drive, watching as she traveled up the long lane to her house. Only when she had parked and got out, did he move down the road toward his own farm.

Bekah immediately called her doctor. He apprised her of warning signs, of which she had none, and suggested she lie down and rest for the remainder of the evening. All should be well, he said, a growing fetus is a lot tougher than most people think, but if she experienced severe pain or bleeding, she was to call him immediately. Bekah thanked him and hung up the phone.

A few minutes later in the shower, the stinging droplets of water camouflaged her sobs.

Chapter Seven

The tender tobacco plant slipped easily out of the loose ground. Bekah shook off dirt and laid it gently on the burlap sack with the others, then reached into the bed and pulled another. She balanced herself on the two-by-eight board laid across two concrete blocks on each side of the tobacco bed and glanced over at Joe. His old body crouched about twenty feet away from her, bent over the strip of thin, green plantlings.

Bekah sat up and arched her body. With both hands, she reached behind her and rubbed the small of her back. A nagging ache had settled there a few days ago and wouldn't go away. She longed to lay on the grass and stretch the kinks out but couldn't. They needed to pull several more bags of plants before noon, so they could set the plants in the field soon after. Workers were on their way to help and she was paying them whether they got them all set, or not. She had to keep moving.

With the back of her hand, she swiped perspiration from her brow and leaned over into the bed again, silently tugging at the plants. They'd been at it for three hours. She was dead tired already. All these plants had to be set today, or at the very least, by early the next morning. She had forgotten how much hand labor raising a crop of tobacco took, and this was only the beginning. She and Joe had made a deal. He would loan her the use of his equipment and they would share his plants, in return for her labor—and her paying for any help she needed, of course. She'd also promised him a quarter of the profits from the crop.

Unfortunately, Joe planted and harvested tobacco the old way, like her grandparents did, and didn't take much stock in some of the "newfangled equipment" that took away some of the hand labor. He swore the end product was better.

She was clearly getting the better end of the deal and knew it. But she feared in her condition, she wouldn't be able to keep up. She hadn't told Joe she was pregnant, and she didn't intend to for quite some time. She didn't consider it lying, perhaps just withholding information.

He wouldn't let her do this work, if he knew. And she worried about later in the summer if she would be able to pull her weight. She would likely be too big by then, and the nicotine the plants gave off was probably not good for the baby.

She'd figure out a way to repay him, somehow, and would just worry about that later.

Bekah filled the last burlap sack and looked over at Joe. He nodded back. They both slid across the boards, to avoid stepping in the bed itself, and deposited the plants at the edge with the others. She collapsed to the cool grass and finally stretched the length of her body out parallel to the bed, her arms covering her face, blocking the noon sun.

"Water?" Joe shadowed over her, handing her a plastic water bottle from the cooler.

Bekah sat up and took the drink. "Thanks. I'll get the sandwiches out too, you ready for one?"

He nodded. Joe was a man of few words.

They ate briefly, in near silence, and then Joe rose and

began piling the bags of plants in the back of Bekah's pick-up. She gathered the remnants of their lunch and stuffed them into a plastic bag, followed Joe's lead, and helped load the truck.

Later, the old tractor moved slowly across the warm pebbly soil as the setter wheel moved with it, carrying the tobacco plants around and then impaling them into the earth. Bekah's hands worked quickly to keep time with the wheel's gyrations. She was doing the job of two people—the help never showed up —and even though Joe was taking the tractor as slow as he could, it was all she could do to keep the cups filled with plants.

There were at least twenty more rows to be set. Her fingers ached from grasping the thin stalks and placing them in the setter cups. They had tried to get the boy down the road to come, but that hadn't panned out either, so they decided to do it themselves.

Joe pulled up to the end of the row and lifted the setter high as Bekah rode it until he stopped. "Need more plants?" he yelled over the engine.

She nodded and motioned that she was getting off.

When she stood, a lap full of dirt fell to the ground, sending up small clouds around her knees. She was glad she'd worn the long bibs instead of shorts; she'd have been mighty uncomfortable now.

She pulled a grimy bandanna from her pocket and mopped at the sweat beading on her neck and face. The worst part of the day was upon them, and even though it was only early June, it was damned hot sitting on a tobacco setter for hours.

Bekah walked to the pick-up and tugged at the cooler sitting in the shade of the tailgate. Propping one swollen ankle on the opposite knee, she unlaced a tennis shoe. "Water Joe?" He was checking the supply of plants. Bekah emptied one shoe of debris and then the other.

Joe nodded slightly. Removing his beaten straw hat, he

wiped his balding head with the dirty faded, blue bandanna he kept in the back pocket of his own bibs.

Bekah pulled two bottles of water out of the cooler. After handing one to him, he tipped it quickly, letting a small stream trickle down the side of his mouth and into his shirt collar. He swiped at his mouth with his hand and nodded toward the road.

"Looks like company."

Bekah followed his line of vision. There was no fence around this field and Joe had plowed close to the road. The vehicle was parked at the opposite end of the field, but Bekah recognized the self-assured walk, the clothes, the way he held his head, immediately. No mistaking Collin Kramer. It had been three days since she'd seen him. He'd called once and she hadn't answered. She unplugged the landline phone after that.

Collin was too powerful, simple as that. He made her feel and do things she'd never felt or done before. And for the baby's sake, she had to stay away from him.

"Damn. What does he want?" Bekah stared as he steadily walked toward them.

"Been riding over your garden lately?" Joe's gaze turned to hers, questioning.

"Not unless it was this morning."

"Well, don't right reckon I know what he wants then. Only thing I know is that there's a dark cloud in the west and we better be getting' these plants in the ground soon or you might not be getting' them in at all."

He was right. They pulled the best plants this morning—all of them—and if it rained and continued to rain, the ones that didn't get in the ground would wither and die before they could get a tractor back in the field. They could lose half their crop. She couldn't afford to go out and buy plants, it was just too expensive. And bagging someone else's rejects didn't exactly appeal to her either.

"Better get him out of here in a hurry then."

Bekah threw back the water, draining the cold liquid from its plastic confines, and watched as Collin drew nearer.

He stopped square in front of Bekah. "We need to talk."

"No, we don't." She answered quickly.

Collin stepped closer. "Bekah, please. I don't want to leave things the way we left them. I'm at a loss here. I don't understand what happened."

Bekah took a step in the reverse, her backside nudging against the truck's tailgate. Her voice lowered, "I know you don't."

"Then let's talk about it."

Bekah glanced at Joe patiently standing beside the tractor. "Not now. Maybe later. I've got a lot to do here Collin, and it's about to rain."

Collin's eyes followed her gaze. "Okay, when?"

She sighed, knowing she had to get him out of there before the storm hit and her heart exploded from the rein she had on it. "Call me."

"You're not answering your phone."

"I will now." Her voice rose. "Look, I've got to get back to work."

Collin looked from her to Joe and back again, and then to the half-set tobacco field. "What are you doing here?"

"What does it look like I'm doing?" She was getting agitated. All she wanted was for him to leave.

Collin cocked his head. "It looks like you're trying to set tobacco."

"Trying? Oh, Joe. Did you hear that? We're trying to set tobacco. *Trying*. That's funny." Bekah glared. She was in no mood to spar with him.

"Ha, ha," he returned. "Now that you're finished laughing,

let's get back to the question. I'll rephrase. Why are you doing this by yourself?"

Bekah looked to the sky. "I'm not. Joe is driving."

"Don't be the comic, Bekah. I may have been raised in the city, but I know that this is a two-person setter and you are only one person."

"Is that right? And you think I can't handle it by myself. Well, I'll let you in on a little secret. I can handle it by myself."

"Really?"

"Really."

"You wouldn't like some help?"

"From who? Tobacco hands don't exactly come easy these days."

"From me."

"You?" Bekah let out a cackle.

Collin glared, clearly not amused. "I can do it."

"I'd rather set them by hand first."

"I can do it."

"You've never set a tobacco plant in your life and I don't have time to teach you. Besides, you'd ruin your loafers and wrinkle the starch out of your shirt."

Bekah climbed up into her seat on the setter and lowered the tray. Joe piled a sack of plants in front of her, his gaze holding hers briefly, and then moved around to get on the tractor. "Thanks, but no thanks. We'll manage." She faced Collin, her back to Joe. "Ready?" she yelled over her shoulder.

He nodded and revved up the engine, then slowly inched forward about a foot.

Collin took a step and followed. "Wait. Wait a minute." They continued to move slowly down the plowed field as Bekah placed the plants in the cups and they started their rotation into the ground, her concentration solely on her work.

"Damn it." He ran forward, next to Joe. "Damn it, stop the tractor for a minute."

Joe looked over his shoulder and saw Bekah's nod. The tractor stopped and he gave a deep sigh. "Losing' time." He looked to the west.

Collin raced back to the rear of the setter and faced Bekah head on. "You're going to listen to me for once, do you hear me?" he shouted.

"You don't have to yell," she shouted back.

"Are you going to listen?"

"I'm listening!"

Collin reached over and took Bekah's hand in his, turning them over to face her palms skyward. Bekah's chest swelled involuntarily as he did so. His touch sent her into shivers internally that she hoped he could not detect and was trying desperately to avoid.

"Look at your hands."

Bekah only looked into his eyes. He shook her hands and she looked downward. "Look at them Bekah."

She did. They were tinged with the brown earth and the green of the tobacco plants. Her nails were dirty and broken. Her palms were rough, but not yet callused. Small blisters were forming on the pads of her thumbs and forefingers where she had pulled and separated plants since this morning. They didn't look like her hands. They looked like her mother's hands, but it didn't bother her nearly as much as it once would have.

She looked up into his face.

"Let me help you," he said. "You're not fooling me. You're not used to this type of work."

Bekah shook her head from side to side and looked to the ground. She didn't want his help. She didn't want him anywhere near her life. It would only complicate things.

Collin lifted her face to look at him. She trembled slightly.

"Bekah please. You told me once that's what people do around here, right? They help each other out. Well give me a chance. Let me help my neighbor. I don't think you'd refuse that from anyone else around here would you?"

She gazed into his face, her hands still in his.

"But you've never...."

"Teach me. Look, there's not a lot of time. You've got at least half of this patch left to set and it's going to rain soon. Let's get it finished."

Bekah pulled her hands from his and dropped them in her lap. She blew a long breath forcefully out of her lungs. "Grab that bag of plants and get over here."

Collin did.

"Are you right- or left-handed?"

"Right."

"Then take my seat."

"But that's...."

Joe jumped down off the tractor and took the sack of plants off Bekah's tray as she slid out from underneath. "I don't have time to argue with you. Sit in this seat. It's going to be hard enough teaching you how to do this with your dominant hand, let alone try it with the other. I've been setting with either hand since I was nine. Sit down."

Collin sat. She laid one sack of plants in front of him and then slid in the other side. Joe placed the other plants in her lap.

"Look," she said straightening the plants in her tray. "Do everything that I do, except with the opposite hand. Separate a plant out from the rest like this." She held up a slim light green plant with two leaves at the top. "Then with your other hand, place it in the cup. Be careful though, because the wheel will be turning and the cup closes in and grabs the plant. It could get your fingers."

Collin nodded, following her movements.

104

"You'll take every other cup. I'll take the others. You've got to get in a rhythm or you'll get lost. The wheel keeps on moving as long as the tractor's moving and the faster it goes, the faster the wheel goes. That's all there is to it. Think you can keep up?"

Collin looked at her confidently. "Sure."

Bekah concentrated on straightening the plants in front of her. "Let's go, Joe!"

The tractor sputtered and Joe whistled and smiled as its wheels dug into the turned sod, the tractor moving at a slightly faster clip than before. Bekah watched the sky turn darker in the west.

Twenty minutes later she said, "You missed one."

"I know."

"We'll have to go back and set them by hand."

"I know, I know. You keep telling me. I'll do it."

Bekah's voice held a slight edge to it, but she was secretly glad Collin was here. It was getting darker by the moment and the wind was whistling around them—she didn't relish getting caught out in the field in a thunderstorm. And she was dead tired.

"Ouch!" Collin jerked his fingers back and swore.

Bekah looked at him and smiled. "Getcha?"

"Damned straight."

"You missed another one."

"Dammit! Can't he slow down a little?"

"It's gonna rain."

"Okay, okay."

"Just forget about it. The pain will go away soon enough."

Collin mumbled under his breath.

"You missed another one."

* * *

Two hours later, Collin's larger fingers fumbled with the plants —pulling, separating them from each other in the burlap bag, making a mess of the process. His forefinger hurt, caught by the setter cup one too many times. His back ached from sitting on the tobacco setter for too long. He had dirt in his shoes, down his shirt, and probably in his underwear. But he didn't care, he wanted to do this. He needed her to see he was a decent human being, deep down.

He watched Bekah's slim, ivory but slightly pinked, arms move the plants in a graceful rhythm, placing them in all the right places at the right time. She'd done this since she was a child, but the fact of the matter was that she hadn't done it for quite some time. That he could tell. Her hands were not callused enough to have done farm work all her adult life. Her skin was too soft and smooth, and obviously hadn't seen years of outdoor work. Even though she was trying to convince him that she was country through and through, and a competent farm woman to boot, he knew that it had been quite some time since she'd farmed.

He missed another one. *Damn.* He glanced to his right. Bekah didn't seem to notice—his first clue something was wrong. She had commented on every plant that he'd missed the entire afternoon, it wasn't like her to let one slip by.

He searched her profile. Her cheeks were pale. Her sunken eyes rimmed by deepening dark circles. Perspiration beading across her nose.

"Let's take a break," he said.

Bekah kept on moving. "No. Keep going. Gonna rain."

"Bekah, you're about to fall over in your seat, let's stop."

"No."

He stopped. He laid his hands in his lap, stopped, and looked at her. The wheel made two entire rotations before she also stopped and turned to look at him. What Collin saw in her eyes frightened him.

Her words came slowly, as if dragged from her mouth. "What...you..."

He eyes rolled back in her head and she fell across the plants in front of her.

"Stop Joe!"

* * *

Bekah's vision grew blurry, her head light. The motion of the wheel didn't help much with that, either. Her stomach churned, like acid eating away at the lining, sending periodic stabbing pains through her abdomen. Damn ulcer. Her arms felt like lead, and lifting each plant became an increasingly difficult task.

I won't throw up. I won't. She would not make a fool out of herself here in front of Collin, no matter how neighborly he felt like being today.

Her mind a fuzzy haze, she turned his way. He was saying something. Stop? No, they couldn't. Had to get this done. She never stopped until a job was finished. *What was he doing?* The edges of her vision were fuzzy and dark. She shook her head to ward off the sickly feeling. Keep moving.

Why wasn't he helping her? Why....

* * *

Collin flung the sack of plants off the setter and jumped before Joe had completely stopped the tractor. He rounded the setter as she started to roll off and he caught her, cradling her body against his as he carried her away from tractor. He sat her in the shade of the pick-up as he shouted at Joe to get water.

With her head in his lap, he dipped her bandanna into the

cup Joe handed him and wrung it out beside her. He bathed her face with the cold cloth. She moaned low, almost a whisper. Soon her eyes fluttered opened, but just as quickly, she moaned louder and clutched at her abdomen.

"The baby..." she whispered.

Collin stopped and gazed into her face. His throat constricted. "What?"

Bekah sucked in a breath. Her eyes squeezed shut tightly. "It hurts."

Her breathing came in short, quick breaths. A tear squeezed from an eye.

Collin mopped the perspiration away from her neck. "Bekah talk to me. What's going on?" Surely, he hadn't heard what he thought.

She whimpered, clutched her abdomen again, and rolled onto her side into him. "Take me...hospital. Pregnant."

A rush of adrenaline shot through him. *Pregnant!*

Not the words any man wants to hear unexpectedly, and if he were honest with himself, he was near panic. And alternately, scared for her. "Pregnant? What the hell?" The rush of pumping blood to his brain made his ears ring. *Was he hearing correctly?*

"Not. Yours." The words came on a whisper. Her eyes fluttered once more, and her hands fell slack in her lap. At that moment, Collin saw the bloodstain growing between her legs, through her bib-overalls.

He sat stunned, and then looked up at the old man hovering over them. Finally, he shook himself out of a trance. *Pregnant?* He dismissed everything but the blood and made a very quick decision.

"We'll take my car. It's faster." He gathered Bekah's small body up against his, one arm cradling under her knees the other at her back. Her head leaned into his chest. Collin walked the length of the field, stumbling over freshly set tobacco plants. He glanced back over his shoulder to Joe. "You coming?"

The old man nodded.

They reached the Mercedes parked just inside the field and Collin slid into the back seat with Bekah on his lap. He nodded to Joe from inside. "Keys are in the ignition. Get us there fast and in one piece."

Joe eyed Collin from outside the car, then slammed the backdoor closed and eased behind the driver's seat. Sliding five fingers around the leather steering wheel once, he twisted the ignition key. He backed the car around, taking one long and serious look at Bekah behind him, and then faced the road. He smoothly shoved the gear into first and eased onto the pavement.

Collin fished his cell phone out of his pocket. He dialed 9-1-1, informing them of their location and that they were heading toward the hospital in Versailles. He tried to ignore the growing stain of red in Bekah's lap and silently feared she'd lost a lot blood. Too much blood. He prayed they would get to the hospital in time.

She was pale and had lost consciousness now, her head laying limp against his chest. He draped his raincoat over them both and held her close to keep her warm. Collin softly kissed the top of her head and sent up a silent prayer.

A county officer caught up with them halfway into town and escorted them the rest of the way to the hospital.

Collin caressed her face and rubbed her arms. He spoke softly, telling her everything was going to be all right, that he would take care of her. He knew she couldn't hear him, and the words of comfort were probably more for himself, than her. An intense emotional feeling washed over him.

He was scared shitless.

Pregnant?

Periodically he glanced up into the rearview mirror, catching Joe's concerned gaze. The old man obviously cared for her. He wondered about the connection, and why Joe hadn't questioned his taking over of the situation.

Fifteen minutes later, they pulled up to the emergency room doors. They were met by a team of medical professionals, a gurney, and a flurry of questions. A male assistant stepped up and Collin handed her over.

Suddenly, his arms felt so empty.

"What's happened?" One nurse fired at him.

Collin spun to look at her. "I don't know. She's pregnant. Hemorrhaging?"

"How far along is she?"

Collin looked at Joe questioning. Joe shrugged his shoulders. "I... I don't know. Not long, I guess?"

The nurses' eyes grew larger. "You don't know?"

Collin shook his head.

"You the baby's father?"

His eyes rounded in surprise. He, the baby's father? What if he was? Surely, there had been no one else recently, was there? Bekah didn't seem the type for casual relationships. Especially since her speech the other night.

He didn't answer her.

Collin took two steps forward to follow them through a set of swinging doors. The nurse hooked his elbow. "You can't go in there. I need some questions answered. We need to register her. Sit over there. Now how far along is she?"

Collin jerked his arm from her hand, shook his head, and looked at her. "I told you I don't know. She just told me."

"What was she doing?"

"Setting tobacco."

She eyed him up and down. "That the way they dress for it these days?"

Collin looked down at himself, covered with dust and dirt. His white shirt was more like tan. Bekah's blood had stained the legs of his trousers. He didn't care.

Collin stared after the double doors that had swallowed Bekah and the team. One still swung inward. He felt empty. Lost. Alone.

And he didn't like it.

Chapter Eight

The nurse let him in to see her sometime later in the evening. Time had stopped the moment Bekah had slumped over on the setter, and he had no clue how long it had been since they took her back.

She was in a private room off the maternity wing. The nurse said the hemorrhaging had stopped. An ultrasound showed the baby was fine. Bed rest was important for her right now. The nurse said the doctor would speak to them in the morning. Everyone assumed the baby was his, and they all spoke as if he had a stake in this child's welfare. And Bekah's.

He didn't correct anyone and found it easier to go with the flow.

The nurse added he could stay long as he liked. Collin did not intend to leave any time soon.

He sat on an old straight-back chair he'd pulled close to the bed—close enough so he could see her face. The nurse had given her something to make her sleep, and he had no clue how long she would be out. It didn't matter. She wouldn't wake up to an empty room. He would see to that.

Bekah's chest rose rhythmically, up, and then down, her

breathing more even and shallow now than it had been when they first brought her in. He wondered how a beautiful, intelligent woman as she could get herself into a mess like this.

It wasn't his baby. Was it? What had she said? *Not. Yours?*

Certainly, that meant it wasn't, although she was a bit out of things.

Besides, they were together just two weeks ago. Too soon for that. Right?

Women just didn't get pregnant these days unless they wanted to. Perhaps he'd been wrong about her. Perhaps she was like all the rest—like every woman he'd ever known. Greedy. Self-absorbed. Always on the take. Well, she had another thing coming if she thought he would support her and this child the rest of her days.

No. He wouldn't back off on his responsibilities. But he wouldn't marry her. She was mistaken if she thought that a premature pregnancy meant automatic marriage these days. Maybe in her world, but not in his. There was a term for it, wasn't there? Gold-digger? Was that it? Old fashioned, but close enough.

Marriage. He'd always thought someday he'd marry. At least in the early years of taking over the business. He'd thought about it, yet there had never been anyone he could see himself paired with for the rest of his life.

But the longer he sat there, the tighter his heartstrings stretched and strained. Soon, he was like a tightrope, ready to spring off the walls. Bekah pulled at him—at his heart. And when he looked into her face, his insides melted like dissolving gelatin in boiling water. His body morphed into a mass of nervous energy. He might explode.

No matter how he felt about the possibility of fathering a child—how he hated to even think about the consequences of that—he also felt protective and caring toward her.

His head was spinning like an out-of-control carnival ride, and none of his thoughts made sense. No sooner had one landed in his head that an opposite notion countered it.

His gaze played over Bekah's face. What would marriage be like with her? She was a beautiful woman. Her ebony hair shone in the low lamplight. Her ivory skin mellowed in the darkness. Her lips were ruby red, even without lipstick and her eyes, closed now, were normally sparking dark coals.

She was incredibly sexy, and smart, and she had a perseverance that Collin understood.

Today, in the tobacco patch, she wouldn't have stopped had she not passed out. She would have continued, no matter what, until finished. Her garden was perfection. She'd even been sympathetic to his hounds that night after they'd ripped it up a second time. At least she'd cared enough to try to pen them up safely until he got there.

She drew him in. She held something powerful within that made him forget everything else. His desire for success. His need for wealth and power. Even his long-term obsession for Erin's body. She made him forget it all. When he was around her, all he wanted was to plant tomatoes, set tobacco, and go to church socials.

What the hell?

No. *Her* lifestyle was not *his* lifestyle. He couldn't live like that.

Trouble was, he once thought he could. There was a time when that was all he wanted. A simple country life as a country veterinarian. A small farm. Some animals. A wife. Kids running around everywhere. He *had* wanted that, hadn't he?

Collin combed fingers through his hair and rested his forehead in his palms. That was a lifetime ago. He was different then. It could never be.

He had to rid Bekah McCauley and all thoughts of domestic

life out of his mind. It just wasn't the lifestyle he now lived. He would never be able to go back to his youthful dreams. Never. Youthful dreams were just that—dreams held as a kid that are impossible to grasp once you've passed the point of no return. And he'd passed that point long ago.

Collin's thoughts drifted back to the night he and Bekah made love. What point he'd passed that night, he wasn't certain. She had weakened him—weakened him of every powerful hold he'd ever had over his emotions; every bit of control he'd had over his body. He had let go with everything in him. He was lost. And then found. He felt things he'd never felt before.

And he had not used protection. He'd just assumed...hell, what had he assumed? That she would take care of birth control like most modern women. Well, Bekah was different. He knew that. Well, he wouldn't assume anything anymore. It would never happen again. Maybe when making love to her, he had assumed way too much; that she would protect herself, and that he could love her and walk away. Thing was, he really thought he could. Now he was so damn confused, he didn't know what he could and couldn't do anymore.

After nearly an hour, Collin pulled the chair up as close as he could, grasped her hand in his, and laid his weary head over them at the side of the bed. Mass confusion ate at him. He needed rest and sleep. His eyes closed and he dozed.

* * *

A sliver of light pierced the darkness behind Bekah's eyelids. She worked to open her eyes, and quickly closed them again. After a few seconds, she tried again—and succeeded. In the dim room, she realized the sliver was a crack made by an open door— with slight movement from beyond.

She rotated her head to the left and noticed the IV dripping fluids into her arm. She remembered. Her right hand moved to her abdomen, and she closed her eyes again, squeezing out a small tear. Had she lost the baby?

Her groggy brain refused to make sense of it all. She tried to lift her left hand but couldn't. Something restrained her.

Slowly, her gaze drifted toward her hand, and she sucked in a silent breath.

Collin sat beside her. His arms lay folded across the bed and his head lay upon them. His hair was tousled and disheveled. The fingers of one of his hands lay curled around hers. Bekah reached with her right hand to run her fingers through his hair, combing the curls into place. Her heart swelled with something she didn't dare try to name. She was touched he had stayed. She didn't have anyone else. Calling her parents was out of the question. Too much of a shock to them right now.

He moved and Bekah placed her hand back across her stomach. He lifted his head and sleepily peered into her face. And smiled.

"You're awake," he said softly.

She nodded. "Yes, just. Collin...."

"Everything's okay, Bekah," he interrupted. "The baby's fine and the doctor will be here sometime this morning to talk with you.

A quick sob escaped her mouth, one she hadn't realized she was holding back. "Oh, thank God," she whispered and briefly closed her eyes. Collin squeezed her fingers, and then dropped her hand and stood.

A thousand emotions rippled across her chest as he slipped his hand out of hers. He looked down and Bekah wondered if she looked a mess. Certainly, she did. How long had she slept? And what was he thinking right how.

His gaze bored into hers, questioning—waiting for her to say something? An explanation. Something. His expressions somehow frightened her.

She ran her tongue across her parched lips. "How did I get here?"

"Joe and I. We took my car. He drove."

"Oh. And where were you?"

His stare penetrated. "In the backseat. With you. Holding you."

Her heart melted a little. "Thank you," she whispered.

"You're welcome," he answered, still staring.

"I guess I owe you an explanation."

"You don't owe me anything." His voice was so matter of fact, Bekah was truly frightened.

"Yes I do."

"No, Rebekah."

She winced at the coldness of his words and at the use of her full name.

"But I want to explain," she continued softly.

Collin leaned forward and placed both hands on either side of her on the bed. "No. You don't owe me an explanation. In return, I don't owe you anything either, got it? Understand something, Bekah. I will support this child, but if you think for one moment because I fathered this child that I will marry you, then you're grossly mistaken. *And* if you think, by getting yourself pregnant, your little country ass is going to hook me and all my money then you can forget it. You won't see one red cent."

Bekah blinked. "Excuse me?" He thought *he* was the father? "Collin, wait a minute...."

"Look. We made a mistake. Yeah, I should have thought to use protection, but I didn't. Maybe you should have thought along those lines yourself, but it was too easy to forget, wasn't it? Maybe you planned the whole scheme. Maybe you did let the hounds out that night. Was it all just a ploy to get me into your

house so we could have sex? Was that it? Well, you've got yourself a baby, Ms. McCauley. But you're not getting yourself a
husband."

He jerked back. Bekah watched the flash of anger cross over
his face and felt it settle somewhere in her own chest. She
fought it as he stalked away and out the door—but the anger rose
and fell inside her chest until she thought her heart might burst.

She refused to give into *his* anger and make it her own. She
would not give that power over to him. Over to any man. If his
ridiculous reaction—and assumption—is par for the course, then
she was better off without him.

Two men had now rejected her because of her baby. Two
men had now walked out of her life. And even though Collin
Kramer was never really *in* her life, her heart ached as if it was
missing out on something incredibly important—if all the other
junk in her life hadn't screwed it all up.

The room was too quiet. His presence had filled it but now
that he was gone, there was nothing. "Get used to it, Bekah," she
whispered to herself. "Being alone was your plan when you
came back to Kentucky. Stick to it."

Silence screamed within the dark, empty room. She should
sleep, but she was wide-awake now. Her gaze drifted to her left,
and a bud vase containing a single, red silk rose sitting on the
bedside table. She groped for the vase and without thinking,
grabbed it, and hurled it across the room, listening for the crash
to break the silence. Wondering if the sound of falling glass
vaguely resembled the sound of a breaking heart.

* * *

It was one-fifteen in the morning. Collin glanced at the clock
over the nurse's station and scowled. What in the hell had just
happened? How had he let himself lose control? Bekah

deserved none of that. He'd be lucky if she would ever speak to him again.

He stopped mid-step in the center of the hallway and ran a hand over his face. Eyes closed, he breathed deeply, an attempt to pull himself together. All the pent-up emotion he'd just let loose at Bekah left his chest devoid of just about everything. As his last breath, words had exited his throat; he felt empty, shallow.

He sidestepped toward the antiseptic-white wall and leaned into it. His head fell, resting his chin on his chest. *She sucks the strength right out of me.*

He needed sleep and pushed away from the wall, thinking how good his bed was going to feel in a few minutes. When he could slide into unconsciousness and forget, at least for a while, everything that had happened over the past few hours—hell the past few weeks. Maybe a shot of his favorite Bourbon and he could forget the tug at his heart pulling him back to Bekah's side.

"Mr. Kramer?"

Collin stopped short and slowly turned. Bekah's doctor stepped toward him. He extended a hand and Collin shook it.

"On my way to check on Ms. McCauley. Been in the delivery room for the past couple of hours or so. Rough labor, then emergency C-section. Mother and baby doing fine, though."

Collin listened and thought of Bekah. What kind of pain was she going to have to endure delivering this baby? *His baby.*

"How is she doing?"

His thoughts jerked back to the doctor. "I...uh, just left her. She was fine."

"Still sleeping?"

Collin hesitated, then nodded—lying. He imagined she wasn't sleeping.

"Good, I'll not bother her now, then. I'll talk to you both in the morning though. I make my rounds about ten o'clock. Be back by then."

Collin could only nod. He didn't want to get into anything with Bekah's doctor. It wasn't his place to say anything. "We'll be here," he said, a tired edge to his voice. Suddenly his brain felt like fried mush.

The doctor grinned and nodded. "Hell, isn't it? Worth it in the end though. Got three kids myself. Wouldn't trade 'em for anything."

The doctor turned, and then stepped back. "Bekah's lucky, you know? I haven't known her long, but I know enough about her to realize she's fortunate to have a man like you at her side."

Collin stared. "How's that?"

"Well, it's good we discovered Bekah's problem early in the pregnancy. Now we'll be prepared for any complications that might arise during delivery. Being in the second trimester, the condition could change a bit over the next four months or so. She may have to go on bedrest, at some point."

Collin stared straight ahead at the doctor. *Second trimester? Four months until delivery?* He didn't know much about pregnancy, but... "Second trimester?"

He nodded. "Oh yes, by the ultra-sound I'd say she's between four and five months along. I've only seen Bekah once prior to this, for the pregnancy that is. I saw her occasionally during her teen years. She's small, but the baby is growing normally. She'll start blooming soon." He grinned and headed toward the elevator. "I'll see you in the morning."

Collin stared past the doctor to a window at the end the hallway. The only thing he knew for sure was that the baby Bekah McCauley carried was not his. That twisted with his head more than the previous several hours had.

Forty-five minutes later, Collin leaned against the open barn door, gazing across the open pasture at Bekah's house. The moon and starlight were the only illumination offered. The windows all stood dark and empty, and stared back like blank, vacant eyes—taunting him with questions about Bekah. How was she? How did he really *feel* about her? What was he going to do? What was *she* going to do?

It dawned on him that everything he had once wanted in life could come true if he wanted them bad enough. He could love Bekah, couldn't he? *Love?* He'd long given up the idea of love. Had thought it would never come his way.

He wasn't in love with her. No. But was he falling in love?

He'd never been tempted to face the consequences of love. Look it right in the face and say *bring it on*. Why now?

What *was* he going to do about it?

If he wanted Bekah in his life, he would also have to accept the child of another man. Did it matter? He pondered that for a moment, staring at the empty house across the field. No, it didn't matter one damn bit.

That was a crazy thought.

He wanted her. He wanted Bekah—for keeps. Forever. He could barely stand thinking of her lonely and pregnant, living across that pasture, without him. Hell, he couldn't stand to think of her all alone in that lonely hospital room.

He turned and headed for his car.

* * *

Bekah blinked and opened her eyes. She remembered a nurse coming in sometime after Collin had left, checking her vitals, changing out the IV bag, and cleaning up the glass and water on the floor. She felt slight remorse at throwing the vase, but it quickly left. Collin Kramer was an ass, and she was better off without him. Then she must have drifted back to sleep for a while—maybe for a long while because she was groggy as hell when she finally woke.

Then, as she focused, she realized she wasn't alone. Someone else was in the room, sitting in the chair at the foot of her bed, watching her.

Collin.

She shifted and rolled to her side, feigning indifference. "What the hell are you doing here?" Her voice was hoarse and devoid of emotion. She pushed herself up to a sitting position.

Collin rose and crossed the room, helping her up, and then sat on the edge of her bed. With a shaking finger, he pushed a strand of hair out of her eyes and Bekah savored his light touch —and at the same time wanted to push him away. Silence fell between them for a few seconds.

"I came to apologize. I was—"

"Out of line? Rude? Ridiculously wrong?" Bekah pulled back, her head settling against the raised bed.

"Yes. All of the above. How are you feeling?"

Oh, don't go changing the subject, Mister. "I don't know what I feel. Or *how* I feel."

"You have every right to be mad as hell. I wouldn't blame you if you asked me to leave, but I'm begging you, please don't. I got it wrong, Bekah. I know what you said, but you were nearly unconscious, and I thought the baby was mine. The entire scenario yesterday was nerve-wracking and unsettling. I made a wrong assumption and..." His words trailed off and Bekah shook her head.

"You are an ass," she said. "You thought I tricked you. You have no clue how wrong you are, you son-of-a-bitch."

Collin dropped his chin. "I deserve that. All of it. And I'm deeply sorry. Your doctor stopped me after I left your room earlier and explained that you're over four months along." His gaze lifted and played over her face. "Bekah, why didn't you tell me what was going on with you?"

Bekah closed her eyes again. "Tell you what? That I'm pregnant with another man's baby? I did. Geez. Give me a freakin' break. I told you while we were still at the tobacco patch."

He hedged closer and Bekah stiffened. "I know, but what about before? Why didn't you tell me *before*?"

"Before what? Before you replanted my garden? Before you invited me to your house? Before you took me on my sofa in my living room?" Bekah glanced off, feeling her heartbeat rise. "It just never seemed to work its way into the conversation, Collin."

"You could have told me."

Bekah sighed, and her gaze fell to his hands. They were so close. She wanted to reach over and draw them into hers but didn't. In addition to all the turmoil of the past few hours, she could see the anguish in his face. She ached to smooth out the wrinkles in his forehead.

"Collin, why would I have told you? For the past month, we've done nothing but argue. We don't believe in the same things. We don't come from the same backgrounds. We have nothing in common—except for a few minutes of—" she paused, unsure how to label what they had, "of sex on my couch and a pleasant afternoon on Memorial Day. That's all we've had. Why would I tell you?"

"Um, because we had sex in your living room and a pleasant afternoon on Memorial Day?"

Bekah shook her head. "No. Besides, I haven't told anyone." Well, anyone here, at least. "There is only one other person who knows, and he's not interested." *Damnit. Don't go there.*

Collin's gaze met hers. "Then he's a fool."

"He's a lot more than that."

His eyes narrowed.

"He told me to get out of his life. So, I did. I am here now. End of story."

"Bastard." Collin shook his head. "I'm sorry."

Bekah watched his chest elevate slightly, then fall as a huge breath exhaled through his nostrils. "So, you don't want to talk about it."

"I don't. Ever."

"Maybe we *need* to talk about him."

"*We* don't need to talk about him, or anything else for that matter. There is no *we*, Collin."

* * *

Collin rose and moved two steps from the bed. No *we*? What did he expect? Did he think he'd walk back in here and she'd welcome him with open arms? Ridiculous. He was going to have to do some heavy apologizing—and fast.

And mean every word.

"Bekah—"

She interrupted. "Collin, look. I'm going to be direct. I *was* angry with you last night. Actually, I still am, but before the anger, I was very hurt."

He started to say something, but she shook her head and rushed forward. "Then I started thinking. I had no right to be angry *or* hurt. We don't have anything to hang that anger on, do we? We've been fighting—something—forever, it seems, but we don't have anything." She cleared her throat and kept her gaze steady on his expressionless face. "Yes, I fought you. Because I don't want to lose my independence. Because I don't want to jump from the frying pan into the fire. I'm sure none of that makes sense to you, and that is okay. I fought *because* of my child. But then— When we... I let you in a little. Into my heart. I assumed that you might be around, and you didn't assume the same. But it's okay. I don't *want* to count on you. I don't want to count on *anyone*. I can make it by myself."

Collin waited for a moment, his gaze playing over her face. "I came back, Bekah. You don't have to make it by yourself. I'll help you through this."

His words jolted her. He *was* back, but what did that mean? "Why? Why would you? I'm nothing to you, Collin."

"Because I think we do have something. Hell, I've been so confused and fighting it myself. And I know we haven't had much time together but what we've had, has been good, and maybe it can be spectacular in the future. But we'll never know if I walk away right now, or if you push me away."

He edged closer and sat on the bed. "Bekah, a year ago I would have run away from you as fast as I could, but everything in me is screaming for me to take a chance. To step forward, out of my comfort zone. I want to help you through this pregnancy. I just want to be your friend to start, so we can grow together and... And maybe down the road, who knows? Maybe we can even be a family. But that is putting the cart before the horse. Just let me be here for you now. Okay?"

* * *

A family?

It was beyond Bekah's hopes and she refused to dwell on it. But to have someone to help her right now would be a wonderful thing. She wouldn't feel so alone. Could she let him?

Emotion balled up inside her, settling behind her eyes. All the cards laid out before her, which would she pick up? Take him up on his offer or send him packing?

Tears pooled behind those closed eyelids.

"No." She opened her eyes and studied Collin's face.

"No?"

Bekah sighed. "Collin. I'm tired and I don't feel like playing a game of *what ifs*. Thank you, but you can't be here for me during my pregnancy. We can't contemplate a potential family—we're not family. We aren't even very good neighbors. I really appreciate your offer, but no. My pregnancy is of no concern to you, so I think it would be best if we settled this right now."

"Settle what?"

Collin was seething mad, it seemed. Well, too bad. Just another incident of him not getting his way. Well, *dammit!* Money can't buy everything. And you can't build a family on mistakes.

"Settle this relationship thing. I don't want anyone in my life, Collin. I want to spend the rest of my pregnancy on my farm in peace and quiet. That's why I came there to begin with. That's my intent from now on. You can help by keeping your animals where they belong. I want to raise my child on my own. For most of my life, I've let someone else call the shots. Not anymore. It is sweet of you to sacrifice your time, but I don't want you to do that for me. I don't want *anyone* to do anything for me. I want to be left alone."

He shook his head, as if not believing a word she'd just said. "You're sure about this?"

She nodded. "Quite sure."

Collin stood and shoved his hands into his pockets, a scowl on his face. "I'm not giving up on this."

"You don't have a choice, Collin."

"Everything is always up for negotiation, Bekah."

"Oh really?" *Arrogant bastard.* "Even human lives? I think not."

"I think yes." Then he leaned closer and took her face into his hands. His mouth sought hers and claimed her lips. Bekah jerked back but he held her fast to him, and she couldn't deny

127

that the pressure of his lips moving across hers, tasting and tempting, sent her into a pleasant spiral.

Please don't do this to me.

Then he broke free and whispered. "I can be very stubborn, Bekah. One quality you have never seen is about to become very apparent—perseverance. When I want something, I get it. I know exactly what I want. And I fully intend to get it."

Then he pulled back, stared into her eyes, and added, "Dr. Benton will be here about ten o'clock this morning. I'm going home to shower. Then I am going by your house and finding some clean clothes and things for you. You might as well give me your house key or tell me how to get in, because I'm not coming back here without what you need."

Bekah blinked. "I'm going home today?"

"I don't know but when you do, I'm sure you want clean clothes."

"I'll tell him I want to go home today, so no need."

"Bekah let me do this."

Confused at the turn, she shook her head. "I am not sure where my keys are. Probably still in Joe's truck. I left them in the console."

"Joe's home. He had someone pick him up last evening. The old guy stuck around for a quite a while, worried about you."

Bless Joe's heart. She'd call him first thing. Resigned, she looked at Collin and said, "If you jimmy the kitchen window a little it will go up. My room is on the second floor. There should be some sweatpants and a T-shirt in the dresser. Maybe you could get my hairbrush, and toothpaste and toothbrush...."

Collin leaned in and gave her a peck on the cheek. "I'll take care of it. Be back soon."

No doubt.

Chapter Nine

"**M**s. McCauley, you have a condition called placenta praevia."

Dr. Benton leaned against the counter to Bekah's right. Collin sat to her left. He had arrived shortly after the doctor entered the room, looking a little smug, slightly more rested, and cleaner, having showered and changed his clothing.

"We see it in approximately one-percent of our patients. What happens is that the placenta either fully or partially covers the cervix, the opening to the uterus. Normally there is no pain, just bleeding—sometimes severe. If it continues until labor, the bleeding can present quite a problem. I'm glad we know now. It would have become apparent when we did the ultrasound we'd scheduled next week. I think the pain you were experiencing yesterday was due to your ulcer, not to this condition. Had you eaten much yesterday? Have you been under a lot of stress?"

Bekah stared past him to Collin. Stress? For months, her life had been nothing but stress. Maybe years. "Yes. There has been stress. As far as eating? Not much yesterday, I guess. Toast for breakfast and a sandwich around noon. I drank a lot of water though."

"Good nutrition is important, Bekah. You have two conditions that require it."

"I know."

"And no more setting tobacco."

"But—"

"Doctor's orders," Dr. Benton said.

Bekah deflated into the bed. Crap. What would she do now?

Collin rose and stepped toward the doctor. "So, what happens next?"

Bekah studied his face and felt her own flush. "Yes, doctor, please tell *me* what happens next."

Dr. Benton looked from Collin to Bekah. "What happens is this. You eat right and no more setting tobacco, as I said. No physical labor of any kind. Bed rest as much as possible. You're in the second trimester of your pregnancy. Sometimes the placenta moves. We'll have to monitor it closely with periodic ultrasounds. If it stays in the position it is now, which is totally covering your cervix, we have no option but to do a cesarean section. Your pregnancy is now considered high-risk."

Bekah sat looking at him. "Complete bed rest? Until the baby is born?"

Dr. Benton shook his head. "Maybe. For now, a few days at least. Your body will thank you. The bleeding stopped before I left here last night. I don't think we're going to see anymore. In a week or so, you can get up and move around the house, but stay home. As the pregnancy progresses, we'll see."

Bekah breathed deeply. "Dr. Benton, did I do anything to cause this? Was it because I wasn't eating right or setting tobacco?"

He shook his head. "No. We don't know why some women

have this condition. Your diet didn't cause it nor the fact you were setting tobacco. What I don't know is whether the physical labor aggravated the condition, or not. And then there was the fall over the weekend. I don't know. That's why you need bed rest. If it happens again, we'll be prepared. You call me at any sign of discomfort or bleeding. And you take care of yourself."

Bekah nodded. "I will."

Dr. Benton glanced at Collin. "See that she does. I've known this young lady since she was little—strongest-willed child I ever met. She gets a notion in her head and you can't change her mind. Don't let her go off and do anything foolish."

Collin nodded, a serious look on his face. "I won't, sir. Promise."

Bekah started to protest, but Dr. Benton continued. "Good. I need to make my rounds. You'll stay the night and if there are no complications, you can go home tomorrow. When you do, bed rest." He glanced from one to another. "I'll see you both in the morning."

"All right," Bekah grumbled. "I understand."

The door shut behind him and Bekah paused a moment before she lit into Collin. "What are you doing?" She pushed herself up to sit higher in the bed. "You have no business here."

"I told you early this morning, Bekah. I intend to be around. You may not like it, but that's the way it's going to be."

"You are crazy."

"For you."

Bekah's eyes widened. "Oh pooh. You're only out for yourself."

"You've redeemed me."

Bekah let out a short huff of breath. "Collin, go home. I don't need you here."

"I'm leaving in a minute, but I'll be back."

She rolled her eyes. "Collin, please. I have enough to worry about. Just do as I ask and don't make a big deal of this, okay?" *Dammit*, she would not cry, but tears were welling up again.

"I'll help you, Bekah."

She shook her head. "This is not helping."

He stepped closer and reached for her hand. "Let me." She pulled it out of his grasp.

"No."

"I weeded your garden this morning."

"No, you didn't."

"I fed your dog."

She glared at him.

"I'm setting your tobacco this afternoon with Joe."

"No!" She sat up even farther in the bed. "You leave my tobacco alone. You know nothing about it."

"Joe does. He needs my help. If you weren't so damn stubborn, you'd realize you do too. He's an old man, Bekah. He can't take this on by himself."

"I don't need anyone's help, Collin Kramer. I don't need *anyone*," she shouted.

Collin sat at the edge of the bed. "Don't shout," he said softly. "It's not good for you to get so upset."

"Upset? *Upset?* You don't want me to get upset? Then get the hell out of here and don't come back."

He nodded, smiling, placed his hands on each of her shoulders, leaned over and kissed her directly in the center of her forehead. "I'm leaving. I'll be back later tonight after we're finished." He cupped her cheek in his hand and smiled. "See you later."

Bekah fumed. He ignored every word she'd said. Amazing. She shook her head and then nearly laughed aloud. The man *is* crazy.

* * *

Collin took Bekah's seat on the setter. Pete sat to his left. Joe drove. The plan was to finish Bekah's crop today, then do Joe's immediately after that. They probably wouldn't finish until tomorrow or the day after.

Collin didn't miss a beat this time. He placed every plant in the setter cup and got into a rhythm darned quick. His aching muscles loosened up with the warmth beating down on his back. He, Pete, and Joe continued down the rows of the tobacco patch in near silence. Occasionally someone would utter something, but mostly they kept their hands busy and their minds on their task.

Except Collin.

His mind reeled with thoughts of Bekah. At first it was sexual. Then something happened the day they'd made love. It started out as an adventure, a one-night stand of pleasure, but it had changed. Somewhere in the middle of loving her, it had all changed. And he *had* loved her. He did. He cringed when he thought about the things he'd said to her, but he'd been scared.

Real scared.

He had a lot of making up for lost time and his arrogant attitude.

With Bekah, the sheer fact that she didn't want anything from him that was so attractive, so appealing. But there was more. An ache in his heart consumed him each time he thought of her. An ache quelled only when he was with her. A fire that wasn't doused by being physically intimate with her but made more intense.

When she lay unconscious in his arms, he thought he would die. Her fragile features tugged at his heartstrings. He had spent most of his adult life taking from people, living off their successes. Suddenly with Bekah, he wanted to give. Protect.

He had an uphill battle in front of him, and he knew it.

* * *

Bekah propped herself up in the hospital bed. She'd napped the entire afternoon, then got up long enough to go to the bathroom, wash up, and brush her teeth. She glanced at the small bag Collin had packed for her—comb, brush, toiletries and even a nightgown—and smiled at his efforts. Perhaps Collin had some redeeming qualities after all—but that didn't change anything.

She ran her brush through her unruly hair, a vague attempt to smooth it out. She longed for something to pull it back with but couldn't find anything in the bag. She wished she had some concealer to hide the dark circles under her eyes. Sighing, she gave her reflection a last glance then returned to her bed.

The rest of the afternoon dragged on. She settled herself in, listening for the squeak of the cart bringing her dinner. Earlier in the day she'd ordered meat loaf and mashed potatoes and green beans, with vanilla ice cream for dessert. Earlier when they'd brought the menu around, it sounded good, but now, she worried about the dinner laying heavy on her stomach.

The orderly arrived about thirty minutes later with the entree. She picked at it and watched the digital clock at her bedside. She fished for the remote control and searched for something to watch while eating. Finding nothing of interest, she pushed the table aside, and the remote with it.

Leaning her head back against the flat pillow, she signed, her eyes closed.

Tobacco. Collin Kramer was out setting her tobacco. He'd come in here tonight with blisters and a sore butt from sitting another afternoon on that setter. Not to mention with sunburn and a greenish-brown stain on his hands. She chuckled. Yeah, she could just about see him. The image was almost as funny had she pictured Matthew on the setter.

Matthew. How in the world had she gotten herself mixed up

with another obsessive, control-freak, Alpha male like Matthew? Obviously, there was something seriously wrong with her.

Matthew had changed his mind.

Matthew had done more than that—he'd thrown her out in the street.

No job, no money, and only the clothing on her back. He'd tried to make it so that she'd lost her pension funds, but she'd managed to convince Human Resources otherwise—the threat of a lawsuit wasn't appealing to them.

If Matthew were in control of any situation, things went smoothly, but the moment the tables turned, he couldn't handle it.

Was Collin like that?

She didn't think so. He'd not run the other way as Mathew had. Collin was running toward her, baby and all.

She'd get Maggie to help her out. She'd have to pay Joe for his work on the farm—there would be no bartering for a while. Maybe, if she got desperate, she'd call one of her brothers. She hated the thought of her family bailing her out—they had their own troubles—especially when she'd been so independent all these years.

Of course, they knew nothing about the pregnancy yet—or how Matthew had treated her.

Dr. Benton called her pregnancy high-risk. She had to think about the baby's best interest, not hers. The baby was the most important thing—her health and the baby's. But how would she pass the time now that she was confined to bed?

"I guess I'll just have to take up knitting or something," she mumbled.

"Oh?" A light feathery touch graced her cheek. Bekah's eyes flew open.

"Collin."

"As promised," he said. He stood at the side of her bed,

looking fresh and clean, his forehead reddened with sunburn. As much as she didn't want to like the thought of him being there, he looked darned good to her right now.

"Hi." The grin on his face widened. "How's my girl?"

His girl. Thoughts of how good he looked vanished. She had to remind herself that she didn't want him there. "You don't give up, do you?"

"Not usually." He laid a couple of packages down on the table.

"Had dinner?" His gaze rose to meet hers, then fell to the half-eaten meat loaf patty. "Like Chinese?"

"No." She lied. She loved Chinese.

Collin opened the bag and pulled out two Styrofoam containers. He lifted the lid on one. "For you, my dear, Rainbow Chicken and rice. Healthy. Carrots, broccoli, pea pods, and chicken there. Do you like egg rolls? I bought a couple of extra, so have one of those too."

Bekah stared. "Put it all away. Take it home with you and warm it up for lunch tomorrow."

"Can't." He shook his head and arranged the items on her table, then turned to another box and sat in the chair next to the bed.

"I can't eat all that. Besides, I had dinner."

Collin shrugged and glanced again to her entree. "Yeah, I can tell you sure dug that. Eat up. You know what they say about Chinese food."

"That I'll be hungry an hour later, I know. But I don't want it. You eat it. In fact, why don't you take it to go." She was grumbly and in a bad mood. Damn him for being so cheerful.

"No way. I've got some Kung Pao Beef waiting for me here. I don't know about you, but I'm starving. Eating Chinese on the run isn't like palming a hamburger while driving. If you don't mind, I'll eat right here." He broke open the bag that held a plastic fork, napkin, sauces, and a fortune cookie and handed it to her. He rearranged the items on her table, pushing her meal toward her. Then pulled up a chair next to her and attacked his own meal.

"I do mind."

He continued eating.

"Did you hear me?"

Finally, slowing the chewing motion of his jaw, he looked up at her. "What?"

Bekah looked up at him. "You're really serious about all this aren't you?"

Collin stopped fidgeting with his food and looked at her. "What?"

"I said, you are really serious about all this, aren't you? What are you going to do, pester me until I give in? Well, it won't work." She turned her face up in defiance.

He stood up and placed his dinner on the bedside table, then reached over and cupped her cheek, bringing her face closer to his. "Dead serious," he whispered. "There's nothing in the world to keep me from doing this, or from you. It will work." His lips captured hers in a sweet, Kung Pao kiss.

Involuntarily, her hand fluttered up to his neck. The touch of his skin on her fingertips sent a shock wave through her. She toyed with a few wispy hairs at his nape. Then drew her hand away and dropped it to her lap.

Think, Bekah, think!

"I want you to stop doing that."

"No, you don't." He smiled.

"You're not serious."

"I couldn't be more serious if I wanted to, Bekah. If it takes me forever, one day I will convince you of that."

Bekah sat stunned. At what, she wasn't sure. Was it the fact that she let him kiss her—and that she had felt something?

"Leave, Collin." She knew her voice trembled as she spoke the words. "I want you to leave."

"Do you really?"

His face was only inches away.

"Now." She felt a little stronger.

"I'm here, baby, and I'm gonna stay."

"I'll call a...a nurse. The hospital administrator. The police, Collin. If you keep doing this to me, I'll call the police. I want you to leave me alone."

He leaned closer. "I don't think so."

"You don't think I would?"

"No. I don't think you want me to leave you. I don't think you want to be alone. If you'd only think about it, I think you'd realize that."

Bekah leaned forward, her eyes narrowing. "You don't know a damn thing about me, Collin Kramer. Not a damn thing."

"I know a whole lot more than you think I do."

"Oh, yeah?"

"Yeah."

"Like what?"

"Like when you were a kid you hated farm work."

Bekah bristled. "Who told you that?"

"That you are an excellent artist. That you earned a lot of scholarship money to go to college."

"It's a lie." She didn't like him knowing so much about her.

"That you lived in New York for the past five years or so. Big magazine editor. And now, for some mysterious reason, which nobody around here knows, you're back."

Bekah crossed her arms and leaned back against the bed pillows. "What did you do, hire an investigator?"

He shook his head. "Had a long talk with Joe this afternoon." He leaned back and stared questioningly at her. "Why are you back, Bekah?"

She wouldn't answer. He had no right to know these things. "You figure it out. You're so smart."

He contemplated that. "I will. Sooner or later." He shifted in his seat. "Look, let's forget this for now. I don't know about you, but I'm starved. I set tobacco for six hours. Let's eat."

Bekah picked up the fork and stabbed a sprig of broccoli, then stuffed it into her mouth. "I'm not forgetting it. So, you got some information out of Joe. Who cares? That doesn't make you an expert on me. And it still doesn't give you the right to implant yourself into my life."

Collin chewed and swallowed. "Joe and Pete and I set the rest of your tobacco. It's all done. Tomorrow we'll get Joe's. I'm sending one of my stable hands over in the morning while I come to get you. I had two of them pull plants this morning. I'll help them finish up in the afternoon, after we get home."

Bekah stared. All of that was a whole lot to take and she wasn't sure on which statement to settle first.

"You set my tobacco?"

Collin looked up. "Yes. All finished."

"And you're going to help Joe tomorrow?"

He shrugged and nodded. "Yes."

She wanted to blurt out the word *why?* But she already knew the answer. Damn him, he was really trying, however futile his attempts would be.

"Collin, I really appreciate your help, but that wasn't necessary."

He smiled and gathered his food container and took it to the garbage can. He must have been hungry because he polished his dinner off in no time. "Just being a good neighbor, Bekah. I'm sort of getting the hang of this."

And I'm not sure how to handle it. "You're not coming to get me, Collin. I've made other arrangements," she said quickly.

His eyebrows arched. "Oh? Who's coming?"

"That's none of your business."

"No one's coming, Bekah."

She fumed. "And what makes you so sure?"

"Who would it be?"

Her mind raced. "My brother." She smiled. He didn't know her brother knew nothing.

"Michael or Kevin?"

Bekah bristled. Joe again. "Michael," she spat back.

"You've told them about the pregnancy."

"That is also none of your business. You are not coming to get me tomorrow, and that is that." She didn't care how she got home. Surely there were ways.

He stood there, studying her for a moment longer. "I brought you here. I'll take you home. Get some rest—I need to get a good night's sleep myself, with everything on the agenda tomorrow—but I'll be back early in the morning."

"You are seriously setting Joe's crop tomorrow?"

"Yes, ma'am."

"How did you do today?"

"Absolutely fine."

"Bet you missed a million plants. How many did you have to set by hand?"

"None, actually. And I set left-handed."

"No way."

"Yeah, Pete hadn't set before, working on horse farms, mostly. He did okay though."

Bekah glanced to Collin's hands, and took a good look at his fingers. He'd tried to scrub them, but tobacco stain ran deep into the lines and crevices of his skin; fingers tinged a faint green-brown. He'd also wrapped both forefingers with a bandage.

"Are you okay?"

Collin wiggled his fingers a bit. "Yeah, I'm fine." He picked up one of his hands and turned it over in the air.

"Your hands are all blistered."

"Better mine than yours."

"Collin...."

He looked back to her face. "Bekah, listen to me. If I didn't want to do this, I wouldn't, but I do. So please eat your dinner and hush. I've had blisters before, a lot worse than this. Don't worry about me." He caught her gaze and held steady.

"I don't want you to do this for me." She heard her say the words, but she wasn't convinced she really meant them anymore.

Collin's eyes never left hers. "I'm not," he replied. "I'm doing it for us."

Chapter Ten

As much as she disliked the thought, Collin had won. As he pulled up to Bekah's house the next day, he glanced toward her and said, "Home at last."

"And none too soon," she replied, glad to be rid of the hospital and surprised by the fact that she could be civil to him and had been happy to see him when he arrived.

"You seemed eager to leave."

"Not a fan of hospitals," she said. Bekah glanced his way and smiled a little. "How could you tell?"

He shrugged and chuckled. "You've been a little testy the past few days."

"Just the past few days?"

He grinned. "Well, maybe a few weeks."

"Touché." She glanced toward her house. "I am so ready to be home. I hope I only have one more visit to that place, deliver the baby, and then get on with things."

Collin stopped the car, pushed the gear into park, and grasped her hand. "Everything will be okay, Bekah."

Her hand in his was comforting, and she wasn't sure who

was more surprised she'd not jerked it away. "I'm so stupid," she whispered.

"No, you're not." Collin squeezed her hand a little tighter.

She turned. "I know nothing about pregnancy or children, Collin. I'm going to be a terrible mother."

One corner of Collin's mouth turned up. "You're going to be a wonderful mother."

Bekah inhaled and let it out slowly. "I just didn't think, I guess. I didn't realize...."

Collin leaned in and touched her cheek. "Don't do that to yourself. You heard what Dr. Benton said. There was nothing you did to cause this condition."

"But I might have aggravated it."

"But you didn't know. Now you do. So we take every precaution. We do what he said. You start eating better, bed rest for a while, no physical labor. And I'll help."

Bekah studied his face. *We?* There was that word again.

He was good for her, in ways. It was nice of him to bring her home. Yes. And his words were comforting. But there was no *we.* "Collin, I thought you understood that—"

Collin stared, his face blank. After a moment, he sat up straight in the driver's seat and looked out over the hood of the car. "Bekah..." He looked at her. "I've been a bastard. I'll admit that. Today I'm trying hard not to be. Right now, I just want to help. Make no mistake, I want to be part of your life, but I'm happy just being here for you. And I'm trying really hard not to be a fucking bastard."

"Collin," she began soft. "Whether you are a bastard or not, my position stands firm. I don't want anyone's help. I just want —I need—to be left alone."

"That's not healthy, Bekah. Especially in your condition. Everyone needs help occasionally." Collin took a deep breath, then exhaled slowly.

"I'm fine. I don't need anyone."

"Not even a friend? What happened to that? Bekah, I can be a friend. I'm just across the fence and I'll always be there when you need me. Someday, you're going to need me."

Bekah shook her head. "I don't think so. A friend is one thing but... Collin, you must understand, I don't want to have to rely on anyone. I need to go this—

"Alone. You already said that."

Bekah lifted the car door handle. "I'm tired, Collin. I need to go lie down. I don't want to fight about this anymore."

He nodded, a rueful look on his face, "I know how you feel," he whispered. "I'm tired, too, but I can't leave this hanging. Just one minute, okay?"

Bekah sighed. "All right. One minute."

"I thought a lot about us last night. I understand your position and I respect it. I don't have to be your lover. I just want to be your friend. Then maybe, someday... Well, you never know. Let me be that one thing to you, okay. That's all I ask. Lean on me occasionally. No pressure. I'll butt out whenever you want, just say the word. But I want you to feel like you can call on me if you need something. You don't have to go this totally alone."

Bekah released a pent-up breath. "I can be a real bitch."

Collin grinned. "Not you?"

"Yeah, me."

His eyes sparkled. "Don't worry, I can handle it."

"Friends, huh? It will never work."

"Sure, it will," Collin stroked an invisible X over his heart with his forefinger and smiled at her. "Cross my heart and hope to die."

"Stick a needle in your eye?"

Collin's eyes crinkled. "Well, I'm not sure I'd go that far, but if you insist."

She shook her head. "I don't insist. No sex, right?"

"Right."

"Just friends?"

"Right."

She paused for a moment. "I think I can handle that." She wondered if he could. For a long moment, she stood staring into Collin's eyes, searching, then started for the house.

After a quick dinner that Collin threw together, Bekah started for the stairway. "Thanks, Collin, for the sandwich. I'm going to get ready for bed now."

He halted her with a hand to her elbow. "You shouldn't be climbing stairs. I spoke with Dr. Benton."

She stared. "Then how do you propose I get to my bedroom? Are you going to carry me up and down?"

Collin grinned. "As appealing as that sounds, I have a better idea." He took her hand. "Come with me."

Bekah followed him down the hallway to another bedroom, the one her grandparents had used when they were older.

He opened the door and they stepped inside. Bekah gasped. Someone, and she guessed it was Collin, had cleaned and transformed the room entirely for her convenience. Fluffy comforters and pillows adorned the bed. In the window, the addition of a small air conditioner cooled the room. Nice, since the house did not have air conditioning. On a dresser, sat a large, flat screen television with DVD player. Books and magazines were stacked on the night table.

"What do you think?"

Bekah blinked. "I think I'm wondering what in the heck you have done."

Collin grinned widely. Obviously, he was pleased. "Pete and I moved everything in late last night. Look over here, what do you think of this?" He stepped to the corner where a small refrigerator sat and opened the door. "Juice and milk and water. No soft drinks, sorry. My orders."

Bekah froze, then scanned the room. Too much. Just too much.

On one hand, she knew exactly why Collin was doing this—to be helpful and friendly and probably because he cared. But who needed this kind of hovering?

Everything—*everything* was out of her control. *Everything!* It had to stop right now.

Her fists involuntarily clenched at her sides. As she looked at Collin, smiling happily before her, she saw Matthew, instead.

He meant well, she knew, but she had to put a stop to it. *Now.* Before it was too late. Before she *lost* all control.

"How dare you," she whispered, then hit him square in the chest with the heel of her hand. "How fucking dare you!" She turned and left the room.

* * *

Collin watched the door slam between he and Bekah and felt his shoulders drop. His hand went immediately to his chest and rubbed. He'd been up past midnight readying everything for her, and this was the thanks he got? *Fuck. I've done it again.* What in the hell happened?

He found her in the living room and was prepared to pounce the moment he saw her but didn't. Clutching a pillow to her chest, staring out the window, Bekah sat curled up in the corner of the couch. Her face held an agonizing gaze, tears running down her cheeks.

He sat quietly beside her. She glanced off. He didn't say a word and waited patiently.

After a moment, she spoke. "You didn't deserve that. I'm sorry."

Collin let out a deep breath. "I don't know what I did wrong."

Bekah shook her head. "You didn't do anything wrong. In fact, you did everything right." She poked a strand of hair behind her ear.

"Then what?" he said quietly. "Obviously, something's wrong."

Bekah closed her eyes. "It... It all came rolling back. How I used to feel when...."

"What Bekah, what all came back. I need to know."

She gazed into his eyes. "Matthew."

"The baby's father?"

She nodded. "Yes."

"What about him, Bekah? I need to know so I don't trigger that kind of reaction again. Tell me."

She sighed and then looked at him. "Matthew had complete control over my life. All decisions were out of my hands. The clothes I wore. My diet. When we had sex. When we didn't. When I worked and who I worked with. Who I socialized with and who I didn't. I don't ever want to live like that again. Ever."

Collin swore under his breath. "I was taking over."

"Maybe a little."

"Maybe a lot. I'm sorry, Bekah. I won't make that mistake again."

Her eyes searched his, and he wasn't sure she believed him. "Please, it's my problem, Collin. You didn't do anything wrong. You were just trying to help, and it was lovely. I know your intentions were good. I'm just screwed up in the head over stuff like this. See? You're much better off to leave now while you can."

Damn. Collin took her hands into his. "Let me explain something to you. I was wrong to assume that I could come in here and take over. I shouldn't have done that. We've not been sailing on even keel anyway, but now that we have an agreement, of sorts, I promise you that in the future, I'll discuss every-

148

thing with you beforehand. I guess I just wanted to make you comfortable...and the fact that you've never asked me for anything makes me want to do it even more." He raked his fingers through his hair, settling his face in both hands, and then looked at her. "Bekah, do you want to talk about Matthew?"

She shook her head. "No," she said quietly. "Not today."

"All right." He was willing to wait—but one day he needed to know more.

"I really just want to go to sleep." She yawned and covered her mouth with the back of her hand.

"Just lay down here," Collin instructed in a soft voice. As she lay there, he tucked the afghan around her and heard her gentle sigh.

"Collin?" she called out softly, eyes still closed.

"Hmm?"

"This friends thing— Sometimes I might need you. Sometimes I might not want you around. That okay?" Her words slurred in sleepiness.

"That's just fine, Bekah," he whispered. He traced her cheek with the pads of his forefinger. Then on impulse, he scooted her over and laid beside her, gathering her close. He wrapped his arms around her protectively, and the feeling that surged through him at that moment was pure joy.

He longed to protect her, care for her, and make her forget about the sonofabitch Matthew.

She burrowed into him. "Just so you understand," she murmured.

He closed his eyes in contented bliss. Bekah McCauley was exactly where he wanted her. He would have to tread slowly. Problem was that patience was never his virtue. He'd just have to make it so.

* * *

Hours later, Bekah woke in her bed and found a tented note on the nightstand, propped up against a couple of books. Smiling, she reached for it, noticing her name on the outside, and opened it.

Bekah. Didn't want to wake you. Finishing Joe's crop today. Should be in sometime later. Please rest. We'll decide about dinner then. If you get hungry, there's food in the refrigerator you can eat or nuke. Don't get up to fix anything. Left a couple of books on the table. Take a look. Just a suggestion. Collin.

Bekah folded the note and set it aside on the table. She picked up one of the books Collin had left. *Pregnancy, Birth, and the Early Years.* She glanced at the other. *Welcome, Baby.* She put the first one down, picked up and opened the second.

Pillows fluffed behind her, the book resting comfortably across her abdomen, she turned pages until her eyelids grew heavy. Soon the book slid from her hands, down to her side, and again she slept.

Chapter Eleven

Collin eased the door open and looked toward the bed. Good. Bekah was sleeping. Returning a lot later than expected, he'd worried she was hungry, bored, or both.

He tiptoed to her side, not wanting to wake her. Carefully, he eased away the book she was reading, and watched her fingers curl into loose fists on her lap. He closed the book and placed it on the side table, careful not to make a sound.

Bekah moaned and curled into the comforter. He wanted to join her there, inside the safe cocoon of warmth, and chase away the chill of the air-conditioned room. He wanted to slide his body next to hers and elevate the level of heat between them with friction—lots of skin-to-skin friction.

But he wouldn't.

It was hard enough keeping his hands off her before he knew of her medical condition, not to mention their new *arrangement*. He wouldn't risk hurting her again for all the money and power in the world, though. Besides, there was something else going on with her. Some sort of insecurity he couldn't quite put his finger on. He didn't know much about this

Matthew character, but he had a sinking suspicion that Bekah's insecurities were due to him.

He'd find out, one day.

Her eyes fluttered and she glanced up. She blinked once, then smiled and held out a hand. He took it, but barely moved from where he'd firmly planted both his feet.

"Hi," she said.

"Hi."

She tugged on his hand. "Sit down."

Collin shook his head. Her sleepy eyes and softened features, coupled with his earlier thoughts of slipping beneath the covers with her had left him more than a little aroused.

"I'm dirty."

Bekah smiled at him. "I don't care. Just for a minute. Please?"

He couldn't refuse. She tugged at his fingers and the rest of him followed. He sat on the edge of the bed, his back stiff, afraid to get much closer. Afraid his body would rein out of control.

"It's late." She released his hand and scooted up against the headboard, pillows behind her. "It's getting dark out already. What time is it?"

Collin glanced at his watch. "Around nine."

Her face screwed into a puzzle. "Working this late?"

Collin shook his head. "We finished hours ago. I helped Joe with a couple of other things." He watched her hair fan out on the pillow, and her chest rising and falling slowly with each breath. He wanted to touch her.

He stood, pushing away the temptation.

"I need a shower." *A cold one.*

"Okay," she said softly, her brows knit. "You're welcome to use the shower here."

Collin took two steps backward and shook his head. "No. I don't have clothes here. I'll run home and shower, then I'll come back and fix dinner. Are you hungry?"

She studied his face. "Not too. I had a sandwich earlier and can grab some fruit if I want something."

He turned slightly. "No, you need a proper meal. Balanced nutrition. Doctor's orders."

"But you're exhausted."

"I'll be fine after a shower."

"I'll be okay, Collin. Go home, take a shower, and go to bed. I'll see you tomorrow." He watched her back stiffen and she glanced off. Hell, he'd pissed her off.

"Bekah, look...."

"It's okay. Just go on." Her emotionless glare pinned him to the floor. "I'm tired."

Collin was hesitant. He was tired too, but he didn't want to be away from her for the evening. Not really. Of course, he was barely a quarter of a mile away. "You're sure?"

Something was off kilter. He watched her face. *What is she thinking?*

Bekah jerked a nod. "Absolutely," she told him. "I'm sure. And I'm tired too. I'll see you tomorrow."

"Call me if you need anything."

"Of course."

He stepped toward the bedroom door, had one foot through it, and then turned. He slowly curled back to look at her. "I'll be in early," he said.

"Collin?"

He caught her gaze. "Yes?"

She shook her head. "Never mind."

What? "Bekah?"

"Never mind. Sleep well, Collin," she whispered.

He studied her face for several seconds. "You will eat something, won't you?"

"I will."

"All right. See you in the morning."

But within the hour, Collin was back.

He rubbed the towel over the last dinner plate and placed it in the cupboard. It was easy to let his mind drift to earlier to earlier in the evening. Thoughts of Bekah sitting up cross-legged in her bed, an ebony wave of hair slung over one shoulder, while he sat across from her rushed through his head. They ate grilled cheese and sliced apples and argued about crumbs in the bed. Then, they settled in to watch the late news.

She'd been hesitant, for sure, when he'd come back. Later, after eating and the dishes set aside, she'd cuddled into the pillows next to him and had fallen asleep. As he thought about that now, how it felt with her warm and soft next to him, an intense emotion crossed his heart—one so full of rightness that he thought it might just burst with sheer pleasure.

He left the kitchen and glanced back at the clock over the stove. After midnight. He longed for sleep and rest. He was used to being physical, often working in the barns alongside his stable hands on the weekends. Riding was physical enough, too. He worked out often as he could to keep in shape, too, but the last few days had taken a toll on his body. He ached in places he didn't know could ache.

But every twinge reminded him that he was doing all this for Bekah. He didn't mind.

At the kitchen door, his hand hit the light switch, extinguishing the only illumination in the house. Collin stood in the hallway letting his eyes adjust to the darkness. Stepping to the right would put him in the living room, safely away from Bekah, where he could sleep on the couch. To the left meant her warmth—throughout the entire night. His body was physically exhausted, his mind emotionally drained, as the decision played over his brain.

Tired feet carried him down the hallway to the left, his hands pushing open her bedroom. A thin shaft of moon glow penetrated the darkness and lay soft across Bekah's face—his sleeping angel. But he felt less than angelic, as his desire for her shot hot and fiery straight through him.

If circumstances were different, he would have stripped out of his clothes and slid underneath the comforter, slipping one arm beneath her shoulders, and the other around her chest, cradling her to him.

Collin shook himself. Not the time or the place for fantasy. It wouldn't do him a damn bit of good to start anything—whatever they shared couldn't go anywhere for quite some time. Besides, she was carrying a baby, and it was a high-risk pregnancy. No way would he compromise her, or the baby's health.

Yet, desire flashed through his body as he watched her sleeping. He ached to hold her, and he thought about what it might mean to love her. *Really* love her.

No. Not going there.

Turning abruptly then, he headed for the couch.

* * *

Bekah woke to the sound of whistling down the hall, and birds chirping out her window. Morning. And Collin was still here.

Last night she had watched him go, her chest tight and her stomach jittery. She'd almost said, *Why don't you bring over several changes of clothing. Maybe you should stay the night.* But she didn't.

That would have been inconsistent with everything she'd said to him the past couple of days. Surely, he thought she was a ditz—her emotions out of whack and her thoughts scattered.

There was no reason for him to stay. No reason for her to suggest anything of the like.

But he'd come back anyway, and she'd not only been surprised, but relieved.

She'd slept better. Felt safer knowing he was in the house, even though he slept on the couch. She'd never been frightened before in the old house before. Why now?

She didn't want to be alone. For the first time in months since she'd come home, she didn't want to be alone. And that was a bit unsettling.

What would she do if she started bleeding again? What if she started having pain and couldn't get to the phone? What if she passed out again?

No. Not going there. She was going to be fine. So would the baby.

The whistling came again from the bathroom, and like a child following the Pied Piper, she rose and followed. The door stood ajar, a diagonal shaft of light penetrating the dark hallway. Silently, she padded to the light and the happy whistle, placed a soft hand on the doorjamb, and rounded the corner into the open space to see Collin looking into the mirror on the bathroom wall cabinet.

Leaning against the frame, she watched him shave. With each stroke, his firm, thick fingers awed her, slicing through the creamy white foam, stripping away the three-day growth of stubble. Methodically he finished the task, splashed his face with warm water, and reached for the towel. He rubbed his face dry while his gaze caught hers and held. Replacing the towel on the bar, he scooped up his razor and shaving cream with one hand, hesitated, and then reached for the medicine cabinet mirror with the other. He pulled it to him, the angle catching her watching him. He stopped.

He waited only a second before he spoke. "Mind if I put these here?"

Bekah blinked. Moving forward, she placed her hand on his and opened the medicine cabinet door more fully. She took the shaving cream and razor out of his hand, scooted lotions and medications out of the way, and placed them on a shelf. She closed the door softly and looked at him.

"I hate clutter." Then she grinned broadly.

"Oh," Collin returned. "Me too."

Bekah stood between the sink and Collin. "Good morning," she whispered.

Collin's right hand slowly rose to her face. One finger traced underneath her eye and Bekah shivered a little at his touch. Then he quickly drew back and said, "I hope you don't mind. I took the couch. It was late, I was tired...."

He paused and she searched his face.

"And I really didn't feel like leaving you."

Bekah studied him. "Oh," she said softly. He'd obviously just taken a shower, his chest still beaded with water. A towel sat low on his hips. Her heartbeat kicked up a notch. Instantly, she recalled their one night of sex. She wanted to step closer, lean into to him. She wanted to press her cheek against his chest —rub up against the small droplets of water clinging to the thick dark hairs there. She ached to wrap her arms tight around the thick trunk of his body, while she drank in the smell of a clean male.

If she closed her eyes, she might even hear the thump of his heart in her ear, blood pumping in and out in a rhythm of contentment and solitude. A sentiment that perhaps was an echo of how she was feeling right now, too.

Dare she hope?

Could she love him?

Bekah pulled back and looked up into his eyes. Collin closed his arms around her and peered down into her face. Their breathing deepened in unison. He cupped her face, skimming his fingertips over her cheeks. His gaze dipped to linger on her lips.

She took a step backward, breaking the connection, her

rump hitting the sink. She needed distance. "Hungry?" she asked, slipping fully from his arms, and backing toward the door.

Collin tucked the towel tighter around his middle, then swivel back to the sink and splashed cold water over his face. "Some. I made coffee. Decaf."

"I can fix eggs, bacon. If you want."

"No." He rubbed his face with a towel. "You need to get back to bed. I'll bring you something, and then I'll head to the office."

"You don't have to wait on me, Collin. I can fix myself breakfast."

He wiped his hands on a towel and looked at her. "I don't mind. You're supposed to be in bed."

"But I can't stay there all day."

He glared. "Like hell you can't, and you will."

Bekah felt her eyes flash wide at his sudden outburst. "Oh, really?" she spat back.

She hated the way he looked standing there, half-naked, his chest glistening and tempting her to fling herself against him. "Don't bother fixing anything. Thanks for staying last night and everything, but just go on to work."

"I am."

"Now."

"If you get out of here, I will." He grabbed the top of his towel.

"Oh!" His fingers gripped the terry cloth at his waist. Bekah whirled and fled down the hall to the kitchen.

By the time she reached the kitchen table, she had to sit. Breathing heavy—and it wasn't because she had exhausted herself walking down the hall—she fought to quell the panic in her tummy. He *exhausted her* by just existing. The thought of what he could do to her, of how he could make her feel—

Stop it, Bekah.

She dismissed the direction of her thoughts and shakily rose to pour a cup of coffee and fix toast. Sounds of him getting ready filtered down the hall. Finally, his footsteps grew louder. She didn't look up as he stepped inside.

Didn't look but didn't have to. She felt the electric charged atmosphere he created in the room as he entered. Heat brushed her cheeks. She stared into her cup.

Finally, Collin turned and headed outside, leaving the inside door open. She lifted her head to gaze at the wood-framed screen door. A few seconds later, his car started and headed down the short lane toward the road.

Her heart jumped in her chest, kicking her ass.

Dammit. She was falling for him. Hard.

And she'd just let him walk out the damn door.

* * *

Collin argued with his secretary. He fumbled through a meeting with a business associate for forty-five minutes, and after that was over, forgot everything they had discussed. He lunched with his mother, counting the minutes until they were finished, tolerating her discussion of her social obligations and volunteer work, and wished he were home sharing lunch with Bekah. When five o'clock rolled around, he gathered a few folders into his brief case and started for the elevator, relieved the day was nearly over and that he would soon be with her again. Whether they acted like they wanted to be friends or lovers, or not, he didn't care. He just wanted to be near her.

But before he reached his car, a thought struck him, and he retraced his steps back to his office.

A few minutes later, the drive to the farm calmed his nerves. His muscles loosened as his fingers undid his tie and unbuttoned his shirt collar. He rolled down the windows and drank in the smells of the countryside as the fresh air sifted through his hair.

His thoughts only on Bekah and getting home, he sped much too fast on the winding country roads. Before he knew it, he had navigated her gravel lane, parked his car, rushed inside her back door, and made his way toward her bedroom.

"Collin...?"

He stopped and retraced his steps. When he saw her sitting on the couch, so small and fragile, so beautiful and so alone, his heart leapt, and his body rushed forward. When he reached her, he paused—gathering her into his arms and next to his body was all he'd thought about *all* afternoon but now that he was here, he wasn't sure he could. Or should.

What did *she* want?

Bekah stood and moved forward, her glare catching his and holding with every step. When she was but a step away, she stood still for a moment, studying his face. Finally, she leaned in and wound her arms around his waist, pressing her cheek against his chest. Collin sighed, looked to the ceiling, and drew her into his embrace.

He reveled in the fact that she'd made the first move.

Thank God. She wants *me.*

* * *

Bekah wasn't sure whether he pulled her quickly into his arms or if she had moved into them of her own accord. Her body had simply surrendered, and she wanted that.

Didn't she?

Yes.

All day long she ached for his heart beating against hers. Collin broke the embrace and brought his hands to frame her face. His thumbs caressed her cheeks as he turned her face to his.

"I'm sorry for this morning."

Bekah shook her head. "No, I am."

Collin smiled. "So, we're both two sorry souls. I promise. I'll try not to get bossy again."

"I'll try not to get mad so easily."

He stepped back and dropped his arms to his sides. "And I'll try to keep my hands off you."

Bekah sighed, watched his face, and grinned. "Me too, I guess."

Collin arched an eyebrow. "You guess?"

Bekah teased. "I mean—" She sighed. "I guess I want to keep my hands off you."

Grinning, Collin reached out and took her hand. "I don't think I can say the same for myself."

She cocked a brow. "Oh?" Feeling braver, she ventured forward. "I have to admit that sometimes..." Her eyes twinkled. "Sometimes I'd just like you to hold me."

"Sometimes, I will."

"Okay."

"Okay."

Collin drew her closer and whispered. "Is this an amendment to our arrangement?"

Bekah looked up into his eyes. "A slight one. Perhaps."

Collin nodded. "Okay. I can handle that. I missed you."

She smiled. "I thought you'd never get home."

Home. "I thought I'd never get here," he said. *It really does feel like home.*

Bekah rested her chin on his chest. "You're here now."

He stroked her hair, and she loved the endearment. "I want to be here. Bekah," he whispered.

"I know."

"I can't stand being away from you," he added.

"I don't even want to think about tomorrow."

"Then don't. We have all night together. I mean. Just to be here. It's enough. I'm not talking about sleeping together...."

Bekah settled into his chest. "I know."

Collin pulled away slightly.

"What is it Collin?"

He shrugged. "I missed you so much today and I started thinking...."

"About?"

"Well, I'm not sure if it's a good idea now or not."

"Tell me." Bekah angled to investigate his face.

"I don't want to go back."

She wasn't sure she understood. "What are you saying?"

Collin exhaled, long. "Today was a miserably long day. I'm literally a figurehead. I could set up an office at my farm and then pop in and out here throughout the day. I'm thinking of cutting way back on my hours in the office."

"Can you do that?"

"Bekah, I own the company."

"But why now?"

He stared at her. "Why not now? Bekah, I can't stand being away from you. You need me. They don't. And—I need you."

Silence settled around them. Bekah searched his face. "There's an extra bedroom upstairs. Why don't you set up an office there?"

Collin stared into her eyes. "I didn't want to appear pushy...."

"Will you forget the pushy stuff? Is that what you want to do?"

He grinned and nodded. "Do you mind?"

Bekah shook her head and smiled. "Collin, will you just move in and stay here with me?"

"You're sure?"

She nodded. "I need you, Collin. I need you more than I really want to admit. But of course, there are still the rules."

"The rules. Yeah. No sex. Friendship, with hugs. I understand."

"There's a spare bedroom upstairs."

"The couch is fine. I want to be down here with you."

"It pulls out to make a bed, I think."

"Are you sure you want to do this?"

She nodded. "I need my independence, but with the baby, and how I'm feeling, sometimes I get frightened. It was lonely today."

"I'll be here."

"Then I won't miss you."

"The trunk of my car is full of boxes."

Bekah smiled. "Then let's get to work."

Collin narrowed his gaze at her. "Oh no, you don't. Back to the bedroom with you."

Bekah whined, "Oh Collin, please. Not the bedroom again. I'm so tired of being cooped up there."

"All right. Stay on the couch. I'll carry in the stuff. You watch. I don't want you to lift a finger."

Bekah saluted him as she sat back down on the couch. "Yes, sir." Then she grinned. "Do whatever you want to the bedroom."

Then as he stepped away, he paused, the smile faded. "Are you sure, Bekah?"

Her face turned serious also. "I'm sure," she nodded. "We just have to remember the ground rules."

He grinned. "No sex. I know."

"I think we should add kissing to that."

His eyebrow arched. "Where did that come from?"

Bekah's chest heaved. "From, oh, I don't know. It just sounds like a good idea."

He shifted his weight as he stood before her and began to count on his fingers. "No kissing, no sex, no sharing of beds...."

"But hugging is allowed," she interjected. "Friends do hug." She smiled at him. He leaned forward, placing each of his palms flat on either side of her on the couch, his lips inches from hers. "Yes," he murmured. "Friends do hug."

Chapter Twelve

T *wo weeks later*

"It says here I can't be in the delivery room unless we go through the approved classes, Bekah. Have you spoken with Dr. Benton about this?"

Bekah glanced sideways from her side of the bed where she was reading. "Talked to him about what?"

"Lamaze, honey. Natural childbirth. Having me in the delivery room. We have to take the classes."

Bekah blinked, trying to make the transition from a heated love scene in her book, to talk of childbirth. "He hasn't said anything about it."

Collin turned back to the book. "Well, it is still early. The book says that classes usually don't start until the seventh month. We have time. When is your next appointment?"

Bekah watched him study the book in front of him. "Next Thursday."

"Hm. Make sure you mention it."

She smiled. "Okay."

Collin turned a page. Bekah watched, amused at the previous exchange. "Collin?"

"Hm?"

"I've been thinking. Before we deliver this baby, don't you think we ought to fix a room for her?"

He read on. "Sure, honey. We'll get started on it right away. Do you think you want an epidural as a backup? You know, just in case there are complications. The book says...."

"I'm sure I'll discuss that with Dr. Benton also. Do you think we should paint the room pink or blue? I really feel like it's going to be a girl, but maybe yellow would be better."

"...and I think if you deliver vaginally, you need to stress that he does an episiotomy. It will heal better, you know. And the book says...."

"You're not listening to me. Pink, blue, or yellow?"

"A yellowed complexion after birth is nothing to be concerned about, Bekah. It's called jaundice and occurs to some extent quite often. They just put the baby under lights and feed him lots of...."

Bekah's eyes grew wide with disbelief. She reached over and snatched the book out of his hand. "Would you please stop?"

Startled, Collin reached for the book. "What are you doing?"

"Trying to get you to forget about this delivery for a minute. I have three months to go Collin. We'll discuss it all with Dr. Benton next week. Now, may I have some peace and quiet?"

Collin stared. "This is important, Bekah. Have you read this book yet? I think it would be really helpful."

She sighed. "Yes, Collin. I've read it and every other book you've brought in here. I'm an expert now on everything from anesthesia to labor positions to vernix caseosa. I know what

Braxton-Hicks contractions are, why Kegel exercises are important, and how to breathe during the transition stage of labor.
What I haven't read myself while I've been confined to bed,
you've read to me at night. I think I could single-handedly
deliver this baby myself. Now please, will you let me finish *my*
book?"

Collin glared. "How could you read that? I mean, when
there's so much to know about what's going to happen to you.
Don't you want to be prepared?"

"Did you hear a word I just said?"

Bekah took both books and set them on the bedside table.
She turned toward him, her head propped up on one hand.
She exhaled, slowly. "Collin, look," she began, "women have
been having babies for eons. Most of them didn't even know
how to read let alone have someone teach them how to breathe
properly during labor. I've read everything I can read on the
subject. I feel quite informed. Dr. Benton will take care of me.
I'll take care of me. And I know that you will darn well take
care of me too. Right now, I'm tired and sleepy, my back aches,
and I want to finish that book before I go to sleep. So, if you
don't mind...."

"I'm pushing it again."

"Yes."

The corner of Collin's mouth drew down. "Sorry."

Bekah grinned. One finger made a trail down the side of his
chin. "You're priceless, you know that?"

"Yeah, sure. So are you." He snuggled down under the
covers and pulled her under with him. "And you like me even
more for it don't you?"

"I like you exactly the way you are. I wouldn't want you to
change one bit."

Collin pulled her closer, his hands playing over her back.
"Did you say your back hurts?"

She nodded against his chest. "Just aches a little. Muscles seem a little tight."

"Turn over, I'll rub your back."

Bekah did. Soon his hands spread wide across her back, kneading and easing the tension out of her stiff muscles. From her shoulders to her hips, his fingers played and teased until Bekah moaned from the sheer pleasure of it. Her silky gown bunched under his palms until the bottom moved up around her waist, then Collin quickly slid his hands under to massage her warm skin beneath.

Bekah shifted slightly, half resting on her side, half on her stomach, one leg curled up and out to the side. Collin himself shifted positions until he knelt behind her, kneading her softening flesh while she continued breathing small moans of pleasure. Soon the gown was lifted over her head and nothing separated Collin's fingers and Bekah's smooth skin but air.

Bekah turned back to face him. She'd become accustomed to the back rubs he'd given her, but lately, they'd turned more erotic and sensual. She wasn't sure if it was the hormones raging through her body or if he indeed turned her on so. At any rate, she'd come to welcome his hands on her flesh, even though it never led to any kind of sex. He seemed content to skim his hands over her body, and she was simply content to let him.

* * *

Collin stared down at the full rounded breasts beneath him, marveling at the switch his life had taken the past couple of weeks. He reached out and gingerly traced one peaked, dusky nipple as he watched Bekah's face. Her eyes closed, her facial features relaxed. Collin slid down on his side next to her. His fingers caressed and fondled the hardening nipple and then he palmed the entire breast. Her breasts had grown more full and lovely this past month of her pregnancy. Heavy and so sensitive to his touch.

He let his hand trail lower to her rising abdomen. She'd avoided visiting her family the past few weeks—her body would give her condition away. Collin knew it was only a matter of time, though. Joe knew, but that was only because he'd been there at the tobacco field that day. And he'd probably told Maggie. Bekah had discussed telling her parents, and knew she'd have to do so soon. Hiding her growing abdomen was easy enough with loose cotton jumpers and bib-overalls but she'd recently mentioned that the charade would have to end. Collin's thoughts deepened as he laid the palm of his hand softly across her abdomen. He made small circles with the pads of his fingers as he thought about the small life growing within her. If he had fathered this child himself, he couldn't love it more. And that was such a mystery to him. He'd never thought of himself as a benevolent person, but this was Bekah's baby, and that made all the difference in the world. And even more than loving the baby, he loved her. He was in love with Bekah McCauley.

Sometimes he wondered about this Matthew, the father of her baby, but until Bekah decided it was time to discuss it, he wouldn't bring it up.

"What are you thinking?"

Collin smiled. "Nothing."

"That's not true, Collin. What is it?"

His eyes held hers. His hand left her abdomen and cupped her chin, pulling her lips close to his. "You're right. I was thinking how it would feel right now to kiss you." His lips touched hers softly.

Bekah waited until their lips parted, his face a breath away from hers. "Liar."

Collin jerked back amused. "Are you calling me a liar?"

"Yep."

"Why?"

"Because that wasn't what you were thinking at all. You face was much too serious. When you're thinking deeply, your face gets all screwed up in a tight ball and you squint your eyes. You were doing that. It wasn't your, 'I'm-thinking-about-kissing-you-look.' I know that one quite well. What *were* you thinking?"

"You think you know me pretty well, don't you?"

"Yep, for the most part. Tell me."

"Honestly?"

"Yes."

"I was thinking how glad I am that we've agreed to hug, and touch, and kiss...."

She narrowed her gaze and smirked. "Well, me too, but that's not what you were thinking, Mr. Kramer."

Collin nodded. "You're right."

* * *

Bekah watched Collin's face grow solemn. Suddenly she knew that whatever Collin was going to say was—well, serious. She wondered if she'd opened a can of worms she wasn't yet ready to open.

"Tell me about Matthew, Bekah."

No. *I'm not prepared for that.* Since Collin had moved in, they had avoided past issues. She guessed it was probably time they faced them. She might as well be first.

Bekah pushed herself up to a sitting position. "Hand me my nightgown."

"What?"

"My nightgown, hand it to me."

He did and watched her put it on. She fluffed the pillows behind her and leaned back.

"Get comfortable, we've got a long night ahead of us."

He leaned closer. "Are you okay with this?"

She nodded, looking into his eyes. "I need to get this out of my system. I want you to know." *Then you're going to tell me everything I want to know about you.* She looked deep into his eyes and began.

"When I was a child, I wanted nothing more than to get off the farm. I hated it. We all worked in the fields, my brothers, my dad and mother, and me. The boys loved it, still do. My mother worked herself to the bone inside and outside of the house. The older I got, the more I knew I didn't want that for me."

Collin listened but didn't interrupt.

"I was a creative child. Sometimes a little sullen and moody, I guess. I liked to spend time alone, either drawing or painting, or writing stories, or reading. And I got good grades. At school I could be me, but at home, the things I liked to do weren't important or practical. It wasn't my mother or father's fault. They just didn't know what to do with me. For generations, our family farmed. When I started talking about college, they didn't understand very well. No one in my family had ever gone to college.

"At first there was the issue of money, but then I earned several scholarships which enabled me to go, so I did. I was finally off the farm. I earned a degree in art and journalism, then immediately moved to New York City. I was determined to take the world by storm. It didn't quite turn out that way.

"One of my college friends and I rented a small apartment in the Village. She wanted to write—I wanted to paint. We worked part-time jobs, making enough to pay the rent and buy a little food, and tried to write and paint when we could, peddling our wares in the city. I found a couple of small shops willing to show my work, and even sold several paintings, but not enough to feel successful. That's when I met Matthew."

Bekah hesitated, studying Collin's face. She took a deep breath and went on. "You have to remember, at this point I'm not a very worldly person. I'm fresh out of college, living in a dream world, happy to be off the farm. Vulnerable and trusting. I'd had a couple of semi-serious relationships in college, but nothing to write home about. But Matthew... Well, he literally swept me off my feet.

"He found my paintings in one of the shops and bought them all. He begged the shop owner to give him my phone number and he did. When he called, he said he wanted to commission more work from me. I was ecstatic because I needed the money. We met, I did the paintings, and he still wanted to see me. He was very impressive in his expensive suits. He wore an air of sophistication that I was totally unfamiliar with. He reeked of money. And I was impressed as well as madly infatuated with him. Before I knew it, he'd whisked me all over the city for late night dinners and dancing, moonlight strolls at his parents' estate, and within a matter of a few weeks had tucked me neatly into his Manhattan apartment and into his life."

Bekah closed her eyes and sighed deeply. Talking about Matthew suddenly made her draw comparisons to her life recently with Collin. Now she knew why she'd run from him so much in the beginning. His flashy lifestyle paralleled Matthew's. The big difference here though, she told herself, was that Collin hadn't picked her up and placed her within his life, she had allowed him to transplant into hers. She opened her eyes to look at him.

"What is it, Bekah?" Her glance fell past his shoulder.

"Thank you for coming here to live with me."

His gaze caught hers. "I don't understand."

Bekah took a deep breath. "You see, when you came into my life, if you had insisted that I come live with you, if you had taken me into your home, I don't think it would have worked. It would have been too much like what Matthew did. Even though I hadn't drawn the comparison until right now, sooner or later I would have had to leave."

"I've tried to let you make the choices about those things."

"I know. You've let me keep my freedom and my dignity. Matthew didn't do that."

"What did Matthew do, Bekah?"

Her gaze caught his again, her mouth turned into a frown, and she continued. "He controlled every aspect of my life. I guess his lifestyle was so different from mine and I was too trusting. And as I said, I was very naïve. Matthew insisted I get a job, so after several weeks of trying, I landed an assistant art editor position at a major magazine. Within a year, I moved up to art editor and more money. I began spending long hours working at the office and with no time to paint. Eventually I stopped painting altogether. Matthew didn't like the stains on my hands. In fact, if there was anything I did that Matthew didn't like, I stopped doing it. He molded me into a person I didn't know, or want to be, and I allowed him to do it."

Pausing, Bekah studied Collin's face. He listened intently, processing her words, but said nothing. She continued, looking downward now, and fiddling with the edge of the blanket.

"He controlled my money, he picked out the clothes I wore, he chose my friends—everything—right down to the color nail polish and type stockings I wore. We did everything for business, which meant we did everything for money. He encouraged me to work long hours to prove my dedication to my job. Then we hit the social scene until late most evenings. That's how it was done, he said. That's how success is accomplished. And I wanted success because I thought I wanted Matthew to be proud of me. I guess I got caught up in it all. After five years, I wasn't Bekah McCauley, farm girl, anymore. I was Rebekah McCauley, career woman and socialite, and Matthew's favorite toy. The charm on his arm. He insisted I lose the dialect and the past. I didn't realize how much I hated it until I got sick."

Somewhere amid Bekah's story, Collin had reached over and grasped her hand. He stared down at their intertwined fingers, then his gaze rose to meet hers. "That's why you didn't want me to call you Rebekah?"

She nodded. "I don't want any reminders."

Collin nodded and smiled back. "I understand. What did you mean about getting sick?"

"An ulcer. I guess it was all eating at me from the inside and I didn't know it. Finally, the pain became so severe one day that I took an afternoon off work and went to the doctor. It was then I also found out I was pregnant. That was in February. I took several days off from work, which infuriated Matthew to no end, but I had to do it to pull myself together enough to tell him."

"What did he say?"

Bekah shook her head and let a small nervous laugh escape her throat. "I thought that there might be a remote chance that he would be ecstatic about the baby and would want to marry me, but that wasn't the case. He ordered me to get an abortion and gave me some money to handle it discreetly."

Collin gripped her hands tighter and pulled her closer. Bekah tugged her gaze from his; a small sob escaped her lips. Then she lifted her gaze to meet his. "I couldn't do it," she whispered.

Collin gathered her close. "I know. I know."

"It was the most terrible thing. I even went to the clinic, but I couldn't do it. When I told Matthew, he gave me an ultimatum —the baby or him. He made it quite clear that if I kept the baby, he wanted nothing to do with it and would deny paternity. I did the only thing I could do."

"You came home," he whispered.

"Yes, and I found you." Her voice quivered softly as she spoke.

"...and you don't know how grateful I am that you did."

She glanced off for a moment. "Collin, I'm not sure what I would have done if you hadn't come into my life. I'm not looking for a white knight or anything, but you sure have been a godsend." She peered into his eyes.

He released a pent-up breath. "Oh, Bekah," he breathed. "Don't you understand? You're the one who saved me."

Her heart twisted. She laid her head on Collin's shoulder and held tight. "I'm not so sure about that."

"Well, I am."

How did this happen?

* * *

More than anything, Collin wanted to make Bekah feel secure and wanted. He wanted to love her and her child. But had he overdone it? He had to know.

"Bekah? Am I too pushy? I swear, I won't be anymore. I don't want to do anything that will force you away from me."

She pulled away and placed both palms flat on his chest. She searched his face. "No. That's just the thing, you're not. Not now, at least." She teased out a slight grin, then went on. "With you, I know you're sincere and concerned about my well-being and the baby's. That's different. Please don't stop. I like feeling the way you make me feel. It's the way you love me, Collin."

Collin leaned in and placed a tender kiss on her lips. "I do love you, Bekah. I've wanted to say that for a while. I just didn't know if...."

Bekah kissed him back this time. "I know you love me," she whispered. "I love you too. But I want you to know that what Matthew did was in no way connected to love. It was power, greed, and control. You love me for what I am, and I love *you* for that. Matthew said he loved me, but it was only for what I could bring to him."

Collin sat quietly for a moment. The trouble was, he *was* like that—or could be—and had been in the past. "I *am* like that Bekah —not with you, but in my business. *I am.* I have to be. Ever since my father died, I had to be. He was—and now I am. I hate it. Right now, sitting here with you, I realize how much I actually hate it."

"Then get out."

"I can't."

"Yes, you can. If you want it badly enough, you will find a way."

He shook his head. "No. It's too late."

"It's never too late, Collin." Then she went somewhere that surprised him. "Tell me about your father."

He blankly stared back. "I can't talk about him. Not tonight."

"Can't or won't?"

"Can't, won't, it's all the same."

"Why?"

"Because I just can't."

"Did you love him?"

Collin pulled away, turning his back to her. "Once. Before he turned into..." He paused, not wanting to go on. He couldn't say it out loud, could he?

"Into what?"

Collin turned back and faced her. "Before he turned into

the same type of man I've become and vowed I wouldn't." He got up and took several steps toward the door. "I can't talk about this Bekah."

"Why? I'm here, I'll listen. I'll help you."

"You can't help. Because to talk about him would mean I'd have to open that door to the past. And I just can't do it. Not yet." He stepped closer to the door.

"Sometimes it hurts but things get better. You need to talk about this."

Collin rotated his body toward her and just stood, his gaze holding hers—then he quickly turned and left the room.

Bekah waited for the slap of the screen door. *There.* Soon after, she heard the slam of a car door and the grinding to life of an automobile engine. By the time the crunch of gravel faded into the night, she decided it was best to let him go. He'd shared more than he'd bargained for tonight, and she imagined he needed a little time to sort through the junk they'd exposed. Funny how learning about Matthew had unlocked a piece of him he hadn't counted on. He'd expected to find out things about her and had ended up looking at himself through a different lens.

Bekah only hoped she could help him realize he wasn't the person he thought he was anymore. Obviously, they still had mountain of work to do, together.

* * *

Hours later, when dawn was just breaking on the horizon and Bekah was busying herself with toast and juice in the kitchen, she watched Collin's vehicle meander up the driven through the window. When he didn't come inside, she went looking. Bedrest, or not. As she stepped off the back porch, she caught sight of him leaning against the plank fence next to the barn, a handsome silhouette against the pink-orange sunrise.

Bekah pulled her thin robe around her, knotted the tie, and stepped across the barn lot toward him. Stepping up next to Collin, she placed her arms across the top of the wooden fence and gazed out across the field at the morning. The sun rose slowly over the ridge in the near distance. The birds were stirring and calling out.

Collin breathed deeply beside her.

She risked a glance in his direction. "Why is it you think you've turned into such a terrible person?"

His blue eyes—bloodshot from the lack of sleep, she guessed—quickly glanced her way, then turned back, fixed on the horizon. Bekah studied his profile. Deep circles rested below his eyes. A stubble of growth hinted on his cheeks and chin. He appeared tired. She wished he'd look at her.

"I asked you a question." Her gaze never left his profile.

Soon he lowered his head, then faced her. He shook his head. "Somewhere, I lost it all along the way."

"Lost what, Collin?" she whispered.

He studied her face. "Me."

Her eyes caught his and held fast. She shook her own head. "I don't believe that."

"It's true. I don't know who I am or what I want anymore."

"I don't believe that for one minute." Then panic gripped Bekah's stomach. Was he saying he didn't know if he wanted *her* anymore? She grasped his upper arm. "What are you saying, Collin? You don't know if you... If you want me?"

His eyes showed pure terror. "No, no, Bekah." He turned and pulled her to him. "I didn't mean that at all. You're the only thing in my life that is right." His hands caressed her hair and back. "Oh, God, I didn't mean that. I don't know what I'd do if I lost you. I need you to help me through this, Bekah."

Bekah sighed deeply against his chest and held onto him a little tighter. "I'm here, Collin."

"I know."

Bekah pulled away and brushed russet curls from his forehead. "Let's get some sleep and talk about it later."

Collin shook his head. "No. I need to talk about it now."

Bekah nodded.

"Just let me talk and get it out. Don't interrupt me. Just let me talk."

"Okay." Bekah held him tight.

He pulled her closer, took a deep breath, and began. "I haven't talked about this to anyone in years. Not since he died. No one understood then, I didn't think anyone would want to even try to understand after it all happened. Not until you.

"Bekah, I need to do this for us. When you spoke last night about Matthew, it just kept running through my head that I was an awful lot like him."

"But you're not," she whispered, then regretted it when she saw the anguish on his face.

"I am. And you need to know that. Maybe I haven't been that way with you, because when I'm around you, I am different. When I'm at work, I'm ruthless and I have been for years. It's business. It's the way things are done. But if I want to keep what we have, I've got to change it. I want to change it, for you and for me, and for the baby." He shifted, staring Bekah directly in her eyes. "Bekah, I want to be a father to your child. I don't want to be what my father was to me. I want to be a real father. Even though biologically I won't be—emotionally I want to be. So, I have to change everything, Bekah. And I need to do it now."

Bekah nodded, afraid to say anything. She didn't want him to stop talking. Then he continued quickly.

"Before my father died, I was going to vet school. That was

my dream. He, of course, didn't see things my way and insisted I learn the business. When I was about to break the apron strings for good and go out on my own, the bastard had the nerve to go and die on me. I've resented it ever since. Mother expected me to pick up where Dad left off, to keep her lifestyle the way it was, and from that day on, I did just that. Before I knew it, the years flew by and I had turned into the man I hated as a child. I became my father.

"I'm just so afraid I can't change, and I won't be able to be what you and the baby need."

Bekah cradled his face in her hands. A small tear escaped one of his eyes. Her thumb caught it and erased its track from his cheek. Bekah's own eyes filled. "You've already changed," she said softly.

Collin shook his head and closed his eyes. "No."

Bekah caught his shaking head and forced him to look at her. "Listen to me, Collin. You have changed. You're not the same man that came ripping through my garden a few weeks ago. You're not the same man that pulled out big bucks to take care of the damages, and you're not the man that denies his feelings anymore like the man who left me the night we first made love. You're not that man anymore, Collin. You're caring and giving. You're a man who fixes me dinner and rubs my back and teaches me how to take care of myself and my baby. You care. You just cut back on your office hours to be with *me*. You *have* changed. So have I. We will continue to change, both of us. The beautiful part is that we'll grow together. We'll learn about each other and complement each other. We'll share in the birth of this child, and how we raise her, and how we love her. You are not your father, Collin. *You* are *you*, and I love you just the way you are. Do you understand me?"

A deep sigh escaped his lips. "I understand. I love you, Bekah."

She smiled. "I love you, Collin." Bekah dropped her hands to his shoulders and hugged him. "You crazy man," she whispered.

Collin threaded his fingers through her hair and pulled her face closer to him. His lips touched hers sending fire throughout their bodies. "I'm exhausted. Let's go back to bed."

"Um..." Bekah agreed as she captured his lips again. "Let's go."

Chapter Thirteen

"When the baby comes, should we have the nursery upstairs or down?" Bekah looked up from her painting. She sat in a lawn chair opposite him— as he worked the garden row with a hoe—mixing a little water with paint, making a pale blue wash. She leaned into her easel and stroked the color across the canvas, subtly blending with the pinks and purples of the evening sky.

Collin stood upright and leaned against the hoe. Bekah set her paintbrush in her tray and focused on him—hot and sweaty, his faded denims hugging his thighs. His shirtless chest gleamed with perspiration, his hair damp and curly around his face. Bekah wished she were painting him.

He smiled, and she nearly melted. She'd grown to love him more than she ever thought possible. She wanted him, and needed him, more than anything or anyone else in the world. She was tired of waiting. It was time. It was getting harder and harder for them to keep their hands off each other. And there was simply no reason why she had to keep her hands off him.

Collin caught her gaze and held on, not letting go. A smile broke over his face, slow and sultry, as she approached. He flexed his fingers around the wood, seeming to steady himself. Bekah wondered if she had that much effect on him,

She grinned inwardly.

Reaching him, she touched his cheek with her forefinger, her gaze still holding his. Her hand dropped and trailed feather light fingertips down his chest until she caught his hand. Then she turned and stepped away. His hand in hers, he followed. The hoe fell softly to the ground.

* * *

In Bekah's bedroom, Collin waited for her lead. His breathing deepened as she ran the palms of her hands down his chest, then followed with her mouth. His eyes closed as she placed softened lips down each rib and then back again to both of his nipples, circling them with her tongue, hardening them with each touch. Pleasurable sensations rippled down his spine as he allowed himself to feel the desire he'd kept at bay since he'd moved in with her. Mixed emotions of allowing her to continue, or forcing her to stop, thrashed through his mind.

He did nothing.

Bekah fumbled with his belt and then the button at his waist, then his zipper. His head fell backward as she made her way down his chest, but now he pulled it upright, and taking her face into his hands, pulled her to him, devouring her lips with his.

"What are you doing to me?" he breathed, and then his tongue plunged deep into her mouth. He sucked and nibbled on her tongue and lips, and plundered what was his for the taking, like a dying man gasping for air. He felt Bekah's hands wrap around his neck and pull him farther into her mouth. Then finally, they slowed, released each other, and stood breathless staring into each other's eyes.

Then she started with his zipper again.

Collin's hands stopped hers. "Bekah, no... We can't do this. I might hurt you."

She smiled. "No, you won't. You're not going to do anything." Her voice turned husky. "Lie down. I'm doing the doing."

He stood before her trying to understand, and then her mouth started another progression down his chest. When she reached his belt, she slowly walked him backward until the backs of his legs hit the bed. Her hands returned to his belt, removed it, and then quickly undid his fly. She slipped her hands around his hips to lower his jeans and boxers all at once. With a slight push against his chest, he fell back on the bed. Bekah removed the jeans, shoes and socks then lay quietly beside him on the bed.

She smiled and he cupped her chin in his hand and smiled back. "What are you doing?"

"Loving you." She sat up and straddled his body.

"You don't have to do this."

"I know. You've been very patient, and so have I."

He caught her arms and pulled her forward. "I can wait forever, Bekah. I want more than anything in the world to make love to you, but I want it to be mutual, I want you to feel it also."

Bekah sat back on his thighs. Her eyes never left his. With one swift motion, she lifted the jumper she wore up and over her head, then unhooked the back closure of her bra, releasing her full, heavy breasts. Her rounded abdomen protruded before her, filled with child. Collin reached out to stroke her breast, and knew he'd never seen anything so beautiful.

"I will feel it," she returned softly. "When you feel it, so will I." She laid her body over his and he wrapped her with his arms.

He stroked her breasts at her sides, then eased her closer where he could touch her fully. Their hands played over one another, his skimmed her hips and trailed under and over her breasts, hers played down his ribs to his thighs and across his hardening stomach. They kissed and nibbled. Collin's tongue traced the shell of an ear, and then lowered to the pulse point of her neck. As he palmed her abdomen softly, he pondered lowering his hand to between her thighs, but not until Bekah urged his hand lower, did he do so.

When his fingers slipped underneath her panties and he touched her there, Bekah visibly shuddered. Quickly then, she rolled over him. His breathing deepened and quickened, and his libido revved up a notch as her hot lips trailed down his stomach, to his naval, and then lower. Collin moaned her name and clutched her shoulders as her fingers slid down his satiny smoothness, and her tongue flicked softly against his aching flesh.

* * *

"If we put the nursery upstairs, then I want our bedroom upstairs," Bekah said later as they wove their way through heavy Lexington traffic toward the mall. "You'll have to move your office down."

"Yes, but we don't have to do that until right before or after the baby is born. I don't want you climbing those stairs while you're pregnant."

Bekah didn't argue with him. She wanted to get the nursery finished soon. Until now, they'd not done a thing. This afternoon's shopping excursion was the first time she'd left the farm in weeks, but not without Dr. Benton's approval. Collin had seen to that.

"I think yellow would be best for the walls, could we stop at the paint store, too?"

Collin grinned across the width of the car. "We'll stop wherever you want, sugar. Just don't forget we've got dinner at Joe and Maggie's tonight. We need to be back by six."

"I know. It's just that since I'm out, I want to get as much done as possible."

"But don't overdo it."

Bekah narrowed her gaze and laughed. "As if you'd let *that* happen?"

He chuckled and turned into the mall parking lot.

The baby department had all the things Bekah realized she needed for the baby but could not afford. She and Collin walked hand in hand throughout the store, commenting on this and that, looking at furniture and clothing and accessories. Her mind whirled trying to take it all in. Collin, on the other hand, wrote down everything in a small notebook he had carried along for just that purpose.

Bekah leaned over his shoulder in the infant clothing department. "What are you writing down in there?"

Collin snapped the notebook shut. "Just taking notes."

Bekah stood beside him, amused at his reaction. "What kind of notes?"

He took her hand and pulled her across the aisle. "What do you think of these, Bekah?" He picked up several layette sets, turned them over as if inspecting them, and then replaced them on the counter.

"They're okay, but I'm more interested in what you're writing down in that little book."

He ignored her and stepped over to the next counter filled with infant sleepers. "I told you, I'm just taking notes."

She followed. "For what?"

"For me."

"Oh, and that makes a lot of sense. Why?"

Collin finally turned to look at her with a smirk on his face. "You're not going to leave me alone are you?"

"Nope."

"Then I might as well confess."

"Might as well."

Collin pulled her closer. He rested his backside against the counter. "I'm pregnant."

Bekah slugged him across the shoulder. "You rat! What in the hell are you doing with that notebook?"

"It's a surprise, Bekah. Just forget it, okay?"

"For me?"

"Yes, for you. How many other women do I live with that are pregnant?"

The corner of Bekah's mouth turned up slightly. "None, I hope...pregnant or otherwise."

Collin held her hands in his, ready to confess. "Look, I know you don't have much money right now. Let me help you fix the nursery. My gift to the baby."

Bekah sighed and smiled. Her heart filled with his thoughtfulness. "I have enough money for paint and curtains and the bed. I hate to ask but if you insist, maybe you could help with some of the little stuff...."

Collin pulled her closer. "Let me take care of it." He whispered softly. His lips touched hers for a mere second, his arms folded around her waist. Bekah nibbled back.

"Well, well, well. What have we here, sugar?"

Collin turned abruptly, and Bekah jolted at the sound of the sultry southern accent. His arm curved around Bekah protectively. Every feature on his face froze.

"It's been a long, long time, baby," the woman said. "A couple of months I would say." She dropped her gaze to Bekah's rounded abdomen, then looked back to Collin's face. "Yes, two months exactly, I think it was. My apartment, you remember?"

Collin cleared his throat and stared back. "I remember perfectly, Erin. And it's been a lot longer than that."

"No, I don't think so," she said curtly, looking Bekah up and down. "Aren't you going to introduce me to your little friend?"

Bekah took the opportunity to assess the woman standing before them. She considered herself a good judge of character, so this one took only a few seconds to evaluate. Words like fake and ditsy quickly came to mind but when she continued speaking, other words started crowding her mind. Words like jealousy, intimacy, and history, also crowded her brain.

Collin pulled Bekah closer. "This is Bekah McCauley."

"And since Collin doesn't have the manners God gave a goose," the woman's high-pitched dialect shrilled, "I'll introduce myself. I'm Erin Kilpatrick." She thrust her hand at Bekah. "An old friend of the family," she added quickly, winking at Collin. "Very close friends, I'll add."

Bekah took Erin's hand briefly, and then dropped it. She glanced down at the gold bangles encircling her wrists and the diamonds sparkling off her fingers. Suddenly, her expensive perfume filtered through Bekah's nostrils. That, and her perfectly coifed hair and tailored suit screamed money. Bekah suddenly felt dowdy in her cotton denim jumper and sandals.

They stood for several awkward seconds. Erin smiled sweetly. Collin fumed. And Bekah wondering *what the hell* was going on—although she had a very good idea. Collin finally broke the silence.

"Don't you have somewhere to be, Erin?"

"No, darling'. Not really. Lunch? You can bring your little friend too if you want."

"We have plans." Collin wrenched himself from between the counter and Erin and stepped into the department store aisle, dragging Bekah along with him. "Nice to see you."

He turned and pushed Bekah ahead of him.

"Nice to meet you...Bekah." Erin's voice rose.

Bekah stopped, ignoring Collin and planted her feet on the floor. She turned back to Erin. "Nice to meet you, Erin."

"Let's go," Collin growled.

"Oh, Bekah?" Erin began again. "What a sweet name, Bekah. Sounds so...country. When *is* your baby due, dear?"

Collin stepped between them. "That's none of your business, Erin."

Bekah laid a hand on his arm.

"Oh, sorry," Erin replied sweetly. "But is it really any of *yours* either Collin?"

Collin's gaze narrowed. "It's every bit my business."

"Really?"

"Yes, Erin. Really."

"Oh. Well, then. I guess the rumors are true."

Collin shook his head, stepping closer. Bekah watched the entire scene from behind him. "What rumors, Erin?"

She smiled sweetly. "Why, the ones that say you've been taken out of circulation by a country bumpkin with a bun already in the oven. I didn't believe it myself. She *is* rather pretty you know, though, in a quaint sort of way. Maybe it's the pregnancy. They say pregnant women just glow, don't they?" She stepped closer and placed her fingers carefully on his chest. "Collin, are you sure this is what you want?" she whispered. "I mean, this isn't like you. And I know what's like you better than anyone."

Collin whirled. He encircled Bekah's waist with his arm and led her quickly away from Erin. Her shrill laughter followed behind.

Bekah waited until his steps and his breathing slowed—until his face turned a slightly paler shade of red—before speaking. He finally glanced her way as they left the mall and walked toward the car in the parking lot.

"Who was that?" Bekah asked.

"Someone from my past."

They walked a little farther before Bekah responded. "Oh. How *far* in the past?"

Collin stopped mid-step and turned, his hands gripping her upper arms. As his angry face softened, he slid his fingers down to hers and grasped her hands. "Way in the past, Bekah. A lot longer than two months, if that is what you're getting at. A lot longer. But I'm going to tell you what she's referring to and then I don't ever want to bring it up again, okay?"

Bekah nodded.

"Erin and I share a long history, since we were kids. We had nothing like I have with you. I went to her after we'd made love. I was confused. I didn't know what happened to *make* me so confused. So, I went to her because she's always been conve-nient—but I couldn't do it. I couldn't have sex with her...because now I know what making love really is. After you, I'll never be able to make love to another woman again. I love you, Bekah. I never loved Erin. It was over with her the first time my lips touched yours." He hesitated, claiming her eyes. "Now, I don't ever want to see her or to talk about her again. Understand?"

"You don't have to shout at me."

Collin's shoulders dropped and he pulled her into him. He hadn't realized how loud he'd been talking. "I'm sorry. She caught me off guard and made me angry. I don't know why I let that happen."

"I understand. She's history."

"Ancient." A smile finally broke his face.

"Before time."

"Before us."

"And that's all that matters."

Chapter Fourteen

M aggie met them at the door with a hug and a peck on Bekah's cheek, and a pat on Collin's shoulder. "Bekah, you look lovely. You come along with me now. We got some woman-talk to tend to." Maggie hooked her arm through Bekah's and led her off to the kitchen.

Bekah turned and watched behind her as Joe whisked Collin off in the opposite direction. His glance fell on her face just as she started to turn back to Maggie. His smile caught hers and held tight, leaving her with an image of sparkling blue eyes and a flash of pearly white.

Stepping through the threshold of Maggie's large country kitchen was like stepping backward in time fifteen years. Instantly reminded of the years she visited there as a child, the memories flooded back. A mixture of cinnamon and yeast came immediately to mind as she recalled Maggie's special cinnamon rolls and how she'd bribe her grandmother every morning to let her get up early to feed the chickens, and then slip off across the field to Maggie and Joe's just as the rolls came out of the oven.

As she glanced about, she realized how things had stayed

remarkably the same, and was somewhat embarrassed to think she'd not visited lately.

"Sit down, honey," Maggie broke the spell of her mind's wanderings.

Bekah shook her head, "Oh no, let me help with something."

Maggie clucked at her. "Nonsense. Not much left to do. I'll mash the potatoes in a few minutes. Beans are on the stove waiting to be dished up. The roast is in the oven. Nothing left but the shoutin'. I just wanted to get you away from the menfolk for a spell. Now sit."

Bekah did. "Maggie? Do you really think I look lovely?"

The older woman sat down, the oak chair creaking beneath her weight. "Honey, you're a Madonna. You look beautiful."

"Really?" Bekah's eyes dropped to her lap; her fingers smoothed the worn denim jumper. "You don't think I look dowdy?"

Maggie grinned and reached across the table to one of Bekah's hands. "Bekah, you're pregnant, and I've never seen you look so beautiful. But I really don't think the pregnancy is the only reason."

Bekah's gaze met the knowing eyes of a woman who had seen quite a lot in her lifetime. She smiled back at her and nodded.

"So. Tell me what you need to tell me."

Maggie sat across the worn oak table from Bekah, her fingers folded together in front of her, and stared into Bekah's face. Sitting across from her was almost like sitting across from her grandmother. Although Maggie was several years younger, she and her grandmother had been close friends. Suddenly, everything she would have wanted to tell her grandmother came boiling out, with Maggie taking the brunt of Bekah's confessions. It was as if her grandmother were there.

"It was a real mess, Maggie, but everything's okay now.

Sometimes I'm not quite sure how it all happened so fast. All that I know is that, for some crazy reason, I'm in love with Collin and he loves me, *and* my baby."

Maggie dropped her gaze, focused on the table. "...and the baby's real daddy?"

Bekah shook her head. "Back in New York. Doesn't want anything to do with either of us. It's as if he never existed."

Maggie's face grew stern. "But he does exist, Bekah."

Bekah breathed and then exhaled deeply. "I know."

"What if...?"

Bekah rose abruptly, picked up the pan of cooked potatoes and began draining them into the sink. With her back to Maggie, she began. "There will be no *what ifs* Maggie. I won't allow it. As far as I'm concerned, Matthew blew it, and Collin will be the father of this baby. Biological, or not, he will be the father."

Bekah turned quickly and replaced the pan on the stove. The older woman nodded and then grinned as she took over. "Grab the butter and milk out of the refrigerator, girl. And if you want, start working on that iced tea over there."

Bekah turned toward the refrigerator, then back to Maggie. "I love him, Maggie. He's the best thing that ever happened to me."

"That so?" Milk splashed into the boiled potatoes.

"Yes."

Maggie's eyes bore into hers once more. "In that case, I only want to ask you one more question. Ever heard of a little thing called marriage?"

* * *

Later, Collin groaned as he slid behind the steering wheel of the pickup. "I don't think I've *ever* eaten so much as I did tonight."

Bekah slanted a look in his direction from the opposite side of the truck and smiled. "You did rather look like you enjoyed yourself."

"That was, without a doubt, one of the best meals I've eaten in my life."

Bekah agreed. "Maggie's a wonderful cook, although some people would say it's a sin what she does with those green beans, but you'll never convince me that a crunchy, half-cooked steamed bean is better than one slow-cooked with bacon or ham drippings. Country cooking. I grew up on it."

"Well, I sure didn't. Not like that. Is that what I was missing out on all my life? That fried cornbread was out of this world. Can you make that?"

Bekah grinned. "Sure."

"...and what was that orange casserole dish, you know, the one with all the brown sugar stuff on top?"

"Um, oh, that was cushaw."

"Cushaw?"

"Yeah, cushaw. It's a kind of squash."

"Never heard of it."

"Did you like it?"

"It was wonderful. Can you make that too?"

"Sure, that is if we had cushaw. You have to grow them. I rarely see them in the grocery store. It's too late for this year, but we can put some out in the garden next spring."

Collin's eyes fixed ahead of him as he drove down the road, nearing Bekah's drive. His sated smile turned into a frown. "Next spring?"

A sprig of panic gripped Bekah. An unwelcome rush of insecurity raced through her. Had she dared suggest this relationship was permanent? It was how it felt to her, and she could only assume it felt the same to him. They had both confessed their love to each other and had been inseparable for weeks, but they had never talked in terms of the future. Was it all just an assumption?

No. Certainly not.

Had this talk of marriage with Maggie made her vulnerable to the idea of him being around forever? It was what he wanted, wasn't it?

Did she? Truly?

Bekah turned and stared out the window. The early signs of dusk blanketed the countryside. Her eyes stung and she blinked rapidly to avoid them spilling over. Marriage. What would he think?

Can I do it?

"What do you think about putting out more potatoes next year? I love garden potatoes. I think we could probably plow a few more rows and store them in that old root cellar out back. I checked it out the other day, it's dry in there. I think if I just fix the hinges on the door...."

Bekah jerked her head back around to him and beamed. Before she realized what she was doing, she crossed the width of the pickup, wrapped her arms around Collin's neck, and snuggled against his chest. She laid a soft kiss on the bare skin that showed through in the space where his shirt lay open.

Collin's right arm pulled her closer to him. "Hey, what's this?"

Bekah shook her head, her face still in his chest. "Nothing," she whispered. "I just needed to be next to you."

Collin laid a soft kiss on the top of her head and fanned his fingers through her hair. "Um, anytime," he whispered back. He passed Bekah's drive. "Mind if we run over to my farm? We've been running around all day and I haven't checked in with Pete. I think he thinks I've been ignoring the animals lately."

Bekah sat back a little and looked at him. "Collin, I'm sorry.

I didn't think about that. You've been spending so much time with me, that you've been neglecting your own obligations."

"No, I haven't. I run the hounds and horses daily for exercise. And I check in with Pete at least once a day. The stable hands do the rest. It just seems lately I've been otherwise obligated."

Bekah chewed on her lip, thinking. "...and are things at work okay. I know you work a few hours a day upstairs, but I hope that I'm not taking too much time...."

Collin slowed the pickup and cupped her cheek in his palm. "You've got all my time, Bekah. And that's exactly the way I want it."

The pickup slowed even more as Collin pulled into his drive, drove back to the barn, and then braked fully. They sat in the cab of the truck for several minutes before either moved, content with holding each other and listening to the mingled beating of their hearts in unison with the night sounds all around them.

"Potatoes, huh?" Bekah finally broke away from him.

Collin looked down at her pert little face, bathed in moonlight and smiled back at her. "Yeah, potatoes and cushaw."

His lips touched her briefly. "Up for a short walk? We can take it slow and easy. I need to work off some of Maggie's country cooking'."

"Sure. Dr. Benton says I can do whatever I feel like doing now, especially since the placenta seems to have moved back to normal. He just doesn't want me to overdo it."

"No chance of that."

"You don't have to tell me that, *Mr. Watch-me-like-a-hawk.*"

Collin's face turned serious. "Does it bother you?"

Bekah looked into his eyes and slowly shook her head. "No," she whispered. "It doesn't."

"I do it because I love you, Bekah."

"I know, and I love you for it." Bekah traced a finger over his cheek. "Ready for that walk?"

Collin nodded, then opened the door on his side of the pickup truck. Bekah slid across the bench seat and out his door. They strolled toward the barn.

Bekah contemplated the question she'd been waiting for the right moment to bring up. Maybe now was it, she thought. "Collin?"

"Hm?"

Bekah slipped her hand in his and turned her gaze to his face. "Have you thought lately about going back to school?"

Collin stopped and looked at her. "What brought that on?"

Bekah resumed walking. "I've just been thinking. You're not too old, you know."

"Of course, I am, Bekah. It's a ridiculous notion."

Bekah shook her head as she watched his profile. "No, it's not, Collin. I think you should look into it."

Collin stopped once more and faced her. His hands traveled up to her elbows and grasped her upper arms. "Bekah, it's just not the right time. That was something I should have done ten years ago. Besides, it would take too much time."

"Only a few years."

His eyes grazed her face. "Not an option. My priorities and goals have changed, and that's the way I like it."

Bekah sighed. "Collin, you should at least think about it."

Collin ran his fingers through Bekah's hair at the sides of her face, cupping her head in his hands. He tilted her face up to his. "You are priceless."

Bekah grinned. "No, you are."

He nudged her nose with his. "We'll talk about it another time. Okay?"

Bekah dropped the subject. "Okay."

Collin's arm dropped around her waist as they walked

toward the barn. He pulled her closer and nudged her ear. "As soon as we check on the animals, I'm going to take you home and love you," he whispered in her ear. "Dr. Benton said things were back to normal, didn't he?"

Bekah tightened her grip around his waist. "Um, that he did. Let's hurry."

Chapter Fifteen

O nly a few stars lit up the still, black night. Collin
pulled Bekah closer as they ambled from his parked
car toward Bekah's house. A late-night chill tripped
over her shoulders and she shivered, welcoming his warmth.

"Cold?" He tightened an arm around her.

"A little," she answered. "And it's so dark. Didn't we leave
the porch light on?"

Collin glanced at the house. "I could swear we did."

A tremor settled near her heart. She was *sure* they had.
Collin was increasingly fearful Bekah would trip on the old
wooden porch steps, and always made sure the light was on
when they left.

Collin's gait slowed. The hairs prickled on the back of
Bekah's neck.

His grip tightened about her waist as they moved steadily
toward the porch. Bekah leaned in, her cheek resting on his
chest. When they reached the steps, Collin stopped abruptly.
Her head rose sharply, and her gaze followed the path of his
toward the porch. A small heap of something she couldn't iden-
tify lay in front of the door.

"What is it?" she whispered.

Collin shook his head. "I don't know. Stay back."

Bekah watched as he soundlessly made his way onto the porch. He moved closer to the object; Bekah stood fast in her spot. Collin kneeled and leaned in. One hand stroked the object. Then Collin's shadowed silhouette bent forward, his head hung.

"Bekah." His voice was just above a whisper. "There's a flashlight in the glove box of my car. Would you get it for me?"

Bekah watched him for a moment and then retreated to his car. She returned shortly, stopping exactly where she had stood before. Collin stood and reached for the light.

"Now, go sit in the car and lock the doors."

Panic shot through Bekah. "Collin, why?"

"Just do it, Bekah. Please. I'll explain later."

"Collin...?"

She saw the flashlight drop to his side and heard his exasperated sigh. "Please, Bekah. Go sit in the car."

Bekah let out a long breath herself, and then then did as he asked. She nudged the button that locked herself in and watched as Collin played the flashlight over the object. She saw him point the beam at the porch light, broken shards of glass dripping from the fixture, then back to play across the porch. Only then could she make out the shape laying before the door.

"Oh, good Lord," she whispered.

* * *

Collin stooped beside the inert figure. The hound lay with his back to him, his paws resting against the door. He ran his free hand over the hound's head, behind his ears, and down the back of his slick tan and white coat. He slipped his fingers under the hound's collar and deftly unbuckled the leather strap, releasing

202

it from his neck. Collin swallowed and blinked back tears as he read the hound's name on the collar tag. It wasn't until he turned the hound over, ready to cradle the animal in his arms and carry him away, that he noticed the pool of blood beneath him—and then the long slash opening the hound's body from throat to gut, threatening to spill his bowels upon the concrete porch.

He swallowed back emotion and shrugged out of his jacket, laying it on the porch floor. Carefully, he rolled the hound onto it and wrapped him up tight, then lifted him and carried him off to the barn. He avoided Bekah's eyes as he passed in front of the car, his brain spinning with how to explain what had happened.

He wasn't sure himself. What had happened? And why?

Blindly, he went through the immediate motions of putting the hound away in the barn until morning—where no other animals could get to him—when he could bury him over at his place. He pushed the anxiety in his gut away on a deep breath until he could find another time to deal with it. Bekah's gaze held his as he motioned for her to unlock the car, and he silently escorted her to the house.

Two hours later, Bekah whispered into his chest as they lay in bed, his arms wrapped around her. "Why would anyone do such a thing?" she said. "I just don't understand."

Collin stared above them at the round glass globe hanging over the bed. Eyes fixated on the light, thinking about the past hour—he'd thought things were getting better. There had been no problems since he'd moved in with Bekah. Why now?

Why that hound? That part puzzled him more than anything did. That particular hound was special. A top breeder, and one of Collin's favorites. Coincidence? Or was it a clear message? If so, that shed an entirely different light on the situation. No local would understand the significance of choosing *that* hound to mutilate.

He turned toward Bekah and gathered her close. "I don't understand it either."

"Honestly, Collin, I've been wracking my brain and I can't come up with a single person who would do that. And why? I've known most of these people all my life. I can't figure it out."

Collin looked past her. "I can't figure it out either, honey, and that's what bothers me. I don't like that they're involving you, either. Especially now. And I don't want you to worry about it, okay? Let me handle it."

Bekah drew back slightly to see his face. "You won't do anything stupid, will you?"

"Honey, I can't do anything until I know for sure who's responsible. I'll probably just do a lot of listening. People can't help but talk about things like this. Eventually it will come out. I just want you to stay out of it."

"Of course, Collin. I don't want you to get mixed up in something right now. I need you with me."

Collin tucked her head into his chest and rested his chin on the top of it. "I need you too, sweetheart."

Bekah settled into his side, and then jumped as the phone rang. "Got it," Collin said, reaching to his right to pick up the receiver. "Yes?"

"Hi, pumpkin. What are you doing?"

Erin, what the f—. "Hello?"

"Don't play games with me, sugar. You know I play for keeps."

Collin hung up and turned to Bekah. "Wrong number." He gathered her close and inhaled the lavender scent of her shampoo, vowing to keep her out of the middle of all of this. *Dammit.* He wasn't in the mood to play games with *Erin.* What the hell did she want, and why would she dare call him here?

How did she even know he *was* here?

She knew better than to fuck with him.

* * *

Bekah put the last letter into an envelope, licked and sealed it, and shoved it and three others into her shoulder bag. A glance out the window confirmed her suspicions. Collin's Mercedes crept up the gravel drive. Hurriedly she shuffled through the clutter on his desk for a book of stamps, finally finding one in the center drawer with exactly four stamps remaining. She swiped them up and stuffed them into her purse, then carefully made her way down the back stairs to the first-floor landing near the kitchen.

The back door slammed, and Bekah jumped. Her shoulder bag fell to the floor and skidded across the waxed linoleum, landing at Collin's feet. The four letters spilled out onto the floor.

"In a hurry?" Collin stared from across the room.

Nervously, Bekah laughed. "Hurry? No, whatever made you think that?"

He reached down to pick up the purse. The letters splayed out on the floor at his feet. Bekah watched in a panic as he scooped them up. He stared at them for a long moment and then turned his face up to meet hers.

"What are you doing?"

Bekah swallowed and bit the inside of her lip. "I was just on my way to the mailbox."

He glared hard, then glanced back to the letters in his hand. One by one, Collin thumbed through them, his face keeping the same blank expression. He tossed them and her purse on the kitchen table, took a step forward, then stopped, hands on hips.

"Why?"

Bekah moved closer. "Collin, I just wanted to get some information for you."

He lowered his head and shook it. "What are you going to

do, pick out the damn school for me, then pack me off like I was going to summer camp? Let's see here, we've got Ohio State, Auburn, Tennessee, North Carolina. Great universities Bekah, but don't you think I should have a little voice in this matter?"

Bekah stepped back. His anger surprised her. Arms crossed, she narrowed her gaze. "It was going to be a surprise, Collin. I was just writing for information. I don't know why you're so angry."

Collin held her gaze for several seconds. Bekah stood her ground, not daring to break the connection. Then he sank into a nearby kitchen chair. In one swift movement, he reached for her and gathered her into his arms. His face rested against her abdomen, his arms wrapped tightly around her waist.

Bekah threaded her fingers through Collin's hair and cradled his head against her. She caressed his temples, and brushed backward a few sun-bleached russet locks, then lowered her hands to his shoulders and kneaded the knotty muscles there.

"Bad morning? Your shoulders are tight."

Collin sighed. "The worst."

Bekah closed her eyes and concentrated only on the movements of her fingers across his rippling back muscles. "What happened?"

"Nothing. Everything. My secretary is out sick. A crazed woman took up camp in my office all morning insisting Kramer Bloodstock insure her llamas and her ostrich, and I just had an argument with Joe. When I came in here and saw the letters, I just lost it." *Not to mention someone's been messing with my horses.*

Bekah stilled her hands. "Back up a minute. Did you say llamas? And an ostrich?"

One corner of Collin's mouth drew up. "Yeah. I tried to tell her we insure horses and some cattle, not exotic animals, but she wouldn't listen. She insisted I come up with a policy, and get this, the ostrich is worth more than all the llamas!"

"What did you do?"

"I drew up a policy."

"What? Was it expensive?"

Collin laughed. "Let's put it this way, she paid cash money and didn't blink an eye. Her policy cost almost as much as I paid for some of my horses. And her Jaguar wasn't more than a few months old at the most."

"What about Joe?"

Collin let out a long breath. "We argued. I just went over there to talk to him about cutting the tobacco. He's hired some Mexican migrant workers at a fair price. They'll begin cutting tomorrow, by the way. Then he mentioned the hound. I guess I said the wrong thing because he got angry."

"He thought you were accusing him, or maybe somebody else around here?"

Collin nodded. "I guess I implied that...."

Bekah drew back. "Collin! How dare you say such a thing? No wonder he took offense."

Collin shook his head. "I don't think he did it, Bekah. Somebody is sending messages, though. Three of my horses are sick. I haven't figured out why yet."

"How do you know they're not just sick?"

"Three of them? All at once? No. Besides, I know my horses."

"Then what *are* you saying, Collin?"

Collin let out a long breath. "Someone poisoned them."

Bekah stared at him. "Poison? How do you know for sure?"

"I've got a vet over there right now doing some blood tests. Everything points to a slow poisoning. Whoever did this was smart. They gave the horses just enough so they would get sick, but not die immediately. When Joe and I discussed it, I guess I was a little angry. It's just that since you and I have been together, things have been better. I've not had any problems with anyone around here for weeks—until the hound."

"It's not anyone around here, Collin."

Collin's gaze trapped hers again. "How do you know?"

She stood and held his stare. "I know."

"I'm not so sure."

"Well, I am."

Collin stood and stared back. "You're so trusting of these people. Don't they ever do anything wrong? Someone wants me out, Bekah. Do you feel the same?"

Bekah stepped back. "*What?* Collin, what has gotten into you? You know I love you. That hasn't changed." She paused then and narrowed her gaze. "Have things changed for you?"

He didn't move. "No. Of course I love you."

"Then why in the world would you ask me that?"

His eyes closed. "This school thing. Do you want me to leave? Do you want me out of here?"

Bekah shook her head, a frown playing across her lips. "Do you think I'm pushing you away? Hell, Collin, maybe it was too much of me to think it, but I thought if you went to school, I'd go with you. Presumptuous of me, wasn't it? Excuse me for making plans for our future." Bekah turned and stalked off toward the living room, then stopped and turned back, her eyes glaring. "Don't worry, I won't make that mistake again."

Before she could take another step, Collin rushed forward and caught her up in his arms. "God, I'm a fool," he whispered into her hair. "I'm sorry."

Bekah cinched her arms around him. "Yes, you are a fool. I love you Collin. I don't want you to leave."

"It's not been a great morning."

Bekah tilted her head back to look at him and placed a light kiss against his lips. "Everyone's entitled to a bad day."

"Not with you around. Every day with you should be roses. Sorry I ruined this one."

Bekah smiled. "It's not ruined. Besides, you know what they say about making up, don't you?"

Collin nodded and grinned.

Chapter Sixteen

"Let me see if I have everything straight." Collin stared ahead through the windshield as he drove, not seeing the countryside, and only concentrating on the makings of Bekah's family. "Michael is your oldest brother and is married to Kate. They have two children, Brian and Michelle. Kevin is the middle child, married to Laura. He has three girls, Emily, Amber, and Holly. Right?"

Bekah grinned. "Yep. That's good for a start. I won't even think about confusing you with any of the others."

Collin glanced at her. "The others?"

Bekah's smile broadened. "Well, yes. There will probably be cousins and aunts and uncles there as well. You see, Daddy has four brothers, and my mother has one brother and two sisters. They're all married except one, and they all have children—and nearly all of *them* have children. I expect most of them will be here tonight."

Collin turned his head to her. "Stick close to me, okay?"

Bekah patted his arm. "I have no trouble doing that." Her gaze held his shortly, and then Bekah glanced back at the road.

Immediately she reached for the dash and braced herself. "Collin!"

Collin looked back to the road in just enough time to brake and swerve wide to the left, nearly avoiding a slow-moving car in front of them. He was thankful nothing was coming in the opposite direction on the narrow country road.

"Damn!" Collin passed the vehicle.

Bekah felt the lump in her throat and knew it was her heart —or a piece of it, anyway. It pounded wildly against her throat. She turned around to look at the black Buick behind them.

"Tourists," she whispered. "I saw the rental agency bumper sticker on the back."

Collin nodded. "Must be looking at the farms."

The manicured paddocks, and plank and rock fences, drew many tourists throughout the year. Not to mention the thoroughbreds. The barns themselves were a remarkable sight. Most of them sported as much security as the mansions the farm owners lived in.

"This road is bad for tourists," she said. "I used to hate it when I was at home."

Collin let out a huge breath and grasped her hand. "You okay?"

Bekah nodded and slipped closer to him. "I'm fine."

They rode in silence for the rest of the way. When they arrived and approached her parents' house, the front door jerked out of Bekah's hand by a gigantic man who swept her up into his arms and whirled her around on the front porch.

"Michael!" Bekah screamed and laughed. "Put me down, you oaf!"

He swirled her once more, then settled her on the wooden porch. "Whew, little sister, seems to me the last time I did that, you were lighter."

Bekah socked him in the shoulder. "Who's asking you?"

"No one, I'm telling you," he returned.

Bekah reached for her older brother and hugged him tight around the neck. "I've missed you terribly," she whispered.

He nodded against her cheek.

"Hey now!" Another male shout came from the doorway. "Leave my little sister alone there, you big ox!"

Michael stepped back and up to his slightly thinner and shorter brother, Kevin. "Make me, squirt."

Kevin puffed up his chest. "Excuse me here, Bekah, while I beat up our brother, he seems to be hogging all the time with you." He shouldered his brother.

"Did you hear him call you a hog?" Michael turned to Bekah.

Kevin grew red in the face. "I did not, she looks beautiful. You're the hog!"

Bekah laughed and stepped between them both, placing a palm on either chest, glancing back and forth from brother to brother. She ignored the audience just inside the door. "Stop it right now, guys. How in the world did you two get along without me to mediate all those years?"

Michael's face grew serious. "We didn't."

Bekah slowly turned. The corners of her lips drew down, her eyes widened, and she blinked to hold back the sting. Her voice began low, "Well, I'm here now and I'm not going anywhere, so you better get used to it."

Michael grinned and then glanced at Kevin over her shoulder.

Collin stood back from the scene, leaning against a wooden porch post, arms crossed, taking in the sibling banter, and realizing how much he'd missed in his own life. He couldn't imagine the jokes, the digs, the laughs, and the hugs like that with either of his sisters. With each passing day he spent with Bekah, he learned more about her, and that he loved her so much more.

But how was he going to keep her without the skills to maintain a happy family? Could he ever be able to carry on like this with his own children? Could he spread the love and happiness within a family like what Bekah had obviously grown up with?

"Collin? Did you hear me?" Bekah tugged at his sleeve.

He shook away the nagging thoughts, his gaze meeting hers. "No, sorry. I guess I was daydreaming."

Bekah frowned. "No, my fault. We got caught up in everything and I forgot to introduce you to my brothers." She turned and introduced both Michael and Kevin to Collin. After shaking hands, Bekah led him through the threshold of the house and into the host of cousins, aunts, uncles, nieces, and nephews. As they wove their way through the masses, Bekah introduced Collin to each—he knew he'd never remember everyone—and prayed she would keep her promise to stick close by his side.

* * *

"Oh, how sweet, another pair of baby booties." Kevin crooned over his sister's shoulder, and then turned to Collin, whispering. "Don't you think it's about time we men head out of here and get into some sweaty, man stuff?"

"Like apple pie and homemade ice cream, you mean?" Kevin's wife Laura piped in on the conversation from Bekah's left.

Kevin bristled up to his full five feet eight inches. "Actually no, I thought a game of horseshoes was more the ticket. However, pie sounds good for later. What do you say, Collin?"

Collin glanced sideways at Bekah who gave him a slight smile. "Go ahead."

Keven patted his stomach and nodded toward the kitchen. "Horseshoes, Kramer?"

Collin nodded. "Definitely. A la mode."

Collin liked this younger brother, and the older one too. They were entirely different. Michael was a tall, husky brute of a man, with a tender heart when it came to his baby sister. Collin observed him for nearly an hour earlier that afternoon playing with the children, keeping them at bay and out from under the women's feet while they were busy in the kitchen. Kevin was the jokester, and very much the protector. The sisters-in-law, the aunts and uncles, the children—the family seemed so close-knit, and Collin wondered why Bekah left home. Ten years can change a person, he knew, but she stepped right back into her sisterly role as if she'd been away at summer camp. This family dynamic seemed unique, so unusual to him, that he couldn't imagine not wanting to be a part of it forever. What appeared more unusual was they seemed to have accepted him right into it.

* * *

As Collin left, a strange feeling of acceptance and rightness came over Bekah. He was almost as at home here, with her family, as she was. He fit right in, and for that, she was so thankful.

The evening slipped by quickly. Bekah opened gift after gift, the women surrounding her and oohing and ahhing to each little sleeper or toy. Each time she said the word, *baby*, she lost one of her clothespins, and her niece counted every time she crossed her legs, announcing that she was going to have at least ten more children in her lifetime. They played other silly shower games, each winner donating her prize to Bekah.

At the end of the evening, Bekah realized she received a lot more gifts than she'd expected. Collin rejoined the group in the living room, and as family members left, he and Bekah huddled alone in the corner of the room, sorting through the gifts.

"Everything's so tiny," he commented as he picked up a miniature sock.

Bekah watched Collin's face. He smiled slightly, and then his lips straightened out into a thin line as he fondled and stared at the sock. She laid a soft hand on his arm. "What's wrong?"

He looked away. "Can I do it, Bekah? Can I be a part of all this? Can I really be a father?"

Bekah drew his face to hers and smiled. "You've already been doing it Collin. You're already a father. Just think how much you've done for me and the baby the past few months."

He shook his head. "I don't know, Bekah. I'm frightened."

"Frightened? Of what?"

Collin's voice cracked as he spoke. "Bekah, what you have here... With your family, I've never had this before. It is amazing. I suddenly know what having a family means. I don't think I ever really had one before. What I have with my mother and sisters is nothing compared to what you have here."

"No," Bekah insisted, "what *we* have here. There's a difference. It's yours now too, Collin."

He stared into her eyes. "Really, Bekah? I can have this too?"

"You already do, they love you." She smiled.

Collin grinned back at her and took her hands into his. "I really like each and every one of them. There all so happy, and friendly, and caring."

"And unique."

He laughed. "That they are." Then his face grew serious. "So, you really think I can do it? I can be a good father to your baby? I can be like this?"

"Our baby, Collin. If you want to be a good father, you will. If you don't, you won't. But all you have to really do is keep on being you and I'll be completely satisfied." Her hands clasped his harder, and she pulled him closer, then placed a quick kiss on his lips. "Now, I guess we better get this haul to the car. Dusk is falling."

Collin rose and pulled her to her feet. "We better say our goodbyes. Looks like several of them have left already."

Arms around each other, they stepped out onto the porch. Michael, the last to leave, hugged his sister goodbye. "Love you little sis," he whispered in her ear and winked at Collin all at once.

"I love you too, Michael. Take care of those kids and Kate. I don't know how they put up with you though," she teased and pinched his nose.

Michael turned, scooped up his youngest, and hauled her like a sack of potatoes across the lawn to their four-wheel-drive pickup. The two kids took up the middle of the seat, Kate and Michael balancing the family on either side. As his truck made a trail of dust down the lane, Bekah, Collin, and her parents waved until they were almost out of sight.

Each turned back to enter the house.

"That Brian," Sarah McCauley exclaimed, "must be the worst mannered child there ever was. If Michael doesn't get a hold of that young man soon, why, there's no telling what that young 'un will be capable of."

"Ah, woman. Leave that boy alone. He's got spunk. Now that Michelle, *she's* the one..." Russell followed his wife through the door, bantering back and forth with his wife about which grandchild was indeed the worst.

Collin slipped his arm in the crook of Bekah's elbow and smiled. Just as Bekah placed one foot over the threshold into the house, she turned at the sound of a car engine. Collin's gaze followed hers.

The car's headlights beamed through the heavy dusk of the late

August night, breaking a path up the lane where Michael's truck had just left. The driver drove a little too quickly, Bekah could tell, probably unaccustomed to driving on a dirt road. The car bounced with each hole in the road hit and then immediately smashed itself into the dry earth sending up dust clouds into the night air.

Bekah turned to face the oncoming vehicle as it approached, her side leaning into Collin. As the automobile grew nearer, it struck a familiar chord, as though she'd seen it somewhere before. When it pulled to a complete stop in front of the plank fence, she knew. The black Buick.

She turned to Collin whose gaze was also fixed on the vehicle. "Is that the car from this afternoon?"

He nodded. "I think so."

"Maybe they're lost."

"Probably."

They stood for a moment before anyone moved. The Buick's windows tinted too dark to see inside. "Should we go down there?"

Collin fixed his gaze on the car. "No, let them come up here. They have to see us."

About that time, the driver's side of the car opened. A dark-haired man emerged slowly, stood, and stared at the porch. Then he stepped forward.

Collin stepped toward the man. Bekah clutched his arm, pulling him back.

"Don't go." Her voice was deep and husky. She slipped slightly behind Collin.

Collin glanced at her. Bekah's eyes fixed on the man walking toward the porch. Her breathing seemed labored. "Why?"

"Because...because I don't want you to."

"He's only lost, Bekah. He probably wants directions."

Bekah shook her head quickly. "He's not lost. He knows exactly where he is."

Collin glanced from Bekah to the man now stopped before them at the bottom of the porch steps. He laid his hand over Bekah's fingers, now maintaining a death-grip on his lower arm. "You know him?"

Bekah's lips set firm. Her gaze was transfixed in front of her, staring at the man. "Yes." Then she directed to the man. "Stop, Matthew. Don't come any closer."

Bekah stood her ground. Matthew placed one foot on the lower porch step.

Collin placed a protective arm around Bekah's waist.

He wasn't quite sure what was happening here, but there was no way Bekah was getting out of his grasp. He made eye contact with the man. "She asked you to stop."

Matthew glared. "I only want to talk to Rebekah. Leave."

Collin glanced at Bekah, who shook her head, her gaze not leaving Matthew. She trembled ever so slightly and then curved into Collin's side. Collin turned back to him. "She doesn't want to talk to you."

Matthew looked at the porch floor. He toed an uneven plank with his leather loafer, hands shoved deep into his pants pockets. Collin's gaze traveled upward to his crisp pleated pants, his starched shirt, and the neat short-cropped hair. He could have been looking at a mirror image of himself a few months ago.

Matthew's gaze rose from Bekah's feet, up her body to her face.

"My, my. We are very pregnant, dear, aren't we? You look quite... Well, let's see, how do I describe it? Matronly—yes. I think that's the word I'm searching for."

"Yes, I suppose you would, Matthew. Does it bother you?

My appearance certainly doesn't bother me." Bekah's voice iced in bitterness.

"Well, as long as I or anyone I know doesn't have to look at you every day, it doesn't bother me a bit. I'm only concerned about my child."

She took a half step toward him. "You gave up your rights, Matthew, months ago. You made that perfectly clear."

"Things change, Rebekah."

"Not this."

Matthew cocked his head at Collin. "Is there somewhere private we can discuss this matter?"

"Nothing to discuss."

"I've come a long way, Rebekah. There are things we must discuss. Be it now or later, we will discuss them. Briefly, I want paternity rights to this child. You can cooperate and we can do it on our terms, or you can fight it and we can do it strictly on my terms. Either way, I win."

"No!" She lunged forward, her arms outstretched. Collin pulled her back and wrapped his arms around her from behind.

"Bekah, not this way." He tugged her backward toward the door.

She planted herself. "Wait. There is something I need to say."

He leaned to whisper in her ear. "Then be quick, because if you think I'm going to stand here and let this man intimidate you, you're dead wrong."

She twisted back. "All right." She turned and narrowed her gaze at Matthew. "When I left New York, you wanted nothing to do with me or this baby. Period. It is too late to change your mind now. Not a judge in this state will award you any kind of custody, Matthew. Not when they know the truth."

Matthew's lips drew up in a smirk. "You're right, Rebekah.

Not in this state. But New York is different. In New York, I have friends. Cooperate with me or you'll wish you had."

Simple as that, and Collin knew he hated this man.

Anger boiled inside him and he could barely control it, much less keep the reins on Bekah. He held her closer and glowered at Matthew. "It's time for you to leave, man."

Matthew chuckled. "Ah. The new boyfriend. How nice Rebekah, a country boy." He glanced about. "Where's his pickup?"

Collin started forward, but this time Bekah blocked his path. "Look," he growled, "matters such as this are better handled in an attorney's office. I suggest you contact me at Kramer Bloodstock in Lexington in the morning. We'll handle it from there."

Bekah leaned against Collin and he felt her physical exhaustion. He tightened his arms around her, wanting her to know he was there for her. That he had her back. Always. Matthew glanced back and forth between them.

"All right," he said and sneered. "I'll find you."

Chapter Seventeen

"Eventually you may have to cooperate."

Bekah sat quietly in the leather wingback chair facing the attorney Collin had hired, considered the woman's words, knowing that she was only doing her job, and said, "Never."

Collin cleared his throat. "Bekah, honey, I know what you want, but you need to hear Patricia out. She knows the situation, and she knows the law. There may come a point where you have to cooperate."

Bekah looked across the desk at the woman. Her caring eyes she trusted. That Collin chose a woman attorney pleased her—she may be more sympathetic to her cause. But the word cooperate was not in Bekah's vocabulary. Not when it came to Matthew.

"I'll not let him have any sort of control over my child."

"The judge may order joint custody. He has the means to support and the right to visitation privileges."

"Then I'll fight the judge."

"You don't fight judges, Bekah." The attorney stared back.

"Then I'll run."

"That would be a mistake."

"Maybe. Maybe not."

Collin breathed deeply and sighed. "Bekah, you're not going to run. We'll work this out to yours and the baby's best interest. Please listen to Patricia."

Defiantly, Bekah raised her chin. "Okay. I'll listen." She sat back in her seat. "But I make no guarantees."

Collin dared a grin.

"I just want you both to know my position. Matthew will never, ever, have paternity rights over my baby." *And I mean that with everything in me.*

Patricia Settle leaned back in her chair. Bekah eyed her as the attorney placed her hands loosely on either sidearm, in a non-confronting manner. Her short black hair framed her perfectly made-up face. Bekah guessed her age close to her mother's. Different worlds, she thought. Could she trust her? Glancing at Collin, Bekah took a breath. Obviously, *he* trusted her. She would trust his judgment.

To a point.

"I think we have some work to do here," Patricia said.

Bekah took another breath. "Let me explain something to you, Ms. Settle. I will be completely honest with you—about everything. And I mean everything. But right now, the word cooperate is *not* in my vocabulary. I don't much like the word negotiation either, and I'm telling you both, I will not be cooperating or negotiating with Matthew." She paused briefly and glanced from one to the other. "And also being straight up and honest, right now I feel more like running than being here."

Patricia looked at her. "Bekah, let's be informal here. Call me Patricia. I'm *not* your enemy. I've been acquainted with Collin and his family for years. *I'm on your side.* You need to trust me."

Bekah's eyes closed, and she exhaled deeply. Inside her

body, she was quaking, and trying awfully hard not to show it. "I know," she began softly. "Collin explained all that to me. It's just very emotional." Her eyes opened. "I do trust you. I trust Collin, and if he trusts you, that's good enough for me. But you must listen to me. Seriously."

"Good." Patricia leaned forward, bracing herself with her elbows on her desk. "Now, tell me everything."

Bekah looked at Collin. He reached for her hand and took it. She recited the entire story to her about her leaving the farm, Matthew finding her in Greenwich Village, the job, the control —everything

"You see," Bekah continued. "I was young and very naïve. Fresh out of college. Looking for the big time. I found it, only it wasn't very pleasant. Matthew wanted a toy, and I was it. He wanted a china doll he could dress up, put his arm about, and parade around the city. He needed it to complete his image.

"At the time, I didn't know it, but he arranged for the editor position at the magazine for me. He controlled my bank account, although he gave me a small weekly allowance. He told me what to eat. He picked out my clothes right down to the underwear, the color of lipstick I wore, how I wore my hair. He made me quit painting because the paints ruined my manicure. I made absolutely no decisions. And I wasn't me."

Bekah's gaze dropped to her lap. She blinked the sting of tears back to behind her eyelids. Saying all of that suddenly made her feel like a stupid little girl. How could she have let him control her like that? Well, no more.

She continued. "I know someone like you probably finds it difficult to understand how a woman could get herself into that kind of position. But I did. I was caught up in it before I knew it." Collin squeezed her hand tighter.

"Bekah, there's no reason to be ashamed."

She stared at Patricia.

The attorney went on. "I deal with women's issues day in and day out. You're not the first, nor will you be the last, to suffer this kind of abuse. I understand."

Bekah shook her head. "Oh, but it wasn't abuse. He never physically hurt me—never really meant to. It was just the one time—"

Collin's gaze burned into the side of her face. "He hurt you?"

She turned and saw the anger there. "Just once. When I left. It got a little rough."

"What did he do to you?"

Bekah's eyes teared. "Just a black eye and a few bruises. Nothing major. A cracked rib or two."

Collin shot up off his seat and glared. "A black eye? Cracked ribs? Why didn't you tell me?"

The tears streamed then. "I didn't want to think about it, Collin. I pushed it out of my head. All of it."

Patricia interrupted. She held out a hand to Bekah. "You've suffered emotional and physical abuse, Bekah, but what you have to remember now is that we, Collin and I, are here to help you get through this."

She looked at Collin. He leaned in and kissed her cheek.

"Can't you see why I don't want a child in that environment?" She felt like she was pleading.

He nodded. "I'm beginning to. Just don't let him pull you down. We're here for you." Collin edged his chair closer to Bekah and placed an arm around her back. She turned her tear-filled eyes to his. "I love you, Bekah. It's okay," he whispered.

Bekah let out a long breath. "I loved my job, though. It was a vast source of pride to me. I worked hard. I didn't know until I quit that I wouldn't have had the job, if not for Matthew. I worked hard and thought they liked my work. I still think that. It was creative—and I enjoyed it. It was a different kind of art, but art just the same. I felt a kind of power there, a kind of control I didn't have in my personal life, so I worked long hours. Matthew took it for a dedication to my work and making money. He liked that, so he didn't object. I ended up working myself into an ulcer, though." She paused. "That's when I found out I was pregnant."

"And he didn't like that idea?"

Bekah shook her head. "That I was pregnant? Ah, no. He was appalled that I had been so careless. Me, the careless one. He hated the idea of being a father. His life was set. Too rigid. Everything in the apartment had a place—and it was never out of that place. A baby would be messy, and in the way. There would be too much stuff, he said. Too much clutter with a baby. He didn't have time. I didn't have time, he said.

"Everything in Matthew's life had sharp angles and crisp edges to it. Neat and precise. No softness. No cuddliness. Nothing that would even suggest a hint of hominess. A baby just wouldn't fit." Her gaze settled out the window behind Patricia. "Which is why I can't figure out why he's here. There is some other reason."

Patricia studied Bekah's face for a few long seconds. "Bekah, why did you say Matthew was appalled at *your* carelessness? Wasn't birth control his responsibility too?"

Bekah snorted. "Oh, no. Birth control was my concern. He expected me to handle it. He didn't want to be bothered. When I suggested at one time we use condoms, he blew up. From that moment on, I used the pill and even sometimes a diaphragm. I wanted to protect myself any way I could. But I got pregnant anyway. Because of the ulcer, I was throwing up a lot and certain foods didn't agree with me. I always took my pill at night, and on some nights when I would be completely exhausted and stressed out, I would eat quickly and take my pill. Then my dinner and the pill would come back up. I guess that's how it happened. I'm not sure. Anyway, I didn't really find out I was pregnant until I went to the doctor about my stomach problems. I found out about the ulcer then too."

Patricia scribbled a few lines down on a notepad in front of her. Bekah leaned against Collin's shoulder. His hand went up to the back of her neck and softly massaged the tense muscles there. His touch gave her more comfort than he probably realized.

"So then what happened?"

"From then on, it's really quite simple. When Matthew found out I was pregnant, he gave me an ultimatum. Either I was to abort the child or leave. I was no good to him fat and pregnant. He couldn't dress me up and parade me around. He never said that, of course, but it was certainly implied. And if I were to have the baby, I'd have to cut down on my working hours, which incidentally meant less money, less social life, and less prestige. In short, he didn't want me if I wanted the baby. And if I wanted the baby, I had to leave. I did and here we are—back at square one and I can't figure out why in the hell he is here."

Bekah rose and paced the back of the room.

* * *

Collin watched her from his chair. He glanced at Patricia, who signaled him to leave her alone. He hadn't realized how much talking about this would take everything out of her. She looked drained.

"I'm going out for some fresh air."

"I'll go with you." Collin rose.

Bekah turned. "No. Let me go alone. Just for a few minutes." Her eyes pleaded, then she whispered. "I'll be right back, promise." Then she left.

Collin stared at the closed door. When he turned to face Patricia, he sat, elbows on his knees and raked all ten fingers through his hair.

"You didn't realize, did you?" Patricia leaned forward in her chair.

Collin shook his head. "No. She'd hadn't opened up that much about him. I knew he had a lot of control over her, but...."

"She needs a little time. She'll be fine. I'm surprised she escaped so unscathed. And Collin, she needs to talk about this from time to time—perhaps some therapy if things go bad. Especially now since Matthew has decided to be a part of this child's life, she may have to learn to deal with it."

"But I want him out of the picture."

"That's what we'll shoot for, but that may not be possible. You have to understand one thing and then you are going to have to convince Bekah of this one thing also: Matthew is the biological father of her baby, and they were living together as a couple at the time of conception. She may have to give a little."

"Easier said than done."

"I realize that, but it may be a reality."

The door cracked and Bekah slipped inside. Collin rose and went to her. He touched her face and traced the wetness over each cheek. Their gazes danced off each other's. Collin watched Bekah's chest rise and then fall as she let out a long breath. His fingers threaded through her hair at the nape and tugged her closer. Their bodies touched, and a sob tore through Bekah's throat.

"Sh... Everything's going to be all right, honey," he crooned. "Everything's going to be fine."

Bekah lifted her tear-streaked face to his. "I wanted you to think I was so strong...."

Collin shook his head. "You *are* strong. You are a lot stronger than any woman I know...and a helluva lot stronger than I am. Bekah, what you've been through— I don't think I could do it."

She placed a finger on his lower lip. "But you did, don't you see. You did it. You've had to live the life your father wanted you to live. You've been living under the control of a dead man for years, and you survived. You made it out, Collin."

"Naw. I don't think so."

"You have more road to travel, and the trip's been long, but you've come a long way."

"So have you."

Bekah glanced away again. "But I fear the rough part is still to come."

Collin pushed back a strand of hair from her forehead. "But we'll get through it together. I'm not letting you go through this alone."

"Why is he doing this?"

Patricia stepped up behind them. "That's what I've been trying to figure out. Let's sit and see if we can make some sense of this." Patricia returned to her desk. Collin and Bekah sat back down across from her.

"Patricia, honestly, I've wracked my brain since last night trying to make some sense of it—and I can't."

"There's a reason," Patricia returned, "we just don't know it yet. There's always a reason."

Bekah shook her head. "This is so unlike him."

"Well, I tell you what, I've got a few more questions to ask, and then we'll call it a day. Sound all right?"

Bekah nodded.

Patricia's secretary interrupted them on the desk intercom. "A call for Mr. Kramer, Patricia." Patricia glanced across the desk at Collin.

"I told my secretary to call if it Vanlandingham contacted the office."

"Shall I put him on the speakerphone?"

Collin looked at Bekah. She shrugged her shoulders. "I think we need to agree on a couple of things first. How are we going to handle all this, Bekah? Do you want Patricia to handle it for you, as your liaison? Or do you want to be present for everything?"

Bekah exhaled. "I hadn't really thought about it." She turned to Patricia. "Can you do that?"

She nodded. "You have to trust me, though."

"But you won't do anything...won't commit to anything with him until you've discussed it thoroughly with me, right?"

"Absolutely."

Bekah looked again at Collin. "All right. Let Patricia handle it." She then turned back to Patricia. "But wait a few days to meet with him. I want him to stew. And I want you and I to talk some more."

Patricia agreed. "I think that's best. I'll put him on the phone. Collin, you answer." She pushed the speakerphone button and nodded to Collin.

"Kramer."

"It's Matthew Vanlandingham. I thought you said you'd be in your office."

"Had other plans. What do you want?"

Matthew paused on the other end. "I want to talk to Rebekah."

"She doesn't want to see or talk to you. All conversations will take place via her attorney. In fact, that's where I am right now. Would you like to set up an appointment?"

"I can be there in a few minutes."

"Whoa now. Wait a minute. I'll have to let you talk with Ms. Settle, Bekah's attorney. She makes her own appointments, and I can assure you, she's usually booked solid."

"I want this thing done. I'm due back in New York."

"As I said, you'll need to talk to her. Now, would you like to call back, or shall I see if she can take your call now."

Silence overtook the office. "Don't give me the run-around Kramer. I could buy and sell you."

"Really? An interesting thought. Now, about the appointment."

"She's there listening to this conversation, I'm sure. Let me speak to her."

Patricia rolled her eyes. "Mr. Vanlandingham? Patricia Settle here. I'm representing Rebekah McCauley and all your inquiries of her are to come to me through this office. Do you understand?"

"When is the appointment?"

"I asked you a question, Mr. Vanlandingham."

"Yes, I suppose you did. I understand."

"Good. Now, according to my calendar, I can meet with you on Thursday at one o'clock. How does that sound to you?"

"I need to be back in New York by Thursday."

"That's the soonest I can make it."

"I *can't* make it then. I have a business to run in New York."

"Then this little fiasco your pulling isn't quite as important as I originally thought, is it?"

Again, silence filled the room. "I'll be there."

"Good. We're on the corner of Lime and Vine. Settle and Blackburn. Any good cab driver can get you here, or I can have my assistant ring you back. And remember, you're not to make any contact with Ms. McCauley. Agreed?"

The line was still. Then they heard a reluctant, "Agreed."

The phone clicked on the other end of the line.

"He's lying."

"Shall we get a restraining order?"

Bekah shook her head. "No."

"He won't bother you Bekah, because I'm not going to let you out of my sight until he's gone."

"Before you go Bekah, there's one thing. Since this child isn't born yet, I think it's probably safe to say that there is no legal documentation anywhere linking Matthew's name and this child together. Would that be right?"

Bekah bounced a puzzled look back at her. "I don't think so. What do you mean?"

Patricia leaned back. "Well, in the state of Kentucky, one thing that is used to establish paternity are legal documents stating as such. For example, a birth certificate. Medical records. Welfare records."

"There's nothing like that."

"Good."

Bekah looked at Collin. He saw a small glimmer of hope in her eye.

"Just make sure that you don't sign anything—anything at all that would link Matthew with this child. If you should deliver tomorrow, don't put his name on the birth certificate. Oh, and by the way, we have time to deal with this problem. Matthew legally can't do anything until the baby is born, and anything he does then has to be done in the state of Kentucky. Jurisdiction happens in the state in which the child is born. There can't be any lawsuit drawn up that concerns a fetus, so he's really wasting his time, unless his goal is to play on your emotions. The other thing is, *if* he wants to establish paternity and *if* you continue to deny his paternity, nothing to be done until the child is six months old. The judge would order a blood test then, but they won't do it until the child is of that age. So, realizing that, understand that you have time to deal with this."

"But after that?"

"But after that, he could legally go along with everything he's threatening. And I must tell you, there are not many judges in the state of Kentucky that think any man off the street is going to claim paternity if he isn't the father. Kentucky has strict child-support laws. When a man makes that commitment, he's making an eighteen-year financial commitment. Frankly, most of the time we're trying to get the men who shirk their responsibilities; when a man comes forward and says he's the father, the judge usually assumes he is."

Collin shifted in his seat and looked from Bekah to Patricia. "So, the fight may come later rather than now."

Patricia nodded. "Yes."

Bekah leaned forward. "So, I don't put his name on the birth certificate. I don't put his name anywhere."

"No. And make sure that baby is born in Kentucky. Don't go out of state."

"I have no plans to do that." She turned to Collin. "Honestly, I won't run. I'm staying put."

"Good." Collin and Patricia both echoed her declaration.

* * *

Bekah slept the entire afternoon and into the evening. Collin insisted she rest, since she'd slept little the night before. In her condition, he didn't want any shock to her system, and without Bekah's knowledge he had contacted Dr. Benton just to apprise him of the situation and get his advice, which was to keep her as calm and rested as possible.

A little after seven that evening, Collin woke her for dinner. He'd prepared a tossed salad and warmed a leftover lasagna casserole from yesterday's meal at Bekah's parents. There was even cake left for dessert.

"Bekah," Collin whispered as he entered the darkened room. Her back was to him, she lay on her side facing the opposite wall. He stepped forward to the room and sat on the bed beside her. He reached out and touched her shoulder. "Time to get up."

She lay still. Collin's heart murmured against his chest. Was she all right? He inched closer to her. "Bekah?"

She turned then and reached out to him. Her arms pulled him down to her and as Collin's body made the ascent toward her, he saw the tears. He slid his body in close to hers and cradled her in his arms. "It's all right, darling."

Bekah shook her head against the sobs. "I hate being like this. I need to be strong. I need you to be strong with me."

"I'm here for you, baby. I'm not going anywhere."

"Are you Collin? You want me to cooperate with him, don't you?"

Collin rolled over onto his back and stared at the ceiling. "It's not that I want you to cooperate with him, I don't want you or the baby anywhere near that bastard, but according to Patricia, most judges are going to award him some privileges. He is the natural father, Bekah, and I'm afraid that eventually some judge down the road is going to award him visitation rights. I guess I'm just trying to prepare you."

Bekah sat up on the bed. "I'll lie. I won't put his name on the birth certificate. I'll tell the judge that he raped me, that we weren't living together. I'll lie, dammit. I don't want him near my baby." Her voice rose with each word.

"Bekah, calm down. I don't want you upset."

She rose off the bed and quickly paced the floor. "Calm down! How in the hell do you profess that I do that! The stinking bastard that ran my life for five years, the one that tried to force me into an abortion, is going to try to take my baby away from me, Collin. And I don't mean just for weekends. He's going to try and take my baby from me for good. And with his influence and his mother's money, he could probably damn well do it. I meant what I said this morning, Collin. If Matthew is awarded any rights to this child, I'll take the baby and run. Then Matthew or no one else will find me. I promise it."

Collin stared at her. His voice was soft, "You wouldn't do that Bekah."

"Like hell I wouldn't."

"I wouldn't let you go."

"You wouldn't have a choice."

Silence spread throughout the bedroom. Collin sat facing Bekah as she stood at the foot of the bed. The telephone shrilled through the room once and then twice. Neither moved, but on the third ring Bekah walked to the nightstand and picked it up.

"Hello," she said bluntly.

The feminine voice bounced back to her in a singsong manner. "Hello? Bekah, isn't it? My, my how I love that name. So country. How are you doing dear? Oh, this is Erin Kilpatrick."

"I know."

"Well, yes, I guess you do."

"What do you want?" Bekah was in no mood to mince words.

"Actually, sweetie, I was wondering if Collin was there? My pussycat is a little out of sorts—and he's so good with animals I thought...."

Bekah tossed the phone on the bed. "It's for you. I'm in no mood to deal with this." Collin watched as she left the room.

He picked up the phone. "Yeah?"

"Sugar?" Collin's stomach turned.

"What do you want."

"You."

"Forget it."

"Oh, baby cakes, aren't you tired of playing house with that little slut yet? I'm sure that fat little belly gets in the way sometimes. Wouldn't you rather come back to something lean and hard for a while?"

Collin shook his head, and then slammed the receiver back in its cradle.

"Bekah!" He shouted and ran out the bedroom. "Bekah? Where are you?" He rushed through house, not finding her, calling her name, then out the back door. Rounding the corner to the front of the house, he saw her; knees drawn up, arms wrapped around them, slowly swinging on the front porch swing. "Bekah," he whispered her name this time and walked to her.

Bekah looked up. Her face was dry now. "What did she want?"

"Nothing important."

"Not going to tell me huh?"

"No."

"You don't have to, I already know."

"Then why did you ask?" Collin sat down beside her. Bekah dropped her legs to let them dangle and scooted over. She pushed the swing back and forth with her feet.

"I just wanted to see if you'd tell me."

"What is this Bekah, some kind of a test?"

She faced him. "I just wanted to see if I could trust you to tell me the truth. You didn't tell me when she called before."

Collin's eyes narrowed at her. "I did not lie to you. I said it wasn't anything important. It wasn't. *She* isn't important. *You* are...and right now that's where I am and where I'll stay. With you."

Bekah planted her feet and stopped the swing. She gazed into his eyes. "Even if I do something you don't approve of?"

Collin swallowed hard. "Even if you do something I don't approve of. I'll always love you, Bekah. But please, just don't leave. You scare the living hell out of me when you talk about running away with the baby."

"I've thought about it. I couldn't tell you or anyone where I would go if I did it. It would be too risky. He'd find us."

"I don't like this."

"I don't like it either. I don't want to leave you, Collin. I love you. But this baby... I can't let him have my baby."

Collin dropped his head in his hands. "Bekah, don't do anything foolish. I honestly respect your rights and any decision you'd make, but I'm begging you, don't do anything rash until you talk to me. Please. I have this fear of you leaving out of here unexpectedly with the baby and never seeing you again."

Bekah touched his face with her fingertips. "I wouldn't do that to you," she said softly.

"Promise?"

She nodded. "I promise."

Chapter Eighteen

When the phone shrilled in his ear two hours later, Collin woke as if in a trance. He reached for the receiver, knocking it off the stand, and then retrieved it over the side of the bed. He fumbled it, and then groggily answered it.

"Hey boss, you better get over here." It was Pete.

Collin blinked to clear his mind, then glanced to Bekah. "What is it Pete?"

"It's the stallion."

Silence. "What's wrong with him?" Collin sat up straight and focused his gaze out the window and across the field to his farm. He saw a light burning through the trees. Bekah rose on an elbow, watching him.

"I think you need to get over here."

"Dammit, Pete, what's going on? Tell me." He was getting angry.

Again, a moment of silence. "He's dead."

"Dead! What the hell? How?"

Bekah gasped. "Who's dead?"

"I'll be right there." Collin slowly returned the receiver and then looked again to Bekah. "The gray is dead. My stallion, Lord Greystoke, he's dead."

Bekah sat up and moved closer to Collin. He sat down on the edge of the bed. She put her arms around him from behind. "Was he one poisoned a few days ago?"

Collin shook his head.

"Then what?"

Collin rose. He had to get over there and he really didn't want to tell Bekah that someone had slit the horse's jugular—at least not now. "That's what I'm going to find out." He pulled on a pair of jeans and a shirt, his socks, and boots. As he belted his pants, he told her, "Stay here. There's nothing you can do. I'll be back soon."

Collin bent over and kissed her lightly on the lips, then left.

* * *

Bekah sat straight up in the bed and glanced about. How long had she slept after Collin left? Seemed like only a few minutes. But something woke her. Dog barking? She stilled and listened, and then sank back into her pillows.

She must be mistaken. Everything seemed normal. Appeared fine. Maybe Collin was back? She listened for signs of him wandering around in the kitchen but heard none. Silence screamed back. But something *had* woken her.

There! Her ears strained against the too still night. Bekah glanced at the clock. She'd dozed for maybe forty-five minutes. Not long. She rose, her ears straining for the sound again as she slowly walked around the bed. Then just as she heard it again, louder this time—and closer—she saw it.

Hurrying across the room, she stared out the window. A wicked blaze licked high into the black night across the pasture.

Red flashing lights moved off the main road and up the hill toward Collin's home.

No. The barn was on fire!

The shriek of a siren suddenly pierced the silence. And suddenly she could smell the smoke.

Bekah ripped the gown from her body and pulled on a T-shirt and a pair of her grandfather's old bib-overalls. The smoke thickened, even in her room, almost choking her. She slipped her toes into a pair of canvas tennis shoes and rushed across the bedroom. The doorknob nearly seared her hand. She then saw the smoke wafting out from under the door.

My God! My house is on fire!

Bekah turned and searched for something, anything, to stuff under the door to keep the smoke out. Jerking the bedspread off the bed, she hurriedly stuffed what she could under the crack. Then rushing to the window, Bekah hit and slammed the palm of her hand onto the rusted window latch, trying to open it so she could escape. *Thank God Collin moved this bedroom to the first floor!*

It wouldn't budge. Taking a deep breath, she tried again, bludgeoning the latch with her palm as the perspiration beaded from her forehead. Quick gasps escaped her throat, and she realized she was doing nothing more than beating her hand to a bloody pulp. She glanced to the other window with the air conditioner. Coughing, she ran to it. The upper window slid open easily and with a huge push, Bekah shoved the air conditioner out of the window. She screamed in triumph.

It was all she could do to haul her eight months pregnant body up and out of the window, but she did, then walked approximately twenty yards away from the house when dizziness gripped her, and she collapsed in the grass's cool morning dew.

* * *

Just when he thought the night was over—as he sat exhausted, with Pete and the vet discussing the past week's occurrences, Collin realized the night's hell had only just begun.

At the sound of the word *fire!* everyone leaped to their feet. Sitting within ten yards of the barn, they hadn't noticed a thing until an early rising stable hand discovered the small blaze in the loft. Within seconds Collin, Pete, and the vet flew into the barn.

"Damnation! When is this going to end?" Collin shouted as they entered the barn. The stable hand beat at the flame with a horse blanket, embers flying. "Get the horses!" he yelled. Everyone scrambled.

Collin ran to the rear of the barn. He grabbed another blanket from an open stall. "Go for water!" he yelled to the stable hand. "And get help. Call 9-1-1. I'll take over here."

The boy ran from the barn. Collin watched as body disappear into the growing wall of smoke. He turned back to the blaze and beat at it until his arms ached, and his lungs bursting from lack of oxygen that didn't burn when it when down.

But he wouldn't stop.

Horses nickered frantically behind him. Pete and the vet shouted, trying to lead the horses to safety. In front of Collin, the blaze grew, and he realized that no amount of effort was going to put the flame down. He coughed and his chest seized, aching to explode. A searing pain ripped through him. He needed air.

Someone pulled at his arm.

"Get out of here, Boss!" *Pete. Pete was pulling him away.*

Collin took a few steps backward and watched in wonder as the fire took hold and in a matter of seconds flashed over his head across the loft.

"*Run!*"

Collin shook his head. Pete pulled at him. He was groggy and disoriented. But Pete kept shouting at him to run. So he did. When they burst through the inferno, the blast of cool morning air hit him like a winter snowstorm. His lungs gasped in defiance of the extreme temperature change. Collin stumbled away from the barn's opening. The siren ripped through the night and immediately the fire trucks were upon them. Within seconds, there was water on the blaze, and within minutes, the barn was destroyed.

Collin, breathing easier now—his head and lungs clear of the smoke—stood in awe at the nearly leveled structure. A few moments earlier, they'd stood there discussing the killing of his horse, and the poisoning, and the mutilation of his hound. Now this. When *would* it all stop?

"Ah hell!"

The tone of Pete's voice frightened Collin. He looked at the older man and followed the direction of his gaze.

"Bekah!" Horror ripped at his gut.

* * *

As he ran, Collin's breathing came in short, shallow breaths. Each inhale ripped through his lungs. His eyes stung, from smoke or fear, he knew not which. His heart pounded against his chest, and his pulse beat a crescendo in his eardrum. His feet hit the ground methodically, one in front of the other as in a pattern, a rhythm. It was the only way he could keep going.

Focused on the burning house in front of him, Collin ran. Flames licked skyward from the second-story window. The nursery. His legs picked up their cadence and with every step, he uttered a prayer that Bekah was safe. That she'd gotten out. That she was alive. His eyes stung again, and not from smoke.

243

He didn't hear the truck pull up beside him. Didn't hear Pete bellow at him until he nearly had to run the truck into him. "Get *in* you stupid bastard! I'm too old to chase you!"

Collin did.

They barreled through the last fence with the four-wheel-drive pickup truck like a knife slicing through warm butter. They pulled up as close to the house as they could get and parked. Within seconds, Collin raced for the house with Pete on his heels.

"Don't go in there!" Pete shouted to him. From where they stood, the heat was unbearable. He was unsure what he would do.

Collin stopped at the side porch and turned. "I have to!" His brain scrambled, thoughts incoherent, except for the need to get to Bekah. He raced up onto the porch. Smoke poured out around the doorframe and the windows on the lower floor. He turned back to Pete. "I've got to get her!"

"Collin!" The shout came from the barn. Both men turned. Bekah stood there wrapped in an old blanket.

As the fire truck pulled up behind Pete, Collin rushed forward, his leaden legs carrying him toward her. With each step, he grew both stronger and weaker. His heartbeat with strength. His body was about to give out. But he finally took her into his arms, clasped her to him, never so happy to have her close.

Sighing, he touched the back of her hair softly, and brushed a few stray strands away from her temple. "I thought I lost you," he hissed.

Bekah turned her face up to meet his gaze. Her frightened, doe-like eyes told him all he needed to know, and he was sure his expression held the same message to her. She grabbed for him and held on. "Thank God," she said. "Thank you, God.

* * *

They huddled in the truck's cab. Bekah curled into Collin, her head resting in the crook made between his neck and shoulder. She held him tight around the waist, and in turn, Collin cradled her close, caressing her face and neck, cradling her bloody hand.

The paramedics checked them over briefly, administered first aid to Bekah's palm, and insisted they both go to the hospital for further examination. Collin was relieved that Bekah quickly agreed. They arrived before Dr. Benton, who examined her and found her okay. They bandaged her hand, and gave her a mild sedative, with strict orders to rest for the next few days.

Three hours later they pulled into Collin's circular drive, the hint of dawn rising with the sun. Pete pulled up to the house alongside them. Collin carried a sleeping Bekah up the front porch steps, through the wide entry, and upstairs to his bedroom. He carefully lay her on his bed, and then stripped her of her smoky clothing.

Bekah moaned softly in her sleep as Collin removed her T-shirt. With a cool, damp washcloth, he wiped away the dark smudges of smoke around her face and neck. He watched her peaceful sleep, devoid of the terror earlier that evening. His gaze tracked lower to her rounded abdomen, heavy with child now that the end of the pregnancy was near. Bekah had still retained the dip in her waist, Collin thought as his hand rested there, and the slightly rounded hips, perhaps a little broader than before, still seemed perfect to him.

He angered a little as he remembered how Matthew had commented about how she looked. *Bastard.*

His breathing labored, he looked at her there. His eyes stung. His throat constricted. *He'd almost lost her.*

Collin stood and stepped across the bedroom to the adjoining bathroom. Quickly he removed his own clothing and showered the smoke and ashes from his body. Inhaling the steam seemed to cleanse his lungs of the acrid, burning taste that accompanied each breath. When he was finished, he thoroughly dried his body, then without clothing, crept into bed beside Bekah and held her tight against him for the rest of the night.

Chapter Nineteen

"I haven't a damn clue, Tom. I wish I knew."

Collin paced his study in front of Tom McKenney, the Woodford County Sheriff, his fingers threading wildly through his hair. "If I knew who was responsible for this nonsense, I would have been at them long before this."

McKenney rubbed his chin and watched Collin. "This isn't the first incident?"

Collin stopped pacing and looked him square in the eye. "Six months ago, Sheriff, you stood in this very room and took a report of vandalism when my hounds were cut loose. At that time, you claimed it was an isolated incident. Then someone crowbarred the locks off one of the paddock gates. *Another* isolated incident, you said. I stopped reporting them after that. A hell of a lot of good it did me."

McKenney narrowed his eyes at Collin. "All right. You've got a valid point. What else has been happening?"

Collin exhaled and shook his head. "I don't know what good it will do—look, I've lost a prized hound to an idiot who left it ripped from throat to gut on Bekah's doorstep. I've lost my best horse because someone slit his jugular, not to mention the others that were poisoned. And now I've lost my barn. I know damn well *that* wasn't an accident."

"It wasn't."

"Arson?"

McKenney nodded. "Both of them, we suspect. The fire marshal speculates that's the case, but we'll wait on the report. There was evidence of gasoline residue at both places. Someone wanted that barn and Bekah's house leveled."

"Well, they got their wish." Collin shuddered, then stalked toward a window and stared between the panes to the smoldering ashes of what was left of his barn. Just across the pasture, the same picture repeated at Bekah's house. He'd lost two other horses that night besides the gray. Pete just couldn't get them out in time. He then turned his gaze back to the sheriff. "What are you going to do?"

He shrugged. "The usual. File a report, put a couple of men on it, and keep on the fire marshal's office to keep us informed. Eventually someone will talk. People who do this type of thing can't sit on it for long. Sooner or later, they blow it. We'll find them."

The sheriff turned toward the door and then back again quickly. "One more thing. I'm a little concerned about Ms. McCauley's involvement in all this. It was one thing when these acts of vandalism were aimed only at you, but twice now, she has been included. I'd stick close to her if I were you. And we're going to keep a man on this place round the clock for a while. I don't mind telling you this whole situation makes me a little uneasy."

Collin closed his eyes. "You're not the only one." He opened them when Tom McKenney left the room.

Collin sat behind his desk, his head in his hands. With the tips of his fingers, he massaged his aching temples, and across the bridge of his nose. He'd slept for a few hours, but it wasn't enough. Inhaling all that smoke had left him with a painful headache. Besides, sleeping was difficult these days. Things happened, and he wasn't about to let anything else bad happen —to him, or to Bekah.

"Collin?" He glanced up. Bekah's voice came to him sweet and soft. Collin fully lifted his gaze to watch her moving across the room toward him. He smiled.

"Bekah..." He rose and rounded the desk, taking her hand.

"You let me sleep too long."

Her pretty face smiled up at him. Thank God she'd gotten out of that fire... "You needed the rest. Dr. Benton told me to make sure you stayed in bed for a few days. I'm sure you don't remember because you were so groggy." He pulled her closer. As their bodies touched, he exhaled heavily into her hair. "God Bekah. I love you so much."

* * *

Bekah wrapped both arms around Collin. One hand rested at the base of his skull and fiddled with a lock of his hair. The other caressed his backbone. Her cheek pressed against his chest and she relished in the warmth and power there. "I love you," she whispered. "Collin, when is all this going to stop?"

He shook his head. "I don't know, darling. Soon, I hope."

"I lost it all, do you realize that?"

A shimmer of panic shot through him. "I know. I'm so sorry, darling."

"All my grandparent's things. Everything they worked for all their lives. All my paintings. The nursery." She sniffled.

Collin framed her face with his hands. "We can replace some of those things. Some we can't. But I can't replace you, sweetheart. I thought I'd lost you."

"Oh God, Collin. I thought I'd lost you." Her arms squeezed

his neck. "I don't think I could have survived that." She jerked back quickly. "My parents! They'll be frantic. I have to...."

"Shush. I've already taken care of that. Joe called them last night, told them what happened, and assured them that you and the baby were all right. In fact, your mother and father and both brothers were over here this morning looking over the mess. They wanted to let you sleep. I told them to come back later this evening."

Bekah breathed a sigh of relief. "Thank you."

Collin's lips brushed hers. "You're welcome."

Bekah turned her head to look out the window. "Was that Tom McKenney I saw leaving?"

Collin nodded and pulled away a little. He sat back on the desk and pulled her to him, his legs straddled her body. "He's finally going to investigate. And Bekah, he and I are both concerned about your safety. You've been involved in this twice now. I won't risk a third time. He's having the house watched twenty-four-seven, but I really haven't had a chance to ask you if this is where you want to stay. Would you be more comfortable with your parents?"

Bekah stared at him. "No, of course not. I want to be with you. I have to be here with you, Collin. You do want me, don't you?"

"Of course, I do. It's just that with this thing with Matthew, I didn't want you to think I was taking over or anything. I wanted you to have the choice."

A grin played across her lips. One finger touched the dimple in his chin. "Collin, I've resolved a lot of this Matthew stuff. I don't feel the same way with you as I did with him. It's different. And I want to be here with you."

He pulled her closer and smiled. "Let's get married."

Bekah blinked and smiled back. "What? When?"

"Now. Yesterday. Tomorrow. Whenever you say."

Bekah looked past him and chewed on her lower lip. She took in a long breath and let it out very slowly. "Collin, I think we have to wait. There's so much going on right now."

"That's why we need to do it now, don't you see? We need each other through all this."

"We *have* each other, Collin. We don't need the marriage certificate for that. I just think there are too many unresolved things going on in our lives and they need to be settled before we think about marriage." She took his face into her hands. "I love you, and before we begin our lives together as husband and wife, I want all this other nonsense out of the way. I don't want to look back on the beginning of our marriage and think about poisonings and barn fires and Matthew. And Collin? I want you to seriously think about where your life is leading you and what will make you happy."

"*You* make me happy."

She grinned. "I know that, but that's not what I'm talking about. There are other things you need to resolve."

"You still want me to think about school."

"I want you to consider it."

"And I want you to think about how you're going to deal with the Matthew situation."

She stared at him. "I think about that every, single day, Collin. It's never far from my mind."

Collin rolled his head backward and looked to the ceiling. His eyes closed for a moment. Then he tilted his gaze back to hers. "There *is* a lot of junk out there to be settled, isn't there?"

"Yes."

"Then I guess you're right. We postpone this marriage conversation until a later date. But I'm warning you, Bekah McCauley, I'm not willing to postpone it for long."

Chapter Twenty

"Clearly, he doesn't have a leg to stand on."

Patricia Settle leaned back in her soft leather chair and smiled across her desk at Bekah and Collin, that next Thursday afternoon.

"What were the demands?" Bekah leaned forward.

"Ridiculous is what they were. Obviously, he has had no legal advice, at least not someone who knows Kentucky law. He left in quite a huff. I think he was heading to the airport."

Bekah's shoulders sagged. She looked at Collin. "Do you think he's gone for good?"

Patricia quickly responded, "No. I think he's gone for bigger guns."

Bekah jerked. "Why do you say that?"

"Well, I'll tell you why. He was none too happy when he left and threatened to be back with a roomful of attorneys."

Collin shifted in his chair. "What exactly did he want, Patricia? And what did you tell him?"

She glanced back and forth between the two of them. "I simply told him the truth. He came in here demanding parental rights, and thus and such, and I calmly told him the way it was. I told him my client did not acknowledge him as the father of her baby. He then blew up. He started spouting about blood tests, so I quickly told him again that my client would not have her child tested unless ordered to do so by a judge. He was quick to jump on that, and then I told him the baby, by law, had to be at least six months old to participate in a paternity test. He didn't like that either. He's a man who wants immediate action, isn't he?"

Bekah nodded. "Anything else?"

Patricia swallowed. "I'm afraid so. He said he wanted you to have an ultrasound and he wanted to be made aware of the results of that test."

Bekah shot a puzzled look at Collin.

"That's ridiculous," Collin said.

"That's what I told him. His reasoning? To make sure his baby was developing normally. He wanted the name of your doctor, too. I politely reminded him that the two of you are not married, and that you do not acknowledge him as the father of your child, and that he has no rights to that information."

"Good." Collin straightened up in his chair. "This guy's getting on my nerves."

Bekah looked from Collin to Patricia. "What else?"

One corner of Patricia's mouth drew down. "He's going to try to make you look bad, Bekah. Along with the ultrasound, he wanted to have you tested for STDs and other communicable diseases."

Collin stood up and pounded the desk. "That's enough. When I get my hands on that fucking bastard...."

Bekah shifted in her seat. "Collin, sit down. That's just Matthew's way of trying to make everything come out his way. He's trying to humiliate me and make me feel inferior by suggesting these things. Forget it, they mean nothing. Right, Patricia?"

"Right. I put it back to him good, again reminding him

that he has no rights. You two are not married and so his demands are pointless. When he left, he was quite angry. We've bought ourselves some time. Time to come up with a decent plan of action, but eventually, we're going to have to face the battle head on. You do realize that, don't you, Bekah?"

Bekah closed her eyes and nodded.

"Just one other thing, Bekah. Do you mind if I put a private investigator on this case? I'd like him to do a little research on Mr. Vanlandingham. I haven't quite figured out his motivation, and I think whatever it is, may be a key element in figuring all this mess out."

Bekah looked to Collin, and he nodded to Patricia. "By all means. Do it and don't be concerned with the expense. Nail the bastard."

* * *

Later that evening, Bekah surveyed the mess in front of her that once represented her grandparent's life work. Collin, who had lost some records in the fire, decided to spend a couple hours at the office trying to retrieve information and make new files from the office's computer database. She stood alone, sifting through the debris on the outer fringes of the disheveled house. With the aid of the gasoline, the fire had spread much too quickly, sparing nothing in its wake.

Bekah bent to pick up a shiny piece of metal reflecting the last of the sun's rays. As she wiped the ashes away, her fingers revealed a small metal frame. Her thoughts jumped back to another time, when she was a child. The frame held a sacred place on her grandmother's dresser. She remembered asking her grandmother once about the wedding portrait and she and her grandmother had sat on the high four-poster bed for a while, and Bekah listened to the story of her grandparents' wedding day.

Bekah looked to the west and the setting sun as she crouched there. Her grandmother had told the story millions of times. Every grandchild heard it repeatedly, but Bekah loved it. The story of the wedding that almost never was. The story of the life together that was meant to be. Between World War II and her grandmother's strict father, the wedding almost didn't take place, but when her grandmother threatened to run away, Bekah's great-grandfather reneged. They married the night before her grandfather caught a bus to boot camp. After two years of separation, they were back together and never apart from that day forward.

Bekah shook away the feelings of melancholy and rose, dusting the frame of its ashes. She turned the piece over. The back was gone, partially charred and burned, and the picture of course was long gone too. Only the memories remained. She turned to her truck as she noticed another pickup coming up the driveway and smiled when she realized that Michael was behind the wheel.

Jumping out of the truck, he sidled close to her and threw his arms around her. "You doing okay?" He spoke softly in her ear.

She nodded. "I'm doing fine."

They separated and then with one arm still draped around her shoulder, walked back to what was left of the burned structure. "Sure did a job of it didn't they?"

Bekah looked up at her older brother's profile. "I don't know why though. It seems like such a waste."

"It is." He looked down at her. "Bekah, I'm worried about you. So is Mama and Daddy. Why don't you come home with me?"

She shook her head. "No, I'm fine. Collin is around most all the time now. When he's not, Pete is here. And they have a deputy covering the house at all times."

Michael looked back across the ashes. "I don't understand all this. Can you explain it to me?"

"I'm not sure if I understand it all either, Michael. We don't know who is responsible for this stuff or why. At first, Collin thought someone around here was trying to get back at him. When he first moved here, he had kind of a bossy, arrogant, know-it-all kind of attitude that people around here utterly disliked. Not to mention that he ruined a couple of tobacco beds and tore up some fences while foxhunting. Anyway, little things started happening, then suddenly in the last two or three weeks, big things started happening. I'm not sure how I got mixed up in all this unless it just has to do with Collin and I living together, and *someone* doesn't like that."

"Do you feel safe?"

"I feel perfectly safe."

He tilted his head at her. "How's this thing with Matthew?"

Bekah breathed deeply. "I don't know. My attorney met with him. We denied everything, which technically is lying, I know, but Michael, I can't let him have any contact with my child."

"Of course, you can't."

"You believe me?"

He smiled. "You know I do, sis." His gaze dropped to her hands. He took the charred frame out of her hands then looked back into her eyes. "The wedding portrait."

"Uh-huh."

"It was a wonderful story wasn't it?"

"They had a wonderful life together."

Michael tilted her chin up with two fingers. "You'll have a wonderful life together with Collin. I know it. It may start out

257

rocky, like our grandparents—it may even seem like it's never going to happen—but it will Bekah. I'm sure of it."

She looked into his warm brown eyes and smiled. "I love you, big brother."

Both heads turned at the play of lights over the dusky horizon. They watched as the approaching vehicle inched its way up the drive, slowed, and then stopped. Bekah reached over and took Michael's hand. Her heart jumped at the sight of the black Buick. "It's Matthew," she whispered. Michael gave a little start and Bekah pulled him back. "It's okay. I'll handle it."

The driver's side door opened. Matthew slowly stepped out and shut the door behind him. He stood a few yards away from them and for several seconds just stared.

"You seem to keep them on a string, Bekah. Who's the brute?"

She ignored him. Michael hedged forward, but she squeezed his hand and held him back. "What are you doing here, Matthew? I thought you'd gone back to New York."

One foot stepped in front of the other for several paces. He drew nearer to them both.

"I'm leaving in the morning. I wanted to see you."

"I'm not interested in talking to you."

Matthew stepped forward once more, but Michael counter-stepped and slid slightly in front of Bekah. "That's far enough," he said.

Matthew glared. "It's not going to work, you know, this little scheme of yours? Denying my paternity rights will not sit well with my attorneys or me. You know I'll fight you every step of the way. I *will* get custody of this child."

Bekah stepped around Michael, who placed a protective arm around her waist. "Let me let you in on a little secret, Matthew, I really don't know if you're the father of this child or not. I was having an affair at the time I got pregnant."

Matthew laughed.

Michael's fingers dug into her waist. She continued. "In fact, there were several affairs. You just weren't doing it for me sexually any longer. I know, the truth hurts, doesn't it? The father could be anyone. And that's what I intend to tell the judge."

Matthew's face fell and his gaze narrowed. "You won't do that, Rebekah. For one, you don't lie well, and for two, that would make you a slut and everyone knows that judges don't award sluts custody of their children."

Michael rounded his sister and stepped into Matthew's space. "Okay, that's enough. I'm out of here." He began walking him backward toward his car. "Time for you to leave."

Matthew's complexion paled as he struggled against Bekah's muscle-bound brother, but to no avail. When he backed up against the Buick, he said. "You can add assault to the list, Rebekah," he said in a shaky voice, then opened the door and sat in the car.

Bekah shouted. "And you can add contempt of court. You were told not to come here."

Matthew glared out the window. "Judges give orders, Rebekah, not attorneys. There's nothing to keep me from you."

"Not yet." Bekah hissed the words.

Michael leaned into the car window. "And there's nothing to keep me from smashing your face in either. Tattle if you want, I'll only deny it. We'll see who the fool is then."

Matthew started the ignition, staring at Michael, turned the car around, and sped out of the drive.

Turning to his sister, Michael said, "Let's get you home and into the safety of that house over there—or I'm taking you home with me. I don't like the looks of things around here."

Bekah, almost frightened at her brother's words, agreed. "All right." She didn't like the looks of things much, either.

* * *

"What do you mean you're going to take matters into your own hands?"

Bekah glared over the breakfast table at Collin the next morning. She watched as he sipped his coffee and looked at her. "Collin, this is ridiculous. It's only been a week. You've got to give them some time."

"They will not do anything, Bekah. Half of that sheriff's department is made up of good old boys. Hell, the other half live down here. Somebody wants me out and if the sheriff will not find out who, then I am. I'm tired of waiting around for him to act."

"That's vigilantism."

"That's called taking care of your own skin. And yours. I don't want you hurt again."

Bekah stared at him. "I still don't think it's anyone around here, Collin. It could be Matthew. It could be anyone. Don't go accusing people, I'm warning you. You have to be awfully damn sure about what you're doing because...."

His head jerked back. "Because what?"

She shook her head. "Nothing."

"Go ahead and say it, Bekah. Because these people some-times take matters in *their* own hands? Isn't that what you were going to say. Isn't *that* vigilantism? I'm not going to go out and murder anyone Bekah, I just want to sort this out."

"I know. I just don't want you getting hurt in the process. And these people down here, they're like family to me."

"Families don't burn down each other's homes, Bekah. Besides, you've been talking about doing a similar thing your-self, haven't you?"

Bekah rose and walked to the coffeepot, refilling her cup. "What are you talking about?"

"You know perfectly well what I'm talking about. Running away."

"That's different." She turned away and looked out the window. Much different.

"How?"

Her gaze fixed on her burned-out house across the pasture. "Because I would save my child's life. I would do anything to protect my baby."

"And I would do anything to protect you. I fail to see the difference."

She turned back to make eye contact. "There's a big difference. You don't have any concrete evidence that what's happened in the past few weeks will ever happen again. I *know* that if Matthew got his hooks into this child he would ruin the child's life. A child couldn't survive in that environment, Collin. I was strong and I was almost destroyed. *That's* the difference."

"I never took you for a coward, Bekah."

His words stung. After all she'd been through? *A coward?* "You think I'm a coward?" Bekah set her coffee cup on the table with a splash and glared.

"A coward runs, Bekah. Why don't you stay and fight. You might win."

"I wouldn't win. You and Patricia have both tried to prepare me for that. Each of you has said repeatedly that it may come down to my cooperation and that I'm going to have to face some type of visitation agreement. I've already decided, Collin, Matthew is getting none of this child. Not one minute. It will come down to the day I'll have to leave, I'm sure of it."

Collin's voice quivered. "Please don't talk this way, Bekah."

She angled her body toward his. "Look, Collin, I promised you that I would talk to you and tell you what I was thinking. I'm telling you now. After the baby is born, if this thing gets sticky with Matthew, I *will* run and hide. I don't want to leave you, but I will have to do it to save my child—not me—but my child."

"I'll go with you." Collin sat and stared at her across the table. "I won't let you leave me."

"I can't let you give up all this for me."

"You wouldn't be letting me. It would be my choice."

Bekah bit her lip. "No."

He rose and stepped closer to her. "No?"

"It would ruin your life."

"It would ruin my life to be away from you."

Bekah stepped back. "Collin, I can't let you go with me. If you keep talking like that, I'll leave without telling you."

Collin looked stunned. "You wouldn't do that to me, Bekah."

She nodded tearfully, but slightly angry with him for forcing her hand on this issue. "I would. Because I love you and I won't ask you to give up your life for me."

Collin turned and pounded the table. "My God, Bekah! You can't go running off to who knows where all alone. You need me."

"No. I don't, Collin," she shouted back. "I can take care of myself. I *have* to take care of myself. And I will do this on my own. I'm an independent woman now. I can handle it."

"Oh c'mon, Bekah. Get off this independence thing. I'm not Matthew. I'm not trying to control your every move. I love you, damn it, and hate to even think about you ruining your life this way."

"Ruining it? No, Collin, I would be lonely, yes... And I would miss you terribly and probably sometimes doubt why I did it, but I'd be saving a child's life, and that right now is what is important to me."

Collin hung his head. "Then I guess if you're determined to do this, I really don't want to know when." He strode forcefully across the kitchen floor and Bekah knew he was angry with her. She couldn't help that. She had to be true to herself. "Forget the promise, Bekah," he added. "*Don't* tell me about it. I don't want to know." He clasped the door handle.

Bekah stared after him. "Is that what you really want?"

He halted and turned. "Yes. And I don't want to talk about it anymore. If you're going to do it, just don't tell me." Then he paused, thinking. "Bekah look, there's something I need to tell you."

She crossed her arms and waited.

"I know this isn't the ideal time, but I have to go out of town today. There's a claim being settled on a thoroughbred in Louisiana. It's a difficult case. I'm leaving on the ten o'clock flight. I won't be back until around six tomorrow evening. I've informed the deputy watching the house and Pete. You'll be okay."

"Why didn't you tell me this when you came in last night?"

"I guess the same reason you waited until this morning to tell me about Matthew. We were both sleepy and exhausted. Look, Bekah, I don't want to leave you on such a sour note. I've got an hour and a half to get ready and get to the airport."

"Then I guess you better get a move on." She gripped her elbows tighter and wondered if it was an attempt to keep herself together—because inside, she was falling apart.

Collin looked at her. "Yeah, I guess I better."

Bekah stewed the entire time Collin showered and packed a small bag for his trip. They'd argued, yes, and she'd been angry with him, but she loved him. It hurt her terribly to think about leaving him, and she knew she'd hurt him when she spoke of it, but if it came down to leaving, that was exactly what she'd have to do. And if talking about it was not what he wanted, she wouldn't do that anymore either. When it came time for her to go, she'd leave. And maybe it would be better for her to do it when he least expected it, not to drag it out for either of them. Maybe.

For several minutes she sat in the den, listening to him prepare for his trip. For several minutes she contemplated going to him, then finally she rose and silently flew up the flight of stairs and down the hall to his—no, their—bedroom. Bekah stood in the doorframe for a few seconds before he sensed her there, and when he did, slowly turned until their gazes met.

Bekah's chest heaved with a sudden influx of air, and fell as she slowly exhaled. He faced her fully and the invitation of his eyes sent her heart jumping in her chest, beating a tattoo against her breastbone that was almost painful. She saw his hand flinch, as if he wanted to reach out to touch her but was unsure of her reaction. Then involuntarily, her feet lead her body to him, and they embraced.

As Collin's arms drew tight around her, Bekah absorbed his heave sigh. "Don't leave me, Bekah. Oh God, please don't leave me."

She closed her eyes and held him closer. "I'm here, Collin. I'm right here," she whispered. "I love you...so much. I love you." *I don't want to hurt you, Collin. Please, forgive me for whatever happens next.*

* * *

At ten-fifteen Bekah glanced at her watch and sucked in a bit of a panicky breath, realizing Collin was now airborne and she wouldn't see him again until late tomorrow. It was the first time they'd been apart for this long, in their few short months together. Bekah wasn't looking forward to spending the night alone.

Her back ached and the stress of the past week had exhausted her. Even though it was still morning, she felt drained

—physically and emotionally. "Maybe a nap is what I need. I've nothing better to do."

She climbed the stairs a little slower than she did earlier that morning, placing a hand on top of each hip. Up until now, she'd been able to carry on her normal duties during the pregnancy, but suddenly her body seemed to weigh her down, and she was achy all over. The bed was inviting, but as soon as she positioned and propped herself to her liking, the phone rang.

She reached for it. "Hello?"

"Bekah, this is Patricia Settle."

"Hi, Patricia." Bekah wiggled her lower back down against the firm mattress.

"Heard you had a visitor yesterday."

"Yes, how did you know?"

"Collin called me from the airport. Are you doing all right there alone?"

"I'm fine Patricia. Collin has a fortress around me. Nothing's getting through here."

"Good. Bekah, I have a question."

"All right." Now she was uncomfortable again. She tried rolling over onto her side.

"What do you know about The Harper Corporation?"

Bekah was silent for a second. "Harper? I used to work for them."

Now Patricia was silent. "You did?"

"I was an art editor for *County by Design* magazine. It was one of their publications."

"Oh, well then, I guess my news isn't really much news to you then."

"What are you talking about, Patricia?"

"Bekah, do you know who Maxwell Harper was?"

"Sure, he owns Harper Corporation. He signed my checks."

"Signed? Bekah, he's been dead for twenty years. He never

signed your checks at all. His daughter is now running the corporation. His grandson is next in line, it seems. You do know who his grandson is, don't you?"

"Patricia, I'm not sure I'm following you."

"All right. Maxwell Harper, the magazine mogul, has a daughter by the name of Arlena Vanlandingham. Her son is Matthew Vanlandingham. Apparently, they share in the controlling interest of The Harper Corporation. They owned the magazine you worked for. Matthew signed your checks, Bekah."

Bekah sucked in a sharp breath and hissed its release. "Wow, Patricia. I suspected Matthew was influential in getting the job for me, but I never suspected it was his company. Why would he keep all this a secret from me?"

"That's what I've been trying to figure out. For some reason, he didn't want you involved too deep in the company. Maybe he didn't think you needed to know—men like him like to operate on a *need-to-know* basis. Especially with women. He only wanted you to know what he wanted you to know. Maybe he didn't want to share in the pie—maybe that's why he never wanted to get married."

Bekah suddenly recalled the conversations, if you want to call them that, about marriage. It was just like having a baby—it wasn't for them, he told her. He wanted to keep things uncluttered, and if necessary, open.

Bekah wondered just how *open* their relationship truly was.

"You may have something there, Patricia, but if he didn't want to share in the pie, then why does he want parental rights to the baby? Wouldn't his child somehow be an heir to all that too? Wouldn't he have to share? Wouldn't he *not* want me, or this child around? I need to think about this. I'm just not sure if it's significant or not. You'll let me know if there's any other news?"

"Of course, Bekah. But honestly, I think the opposite of what you are thinking is true. If the child you are carrying is his, he wants to keep the wealth in the family. Wants to keep the child close—and he doesn't want you involved. But listen, don't wrack your brain with this now. Think about how we might be able to use this information. It may be more significant than we know."

Bekah thought for a moment. "Patricia? Something just occurred to me. Can your PI get a list of the major stockholders in Harper?"

"Possibly, he's still in New York."

"Good, see if you can find him and tell him to get it, and any information he can find out on any of them, personal and business. And see if he can do it quickly."

Patricia paused on the other end. "Bekah, what are you thinking?"

"I don't know yet. Speculation, but could be something. Just get me that information."

Chapter Twenty-One

Bekah glanced nervously at her watch. Since the call came from Patricia thirty minutes ago, with the information she wanted from the private investigator, she'd done nothing more than rest and think. Why Mathew kept his business identity a secret from her was a mystery, but she was more interested in what she needed to do next. Her mind whirled with activity, and before long, she'd formed a plan. One that might possibly rid her of Matthew for the rest of her, and her child's lives, forever. If she could pull it off, she was sure of it. If she failed, she was risking everything. But she had to do it. And now that she had clarity, Bekah realized that it couldn't be put off any longer.

They would settle his thing with Matthew by nightfall.

She reached to the nightstand drawer and pulled out the phone book, searching for a travel agent. As she dialed the number, she mentally rehashed her plan. She smiled and knew it was good. The phone clicked on the other end.

"Travel Dayz. How may I help you?"

"Hi, I'd like to book a seat on your next flight out to New

York City, with a return trip tomorrow morning. Or even better, a red-eye late tonight."

With the arrangements made, Bekah knew she'd have plenty of time to do what she needed to do and return home before Collin's return tomorrow evening. And, when he returned, she would hopefully have the best of news. Then perhaps they could talk a little more seriously about the possibility of marriage in the coming weeks.

* * *

The cab driver threaded the taxi throughout the busy Manhattan streets. Bekah cringed each time she heard a horn blast, a shout, a whistle, a siren. Statistics, Bekah thought. New York was nothing but a bunch of statistics. The noise magnified and in turn, increased her anxiety. She was grateful she was only here for the afternoon and would be returning home on the overnight flight to the solitude of the country.

"Looks like we're stuck for a few minutes, lady." The driver turned back smiling. His toothless grin and unshaven face nearly nauseating her. The pain in her lower back had eased a bit, but the cramped space on the airplane left little room for a pregnant woman. Not to mention that her stomach was already a bit queasy.

Bekah glanced out the window trying to orient herself to her surroundings. This wouldn't have been the way she would have come. "How far are we from the Harper building?" she asked.

He angled a glance down the street and rubbed his chin with his fingers. "Not far, really. About three or four blocks down then left. We'll be out of here in a jiffy though. Don't think you need to walk far in your condition."

Bekah reached down for her purse. "I'll be fine, what do I owe you."

He told her and she settled with him, tipping him gener-ously. He smiled again. She exited the cab on her left and wove her way through the honking, halted traffic, glad she could escape the stifling closeness of the taxi.

As executives and tourists rushed by, she walked slowly, glad she'd worn comfortable sandals. Her feet had grown unac-customed to heels. She'd not worn them but once or twice since returning to Kentucky. It seemed odd being here, suddenly thrust back into the chaos of the city in which she'd lived for some time. She wondered how she'd stayed so long.

A small child with a young couple passed her and she thought of the baby she was carrying. How glad she was that her child would grow up in the country. City smells were suddenly nauseating and about to choke her—and the noises deafening. Suddenly, she longed for a crisp babbling brook, or just her back yard at Wind Ridge, but Wind Ridge was hardly there anymore.

It would be though, again. One day. No need to fret about what was gone. Her land was still there. The house may be gone but what remained in her heart would be there forever. And that was what she was fighting for today—her baby's rights to grow up where he, or she, needed to be. Soon this would all be over.

She walked on, even though the twinges raced across her back. Eight months pregnant was no time to take a trip—and she'd been surprised no one questioned her flying—but when it meant something as important as this, as her child's welfare, the discomfort didn't matter.

As she neared the Harper Building, Bekah stopped and stood in awe of the magnificence of the structure. Why Matthew never confided in her, never at all even hinted of the magnitude of his wealth was a mystery—and it burned her to her very core.

Perhaps though, not so much a mystery. Matthew was a

greedy, money-hungry son-of-a-bitch. He wanted her, but he didn't want to share his wealth with anyone.

And now, he suddenly wanted the baby too? Made no sense. Matthew doesn't share—not even with his own child. There was more to this.

The closer she walked, the angrier she became at the lies and the games Matthew had played. For five years, she assumed he held a position in the firm similar to hers. They never lunched together—too inconvenient, he said. No time. His lunch hours were for clients. His long hours mirrored hers so there were days they never crossed or meshed.

Such an idiot! How could I have been so gullible? Why didn't any of this seem unusual?

Because at heart you are still a trusting county bumpkin, Bekah.

"Then so be it." She wouldn't have it any other way.

Through the double glass doors, she walked to the center of the lobby. A receptionist sat at a circular desk there and Bekah stepped up to it. The older woman looked up from her work. "May I help you miss?"

Bekah smiled at her. "Could you direct me to Matthew Vanlandingham's office please?"

The woman's face remained blank. "Do you have an appointment?"

"No," Bekah replied.

"I'm sorry miss, but Mr. Vanlandingham's suite of offices is not disclosed unless you have an appointment and I've specifically been given your name to admit you."

Bekah closed her eyes, a half-grin on her face. She shook her head. Leave it to Matthew to protect himself so. Looking straight into the woman's eyes, she said, "He'll see me. Call whomever you need and tell them to tell Mr. Vanlandingham that Rebekah McCauley is here to see him. I assure you, he *will* see me. Tell him I have a proposition he won't refuse."

The receptionist glared back through her half-glasses. "A proposition? In your condition? Just what do you think we are here, miss?" Her nose turned upward at Bekah's wide-eyed stare. "At any rate, we don't operate that way. You must be cleared twenty-four hours in advance. Now I suggest you go home and call to make an appointment." She looked Bekah over from head to toe. Bekah suddenly felt self-conscious in her maternity dress and sandals. "That is if he agrees to see you."

Bekah stepped closer. "I don't have twenty-four hours. I just flew in. I've been stuck in traffic and I walked the last four blocks. I'm on a return flight home in six hours. I *will* see him today. So, if you don't have the guts to face up to Matthew, dial the damn thing and give it to me. I'll handle it."

The woman's eyes grew wide. Taking a deep breath, her gaze swept across Bekah, to her work before her, and then to the phone. "What did you say your name was?"

Bekah wanted to smile in victory but didn't. She kept a cool exterior. "Rebekah McCauley," she said slowly.

The woman dialed. Bekah watched her fingers, but the woman shielded the phone from Bekah's view and turned her back to her. *Not only efficient, but also loyal.* Then she heard her hushed voice.

"Madelyn? This is Grace at the front desk. Listen, I have a young woman here who wants to see Mr. Vanlandingham." Grace paused. "Uh-huh. She doesn't have an appointment, but she insists he will see her. Her name is Rebekah McCauley."

Grace held the phone to her ear for several seconds. "All right, I'll hold."

She turned her body back to face Bekah. "He's in a board meeting. She's checking."

The look Grace shot Bekah said *you-better-be-someone-*

important- because-I-don't-want-to-get-blamed-for-this-interrup-tion-if-you-aren't. Bekah stared back. Grace perked up when hearing the phone click back to her.

"Yes, Madelyn. We'll be waiting." She laid the receiver back in its cradle and looked up to Bekah. "We do not disclose the location of Mr. Vanlandingham's suite. Someone will be here shortly to escort you. You may wait over there." She pointed to a grouping of chairs next to the wall.

Grace was quite obviously relieved she wasn't in trouble after all, Bekah thought. Leave it to Matthew to make this place harder to penetrate than Fort Knox. His opinion of himself was quite high. But no surprise there. No wonder he didn't want her to know anything about his business life. How long did he think he could pull off this shenanigan?

A few minutes later, she was approached by a young man in a black suit, who greeted her by name and asked her to follow him. She did.

After her escort stopped the elevator on an unmarked floor, Bekah watched as he keyed in a series of numbers in a computer panel hidden in the wall. The doors suddenly opened, and Rebekah was greeted by a young woman wearing standard busi-ness attire, the same style suit Matthew used to insist she wear to work, the same heels, the same simple jewelry. Bekah followed her from the lobby into a room of cubicles where many men and women worked, each looking like clones of the other, only in different hues. Rebekah knew Matthew liked consis-tency, but she never dreamed he'd carry it this far.

As they walked, Bekah glanced down at her own loose flowing jumper and instead of feeling dowdy and fat, held her head up high, lifted her shoulders, and walked her pregnant body behind the main clone with a confident air and a smile on her face, ecstatic that she had escaped this menagerie.

Bekah followed through a thick oak door and into a plush

inner office receiving area where she sat and waited. Another clone sat behind the desk. She glanced up and nodded to the retreating clone, then she smiled briefly at Bekah and returned to her work.

Glancing around the room, Bekah's took in everything. Sleek draperies made of fine silk, rich carpeting, stately furniture waxed to a dark lustrous patina, and beautiful paintings completed the picture. Including one of hers. Bekah rose, and then walked across the room to the painting. It was an early work in watercolor of a woman on a beach. She hated it. She'd always hated it. Others might look at the painting and comment on the beauty and the serenity it offered, but to Bekah the colors were all wrong and whenever she looked at it, she felt anything but calm.

"Quite a nice representation of the artist's talent, isn't it?"

Bekah closed her eyes slowly and inhaled. Matthew's voice behind her grated along the nerves of her spine—and she loathed the feeling. Turning, Bekah investigated the face of the man she'd lived with and thought she'd loved for five long years —but she realized at once she had never loved him. She didn't know him. Not anymore. Here, in this office, in his own surroundings, she didn't know him. And she would conduct her business today in the same manner she would have conducted business with any of her clients while working at the magazine. This man had turned her life upside down and inside out for the past five years—and it was going to end today. Right now.

"Matthew." Bekah was surprised at the icy tone of her voice. "I'd like to talk to you privately." Matthew glanced past her shoulder at the painting and then back to her face.

"You didn't answer my question."

Bekah glared. Diversion. Always one of his tactics. "I didn't come here to talk about a painting. I have more important matters to discuss."

"But it's your painting."

"No, Matthew, it's yours. You wanted me to paint it. You chose the subject and the colors. And then you told me never to paint again. Why you have it hanging here, I haven't a clue. It obviously means nothing to you."

He studied her face. "It matches the decor."

It was like a slap in the face. Bekah took it and stared back into his eyes. Just like him. If it served some purpose, it was okay. *It matched the decor.* No sentiment. No feeling. Like everything else in his life. "I want to talk to you privately. If you don't want to talk, then fine, I'll leave." She took a half step toward the door.

He grasped her arm. Bekah jerked it away.

"In good time," he said. "Let's order up some coffee, perhaps lunch."

Bekah's abdomen grew tight with anger, but she tamped it down. She *was* the one in control here, she told herself. "Now, Matthew, in your office—privately. Or all your dirty linen will be aired in your outer office for all your clones to hear. We have something to discuss—right now. We do it privately or do we do it right here. Right now."

Matthew swallowed and she watched his Adam's apple bob.

* * *

"How did you find me?"

Bekah stared at Matthew from across his huge cherry desk, landscaped with neatly stacked piles of papers and files. "Don't you really mean, how did I find out about you and Harper?

"That too."

"Guess your security wasn't as tight as you thought, huh?"

"My security is fine. I just wanted to know how you found out about Harper."

276

Bekah smiled. "Interesting notion, isn't it? That I can find out things about you now, and I didn't have a clue for all those years."

Matthew leaned back in his chair and folded his hands together across his stomach. "You're not capable of this Rebekah. Your new boyfriend with you? Is he sitting downstairs waiting to physically attack me like some barbarian? Is he encouraging this behavior of yours?"

Bekah lifted her chin. "I'm here alone, Matthew. I make my own decisions. I don't need a man to make them for me. Let me let you in on a little secret. That's not the way it's done out in the real world."

Matthew glared at her. "So, tell me why you're here. Have you decided to give a little? What is this proposition you speak of? Or was that just hogwash?"

"You think I came here for hogwash?" She laughed.

"I think whatever you came here for, you are too naïve to pull off."

She glared. "I'm never giving in to you Matthew."

He rubbed his chin. "Hmm, I don't understand. Sooner or later, you will conclude that you won't win."

"Interesting notion," Bekah mused. "We'll get to that. Right now, I have a question for you, and I'll be direct. Why in the world do you want to have anything to do with this baby?"

He gazed into her eyes and after a long moment, spoke softly. "Because it's a part of you, Rebekah, a part of us. I love you and I want to be able to hold in my hands the result of that love."

"Bullshit." Bekah shook off an offending chill. "You don't love me."

Matthew rose and walked around his desk. "Of course, I do. I always have." Bekah stood and backed away, tilting her chin up in defiance. Suddenly wondering if she'd made a mistake; wishing she'd never come. When his forefinger hooked under her chin, he drew her face closer. She felt repulsed but allowed him. When their lips nearly touched, Bekah backed away.

"No," she pushed him backward, "that act doesn't work anymore, Matthew."

He ignored her, his voice lowered. "Consider coming back here to live, Rebekah. We can all be together, the three of us. A happy family."

Laughter bubbled up from somewhere deep inside her, and she let it out in slow, deliberate bursts. She laughed long and hard—a good cleansing, releasing laugh. An emancipation.

Matthew stared, frowning.

"This is so unlike you Matthew. Whatever the reason for you wanting this child, I know it is not out of love for me. If you loved me, Matthew, you wouldn't have tried to force me into the abortion. You wouldn't have given me the ultimatum. You would have understood and loved me regardless. You don't love me. You never did." Bekah paused.

"Whatever the reason you want this child in your life, it must be a good one, and I'll bet that somewhere along the line money is involved. And I think that's pretty awful." She watched his blank face. "Then again, I don't know why I should have expected anything else from you."

Matthew backed away and rounded the desk. He paced the room behind it, then stopped at the liquor cabinet and slowly, methodically mixed himself a drink.

Bekah sat, heard the clink of ice in the glass, and the gurgling of the liquor as he poured. She waited. It was time.

When he returned, he stood in front of her and leaned against the edge of the desk, facing her. He sipped his drink. Bourbon. She could smell the smooth potency of the whiskey. Towering above her, Bekah knew exactly what he was doing. It was a gesture of power—of dominance. And she didn't have to give him that advantage.

She stood and circled the wingback chair, putting it between them. She felt his gaze following her, then faced him, gripping the top.

"So why are you here?"

She stared at Matthew for several long seconds. "Give it all up, Matthew. Leave me alone and pretend I, and this baby, do not exist. I'm not asking you for a single cent. I don't want child support or your emotional support, not that that would ever be offered. I just want to be left alone."

"Alone and with your new boyfriend, you mean."

"Yes."

"And you don't need my money because he has plenty, right?"

"I'm supporting myself, Matthew."

"No, you're not. You're even living in his house now. Arson, wasn't it?"

Bekah froze. Her fingertips dug into the leather chair. There was no possible way he could know about that. "You didn't." She had loosely suggested the possibility to Collin, but she never really though him capable of something of that magnitude. Angry, she rounded the chair. "I was almost killed! All my grandparents' things are gone! How dare you." She pummeled his chest with her fists.

Matthew grabbed her wrists. "Rebekah, stop. I didn't do it."

Bekah froze, her arms in his grasp. "Then how did you know about the arson?"

"There are ways."

Bekah jerked her hands away and stepped backward. She still wasn't sure if she believed him or not. "You're having me watched."

"Like a hawk."

"You bastard."

"No, your child will be the bastard, Rebekah, unless you give him over to me. Then he'll be my son. He'll be someone important. And I can give him so much more than you ever could. All you can offer him is a life of poverty on that so-called farm of yours where he'd grow up as an illiterate, Kentucky hill-child without a shred of decency. He'd be the local bastard, Bekah. I can give him so much more."

Near tears, but determined not to let it show, Bekah shook her head and glared. "It will never happen, Matthew."

"It will."

"No, it won't." Bekah stepped backward and repositioned herself behind the chair, struggling to keep her voice calm. "Matthew, let me tell you something. I want you to forget all this. Now."

He shook his head. "Never."

"Are you going to force my hand?"

Matthew stared. "Ah, here it comes... The proposition. What is it, Bekah? You think you have something on me?"

Bekah looked past his shoulder and took a deep breath. Reaching deep into her purse, she took out a large manila envelope. Walking to his desk, she said, "When you have a minute, read this." Then, she turned toward the door. "Oh, and that's just a copy. The original is in my attorney's hands with instructions of what to do with it if I don't call her within the hour. So don't get any ideas, Matthew."

He looked at her, and then glanced at the packet on his desk. Bekah's hand rested on the doorknob. She turned it.

"Wait, don't go."

Bekah smiled. His curiosity was getting the best of him. She stepped closer to his desk as he picked up the packet and withdrew the few papers there. He scanned them and then slapped them down on his desk and glared at her.

"You wouldn't."

"I would."

Bekah lifted her chin. "I think your stockholders would be quite interested, in particular one Mrs. Arthur Corrigan. It seems she is very much Pro-Life. Even has been known to sit in front of abortion clinics a time or two. Was once arrested for her cause, I understand. Yes, I think she'd be interested in your trying to force me into an abortion. She does own quite a lot of stock in Harper, doesn't she Matthew?"

His face turned white.

"And Martin McGann. Owns a good chunk of the business also, doesn't he? Do you know what his pet project is, Matthew? He volunteers his time at a spouse abuse center. He abhors abuse of another human being's life. Had a daughter who was killed by an abusive boyfriend. Be it physical or emotional, he doesn't stand for it. He has put quite a lot of his money into spouse abuse centers around the city. He even sits on the board of directors for the local council on abuse."

Matthew's eyes bored into hers. "I didn't abuse you, Rebekah. I gave you everything. You can't claim I abused you."

Bekah swallowed hard. "I used to think that too, Matthew. I was wrong. You did abuse me. Yes physically, once, but mostly emotionally. You took my person, my body, and formed me into what you wanted out of me and discarded the rest until I was simply a shell of a woman. Not me. You controlled me until I wasn't me anymore. And I'll be damned if you'll do this to my child. That's why I'll spread the news Matthew. And you've provided me with the perfect forum for doing that."

She paused, and then added. "Oh, and I have pictures of the bruises. Look a little deeper in that packet. I believe you'll find them."

He stepped toward her and Bekah stepped back. "You'll keep our private business to ourselves, Rebekah," he said.

She planted her feet. "Oh, so you don't want the story of my abuse and your forcing me into an abortion *and* my escape to freedom plastered all over the front of your rag, Matthew? I think *The Global Review* is the perfect forum for a man of your stature to have his dirty linen aired. Especially since you own the magazine."

Matthew paled. Bekah could tell he was seething on the inside.

His exterior was showing extreme control, but his battling insides were messing with his emotions.

"You're forgetting one thing, Bekah. I control what gets into those things." He spoke slowly and precisely.

"Oh really? It seems to me that a man who controls several major and minor publications doesn't have time to oversee what content goes into every publication. Remember, I used to work for you Matthew, and even though I didn't know it, I'm sure there is some disgruntled employee out there somewhere who does know it. I'll find him or her."

"My employees are loyal. You don't have a leg to stand on. They wouldn't print garbage such as this."

Bekah turned and walked toward the door. "Well then, that leaves me one other option. I'm sure your competitors will be interested. And remember, Matthew, my lawyer has the original copy of that. And there are identical packets ready to send to each of your stockholders, and your competition. Drop the entire thing Matthew, or I go to anyone I can think of and publish it."

Matthew laughed nervously. "Publishing is not that easy, Bekah. You don't just walk in and...."

"They'll want this, Matthew. I've already made contacts." She hadn't, but he didn't know that. "You forget I worked in the publishing business for five years. I have contacts. Drop the entire issue."

Matthew stared. "We'll discuss this later."

"I don't have later. I'm leaving tonight. I'll give you until tomorrow morning before I make my first move. Do you understand?"

"I need time."

"Need to go discuss it with mommy?"

He threw her a nasty look. "As a matter of fact, yes."

Bekah smiled sweetly then turned to walk out the door. "Then give her my love," she said over her shoulder as she left.

* * *

The elevator operator looked straight ahead as he punched in the codes locking the doors.

Bekah breathed a long sigh of relief. She had ignored the increasing twinges of pain racing across her lower back while in Matthew's office. It had taken all her control not to show her panic to Matthew, but she had known she had to leave there immediately, and that she somehow had to get an earlier flight home.

Then it hit her. The intense pain shot across her lower back, nearly taking her to her knees. She grasped the rail beside her, an uncontrollable moan escaping her lips. The operator glanced back.

"Are you all right miss?"

Bekah gripped the rail and straightened up. She nodded. "I'm fine," she whispered.

Then another stabbing, squeezing pain. This time she did go to her knees and the operator was at her side. "You're in labor."

"No, I'm not," Bekah insisted, panic in her eyes. *I can't be in labor! I will not have this baby in New York!*

The man felt her forehead and took her pulse. She watched

his face as she knew her own was screwing up in pain. The elevator screeched to a halt. The doors opened. "My wife's had four kids. You *are* in labor. I'll call an ambulance." He rose to open the case in the wall holding a phone.

Bekah started to protest, then the searing pain flashed across her back again and she felt a gush of water release from between her legs. "Oh no!" She lay on her side on the elevator floor holding on to her tummy and nearly wept, praying this was all a bad dream. Then the unbearable pain took over and she lost all sense of time and place for several minutes.

People. Shouting. Someone lifting her. A siren. And then she was temporarily out.

When she woke, faces were all around—people talking, calming her, reassuring her that she was fine. They took her outside and the lights were flashing. The doors to the ambulance closed and the siren started. All she could think of was that she was now one of those statistics. Faces, all around her in the ambulance, and she fixed her gaze on one.

Matthew.

Chapter Twenty-Two

The flight was long, his business in Louisiana nearly wore him out, and Collin ached to hold Bekah in his arms again. One night without her was one night too many. So much so, he'd cut his business short and left on the earliest flight out that morning. He'd decided late the night before that the idea of her leaving alone was ridiculous, and if she felt compelled to run, he would do it with her. In fact, he'd found a nice little ranch in southern Georgia he thought she would adore and as soon as the baby was born, he'd take her to see it.

Leaving his briefcase and his jacket in the car, Collin bound up the steps to the side entrance of his home, her name on his lips even before he opened the door.

"Bekah?" he listened. "Sweetheart? I'm home."

His words echoed off the walls like those in a cavern. It was too still and too silent. Collin's breath caught in his throat. "Bekah?" he said a little softer this time.

"She's not here."

Collin whirled to the voice. Pete walked through the open

door behind him. Panic welled up inside his chest and each muscle in his body grew tense. "Where is she?"

Pete looked at Collin for only a few seconds. "I don't know. She took the pick-up out about noon yesterday. She didn't come back last night."

Collin wondered if his eyes reflected the horror he felt in his heart. "Did you talk to her?"

"Nope. I watched her from the barn. I just thought maybe she was spending the night somewhere, but I don't think she had a suitcase with her."

"Then she didn't plan to stay anywhere long."

Pete shook his head. "Can't say. Maybe she put a bag in the truck earlier in the day, I don't know."

Damn it all to hell! Collin turned and paced the floor in front of Pete, raking his fingers through his hair. "There's got to be an explanation. Got to be." He turned to Pete. "Look, I'm going to make some phone calls. Ask around outside. Maybe someone heard something. We'll talk later."

Two hours later Collin sat in his study. He tilted the half-full shot glass of bourbon and watched as he rotated it between his fingertips, its amber essence swirling lazily. He had stared at it for the past several minutes. Then quickly, he threw back the drink and let the liquid slide down his throat. It was as smooth going down as the previous three. Collin banged the glass down on his desk.

There had been no word from Bekah, and it seemed no one had spoken to her yesterday. Her parents hadn't heard from her, and even though Collin had not wanted to upset them, he felt they needed to know the truth. He'd called Michael and had him break the news to them. Michael called back reporting that no one there had seen or talked to her in days. The entire damn situation was frustrating, and he was getting nowhere.

Panic wanted to settle into his heart, his brain, and his

body. He wouldn't let it. Collin refused to think the obvious, that she'd left him. Even when he thought of their argument the day before, when she threatened to leave and not tell him, he didn't think she meant it. Nothing made sense. None of her personal things were gone—not even her makeup—which convinced him more that wherever she went yesterday, she had not intended to stay long. And that meant she could be in trouble.

On impulse, Collin picked up the phone and dialed. "Tom McKenney, please."

He waited for Tom to come on the line. "McKenney here."

Collin began, "This is Collin Kramer. I need your help."

"What is it now, Kramer, stub your toe?"

"Damn it McKenney, I'm in no mood for your jokes. Bekah is missing."

Tom seemed to take a sudden interest in the conversation. "How long?"

"No one has seen her since about noon yesterday. She left in the pick-up, without a suitcase. Unfortunately, no one knew where she was headed, and no one has seen her since."

"Where were you?"

"Louisiana, since yesterday morning. Business."

Tom exhaled deeply. "I like Bekah, Kramer. And with everything else that's been going on over at your place, I think we need to investigate this situation. I'll get right on it. In the meantime, you try and see what you can dig up. Wrack your brain if you must but think of anywhere she might have gone, or anyone she might confide in. I'll look in the more obvious places."

"Such as...."

Tom cleared his throat. "Such as the local hospitals and the morgue, son. You say she was driving a pick-up?"

Collin's heart stopped at the word morgue. "Yes," he said

softly. "An older model green Chevrolet." His brain was going to short-circuit any second.

"I'll get right on it."

Collin replaced the receiver, walked to the bar, and poured another double shot of bourbon. When the last of the amber liquid had passed his tongue, he turned in anger hurled the glass against the fireplace hearth.

* * *

"I want to go home!" Bekah wailed in the labor room of the hospital as the nurse prepared her for an epidural. "I want Collin!" The doctor examined her and watched the fetal monitor.

"You can't go home, Ms. McCauley, you're in labor."

"But I can't be," she winced with the next pain. "The baby's...not due for another...month yet."

"But you are. And you're staying right here." The doctor was kind enough, but he wasn't Dr. Benton. And she hadn't prepared to do this alone. She'd prepared to do this with Collin. *Collin! Oh Lord, he'll be furious with me for coming here. Should I call him?*

"Have you had any complications with your pregnancy?"

Bekah nodded, her thoughts turning back to her present situation. "Placenta praevia in the second trimester. But the placenta had moved when I had my last ultrasound."

She noted the concerned look on the doctor's face.

"What does that look mean?"

"That means we tread carefully. Your labor progressed rather quickly at first, but now seems to be slowing down. We'll have to monitor it closely."

"False labor?"

He shook his head. "No, the amniotic sac has broken. The baby will be delivered soon. Who's your doctor in Kentucky?"

"Dr. Richard Benton in Lexington, will you call him?"

"We need to contact him and see if he'll fax your records. Any objection to that?"

Bekah shook her head. "Of course not."

"You're stabilized now, and we'll do an ultrasound in a few minutes, just to check the location of the placenta." He glanced at his watch. "Since it's the middle of the night, I think we'll wait till morning to contact him, do you feel comfortable with that? I assure you, you're not going to deliver this baby anytime soon. You've only dilated to about four centimeters. You've a way to go yet."

Bekah wanted to trust the man. "No. Call him now. Please. Do you think we'll have to do a C-section?"

He shook his head. "I can't tell yet. We'll have to see. You have no bleeding and that is a good sign, but we'll just have to see."

Bekah nodded.

A nurse poked her head through the door. "Dr. Carpenter, the baby's father wants to know if he can come in to see Ms. McCauley."

"No! He's not the father!" Bekah shouted it a little louder than she had intended.

"But—" Both nurses and the doctor stared at her.

Bekah continued, "He is *not* to come in here. He is nothing to me or my baby." She narrowed her eyes at the doctor. "I swear to you, if any of you let that man in here, the delivery room, or anywhere near me, I'll get up and walk out and have the baby on the street. Do you get the picture?" They each looked at her, dumbfounded by her anger. "And that goes for after the baby is born too. I don't want him anywhere near my child!"

A sharp pain began to ripple across her abdomen, crescendo

to a peak, and then fade away, leaving Bekah panting. Monitors started bleeping warning signs.

Dr. Carpenter bent over her and placed a cool hand on her perspiring forehead. "Calm down. You can't get this upset." He glanced at the monitors. "Your heart rate and blood pressure are elevated. We get the picture. Don't worry, he won't come near you or the baby."

Bekah relaxed. The doctor turned to each of the nurses. "Make sure that the word is spread. What's his name, Ms. McCauley?"

"Matthew Vanlandingham...and he's not to be trusted. Oh, and doctor? When you call Dr. Benton, will you tell him to call Collin Kramer? He'll know how to get in touch with him. And tell him I need him. Now."

* * *

Collin drove throughout the afternoon searching for anything that might lead him to Bekah. Her truck, someone who had seen her—something, but it was all in vain. He was fast becoming frantic with worry. Tom McKenney's search was fruitless, leaving Collin with fewer worries of finding her dead or injured somewhere. If he could only find her truck. Then he might be able to get a hold on her whereabouts. Maybe.

By late afternoon, he decided that maybe she *had* left him. Maybe she took nothing with her just to throw him off the track. Maybe she left for good and if she did, it would be damned impossible to find her. But he had to try. Once home, he lost no time retrieving things he might need for a few days. If it took him days, weeks—maybe months, he wouldn't stop. If he had to, he would hire a private investigator. *Private Investigator?* Patricia! Perhaps the one she'd hired to check out Matthew.

He lifted the receiver to his ear and dialed. "Patricia Settle, please."

"May I ask who is calling?"

"Collin Kramer."

The receptionist continued, "I'm sorry, Mr. Kramer, Ms. Settle is out of the office today. May I take a message? She checks in periodically."

Collin paused for a second or two. "You don't happen to know the name of a private investigator she's been using recently, do you? For the McCauley case."

"Sorry Mr. Kramer. I'm just a temp. Everyone is on vacation here. I'm just answering the phone and taking care of the mail. Would you like to leave her a message?"

Collin closed his eyes. "No... No thank you. When will she be back?"

"Tomorrow, I believe."

"Thanks. Just tell her I called." Collin replaced the receiver.

His shoulders drooped and he let his head fall back. Collin inhaled deeply and then let the breath out very slowly. *When in hell was this damn thing going to end?* He turned quickly, and then did the only thing he knew to do. Throwing a few essentials in a bag, he then tossed it at the foot of his bed. Confident that Tom McKenney was doing what he could, and that Michael was combing her hometown area for news, he felt he could leave and search himself. He surely couldn't sit around and wait for her to come home, because he was deathly afraid that that wasn't going to happen.

Collin picked up the bag and hurriedly walked across the bedroom to the door. The phone rang behind him and in his hurry, he almost ignored it. Then thinking better of it, he jogged back to the nightstand and picked up the receiver.

"Kramer," he answered.

"It's McKenney. We've found Bekah's truck. It's at Lexington Blue Grass Field."

* * *

"We're going to help you sit up, Bekah, and hang your legs over the side of the bed. Curl over into a ball for us, okay? We're going to have to try it again."

Bekah did as the nurse said, but it wasn't easy. She'd been in labor for hours and was in constant pain. Her body shook uncontrollably, as she held onto two nurses' hands. An hour or so earlier they administered the first epidural, which hadn't taken. She had consented to the epidural at the doctor's urging because of the pain she was experiencing, and because of her state of upset. Her body was in enough shock going into labor early and her brain was having trouble comprehending what was happening to her, so she agreed. The epidural would alleviate the pain, Dr. Carpenter had said, and she'd be anesthetized, if she should happen to need a C-section.

Bekah agreed. When Dr. Benton called, he also agreed. But the first epidural still left her in pain, and now that her labor had progressed, the pain was almost unbearable.

"You're going to feel a little pop and a sting when I insert the needle." The anesthesiologist talked softly to her. A nurse swiped at her clammy forehead with a damp cloth. Another contraction hit her and grew into a mountain of pain as she sat curled there, then her body took over and started quaking convulsively.

"She's probably in transition."

Bekah wanted to scream, but didn't. Internally she cried and bore the pain, her body out of control. As the nurses held her steady, she felt the anesthesiologist probe along her lower spine, and then the promised pop and sting, which was minor to everything else happening to her. One contraction after another wracked her body. Then soon, or maybe not because she'd lost all track of time, they helped her lay back and covered her with warm blankets.

Soon, she stopped convulsing but the pain continued. *Oh, Collin, I need you.*

"Bekah, we need to do another pelvic. I think you're close." The nurse watched the monitor measuring Bekah's contractions. "Get ready. I'm going to do it now." She slipped her gloved fingers into Bekah's vagina to measure her cervix.

Bekah cried out. A burning encircled her pelvis from her abdomen to her lower back. Then she suddenly felt an incredible urge to push.

The nurse nodded to another by the door. "Get Dr. Carpenter. She's at ten." Then she turned to Bekah. "I know you probably feel like pushing, but don't yet. It won't be long. You're still feeling pain aren't you?"

Bekah's wild-eyed stare answered her question.

"Well, it won't be long now." She watched the monitor. "Here comes another. Get ready." She grabbed Bekah's hands. "Breathe, honey, breathe."

* * *

When they found Bekah's truck in the long-term parking area of the airport, Collin had hope. All he had to do was find out what plane she left on and to where. With Tom McKenney's help, they soon eliminated all the airlines except Delta and within a matter of a few minutes discovered that she had indeed left out of Lexington on a 1:30 pm flight to New York.

"New York?" Collin looked at the man at the ticket counter in astonishment. "I don't understand. Are you sure?"

The man looked from Collin to Tom and shook his head.

"Yes, sir. A Rebekah McCauley left on a 1:30 pm flight from Lexington to LaGuardia yesterday afternoon."

"When did she book the flight?"

The man looked back at his screen. "Yesterday morning."

Tom McKenney looked at the man and then to Collin. "Was there a return flight booked?"

The man's gaze once again dropped to his computer screen. "Yes. For 10:50 pm last night."

"Was she on it?"

The man looked Collin straight in the eye. "No."

Collin stared at the man then looked past Tom's shoulder. "She's in trouble."

"Not necessarily, Kramer. We need to find out why she went there in the first place. You don't think she wants to get back with Vanlandingham, do you?" Collin had explained the situation with Matthew earlier in the day.

"No! Dammit, she despises him. Vanlandingham has something to do with this. It's crazy. I don't know what to think."

They turned away from the Delta desk. Tom asked, "So what do you want me to do?"

Collin looked at him. "I don't want you to do anything. From now on, I'll handle this. You just keep looking for the arsonist."

"What are *you* going to do?"

Collin glanced back at the Delta desk. "I'm going to New York."

* * *

The second epidural didn't work either.

"Hold your breath, Bekah, and push hard."

One nurse was at Bekah's back curling her body up like a comma, the other was at her feet, one foot in each hand. Bekah pushed against her. Bekah strained, her eyes open, and felt the baby move lower into the birth canal. Then the contraction was over, and Bekah had a brief respite.

"Good, Bekah. Now relax for a second." Bekah slumped back slightly against the nurse behind her. "You're doing great. The head is crowning."

Bekah looked up as Dr. Carpenter entered the delivery room.

"How are we doing here, Bekah?"

Another contraction rolled in and Bekah urged her body forward and braced against the nurse's hands once more. As the pain peaked, Bekah pushed. Dr. Carpenter sat at the foot of the delivery table. "Good, Bekah. The head is crowning nicely. Now, during the next contraction, I'll have you stop pushing for a minute. I know it will be hard but remember your breathing."

Bekah nodded. The next contraction came rather quickly and when he asked her to stop pushing, she tried her best to accommodate him. But she couldn't.

"I can't stop," Bekah cried breathlessly.

"Try to Bekah. Give me a second. The baby's head is out."

Bekah heard a small cry and she gasped. "Is that my baby?"

The nurse chuckled. "Well, it's certainly not mine, honey."

"I'm suctioning out the mucous from its nose and mouth. Now, on the next contraction, Ms. McCauley, you're going to push when I tell you and you'll have a baby."

Bekah took a deep breath. She could feel the rising of the next, and what she hoped to be, her final contraction. "Oh, she's coming."

Dr. Carpenter gently pulled one little shoulder out and then another, the rest of the baby's tiny body following quickly."

Bekah's daughter let out a screaming howl. "You're right, she's here," Dr. Carpenter exclaimed. He held her up for Bekah to see. "And looking wonderful!"

Bekah looked at her child, all blue and white and icky, small smudges of blood on her forehead, the umbilical cord still pulsating, still attached to her own body, and the tears rolled. Her baby girl cried, and Bekah reached out. Dr. Carpenter laid the infant child on Bekah's chest and covered her with a warm towel. Bekah laid back on the propped bed and cooed to her newborn baby. She traced her tiny features with one finger and placed a kiss on her tiny nose.

"Good morning, sunshine," she crooned to her daughter, her words falling off with emotion as she spoke. "I sure am glad to see you all safe and sound."

Bekah felt another stab of pain.

"Good afternoon, you mean. Here. Let me clean her up and do a quick exam. I promise I'll give her right back." Bekah reluctantly let her go to the nurse, then breathed through her last contraction.

Later in the recovery room, Bekah nursed her daughter for the first time. She held baby Colleen close to her chest and cooed to the baby until sleep claimed them both. Bekah's last thought was of Collin, and why he hadn't called.

Chapter Twenty-Three

Matthew eyed the infant from the hallway, looking through the thick glass window. He smiled as he watched the nurse lay his child, swaddled in a baby blue blanket, in the tiny bassinette. He knew it was his child. He'd even heard Bekah call him son. Even though they wouldn't let him in, he could still see and hear well enough. When they moved Bekah to a private room, he'd trailed not far behind. Now, he followed the nurse and watched as she laid his sleeping boy in the nursery with a half a dozen other infants.

He turned smiling, then moved down the hall to the elevator and punched the button for the second floor. When the doors opened, he perused the sign showing directions to different offices. Finding the one he wanted, he followed the directions and turned right.

A small blond woman looked up from her work when he entered and flashed him a toothy smile. "Hello, sir. May I help you?" She laid her pen down and kept her gaze on Matthew.

Matthew charmingly smiled back. "Yes. My wife just delivered our son a few moments ago, and I was wondering if I could fill out the necessary paperwork for the birth certificate."

The woman's eyes widened. "Well, sir, generally we are notified by the physician and then we bring the proper paperwork to the room."

Matthew glanced at the woman's nameplate and grinned. "Ms. Winters, I'm sure you understand, being a woman and all, my wife is entirely worn out. It was a long and hard labor. She is resting, so I thought I'd just go ahead and get some of the paperwork done for her so she wouldn't have to bother. She's got so much else to worry about, you know. Besides, this is our first child, and my son. I'd really like to fill them out." He smiled at her again. "What do you say?"

"The paperwork doesn't have to be completed today, sir. As long as it's completed before your wife and the baby leave the hospital. Some people like to think a while about names, you know."

He nodded. "That's something that we entirely agree on. You see, he's going to be named after me."

She smiled back at him. "And it would be kind of special for you to fill out the paperwork yourself?"

"Exactly." He flashed her another grin.

She smiled back. "Okay, well, this is against protocol, but I'll give you the form. If someone happens to bring another one to your wife's room, make sure she doesn't fill out a duplicate. We could have all kinds of problems there."

He laughed. "Oh, of course." Matthew watched as she fumbled through a file in her desk, her fingers sifting through until she found the right form. It was a single piece of paper she handed him, and he laid it down on her desk and immediately began completing the questions.

He filled it out completely, smiling as he placed his name in the spot marked *father*, and even more so when he completed the child's name as *Matthew Allen Vanlandingham II*.

* * *

"Tsk, tsk. What have we here?" One of the nurses picked up tiny Colleen and cradled in her arms. She glanced out over the sea of cradles to the other babies wrapped tightly in their pink and blue blankets. "Not a ribbon in this pretty hair and wrapped in an old blue blanket. Those orderlies must have forgotten to pick up the laundry again." She crooned to the baby and walked to the back of the nursery to change her. "Was this old blue thing all they could find darlin'? Well," she whispered as she held Colleen close to her cheek, "we'll just have to take care of this little problem."

She hummed to the child as she diapered her and dressed her in a clean undershirt, then as she held her in one arm, brushed her hair up into a tiny curl and then taped a tiny pink ribbon in front. After wrapping her in a new pink blanket, she held her up to inspect her handiwork.

"Now you're ready to go see your mommy, pretty one. And I'll bet she'll be mighty happy to see you."

Chapter Twenty-Four

I t didn't take long for Collin to get a flight to New York but trying to figure out how he would find Vanlandingham was another story. He'd hit dead-end after dead-end, with his limited knowledge. He needed to hear from Patricia and the PI before he could move forward. Nearing eight o'clock that evening, he found a hotel and checked in.

As he sprawled exhausted across the bed, he stared at the ceiling. His heart ached from the pain embedded there. He needed to find Bekah, to hold her, to kiss her again. He needed *her*. Not knowing where or how he was going to find her was tearing his gut out.

His eyes closed and he briefly dozed. One arm rested against his forehead, his mouth fell slack. As he drifted, his subconscious took over, and Bekah's face swirled. Just out of the flames—just out of reach—and he woke with a start sitting straight up in bed. His heart beat wildly, and his pulse raced. An unwelcome sensation of dread washed over him, and he feared if he didn't find her quickly, she might be lost to him forever.

He rose, shrugging out of his clothing and stepping into the bathroom. He turned on the hot water. Collin stepped inside the steamy shower, the stinging droplets massaging his tense and tired muscles. He rotated his neck, stretched the weary muscles of his back, and for a short-lived respite, thought of nothing.

After, he dried his tired body and fell naked into the cool sheets. Just as sleep fully took him under, his mind jerked alert. He sat up, thinking for a few seconds, and then picked up the phone and dialed.

It rang three times before answered. "Hello?"

"Patricia, thank God. Where in the hell have you been?"

"Collin? What's wrong?'

He exhaled deeply. "Do you have any idea where Bekah might be? She has disappeared."

"Bekah? Why, I just spoke to her yesterday morning."

Collin closed his eyes and said a small prayer. "Then you're the only one. What time did you talk to her?"

Patricia thought for a second. "Mid-morning, I think. About an hour after you called me from the airport." She paused. "Are you still in Louisiana?"

"Actually, I'm in New York."

Collin sensed the surprise in her voice. "New York? Why?"

"Bekah is here somewhere. At least she took a flight here yesterday afternoon, but she didn't make the return flight home last night. What did you two talk about yesterday?"

Patricia was silent for a moment. "You say she flew to New York?"

"Yes."

Silence filled the phone line. "I think she went after Matthew."

Collin's shoulders dropped. "Why would she do that, Patricia?"

Patricia exhaled slowly. "Because of something I told her yesterday."

"Okay, what is it. What did you tell her?"

"Collin, have you ever heard of The Harper Corporation? They are a major publisher of magazines and scandal sheets. Matthew Vanlandingham and his mother *are* The Harper Corporation. The PI called in with the info yesterday morning. When I told Bekah, she started thinking, and then asked me to find out some information about the major stockholders in the corporation. I did and called her back. She said thanks and that's the last I heard from her."

Collin sat silent for a moment. "So she's going after Vanlandingham?"

"That's how is appears to me."

"Damnit!"

"But you can't find her, right?"

"Yes. And it worries the hell out of me. Patricia look, here is my number at the hotel. If you hear anything at all, call and leave a message."

"Sure Collin. Let me know what's going on. Oh, and the name of the PI is Max Cooper. I'll have him call you. Keep in touch."

Collin sat holding the phone until it began clicking in his ear, and then replaced the receiver.

* * *

"Here she is Ms. McCauley. All bright eyed and bushytailed this morning. Why just look at those blue eyes, darker than a midnight blue night. Almost black." The nurse glanced at Bekah. "But then of course, they're just like yours."

Smiling, Bekah took her tiny daughter from the nurse and cradled her in her arms. She was indeed beautiful and did have such dark, big eyes. Not to mention lashes you could kill for. Already, she's a heartbreaker. Collin would absolutely go crazy.

Collin. According to Dr. Carpenter, Dr. Benton had relayed her message to Collin, but she'd heard nothing from him—and that frightened her. For the past several hours, she'd looked for him to step around the corner. At every footstep that hesitated outside her door, she jerked alert and waited. Yet, he had not called—he did not come. Perhaps not coming simply meant he didn't *want* to come for her. Perhaps he was tired of fooling with her problems. Maybe he didn't want her anymore. Maybe he didn't understand why she was in New York in the first place, and he refused to come. *Oh, God. Does he think I've gone back to Matthew?*

She had to reach him. Somehow.

Colleen cooed, pulling her attention back to her baby. Bekah looked at her young daughter and smiled. The infant rooted at her breast, squirming around so that she knocked the pretty ribbon off her curl. Bekah tried to retrieve it, but it slid to the floor. She shrugged and then tried another attempt at breast-feeding. Each time, Bekah felt a little more successful. This time Colleen latched on quite nicely, and Bekah's heart filled with joy.

Her daughter. No one else's. Matthew would surely give in to her demands. He wouldn't dare cross her. Once Patricia received the envelope in the mail, she would go ahead with the plan for her. And since Matthew hadn't told her he'd drop everything, as soon as she could get home, she'd give Patricia the go ahead.

"Oh, what a lovely sight!"

Bekah glanced up at the woman entering her room. She was an older woman with gray hair pulled back into a bun. Bekah smiled.

The woman stepped closer. "Nothing more beautiful, I say, than a mama nursing a newborn babe. Turns my heart to mush," she said softly as she approached. Laying a finger on

Colleen's forehead she mused, "And such a handsome young man."

Bekah lifted her gaze to the woman. "She's a girl," she said politely.

The woman looked at Bekah oddly and glanced to her clipboard. "You're Rebekah McCauley, right?"

Bekah nodded.

"But the birth certificate information says you had a boy."

Bekah stared at the woman, a little puzzled. "This is my daughter. I gave birth to a girl." She reached for the paper. "What kind of information is that you have there?"

The woman handed it to her. "This is so confusing. You see," she pointed to the form Bekah now held in her hand, "I was sent up here by records to check on something. Whoever filled out this form forgot to complete a couple of lines. We need that information before we can send off to the state Vital Statistics to issue the birth certificate."

Bekah was not only confused but now angry. Her chest grew tight. She read over the information on the paper saying Matthew was the father of her baby, and that the child was a boy. He had the gall to name the child after him!

Bekah looked at the woman. "I don't know who completed this form, but it wasn't me, and the information is all wrong. I'm destroying it." Bekah ripped the form into tiny shreds. "Is this the only copy?"

The wide-eyed woman nodded. "I believe so."

"Good." Bekah continued," Make sure it is, and if there are any others, I want them destroyed also. There is a crazy person out there trying to convince everyone that he is the father of my baby. He's not to be trusted. Don't let him fool anyone in that office again. And bring me a new form so I can fill it out correctly."

The woman nodded and then scurried past her bed. "I'll do

305

that right away, Ms. McCauley. I'll get to the bottom of this for you." She hurried out the door.

Bekah breathed a sigh of relief. If only the rest would be so easy.

The baby nursed and Bekah tried to remain relaxed, but she was furious Matthew had attempted to circumvent the birth certificate. Attempted, hell! He almost succeeded. Shivers of dread ran down her spine. If he could do that, what else was he capable of?

A lot. She couldn't afford to wait any longer.

Colleen had nursed on both sides now, so she gently lifted the sleeping baby and laid her in her crib beside her bed, then lifted the telephone.

* * *

"I'm getting tired of this," the receptionist muttered. "Don't people know the procedure? Doesn't anyone follow protocol anymore?" She shook her head.

Collin glared at the woman. After coming this far, and getting this close to Bekah and Vanlandingham, he wasn't going to give up. If he had to take every office by storm in this damned building, one by one, he would find Matthew Vanlandingham. And hopefully, Bekah.

"All I want to do is talk to him. He'll see me."

Grace rolled her eyes behind the half-glasses. "Sir, I have strict orders. I do not release the knowledge of Mr. Vanlanding-ham's suite of offices, nor do I call up and ask to have someone admitted who is not on the list today. Your name is clearly not on the list. I suggest you make an appointment for another day."

"I don't have another day."

"Well, sir, my orders are clear. I simply can't help you."

"I need to see him." Collin feared he couldn't rein in his

anger. He stepped as close to the round desk as he could get, gripped the edge until his knuckles turned white, and lowered his face. "There is nothing that will stop me. A woman's life may depend on my seeing this man. A woman I happen to love very much. I will stop at nothing. Do you understand me?"

The receptionist sat back in her chair, as if attempting to put as much space between her and Collin as she could. She nodded, then picked up the phone.

Collin grinned. But when he heard her say the word *security* come out of her mouth, his blood boiled.

He turned to leave. Surely there was another way.

He tore through the lobby and ran out the door. The last thing he needed was to be detained by some rent-a-cop. Stopping briefly to adjust to the sunlit day, he began walking—but then he stopped.

Directly in front of him, in the alley beside the building, sat a black limousine. The back window was down, and Matthew Vanlandingham sat talking to a street vendor, buying the morning paper. Collin wondered how he could be so lucky. Now if only the stinking car doors were unlocked.

He rounded the car as any disinterested pedestrian would, then as he reached the other side, jerked up on the door handle. A rush of adrenaline released as he found no resistance to his pull, and swiftly opened the door and sat next to Matthew.

Vanlangdingham's frantic eyes spun toward him. Collin watched them turn to venom upon recognition. He also sensed the driver's reaction to his intrusion, and felt him grab jerkily for his door handle. Matthew waved him off.

"It's all right, Spencer. We'll let him stay." He then turned back to Collin. "But only for a minute. Stay parked."

Collin sat back comfortably and looked over the man sitting next to him—the epitome of self-absorption—and felt like retching. If this man hurt Bekah, no doubt he would kill him.

"Where's Bekah." Collin glared.

"Man of few words. Direct and to the point. I like that."

"Where is she?"

Matthew eased back and perused Collin, from head to foot. "Why do you want the little tramp? She's carrying my child, after all. Why would a man want another man's child? I don't understand it."

Collin knew his ploy. Get him angry. Well, he was succeeding. "I don't need your moralizing any issue concerning her or her child. You are the bastard that let her down when she needed you."

"And you're the bastard who's going to pick up the pieces?"

Collin inhaled deeply. "I've been picking up the pieces all summer after you broke her. You're not going to get to her again. I know she's in New York, and I know she's been to see you. Where the hell is she, Vanlandingham. If I don't get some answers soon, I'm going straight to the police."

Matthew laughed. "This isn't Kentucky, Mr. Kramer. This is New York. There are bigger and better mysteries to be solved than a woman who's been missing for a day or two. Besides, what would you tell them? You have no concrete evidence to link her with me. I assume if Bekah came to New York, she did so of her own free will. I assure you I had nothing to do with it, and I'm telling you that I haven't seen her. In fact, I don't want her Kramer. I only want the child."

Collin narrowed his eyes at the weasel. He felt like coming across the seat at him, but he didn't. "Why? You don't strike me as the father type."

"Oh, and you *are*, Mr. Business? Seems you put quite a lot of time and effort into that little moneymaker you own. So, you're going to be the super-dad to my child? I think not. Besides, the fact remains that the child is mine." He leaned forward into the space between them. "And I take what's mine and run with it."

Collin swallowed. How in the hell did he know about his business? What else did he know about? He felt his cheeks heating up. "Tell me where Bekah is."

"I haven't seen her."

"Like hell, you haven't."

Matthew shook his head. "Not since I left Kentucky. Until that child is six months old, I will leave the two of you alone. But after that, watch out. Now get out of my car. I've an important date with my mother and I'm late. You know how mothers are, don't you Kramer? You have a mother, don't you? Oh, that's right, it's your father who is dead."

Collin gripped the door handle. *Ignore him.* He recognized the statement for what it was--something to get him riled up. Well, it wouldn't work. "This isn't the last of it Vanlandingham. I'll be back, and you damn well had better put my name on that list out there or I'll tear this place apart looking for you. And I might not be alone. Got it?"

Matthew simply glared at him. Collin opened the door and stepped one foot out of it then turned back to him. His voice was low and determined. "If you hurt her— If you do anything to her at all, I'll kill you."

* * *

Bekah replaced the receiver. Patricia was out and she didn't want to leave a message, not with information as important as this. She'd try a little later. Colleen slept soundly, so Bekah took advantage of the time and tried to sleep as well. She trailed one finger along the infant's soft face, then took hold of a tiny hand and smoothed the fingers out of a clenched fist. Propping her head on her arm, Bekah watched her baby sleep and smiled, her pleasure interrupted only with nagging thoughts of Collin.

She debated calling him but felt that the ball was in his court. If Dr. Benton told him what happened, and he didn't come, there was only one possible reason. He didn't want to. At the realization, tears stung and flooded her eyes. Her heart ached, her mind having difficulty comprehending the about-face. She cried until she finally slept.

Bekah felt the touch almost instantly—then movement as Colleen stirred under her hand. When her eyes opened, she bolted up in the bed and saw him—Matthew! And Colleen was in his arms. She grasped and he stepped backward. Then Bekah saw the woman. Arlena.

"Give me my child, Matthew!" Frantic, she leaped from the bed and clutched at the child.

"Easy Rebekah. I only want to see my grandchild." Bekah froze. She turned to Matthew's mother.

"You are behind all this, aren't you? I should have known."

Arlena Vanlandingham raised her chin and studied Bekah. "This is my grandchild. My only grandchild. I'll not have you take him away from me."

Bekah could only stare at the woman. The words she wanted to say would not come. The contempt she felt for this woman was fiercer that anything she'd ever felt in her life. "This is my child, *my child*." She turned to Matthew and reached for Colleen. He stepped backward again and laughed. "Give me my baby."

"I only want to hold him, Bekah."

Bekah stepped closer again. "No, give her to me."

Matthew was playing a game. He stepped back again, closer to the door this time and angled his body toward it.

Bekah lunged and shouted. Surely if she yelled someone

would come to help her. "I said to give her to me, Matthew. I want my baby!"

Matthew started to step back again then stopped at her words. Bekah reached once more, and he let her take the child. "What did you just say?"

"I said to give her to me." She turned, cradled the baby in her arms, and returned to the bed, holding her close. Matthew's gaze fell on his mother and they exchanged a look that Bekah didn't understand.

"We're not idiots, Rebekah, the child is a boy," Arlena began.

Bekah shook her head in disbelief and looked at her. "No, the child is a girl." She turned to Matthew. "And by the way, your attempt to get at Vital Statistics failed, Matthew. Don't ever try anything like that again. Trying to put your name on the birth certificate was one thing but changing the sex of the child is something entirely different. What did you think you were doing?"

Matthew stepped forward, a confused look on his face. "But it's a boy."

"No Matthew, she is a girl. Would you like me to prove it to you?" Bekah looked at first one astonished face and then another. She then laid the baby in front of her on the bed and undiapered the child. The look she saw on both their faces was amusing.

"What's wrong, Matthew?" She wanted to smile. Obviously, Matthew was for some reason counting on a male child. His mother too.

"I'm disappointed in you Bekah. I thought you gave me a son."

Typical. A glimmer of hope welled up inside her though. "No, Matthew, she's a beautiful daughter."

"But not as desirable." Arlena Vanlandingham stepped back

from the bed and looked at her son. "Forget it, Matthew. You still have time. Let this one go. You don't have time to father a child who is not going to matter in the long run." She walked to the door.

Matthew started to follow her.

"Wait a minute," Bekah called after him. "What in hell is going on?"

He stopped and turned. "That child is neither valuable nor desirable to me, Rebekah. You're welcome to her."

Excitement welled up inside her, but she was cautious. "I want to know why, Matthew."

"Because I needed a son to satisfy the conditions my grandfather's trust. Simple as that."

Money. All she needed to know, and what Patricia had suspected from the start. Bekah shook her head. "I pity the broodmare who hooks up with you next time."

"That's not your concern."

"No, but my child is my concern."

"I don't want anything to do with your baby, Rebekah. She's all yours."

Elation zinged through her, but she had to see this to its end. "Will you legally document that statement?"

He nodded. "I'll have the papers drawn up and get with your attorney. Of course, this means you'll relinquish any support from me, do you understand that?"

"I don't want anything from you, Matthew."

"Good. Someone will be by with a draft of the document this afternoon."

* * *

At odds with himself, Collin returned to his hotel room, his anger barely under control. He felt helpless. In a city this large, anything could happen, he knew. Finding her suddenly felt like searching for a needle in a haystack. Eyes closed, he could see Bekah the night of the fire—frightened, so terrified of losing him. Why didn't she leave a note? Call him? What changed her mind from the last time they had talked?

He never would have gone out of town, had he thought she still held notions of leaving. He never expected she would do it —and certainly hadn't thought she would now.

He glanced across the room and noticed the red light blinking on the phone. A message? When he retrieved it, he felt energized. Suddenly taking a new interest in his quest, he picked up the phone and dialed Patricia's office.

She answered on the first ring.

"Answering your own phone today?"

Patricia smirked. "The temp didn't come in. Have you heard anything from Bekah?"

Collin let the phone lay silent for a second. "No, I did see Vanlandingham. He denies seeing her. The bastard is lying, though. I can see it in his beady little eyes."

"Well, listen to this. I got a package in the mail this morning from Bekah. I think it must have been here yesterday, but this crazy temp has my office torn upside down. I can't find a damn thing, least of all the mail. Anyway, I came upon it this morning. I think Bekah's trying to blackmail Matthew."

His back straightened. "What? How?"

"Well, according to the document she typed up, it looks like she's using some of Matthew's own tactics against him. She has the story of her emotional and physical abuse, and the attempted forced abortion, ready for his gossip rags. If they don't bite, she's ready to take it to the competition. There are also copies of letters addressed to each of his board of directors. One of which is a major pro-lifer, and the other sits on the advisory council for a spouse abuse center. Looks like she planned to give him an ultimatum. Either Matthew was to drop all efforts at securing paternity rights, or she'd ruin him."

Collin grinned. "That's my sweetheart. But why do you think she did it now, instead of waiting for me to get home?"

"I think she wanted to strike while the iron was hot. You know how desperate she was to get this thing over with and get Matthew out of her life. I guess she saw the opportunity and grabbed it."

The phone fell silent again. "But that doesn't explain where she is now. Obviously, she approached Matthew. For some reason she didn't get on that fight home. That still doesn't give me anything to go on. I can't begin to even know where to look."

"Have you contacted Max yet?"

Collin sat stunned. He hadn't thought about the PI since this morning. "No. I mean, yes, but he was out. I'm waiting for a return call."

"Let me. I have some other business to settle with him anyway. I'll give him your number and all the information. I'm sure he'll get right on it. Oh, and he'll want the money up front. And listen, you sound terrible. Why don't you try and get some sleep."

Collin laughed sarcastically. "Sleep? It's overrated."

* * *

With a copy of Matthew's document in hand, Bekah dialed the airline from her hospital room. In the morning, she was going home. First order of business was to find Collin, the second to talk with Patricia. What she would find in Kentucky, she didn't know, but she was already forming a plan.

If Collin were through with her, she'd find a way to move on —much as she didn't want to. She could go to her parents until she had time to rebuild. It would take several months but it would be worth it. She could afford to build a modest home, she was sure. And her brothers and father were quite handy with a hammer. She was also sure they would be more than willing to help her out. If only she could go home to Collin and he would want her again. That didn't appear possible. If he wanted her, he would have come.

Bekah stared out the window into the city streets. She'd go back to his house only long enough to gather what few belongings she had, and then she would leave, forever.

* * *

The phone rang and Collin raised one eye. He had slept as Patricia suggested. Perhaps the knowledge that Bekah had not intended to leave him relaxed him somehow, but as soon as he woke, it hit him that he still had no clue where she was.

With a heavy hand, Collin reached over to snatch up the phone. "Kramer," he answered groggily.

"Max Cooper, here. I've found your girl."

Collin sat straight up in the bed. "Where? Is she all right? How can I get to her?"

"Whoa, hold on there. Let's get one thing straight at a time. First, she's okay. Second, I can take you to her. And third, get your ass down in the lobby and we'll go right now. I'm down here waiting on you and I've got other fish to fry. Patricia said you'd have the cash, right?"

Collin hopped on one leg, pulling on his pants, while cradling the phone under his chin. "Yeah, right. Got it. You're not holding out on me are you?"

"Naw. I just like to get business straight from the top. Get down here fast, I've got a lot of work to do tonight."

Chapter Twenty-Five

For all the times she'd flown alone, Bekah had never realized how difficult it would be to travel with a child. Thankfully, she didn't have all that much to carry. The hospital gave her a diaper bag with supplies, and a car seat. Colleen's milk, of course, was portable and quite accessible. The only other thing she had to worry about was her large purse.

For a first-time flyer, Colleen did quite nicely. The flight attendants made certain Bekah had everything she needed, and with the aid of a blanket, she was able to keep her newborn fed and happy for most of the trip. She even managed to doze for a few minutes. She looked forward to her arrival at Blue Grass Airport.

They landed without event, and since Bekah had no baggage to claim, she went directly to the parking lot to retrieve her truck. As she drove, thoughts of Collin ping-ponged in her head. What would she say to him? Should she go back to his farm? Perhaps it would be best to go her parents'. She didn't know if she could bear to see Collin right now. *He probably thinks you left him for good.* But he knew about the baby, right?

Dr. Benton told him. *Maybe he's angry because you went to New York.*

Thing was, she was confused. Didn't know what to think. Or do.

So, she simply drove.

* * *

"I'm sorry Mr. Kramer. She was released this morning."

Collin swore. "How is she?" Max Cooper had told him she was in the maternity ward, but he didn't know why. Collin assumed complications with the pregnancy.

"The records indicate everything was normal—normal delivery, the baby is doing fine. Ms. McCauley is fine."

Collin's eyes widened and stared at Max. "She had the baby? Oh my God." He turned back to the receptionist. "You say she's fine? The baby is fine?" His insides shook like jelly.

"Yes, Mr. Kramer. Everything is normal."

"Relax, Kramer. Women have babies all the time."

He turned to Max. "Relax! Hell, I can't relax. She's had the baby and I wasn't here to help her. Now she's on her way home. That's where I'm going."

Collin turned and headed down the hospital corridor.

* * *

The house stood still and looked empty. Collin's Mercedes was not in the drive. Obviously, he wasn't at home.

Her shoulders slumped and she exhaled deeply. It's just not to be, she told herself. It's just not to be. She tore her eyes away from the house and looked across the pasture to the burned shell of her grandparent's house. *Memories.* Old ones and new ones. Tender ones and not so tender. She longed to see the white frame house again sitting on the slight rise above the pasture. She longed for one last look at her grandfather crossing over the hill behind his home as he took off to pick blackberries or go fishing. Or to see her grandmother gently rocking on the porch, always something to do in her hands, watching for an occasional car to go by so she could wave. That wasn't to be, either. The best she could hope for now was a nice enough tobacco crop and enough collateral on the farm to rebuild.

The most difficult part would be looking across the fence to this house.

Glancing down at her sleeping daughter, snoozing snugly in the car seat, Bekah longed to see Collin hold her in his arms. How much she wanted to be a family. How much she had wanted it all.

Carefully slipping her arms around the sleeping child, Bekah lifted her to her chest. Since Collin wasn't here, she figured she might as well get those few personal things, and then be on her way to her mother's. In fact, it might even be a good idea for her to call her mother from here and warn her that she was coming and that the baby was here. She wouldn't want her to have a heart attack the moment she arrived.

Upon turning the key and opening the door, Bekah took in the strange solitude of the old mansion. Her sandals clicked across the wooden parquet floor, echoing in the cavernous hall. So empty, Bekah felt it mirrored her own soul. Without Collin, would she feel like this forever?

As she approached the phone stand, Bekah noticed the answering machine blinking with several messages. Without thinking, she pushed the play button.

Dr. Benton's voice came first. She listened as she heard him tell Collin that she was in New York, in labor, and at which hospital to find her. His last statement was to call him. The next message was from Patricia, urgently asking him to call her. The next from Michael. *Michael?* He wanted him to call immediately. Then one from Tom McKenney and several others about business. One man in particular left three messages, and was irate, wondering if Collin ever returned his calls, and what was the damned rumor about him trying to sell his business? *Collin's trying to sell his business?*

Bekah listened until the machine trailed off. She stared into the distant hallway and thought about what she had heard. "He didn't get the message," she said aloud. "But where is he? He's obviously been gone for days."

Oh my God! He's been out looking for me!

Suddenly the tiny baby hairs on the back of her neck stood on edge. A soft muffle reverberated through the hallway behind her. She turned slowly, still holding the sleeping Colleen in her arms, and when she did, found herself face to face with the nose of a slick, black handgun. On the other end of the gun was Erin.

Bekah gasped and tried to back away. In her hurry, she hit into the phone stand and knocked the phone and machine to the floor. Soon the annoying beep-beep-beep of the disconnected receiver echoed off the walls of the hallway. Bekah clutched Colleen tight in her arms.

"You had to come back, didn't you?" Erin stepped slowly to her. "You just had to freaking come back."

Bekah breathed deeply and set her gaze on Erin's face. As frightened as she was on the inside, she'd be damned if she'd show it on the outside. "I never intended not to come back, Erin."

"And now you've got the baby." She edged closer. "The dear sweet little baby."

Erin kept the gun pointed at Bekah's head. She held it steady with one hand, the other bracing her wrist. She stepped slowly around Bekah, circling as if she were prey.

"What do you want with me, Erin?"

"I don't want anything with you. I want Collin back."

Bekah swallowed. "You never had Collin, Erin. You were just convenient. He told me so." Bekah watched Erin's eyes narrow to tiny slits. Her hands started to shake.

Erin chuckled nervously. "You're lying. I want him back and I'll get him back. I've already made that decision."

Bekah inhaled deeply trying to calm her jumpy insides. "I've gathered that already, but don't you think that's up to him?"

"He doesn't know what he wants. He only thinks he wants you. You know why, don't you? Cause he knows you can have kids."

Bekah noted a hint of sarcasm in Erin's voice and the gun slipped a little lower, now aimed directly at Colleen. Bekah had to play the game and hoped she could do it. "Does Collin want kids? We never really discussed it."

Erin's gaze narrowed. Bekah noticed how her hair seemed to have lost its shine since the last time she'd seen her. Her skin seemed sallow and limp. Her clothing hung in folds on her thin body. This woman was not altogether.

She nudged the gun at Bekah, stepping closer. "You know he wants kids. That's why he didn't want me. I can't have kids. Oh, I was good to have around for a while, for kicks, I guess. Or for whenever he got the urge. And that was okay because we had each other. But after you came along he forgot all about me." Her gaze moved past Bekah's face. "I was his first, you know."

Bekah shivered. She'd had enough of this. "What do you want?"

Erin looked back with glaring eyes. The gun leveled off again—aimed straight at Bekah's head. Erin held the position for what seemed a small eternity, then her eyes glazed over and she pointed the gun at Colleen.

Bekah uttered a silent prayer, hoping God would forgive all her past sins, and that if he couldn't spare both her and Colleen, that he would at least spare her daughter. Silently, she raised a hand to her precious child's head and cradled her close against her. For the first time since she'd turned and saw Erin, she broke the connection with her eyes. She nuzzled her baby's sweet smelling hair and again prayed for God to keep her safe. A tear rolled down her nose and landed in the downy hair on her daughter's head.

"You know I set fire to your house don't you. And the barn of course."

Bekah's head rose slowly. The gun was still there. "I guessed as much—but not until a few minutes ago. Do you hate me that much?"

Erin snickered. "I hate you that much. I wanted you to die then, but you didn't. So you'll have to die now."

Bekah swallowed. She stared long into Erin's face, and refused to give Erin the satisfaction of killing her with her head lowered in defeat. "Just kill me, Erin. Leave the baby alone."

"I'm going to kill you both."

With a thundering crash, the walls caved in around them. Broken glass flew, Colleen startled and flinched against Bekah, and wailed out at the explosion. Erin's body flew sideways. Bekah ducked and ran to a corner, shielding herself and Colleen from the flying debris. A shot rang out and Bekah clung to her baby and rolled into a tight ball in the corner. She heard Erin scream and gasp. Frightened tremendously, she risked a glance toward the commotion.

Two men with their backs to Bekah struggled to control Erin. One man looked surprisingly like Pete, the other? She was afraid to hope. The gun lay on the floor. Bekah rose, glancing about, trying to console her screaming child, and kicked the gun to the far corner of the room. The wide glass veranda doors had been shattered. A bullet-hole crested the splintered wood in the Palladian window above. And as her gaze lowered, she saw him turn and look at her. Their eyes met and Bekah felt her lungs and her heart expand.

Collin.

In a matter of seconds, the sirens were deafening, and a flurry of activity encompassed the room as Tom McKenney and a deputy rushed in. After quickly assessing the situation, they cuffed Erin and took her outside, as Pete explained to Tom what happened.

Bekah had not moved. She stood staring into Collin's eyes, wondering which of them would make the first move.

"Bekah..." Her name flowed soft and sweet from his lips and she wanted to cry. Her eyes stung, and her lips quivered.

"Collin?" She sobbed. "Oh, Collin...."

＊ ＊ ＊

It only took him one leap to get to her. Before he realized the control he thought he possessed was gone, he devoured her. His lips were all over her face and her neck. His hands were in her hair. Kisses trailed over her eyes, tasting away tears. His own fell in rivulets down his cheeks. "Oh, Bekah," he whispered. "Oh my God, Bekah. I couldn't find you."

She cradled a fussy Colleen between them. Her eyes met his again. "I thought you didn't want me anymore."

"Oh my God. Never. You have to believe me. I will always want you." He held her closer, fully aware of the baby between them.

"Never?" Bekah placed a palm on his cheek. "Always?" she whispered.

He looked at her long and hard. "Always."

She smiled and the tears rolled again. "Would you like to

meet your daughter?" Her smile faded. "That is, if you still want her for your daughter?"

How could I not? "She's a part of you, Bekah. Of course, I want her," he whispered.

Bekah sighed. "Matthew doesn't. He wanted a boy. Something about his grandfather's will."

Collin wondered just how much a miracle this all was. This whole thing, he decided then, from beginning to end. That they had ever gotten back together was a miracle. And he never wanted it to end.

"Her name's Colleen. I named her after you."

Collin brought his gaze to hers and held it there for several seconds. His chest rose with each breath he took. Pure emotion puddled in Bekah's eyes. Then his gaze dropped to his new daughter.

One finger trailed the tiny cheek and he smiled as her little lips curled up. "I'll love her just as I would if she were mine... I would have been there, you know. If I had known. I would have been there."

"I know. I prayed you would come. I didn't know...."

Collin clasped them both to him. "Oh, God, Bekah. I'm so sorry you had to go through all that alone."

She touched his face and smiled. "It's okay now. The baby's here. I'm here... You're here. We've crossed all the obstacles, Collin. Maybe now we can get on with our lives."

"You have no idea how much I love you."

"I love you, too, Collin." She smiled and bit her lip before going on. "I know should wait for you to ask this—but let's get married?"

"Married? You actually think we can make it?" Collin grinned.

"I know we can make it."

"We could join the farms."

"And rebuild?"

"If that's what you want." Collin narrowed his eyes and looked at his beautiful wife-to-be teasingly. "That ridge that runs along the back of both our farms would be a perfect place. A bit windy, perhaps, but the view over the creek would be awesome."

"Wind Ridge II?"

He nodded and grinned. "I like the sound of that. But there is one more obstacle."

"Oh?"

"Do you want get married before or after I finish vet school?"

Bekah smiled even broader. "I'm not going to wait until you finish school, Collin Kramer."

"Good." He took her into his arms and planted a long, slow, and easy kiss on her lips. "I was hoping you'd say that."

Bekah's lips glided over his, then she pulled away with a serious look.. "Can we send the letters now?"

Collin nuzzled her neck. "Send them."

"And what's this about selling the business?"

His tongue traced her ear. "It's sold."

"Did you get a fair price?" she whispered.

Collin stopped his ministrations and placed his hands on either side of her face. "Actually, no. But money isn't everything, you know."

Bekah's head fell back, giving Collin full access to her neck. He took advantage of the moment and nibbled behind her ear, sending Bekah into a giggle.

"Umm, I know. You certainly can't put a price on this," she said.

Collin smiled.

* * *

The End

Hi there, Maddie here. I hope you enjoyed Bekah and Collin's book! I've written several romantic suspense stories—perhaps you'd like to try another?

Double Crossed is about a woman in jeopardy. She thinks her husband is dead...but has she been double-crossed?

Scroll on to read the first chapter.

Trooper Brutally Murdered On Black Bear Mountain

The Knoxville News Sentinel
Associated Press

Black Bear, TN: A Tennessee State Police Trooper was killed in the line of duty Thursday morning in the foothills of the Smoky Mountains outside of Black Bear, Tennessee. Black Bear is approximately one hour east of Knoxville.

Trooper Robert T. Cooper, a four-year veteran of the Tennessee Highway Patrol, responded to a distress call from a motorist around two o'clock in the morning while working his routine shift. The female caller indicated to dispatch that her car had stalled on a secluded mountain road and she required assistance.

Records show Cooper radioed his arrival at the stranded motorist's vehicle at 2:18 a.m.

Approximately one hour later, a passing motorist discovered Cooper's burning body lying beside his cruiser, lights flashing, the driver's side door open, and the engine running. Cooper died at the scene.

A native of Florida, Trooper Cooper relocated to Tennessee five years ago, and currently resided in the community of Black Bear, Tennessee, with his wife of one year.

An investigation is in process.

Double Crossed

Two years later

He wished he could see her legs.

Although her frame was small, with narrow hips and a wasp-like waist, her legs, as they say, went all the way up. The woman wore a pair of low-slung black trousers that hugged tight to her hips and thighs, showing off some of her best assets. A white knit sweater clung to every curve of her upper body—and those curves were damn appealing. Although she wasn't an overly tall woman, the illusion of tall and thin was accentuated by her outfit. The finishing touch, a pair of black boots sporting heels that looked a little too high to be teacher attire.

At least no teacher he ever had ever dressed like that.

But the thing that snapped Michael Lassiter's libido to embarrassingly quick attention was the mane of blond hair, coupled with steel-blue eyes set like perfect jewels against the backdrop of black and white.

Cold as steel blue eyes? Perhaps. That's what he wanted to find out.

Yes. He knew they were blue even though he wasn't close

enough to see them right now. He had stared into them a whole lot lately, though—into the photo in her file. He'd studied this case, and Kate Cooper, for weeks. He glanced to that manila file folder, now laying open across the passenger side of his cruiser—said picture staring back up at him—and frowned.

Not the open-and-shut case they'd once thought. No. That feeling was stuck in his gut. This all went much deeper.

Dammit.

As he sat parked next to the Black Bear Elementary school playground, his gaze lifted, and he returned to examine every inch of Kate's body while she crossed the schoolyard. His breathing deepened as he took in the sexy hitch in her step, every subtle expression on her face. He scowled. Another place, another time—perhaps if he'd spotted her in a bar, or at the mall —he'd have approached her and made small talk, perhaps asked for her number. Pursued her. Admitting his attraction to her now, even to himself and while during a case, was against his own personal moral code.

Hell, she was a good-looking woman. What was not to be attracted to? After all, he was a hot-blooded, All American man. Right? And he was also a professional who know when to cut off the desire and tuck it back inside his jeans. But she conjured up all kinds of scenarios when he looked at her, and his brain raced with thoughts of how physically attractive he found her, and how he could be incredibly interested in her—

If things were different.

But things weren't different.

Clearing up the mystery of Rob Cooper's murder was the goal, not romancing the object of his investigation. Sure, he never thought he'd end up undercover in Cooper's wife's class-room, but here he was, posing as a school drug cop to get into her life.

Somewhat.

But not into her panties.

That was not part of the deal.

He had expected her to be beautiful. The picture was an obvious giveaway. What he hadn't expected was for curvy blonde quicken his pulse the way she had once he'd set eyes on her in real time. But she had. And it was all he could do now not to imagine that halo of flame unleashed from its single braid, fanning out around her on a pillow.

His pillow.

Dammit. Forget it Lassiter. This you don't need. Not now.

He watched her round the corner of the school building, calling out to a child. His heart raced, unable to keep his mind from wandering. How her lips might feel pressed against his. How soft she was. How passionate. How deep he could slide into her....

And how the hell Rob Cooper could double cross a woman like that.

He washed his hands over his face, shaking his head.

Fuck. Give it a break.

Perhaps Jenkins was right. Perhaps Kate Cooper's image of the squeaky clean, widowed schoolteacher was a hoax.

"You could have made this a lot easier, sweetheart," he mumbled, "if you were about a hundred pounds heavier and a foot shorter. Maybe about fifteen years older. With bad teeth."

But she wasn't. She was a beautiful young woman. One he hoped wasn't mixed up in the hottest drug-running operation to hit this area in years. One he hoped to hell wasn't hiding away a husband who was supposed to be dead.

* * *

Doug Harvey waved her into his office. "Kate. Come in. We need to talk."

With an inward groan, Kate Cooper seated herself in an overstuffed chair facing Doug's desk and glanced about her surroundings.

Uh-oh. Now what?

The tiny principal's office Doug inhabited was cluttered with trophies—the Black Bear Cubs excelled in sports, football in particular—along with shelves full of pictures, dusty books, and out-of-date professional journals. He turned away and her patience grew thin as he picked up a green file folder from a stack to his left and flipped through it.

Stop it! It never failed that when she was called to the principal's office, she didn't quaver with anticipation. Even after eight years of teaching, she hadn't shed the fears she had harbored as a child of being told to "go to the office." She watched him in quiet prospect as he scanned the folder's contents before looking up at her.

"I wish there were some way around this. Believe me, I don't like springing this on you now, right at the start of the school day, but I have no choice."

"What?" She was half afraid to ask.

"New student." He handed her the folder. "Glance over this now but spend some time with it later, when you have a minute."

Hesitant, she took the folder, her gaze meeting his for a second. Surely it couldn't be that bad? She shuffled through school and medical records for a twelve-year-old boy named Danny Jackson. She came across psychological reports and suspension records. Finally, her fingers rested on a release form and grades from a rehabilitation hospital near Knoxville. The child had been admitted over the summer for possible alcohol addiction.

"Alcoholic?" To say she was dumbfounded was an understatement. "How in the world...? We don't have these kinds of problems in Black Bear."

"Evidently both his parents are addicts. Bad family life. He's with foster parents now and won't be going back with his real parents. He's up for adoption but you know how that goes, no one wants a half-grown kid. Especially one with problems."

Kate bit her lower lip. "It's going to be difficult, don't you think? He's nearly thirteen—and with fifth graders?" Her concern was not only for how awkward this could be for the boy, but how the other students would react.

"I know you can handle it. He missed one entire year of school. Academically, fifth grade is where he should be. Kate, the boy has been a victim of abuse and is, according to his foster father, somewhat defiant. The kid has had a hard life and is street smart." He drummed his fingers on his desk pad. "I understand he's calmed down somewhat since rehab, but still, we've got to be alert to any signs of violence."

She nodded, trying to quell the anxious feelings creeping up in her gut.

"Public schools have failed him in the past. I don't want that to happen here. Not at Black Bear Elementary, and not on my watch. I know you won't let it. Let's start him out in fifth grade and we'll move him up when we see that it's appropriate. I'll rely on you to tell me when."

Doug rose and took a step toward the door. A crowd of noisy students burst through the front school entrance just outside his office. Kate opened her mouth to speak.

He glanced impatiently toward the hallway. "Look, let's talk later." Before she could respond, he'd turned and left, shouting at a couple of boys rough housing near the trophy case.

She stared at the folder in her lap. *Oh boy.* What could she say? She couldn't refuse. She didn't have that option. Yes, it would be a challenge, but she could handle it.

Couldn't she?

Ten minutes later she rounded a corner and spotted the child who must be Danny. No doubt. Had to be him. He stood taller than most of her students. His dishwater hair furled around his head in an unkempt fashion. He wore stiff jeans and high-top tennis shoes and an orange UT football jersey, like any other school-age boy, but somehow he looked...different. Hard. Would most people suspect all he'd been through?

Her heart went out to him. He looked as if he wanted to be anywhere but here.

Can you really blame him? He's too old. It's going to be tough.

His gaze met hers. She felt every inch of his stare. As she approached, he held a bead on her like a hawk with hard, glaring eyes. Eyes that knew and had seen too much in his young life. She was certain of that fact.

He leaned into the doorframe, flanked by two adults—the foster parents, she assumed—who stood stoic but on guard, as if their sole purpose were to grab the kid should he decide to bolt. The foster father's face was stern and proper. The mother's thin-lipped smile said she meant business. Kate felt like they were getting ready to hand over their prisoner to her, the warden, and wondered if that was how Danny felt, too.

Tucking the folder under her arm, she approached the trio and extended her hand. "I'm Mrs. Cooper. You must be Danny." She looked directly into the boy's eyes.

He stared at her outstretched hand, glanced to her face, and then out into space. The man beside him briskly took her hand.

"I'm Tom Elliston." He nodded toward the woman. "My wife, Anna. I assume Doug told you everything. We don't expect no trouble out of the boy." He handed Kate a piece of paper. "Our phone number and address are right here. Don't think nothing of calling if you need anything or if he gets out of line. We expect him to be good. If he gives you any problems, just let me know and I'll handle it."

Kate wasn't sure she liked the way Mr. Elliston talked about Danny, as if he weren't there. She glanced at the mother, who remained quiet, meekly letting her husband commandeer the conversation. Danny, meanwhile, projected annoyance and frustration. But he took in a whole lot more than she or anyone else realized, she imagined.

"Mr. Elliston, I assure you I'll call when necessary," she said firmly. Her classroom was filling with students and she felt it high time to get Danny inside. "Danny and I will find him a desk now. Everything will be fine." She nodded, indicating that it was time to go in. She didn't, and wouldn't, touch the boy, not knowing how he would react. Still, she could feel him tense as they entered the classroom and she led him across the room and showed him his desk.

In a hurry to get the day started, she gathered all the necessary forms and put them into Danny's school folder, printed his name in bold letters with a red magic marker across the top, and placed it on his desk. "We'll go over all this in a few minutes, Danny, when all the other students arrive. Are there questions I can answer for you now?"

He looked straight ahead, his face blank. "Nope."

* * *

"Do the odd numbered problems for homework. I'm giving you time to work on them now." Kate finished writing the page numbers on the board and turned back to face her class. "If you should need help, ask. Don't wait until you get home and find you can't do them."

She watched her students fumble with paper and pencils, turning to the correct pages of their books. Glancing Danny's way, she grimaced. It *had* only been three days, but she was concerned about his reluctance to get involved in the school atmosphere. He refused to talk in class and was a loner. He reacted to her only when spoken to directly. Otherwise, he existed in his own world.

He thumbed through the pages of his math book, resting his chin on his clenched fist. He glanced up, then to the classroom door. Kate followed his gaze as Doug Harvey's face peered through the tiny window.

She stepped across the room and held the door partially open.

"Yes?"

Doug peered beyond her into the classroom. "How are things? New kid?"

She shrugged and tried to avoid looking back at Danny, not wanting to raise his suspicions. Her glance raked over the entire classroom. "For the moment, we're fine. He doesn't talk much."

"You need anything?"

She shook her head. "No. I'll let you know."

"Good. By the way, the DARE officer is coming by today."

"What?"

"Trooper Lassiter with the drug program. Remember? We talked about it after the faculty meeting last week. Said he'd be by to talk to your class. Just a little pep talk to get them hyped. Be here in," he glanced at his watch, "soon, I'd say. He called about thirty minutes ago. I've been tied up. Told him I was sure it would be convenient."

Convenient? Not convenient...

Heat rose to her cheeks, but it was the shock of alarm coursing through her body that startled her more. She wasn't ready for this but what choice did she have? "All right," she said, "All right. I'll work it out."

He left. Standing there, she sucked in a cleansing breath,

and watched Doug stroll down the hallway, stoop to pick up scraps of paper, and peek his head inside classroom doors. Her thoughts turned to the trooper.

Not now. Not ready for this.

She released a pent-up, dizzying whoosh.

She had no choice—she *would* do this, it was her job—but it wouldn't be a picnic. And right about now any excuse not to like the officer, like showing up unexpectedly, was something she'd grab at.

Her chest tightened, a little bit of anger rising inside, along with something else.

Alarm.

She had to diffuse it. A spiraling rush of emotions sped over her, aimed at a man she had never met. Even more disconcerting were the niggling tremors of trepidation emerging from somewhere deep inside.

Why had she agreed?

Mistake. Big mistake.

Panic. Yes. That was it. Anxiety.

Alarm rippled across her chest, tightening like rubber bands. She found it difficult to take a breath. Maybe she needed to dig up that little-used bottle of Xanax her doctor had given her after Rob's death.

No.

Get a grip, Kate.

The last thing she needed was drugs.

She inhaled, exhaled, and moved to her desk.

Her mind drifted to the day Doug Harvey said her students would be working with a drug officer on a prevention project this semester. Then, she hadn't exactly thought through what that would mean. Later the nightmares returned, and she had questioned why Doug would suggest she do such a thing in the first place. He knew her history. Her past.

337

Hell's bells. He probably thought it might be therapy, or something. Damn him. Last thing she needed was more therapy. Let alone working side-by-side with a man who worked in the same profession as her husband—correction—the profession that had *killed* her husband.

Fact was though, after looking over the materials the trooper had left with Doug, she knew she couldn't deny her students the opportunity to get in on the program.

Even if it meant working with him.

Even if there were nightmares.

Her students were that important.

Okay. Keep your chin up, be professional, let the man do his job.

Think about the children. About Danny.

These children were her own substitute children, replacements for the child she would never have—the child she imagined as a smiling imp with onyx hair and midnight blue eyes, like her father's—eyes so unlike her own blue ones, or her mop of white-blond hair that could only be described as unruly.

She had wanted Rob's child. It would never be. But she still had her students. And that was why she had agreed to work with this program.

A hand shot up across the room, shattering her musing.

"Kyle?"

"Ms. Cooper? I need help."

"Sure." Kate smiled and moved toward his desk, ignoring the flash of movement in the open door to the side.

Brown. Uniform. Trooper.

He's here.

A flicker of dread swept through her tummy. She pushed it away and ignored the specter of her past as best she could while leaning over Kyle's desk, worming the answer out of the boy.

Only then did she glance at the open door. Trooper Lassiter could wait until it was convenient *for her.*

She straightened and strolled toward the door, stopping to spot check some of the other student's work on her way. She lifted her gaze and looked him square in the face.

His grin nearly took her breath. Nestled amidst striking features—firm chin, high cheekbones, thin lips, evenly tanned skin—his smile captivated. She tried not to think about that as she held out her hand.

I'm damned irritated with you and in a bad, bad mood. But his smile broke through any annoyance she felt. Dammit.

"Trooper Lassiter? I'm Kate Cooper."

Her trembling hand stayed between them, untouched. He didn't take it. All she could do was stand there and run her tongue over her suddenly parched lips.

He looked at her as though she was not the person he expected. But after a moment, he took her hand anyway, his grasp firm—leaving her palm warm, her fingers tingling.

Spellbindingly handsome, he could take a woman's breath away. Military-cut sandy hair, chocolate brown eyes, the broadest shoulders she'd ever seen.

Except for Rob's.

Shaking, she took a step back, putting space between them.

"I— I'm afraid this is an inconvenient time. We're getting ready for a...a math quiz. And then recess." She cast a nervous glance at her class and back to him again. "Could you come back in about, oh, thirty minutes?"

Was she babbling? She really couldn't tell. But her babble was the truth. She did plan to give a pop math quiz this afternoon. And there was recess. She needed to get these kids outside so they could run off steam.

And she needed a moment to gather herself.

"Definitely." He nodded. "I need to talk to Doug anyway. I'll be back in thirty."

"That will work. Thank you."

He tipped his hat. "Thank *you*, Ma'am."

He left and she turned toward her class, steadying her shaking hands on the solid oak of her teacher's desk. Behind her, the door closed with a soft click. Time. She needed time to collect her thoughts and her sanity.

I am a bumbling idiot.

So familiar....

Uniform.

Spit-shined shoes, knife-sharp pant creases, starched soft brown shirt, the hat, the belt. The 9 mm strapped to his side....

Her throat ached to release a sob.

A hand in the back of the room caught her eye. Danny.

"What's that cop doing here?" he barked. "He coming back?"

Thrust back into reality, Kate gave him her full attention. Several students' heads turned the boy's way. It was the first time they had heard Danny speak out in class.

"All right. I see puzzled faces. Let's put our things away and I'll explain." She waited as they folded papers and stashed away pencils and books.

* * *

Get *Double Crossed* today!

About Maddie James

Maddie James writes romance with a pulse—sometimes sweet, sometimes spicy, and always steeped in small-town charm. From cowboy heroes and mountain-town secrets to ghostly whispers and edge-of-your-seat suspense, her stories deliver heat, heart, and a guaranteed happily-ever-after.

With over 70 titles published and a loyal base of romance readers, Maddie's work has been called "captivating," "steamy and suspenseful," and "the perfect blend of heart and heat." Whether you're in the mood for a stand-alone escape or a full-on series binge, Maddie serves up stories that satisfy.

You'll find rugged cowboys, strong heroines, maybe a ghost or two—and always a twist that keeps you turning the pages. Her books span contemporary westerns, romantic suspense, and paranormal romance, all wrapped in the warmth (and sometimes heat!) of small-town life.

If you love romance with heart, sass, and just the right amount of danger, you're in the right place.

And if you're in the mood for emtional upmarket women's fiction, look for her pen name, Madeleine Jaimes.

Learn more at www.maddiejamesbooks.com